GRUNTS!

MARY GENTLE
GRUNTS!

BANTAM PRESS

LONDON · NEW YORK · TORONTO · SYDNEY · AUCKLAND

TRANSWORLD PUBLISHERS LTD
61–63 Uxbridge Road, London W5 5SA

TRANSWORLD PUBLISHERS (AUSTRALIA) PTY LTD
15–23 Helles Avenue, Moorebank, NSW 2170

TRANSWORLD PUBLISHERS (NZ) LTD
3 William Pickering Drive,
Albany, Auckland

Published 1992 by Bantam Press
a division of Transworld Publishers Ltd
Copyright © Mary Gentle 1992

Reprinted 1992

The right of Mary Gentle to be identified
as author of this work has been asserted in accordance
with sections 77 and 78 of the Copyright Designs and
Patents Act 1988.

A catalogue record for this book is available from the British Library

ISBN 0593 019563

Typeset in 11/12pt Times by
County Typesetters, Margate, Kent.

Printed and bound in Great Britain by
Mackays of Chatham PLC, Chatham, Kent.

AFTER ACTION REPORT

Grateful thanks go to (in alphabetical order): Ashley Bird, Michael Fearn, Neil Gaiman, Michael Gearing, Roz Kaveney, Alex Stewart, and various members of the old Battlegroup, and Five Company.

And especially to the man without whom this book would be in far better taste: Dean 'Pass me another elf, Sergeant' Wayland . . .

Thanks for the inspiration, guys. The orcs would be *proud* of you.

GRUNTS!

CONTENTS

BOOK 3: WAR CRIMES 205

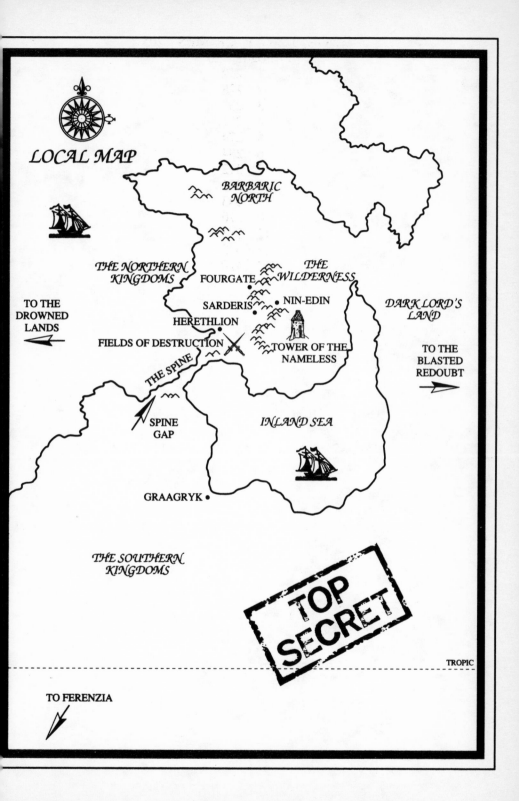

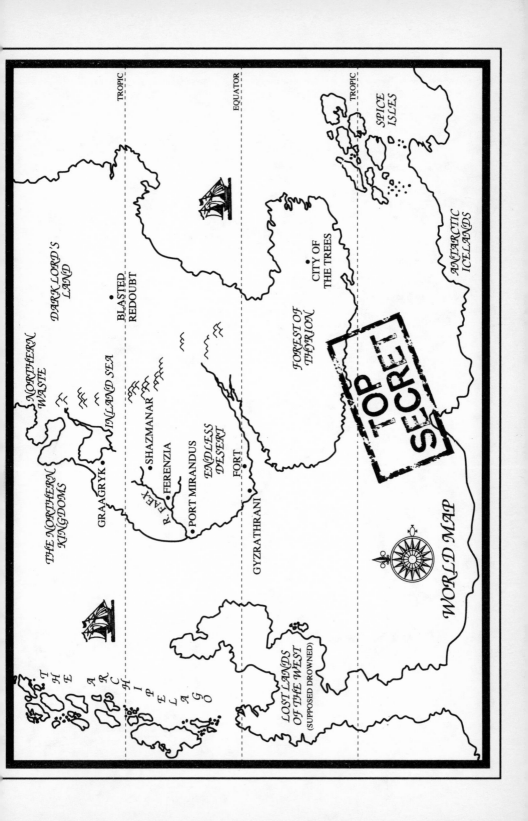

A NOTE ON
ORCISH PRONUNCIATION

A linguistic slur has it that Orcish is a monosyllabic language because orcs have difficulty memorizing more than one syllable at a time. This is not true. Many Orcish names consist of as many as three, or even four, syllables. They are pronounced as follows:

Ashnak	ASH-nak
Barashkukor	BA-rash-KU-kor
Chahkamnit	Chah-KAM-nit
Dakashnit	Da-KASH-nit
Imhullu	Im-HUL-lu
Lugashaldim	LU-gash-AL-dim
Marukka	Ma-RUK-ka
Razitshakra	RA-zit-SHAK-ra
Shazgurim	Shaz-GUR-im
Varimnak	VA-rim-nak
Zarkingu	Zar-KING-u

GRUNTS!

BOOK 1

BROTHERS IN ARMS

1

I N THE TOWER of the nameless necromancer it is always cold.

The big orc's breath smoked odorously on the air. He pulled the buckles of his breastplate tighter round his muscled body. Frost sparkled on the laminated black armour sheathing his shoulders, arms and bowed thighs. The sorcerous cold bites into orc-flesh as no ordinary winter can.

'I come,' he rumbled.

He slung the war-axe and warhammer from his broad, hairy shoulders; and pulled the winged iron helm with its nasal spike more firmly down on his misshapen skull. Even standing to attention he slouches forward; his knuckles hang down beside his knees.

'Hurry,' the familiar whimpered. 'Master calls: hurry–hurry–hurry!'

The orc drew his knobbly foot back, aimed, and kicked the familiar's lean, hairy buttocks. The familiar shot down the corridor, bouncing off the walls several times.

'Don't give orders to Ashnak of the fighting Agaku!' The big orc guffawed, striding up the nine hundred and ninety-nine steps to the tower's top chamber.

Ice congealed on the onyx walls. A sorcerous frost snapped at his clawed fingers. He slapped at dirt and dung on his plate armour, shook his tusked head, and raised a great fist to hammer on the oaken doors. Before he could, they drifted silently open. Light from the tower's single high window slanted down.

21

The nameless necromancer sprawls in a chair made from the bones of his enemies.

His patchwork robes glittered with the silver thread that sewed together their many disquietingly shaped small pieces of leather. At his feet his staff glowed, quiescently, with the light of dark stars. His head was bowed. Ashnak judged him old, as Man-flesh ages, two or more centuries; but still with the disgusting smoothness of human youth.

'Master!' The orc fell to his knees in the darkened tower. His plate harness and weapons clashed loudly in the sorcerous silence.

'Lord Necromancer!' he shouted.

The nameless necromancer started violently. Wine spilled from his bone cup down his black robes. His virulent green eyes opened.

'Um . . . Who . . . ?'

The nameless necromancer rubbed a pale, slender hand across his mouth. The skull wine-cup slipped from his other hand, soaking his robe of skins and bouncing off across the flagstones.

'Wha' . . . ?'

'Ashnak,' the big orc reminded him. 'Ashnak of the warriors! Ashnak of the fighting Agaku!'

'Uhnnnn . . . Ashnash . . . Now wha' did I . . .'

Ashnak, as patiently as is possible for an orc (and a Man-smart Agaku who is facing sorcery can be very patient indeed) said, 'You summoned me, master. Ashnak of the—'

'—fighting Agaku, yes, I *know*. Don't *shout*, scum.'

The nameless necromancer leaned his head over the side of the bone chair and was noisily sick. Another of the lean brown familiars shot out from under the dais and began to lap up the vomit.

Something else scurried in the distant shadows. Ashnak stiffened.

'Damnation!' The wizard hiccuped, and pointed an unsteady finger. Golden forked lightning spiked from his hand to the corner of the chamber.

The blast rattled even Ashnak's ear-drums. Stone-chips flew from the black masonry. The offending rat, missed by three yards, scuttled off into the dark.

'I have a task for you, Ashnak.'

As always after the operation of sorcery, the nameless necromancer's voice sharpened and became alert.

'You may take three other warriors with you. No more than three. You are to go in secrecy to where my agent awaits you. I will give you a talisman for recognition. Then you are to be guards while a task is performed for me. After that, you will be told what to do.'

'Yes, master!'

Ashnak prostrated himself, iron weapons clanging on the flag-stones, and banged his forehead three or four times against the stone floor. It was not something that particularly hurt him, and it tended to placate the nameless necromancer.

'At once, master!'

'You give me a headache, Ashnak,' the nameless necromancer said, reaching for a bottle spun from the silicon bones of a foe stranger than is easily comprehended. 'Go *away*.'

Two pairs of eyes surveyed the outside of the tavern from slightly less than three feet six inches above ground level.

'We're never going to get our gear out of our room,' Will Brandiman said.

'Not without running into the Assassins' Guild,' Ned Brandiman concluded. 'They're bound to have got back here before we did, right, Will?'

Will Brandiman picked up his trailing skirts and faded back from the alley entrance. The laced bodice was uncomfortably tight, restricting his access to the throwing knives strapped under his arms. He coiled the child's skipping-rope and stuffed it into a pocket.

''Fraid so, Ned.'

He glanced at his brother. Ned's pink-frilled frock had become stained with town dirt, and his brown hair (too short really to plait) was coming out of its braids. He didn't suppose he looked much better. He rubbed his hand over his chin, and reflected on the odd advantages not having to shave more than twice a month can give.

'I wouldn't trust this disguise at close quarters,' the halfling said, 'though it's served us well enough today. We got the job done. Now let me see . . .'

'We have to get that crowd out of the tavern room, right?' his brother halfling asked.

'Right. And in such a way that the Assassins' Guild people have to come out with them. So . . .'

'So it's simple.' Ned pointed above his head at the thatched roof. 'Set fire to one of the houses over here. Everyone'll come rushing out – the Guild too, because you can't refuse fire-fighting duty. Not publicly. We go in, get our stuff, and leave.'

Will raised his eyebrows, pleasantly surprised. 'What would I do without you, brother? Very well. Let's find some dry thatch. And, for preference, an occupied building.'

'Why?—oh.' Ned grinned. 'Cries for help'll bring 'em out running.'

'Exactly.'

The last of a long summer twilight shone in the west. The flint and steel bristled sparks on to tinder. Will carefully set fire to three strips of cloth ripped from his dress, and poked them up under the low eaves with a stick.

They retreated into darker alleys opposite the tavern.

'FIRE!'

Raw-throated screaming started.

The tavern emptied a crowd into the winding street. Shouts filled the air. Men and a few elven-kind and dwarves calling for water, buckets, billhooks and sand. Invisible in firelight, the brothers slipped past them into the echoing, empty tavern, sprinting upstairs to their room.

'Let's move it!'

Will ripped his dress over his head. His short, stocky frame glowed in the light from the burning buildings. Fingers fumbling, he pulled on shirt, trunk hose, fine mailshirt and doublet. He buckled on his sword, checked the placing of throwing daggers and poisoned needles; and ran over to join Ned where the elder halfling was throwing every piece of gear from dark lanterns to heavy-duty crossbows into the brass-bound chests.

'Lower 'em down from the back window with the rope,' Ned said. 'We'll go out and round the tavern—'

Will darted across the room and laid the palm of his small hand on the door. He frowned, opened the door a crack, and looked into roaring flames. All the tavern's stairs blazed.

Burning thatch floats.

'We'll jump down after,' he corrected, shutting the door and coughing. 'It's only one floor.'

'One floor in a Man-building!'

'If you'd rather roast, Ned—!'

Grinning at the expression on his brother's face, Will opened the back window and hefted the first chest up on to the sill. Braced, he lowered it by the rope; lowered the second chest; and scrambled up on to the window sill. He took careful aim and jumped.

'*Arrhhh!* You little turd!'

In a tangle of knees and elbows, Will got himself together and found the inn yard empty except for the Man he'd landed on. The fat human ostler, still sprawling, opened his mouth to yell again, and Will hit him on the temple with the hilt of his dagger. The Man fell backward.

Ned Brandiman's feet hit square on the Man's chest, cushioning his jump also. The Man choked, lips turning blue. The halfling pulled the last pink ribbons from his hair and shook out the braids. He chuckled.

24

'Fast work, Will.'

'No problem, Ned.'

A Man's voice bawled, *'Oi! You two!'*

Will spun round and ran towards the burly man in working clothes at the yard entrance.

'Help! Sir, help us! The tavern's on fire, we were only saved by the heroism of this Man – and I think he's injured; please, help!'

The stranger, a brawling-looking redheaded man, loped across the inn yard and knelt down by the ostler. While he prodded the recumbent form, Will took a swift look around. No sign of Ned, but the stable doors were open . . .

Will palmed a knife as he came up behind the redheaded man, and sliced neatly through the jugular vein with the man facing away from him, so that the gout of blood sprayed across the unconscious ostler. He stared thoughtfully up at the tavern. Smoke coiled out between the eaves. He bent and put the red knife in the ostler's hand.

'Will! Here!'

Straining to lead a sweating pony, Ned Brandiman staggered out of the stables. Will grabbed a couple of empty boxes and, climbing on them, fixed the brass-bound chests either side of the saddle, and finally leaped up behind Ned as his brother flailed a horse-crop nearly as tall as himself, cracking it against the pony's flanks.

The hot wind from the fire blew in his face, and Will grinned widely. The poor quarter's houses and low dives flashed by, lost in the dung kicked up by the pony's hooves. He shook Ned's small but muscular shoulder.

'Slow down!'

His brother heaved on the reins. The pony reluctantly fell into a walk. Ned soothed it, until the flattened ears relaxed; and Will sat straight-backed in the saddle as they paced with dignity through the merchants' quarter, and the night that here was quiet, towards the sleepy guards on Ruxminster's city gate.

The orc encampment steamed gently in the sunshine.

Barashkukor, leaning scabby elbows on the parapet of the Nin-Edin fort, gazed down from the mountainside at a wilderness only the vultures could love. He tilted his dented helmet back on his head. 'So what *do* you get if you cut the legs off a warrior?'

Marukka gave a baritone chuckle, waving her jagged sword in the air for emphasis. 'A low-down bum!'

Barashkukor groaned, but quietly in case she should hear him. The young female orc towered above him by a good twenty inches.

25

'And what,' she pursued, 'do you get if you cut the arms off a low-down bum?'

Barashkukor leaned his pole-axe up against the stone parapet, abandoning all pretence of sentry duty. He scratched at the scabs on his scaly chest, and pulled his scruffy brigandine open – the metal plates sewn into the jacket poked through the worn lining, pinching his tough hide. The hot air sang with emptiness, and the mountain fort glowed like an oven.

'What *do* you get if you cut the arms off a low-down bum?' he repeated.

'An 'armless low-down bum!'

Barashkukor giggled sycophantically. The female orc planted her bowed legs wide, fists on her hips, and bellowed. Her bright orange hair, caught up into a horse-tail on top of her skull, shook wildly. The rusty mail and plate armour in which she clad herself jingled, as did the knives and maces hanging from her wide leather belt. Her vast breasts strained the buckles of her brigandine.

'And *what—*'

Barashkukor sidled along the parapet towards the steps. The rest of the orc band sprawled in the bailey, in the noon heat, around the cooking-pit. Only a few roofless buildings and the outer defences remained of this fort. Barashkukor found it rather homely.

Marukka's sword-point slammed against the wall an inch in front of his face. He halted and assumed an expression of extreme attentiveness.

'—what do you get', she demanded, 'if you cut the *head* off a 'armless, low-down bum?'

He considered it in proportion to the nearness of her jagged weapon. 'Ya got me. What do you get?'

'A headless chicken.'

Barashkukor said incredulously, ' "A headless chicken"?'

'Well – would *you* stand and fight, with no arms and no legs?'

Marukka slapped her bulging green thigh. Her jaw dropped, and she wheezed. Tears leaked out of the corners of her beetle-browed eyes.

'That's good! Isn't that good? I made that one up myself!'

Barashkukor showed all his fangs and tusks in a grin. 'Real good, Marukka. You slay 'em.'

'Sure do.' She stroked the sword complacently and tucked it back under her belt. 'Shouldn't be surprised if I was good enough to be paid. Stinkin' *Men* get paid for jokes. I seen that once. I was in a city, once, you know—'

I know, Barashkukor thought. 'How about a game of Orcball?' he suggested hastily.

26

'Good idea! Aww . . . We ain't got a ball.' Marukka sniffed. She stomped down the steps into the bailey. ''Ere! Whose idea was it to *cook* the dinner?'

The largest orc, who was (it need hardly be said) the band's leader, pointed silently at one of the smaller orcs. Marukka advanced, drawing her sword. The small orc backed away.

'I didn't! It wasn't my idea! I wasn't even here— *urp!*'

Marukka's jagged blade whistled through the air. There was a *whup!* and something relatively round bounced and landed at Barashkukor's feet, still blinking. The orc-band scrambled to their feet with enthusiasm.

'We got a ball,' Marukka announced. 'Let's *play!*'

A voice through his nightmare said:

'What's that smell?'

Will Brandiman moved his head fractionally and winced. A blaze of pain subsided. It was no nightmare. He tested his wrists and found them cord-bound. His lock-picks, by the feel of it, were still sewn into his cuffs. His ankles throbbed, tied much too tightly.

'Roasting pony?' he guessed thickly.

'One day you're going to wake up to the smell of roasting brother,' Ned grumbled.

The ground was hard and damp under his face. Will strained to lift his head. The brilliant moon blazed in his eyes, and he flinched. There was no locating the source of the pain as yet, but he had a small bet that it would be a head wound, and an unprofessional one at that.

'Orcs,' he concluded, sniffing.

A bare foot, hard as the hardest leather boot, kicked him in the ribs. The force of the blow threw him over on to his back. He stared up at a broad-shouldered, squat-legged orc in shining black plate harness. The orc opened its tusked mouth and spat accurately into Will's eye. The saliva stung.

'Orcs,' Will marvelled. 'Well, you can't be that stupid. You managed to surprise me and my brother, and that isn't often done – *ahh!*'

A slightly smaller orc leaned over Will's face from behind him, and shoved the muzzle of its hound-faced bassinet helmet open. The fanged and tilt-eyed face was upside-down from Will's point of view and (he thought) none the better for it. The orc gave a light contralto growl. 'Show respect! Do not speak before Ashnak!'

Will managed to roll himself up into a precarious sitting position. Ned, a bundle of rope, lay a few feet away. A fire burned. The shelter

27

of branches and bracken that had concealed this dip in the ground and the cave entrance were scattered about; the brass-bound chests were open and their contents looted. One of the heavy crossbows hung at the belt of the armoured orc. Will raised one eyebrow in a rare respect.

'Agaku,' he guessed. 'The Man-smart Agaku.'

The armoured orc smiled, showing polished yellow fangs. 'I have not met many, Man or elf-filth or halfling, who are smart as the Agaku.'

Will managed to wipe his face against his knee, cleaning off the last of the acidic saliva. His eyes still ran, blurring the night sky, so that for a panic-stricken moment he was not sure how many orcs surrounded them.

Ned's voice, thick with pain, said, 'A scouting party, I'd guess, since there's only two of them. Will—'

'Yes, yes, I know. It's difficult.'

A spark from the fire drifted through the air and lodged against his cheek, burning. He shook his head violently, and then groaned. The fire had been set in the cave-mouth, not visible from the moorland above, and the charred carcass of the pony appeared to have been extensively chewed.

'You're getting rid of the evidence,' he marvelled, looking up at the larger orc. 'Ashnak, was it, that she called you? Master Ashnak, you and I must talk. I'd find it more convenient if you cut at least my ankles free, since I think that if you don't, I'll lose the use of my feet.'

The ground swooped dizzyingly away as a clawed hand grabbed the back of his doublet and swung him up into the air. The female orc's helmeted face grinned into his from a distance of six inches. Her tusks were long, curved, and capped with bronze. Her whiteless eyes gleamed. She hefted a spiked morningstar in her free hand.

'You little halflings, always so tricksy,' she said, in guttural admiration. 'Mark me, Ashnak. They're on some quest for the Light. If we heed their pleas and free 'em, they'll have some miracle later on, and bring us down in our pride. I've heard Man-tales. *I* know how it goes.'

The spiked pole swung up, poised, swung down—

'Not without my orders, Shazgurim!' The large orc wrenched the morningstar away and belted the other orc with the smooth end, sending her crashing against the earth-wall of the dip in the ground. Will tried his best for a tuck-and-roll fall – being tucked reasonably well already by his bonds – but a sharp rock caught him in the gut, and it was a minute and more before he dragged enough air into his lungs to breathe.

He heard Ned say, very reasonably, 'A bargain – our equipment, which you can use, for our lives, which you have no use for.'

An owl hooted twice, and then hooted twice again. The owl is not necessarily a moorland bird. Moving almost as silently as halflings, two more armoured orcs slid around the tor and over the side of the dip and brandished their war-axes in salute to Ashnak. Will groaned as he rolled over, the cords at his ankles cutting into him like wire.

'They're alone,' one of the orcs grunted. 'No smell of strangers: Men or wizard-filth or squat dwarves.'

The smallest orc, which in the flickering firelight Will thought might be another female, gave a high-pitched giggle. 'No smell of magic, no. None. None!'

He saw Ashnak open his fanged mouth, knew that the orc's next words would be *Kill them!* and played his last card. Fortunately, as usual, it was a fifth ace.

'Hold your hand!' he cried. 'In the name of the nameless necromancer!'

Ned, at his side, made a noise that might have been a groan or a whimper. '"In the name of the nameless"?'

'You know what I *mean*. In the . . . Oh, the hell with it. Orcs!' Will exclaimed, loudly. 'Strong though you are, I know your kind fear magic. Do you really wish to risk offending the nameless necromancer?'

The big orc motioned with his hand. The two scout orcs vanished up on to the moorland again. Shazgurim stood, rebuckling the plate armour on her forearms, and scowled at Ashnak's back. Will noted it. As Ashnak approached, he flicked the hair back out of his eyes and gazed as fearlessly as he could at the orc.

'Hhrmmm . . .' The orc squatted down. In the firelight Will could just make out the clan tattoos on his horny cheeks. Polearms slung across his back, black armour thigh- and arm-defences, engraved breastplate – this is no orc bandit, Will thought. He assumed a dignified confidence.

'And just why', the orc growled, 'would it offend my master the nameless to slice your skins from your bodies, and cook them, and feed them back to you, before we leave you impaled by your arses on our spears for the ravens to rip at?'

'You have a wonderful turn of phrase.' Will paused. 'Your master?'

'Yes, little coney. *My* master. Whose name you have made filthy in your halfling mouth, so perhaps I will feed you live coals after I feed you your skin.'

29

Ned Brandiman groaned.

'Bloody hell, Will! We're not even *at* the Grey Crag. We're not inside twenty miles of the place!'

Will sighed. He looked up at the orc's face, upon which confusion was giving way to comprehension with surprising rapidity.

'I have a certain talisman about my person,' he said. 'If I were you, I'd cut me free and let me reach it out, there are poison needles in the matter, you see.'

Shazgurim growled, disgusted. 'Talisman. By the rotten bowels of the Dark Lord! Ashnak, you mark my words, we shall live to regret this.'

The jagged knife sliced the cords at his wrists and ankles. When they saw how he could not move, the big orc chafed his flesh between horny hands until Will, yelping, managed first to stagger to his feet and then, while they cut Ned free, to reach into the booby-trapped pouch and extract an inert cube of amber.

'Say your word.'

The orc's brow furrowed. Ashnak at last muttered: 'Zerganu-baniphal!'

The amber cube pulsed once, warming Will's hand. He tossed it to the orc, said 'Banidukkunishubar,' and watched it glow with as great a light. 'I won't say, "Well met." We are twenty miles off the rendezvous and you've eaten my pony.'

'*Our* pony,' Ned Brandiman corrected. The brown-haired halfling stretched his arms and legs in turn, and looked up at the orc from about waist-height. 'You're a warrior by the look of you – what's the nameless doing sending the Horde? We don't want you clumping around telling the whole world where we're going. We don't work that way.'

Shazgurim slouched over, tipping the visor of her steel bassinet back on her head. 'Just how do you two work?'

Will and Ned looked at each other.

'Ned and Will Brandiman,' Ned introduced. 'Notorious 'alflings. Sir and madam, you are looking at two of the greatest professionals it will ever be your good fortune to meet. As to what we do, we find lost property.'

Shazgurim snorted. 'And is it usually lost before you two "find" it?'

'Now that you come to mention it . . .'

Ashnak nodded his great tusked head. 'Thieves. Our master the nameless said there would be thieves.'

'We prefer the term *adventurers*. It sounds so much more respectable.' Will brushed himself down, and strolled across the dip

30

to look at the ransacked chests. 'You realize it will be necessary to return the tools of our trade? And, now I come to think about it, we have no transport. I think it would probably be advisable for you to detail one of your warriors to carry these chests for us.'

2

THE SQUAT ORC warrior, Imhullu,
peered over the weathered edge of the tor.

'Bandit country,' Imhullu opinioned. 'Thick as fleas down there,
they'll be. And we've got to get those two little rats through it in one
piece?'

Ashnak of the fighting Agaku leaned his back against a sun-hot
crag, ripping the flesh from a still-twitching rabbit. The warm blood
soothed his throat wonderfully. He wiped the back of his hand across
his tusked mouth. 'I asked for my war-band with me. The request was
not granted.'

'Oh, well . . .'

No further reference was made to the nameless necromancer.
Ashnak crunched the rabbit's bones and then, careful not to skyline
himself, took off his helmet and looked over the edge of the tor. His
long, peaked ears unkinked. Perfectly still, his hide a weathered
brownish-grey, he might have been rock himself.

The high crags of the moorland went down to green dales, and
tame rivers, and the chimney smoke that spoke of Man's habitation.
Ashnak squinted into the wind. To the south, wrinkled bare
mountains rose up. Signs of habitation ceased well before the
foothills of those crags.

Turning his head, he made out how the moorland went around in a
great curve, a hundred miles and more, all of it villaged, and finally
became a distant spur of the mountains. Deceptive soft countryside.

He could feel the tension of it from here, waiting for the final accounting.

'Quicker to go across than round,' Imhullu said. 'If I had fifty picked warriors, I wouldn't think twice about it. By the Dark Lord's balls, our fighters could do with some raiding! Burn a few homesteads, eat the stinkin' Men!'

'Not this close to the Last Battle.'

Squinting, he could from time to time make out Shazgurim scouting. The orc shambled from cover to cover, blending into the rocks wherever she stopped, and finally vanished over a concealing hill and – presumably – down towards the cart-track that was the nearest to a road they had seen for days.

There was no sign of Zarkingu. But then, Ashnak thought, passing a hand wearily over his tough-hided brow, there wouldn't be, would there? Agaku and sorcery don't mix, and she's a magic-sniffer, which makes her crazy as a bedbug, right? Right.

'You could send one of us with one of the rats cross-country, Captain, and the other round the long way.'

Imhullu's suggestion clarified his mind. He said, 'No. We'll stick together. We'll run it. Straight across to the mountains. What is it: fifty miles? We may have to carry the halfling scum, but we can do it in less than a night and a day – or we're not fit to be called Agaku. We'll move after sunset.'

Night came cloudy. Ashnak breathed a sigh of relief. He roused the three warriors and set them to running. The halflings, reluctant at first, ran nearly at orc-speed when Shazgurim and Imhullu set about them with whips, and for nearly half the night; at which point Ashnak picked up the younger of the two halflings and ran with him tucked under one arm, letting Shazgurim carry the other. With the two chests, that made four loads, and they laughed gutturally towards dawn, practising swapping loads by throwing them between each other without stopping. The warriors only dropped the halflings twice, and neither time was an accident, so Ashnak found it unnecessary to discipline them.

Night-vision showed him fewer and fewer villages, and fewer dogs howled as they passed by. In the cold grey before dawn, when Ashnak was particularly alert, he heard the jingle of horse tack and the shouts of Men.

'It's the cursed horse riders,' Imhullu snarled. His feet pounded the earth, beating down the green corn.

Ashnak threw Will Brandiman underarm to Zarkingu who, to his surprise, caught the halfling. 'Race, Agaku! I'll delay them. You know where we are to meet! Go!'

The dew began to fall on him as he slowed. The noise of their jingling weapons and armour faded, drowned out by the approaching beat of hooves. Ashnak squinted into the grey light, planted his feet firmly in the earth on the far side of a field-ditch, and unslung the pole-axe from his back.

'*Hai!*'

With a shout and a horse-scream the first rider cleared the ditch. Ashnak thrust the pole-axe point first, struck home between the horse's eyes and killed it with that blow. The rider – a Man – flew off somewhere to the side and landed hard. Ashnak was already swinging back to hack at the legs of the second horse.

'We have him! Here! He's standing ground!'

Grey shapes appeared to the left and right. Ashnak impaled the second rider as he fell, put his foot on the Man's chest and ripped the axe free, and swung up into guard position, grinning.

'Peace!' he bellowed. 'I surrender!'

He beamed with what he knew would not be recognized as sheer curiosity. The riders obviously took it for ferocity. When a circle of a dozen surrounded him – and he could have dealt with that number, they were mostly raw levies by the looks of them – he snarled and threw down the axe. It was still a goodly number of minutes before one female Man dismounted and chained his wrists together. After that there were kicks and blows, but orc-hide is thick. He winced, all the same, for the look of the thing.

By the time he had been dragged the mile or so to the nearest village, and imprisoned (of all places) in the local church – it being the only stone building, he concluded – his boredom threshold had been reached. The other three should be well away towards the mountains. Still, there was a chance they might run into their share of trouble, burdened with two troublesome halflings . . .

Ashnak spat on his hardened hands and began to bend the iron bars on the church door.

A voice became audible on the other side:

'—have him in here?'

He moved quickly and surprisingly quietly back into the body of the church. There was an altar to one of the smaller gods of Light, which troubled him only a little. There was no sign, he noted, of a stone for sacrifices, or any of the usual religious furniture.

'So!' Surrounded by ten or twenty armed warriors, a female Man entered through the doors. Most of her guard were Men, with a few dwarves, and – Ashnak growled – two or three of the elven filth, with bows.

Then he saw her face, and congratulated himself on his curiosity.

34

'This is nothing but an orc warrior, master mayor. Why have your villagers bothered me with this?'

And the voice too, Ashnak marvelled. So that's the way of it, is it? Or is it? Can it be possible?

The village's mayor, a thin and shabbily dressed man, stuttered, 'But it's an orc! An *orc!* Look at it!'

'I know an orc when I see one.'

Ashnak hunched further forward to disguise his height, being almost as tall as the Men there. He lurched forward a couple of steps, deliberately looked up into her face and flung his hand across his eyes. He dropped to his knees and banged his head against the stone paving. 'Master! Nameless! Nameless master!'

There were gasps, exclamations. When her voice spoke again, it was steely.

'I am not nameless. I am called The Named.'

Ashnak rose up on to hands and knees. It was a handy position from which to assess the arms present – his own weapons having been removed, he would need replacements. Then he looked up at the female Man.

'You are not the nameless?'

The Named said, 'He is my twin.'

Ashnak studied The Named. He nodded, and got to his feet. 'You have his face entirely. There must have been something sorcerous in your birth, to bring you male and female so identical from the same womb.'

The woman's short hair was the colour of buttercups, or clear fat when it is boiled from living bones. Her pale, tilt-eyed face had an almost orcish beauty. He guessed this might make her shunned among her own kind. He showed his back fangs in a grin.

She raised her hand and struck him across the face.

Not braced for it, Ashnak fell to one knee and then toppled over on to the stone floor. The magic of her augmented strength buzzed in his head. He felt his mouth, cutting the hide of his hand on a broken tusk.

'Lady!' Ashnak cowered.

'Yes!' she said. 'I am his twin in power, also, but my power is given to the Light.'

On cue, sunlight slanted down from the church windows, shining back unbearably from the woman's mirror-finish plate armour. The gold Sun embroidered on her surcoat, insignia of the Order of White Mages, left after-images dazzling across his vision. He raised a hand quite genuinely to block the sight.

'You must understand,' Ashnak said painfully, slurring his words a

35

little, 'to a warrior, none of this means much. Wars are wars. Power is power.'

'That is the Dark's heresy!'

'I am a warrior. I am of the fighting Agaku! That is all I know, and all I need to know!'

'And all you need to know of me is . . . poor creature: I am merciful.' She turned on her heel. The rest of them followed her out – elven-filth in their wood green, carrying bows taller than their tall selves; engineer-dwarves with food-stained beards; Man-heroes with the smell of horses about them.

Not looking back as she left, The Named said, 'Confine him here for judgement, master mayor, until the Last Battle has been fought and won. That will be before this harvest-time, I promise you. Now we must ride. I must be in the city of Sarderis before noon.'

Ashnak suffered the village blacksmith to load him with chains, while he listened with the keen ears of an Agaku for The Named's party to saddle up and go. The noise of that came as dawn properly lit the sky. Ashnak sighed and breathed out, snapping the chains. He was as tall as a Man, and something on the order of four times as heavy-set. A little greenish blood trickled down from his muscular arms.

He reached out and took the blacksmith's hammer, smashing the Man's skull with it; and used that weapon to walk through the village to the armoury and collect himself what staff-weapons and projectiles might prove useful. He met no one capable of stopping him, and no one capable of outrunning him to get a message to the absent forces of Light.

The sky above turned blue and pink, clouds shredding away from the sun. Gold light fell welcome and warm on his hide. Ashnak trod through the dewy grass of the village green, avoiding the fallen bodies, relaxing in the day's beauty.

He tightened the carrying-straps on his new war-axe, sniffed the air for direction, and began to jog, picking up speed, due south towards his warriors and their cargo.

Will Brandiman carefully stretched the seams of his shirt over the candle flame. Fleas sizzled and popped. He glanced over at Ned, who was scratching furiously at his crotch.

'I told you she had crabs,' he observed. Ned snarled.

The wind in the high mountains did not penetrate as far down through the cave system as this cavern. Will could still hear it battering at the living rock. He shuddered. His whip-welts stung, despite copious applications of a salve they possessed far too little of.

The grime of sweaty running clung to his skin; his bowels were emptying themselves with dismal irregularity; and suggesting cooked food to the orc warriors seemed the shortest way to an unsung death.

He gave up and shrugged the shirt back over his small, stocky shoulders; and fastened his trunk-hose. Next an arming-doublet, mail pointed to it; then an over-jerkin; and then a furred cloak. The cold of the rock still made him shiver. He cupped his hands over the candle-end.

'Where are the other two?' He nodded at Zarkingu's back. Orcs do not perform acts of magic, they hate and fear it, and for that reason are uncommonly good at sniffing it out. The small orc was cuddled into a heap around the shaft of her warhammer, staring listlessly up the passage.

'They're scouting. Doesn't it make you feel so bloody secure', Ned said bitterly, 'knowing they're guarding us? When they said the contract included an armed escort, this isn't what I had in mind!'

'I can smell magic,' Zarkingu crooned. 'I can smell magic . . .'

'I can smell shit, sweat and orc,' Ned said with asperity, 'but do I complain about it?'

Will pulled his woollen cap down firmly on his black curls. He shuffled over to sit beside Ned. The same greasy pack of playing-cards (three of the major arcana missing) gave them a hand each; and an excuse for sitting together. Completely silently, and therefore not suspiciously.

Will moved his left hand rapidly and unobtrusively in the Thieves' Guild finger-talk.

—*Is the fourth one dead? That leaves them without a leader. That makes them dangerous.*

Ned frowned at the cards he held, scratching through three layers of cloth at his lice-infested pubic hair. He used the movement to finger:

—*They probably plan to kill us anyway when we complete the contract.*

—*Is she right about magic?*

—*I think so.*

—*So we stick to the original plan?*

—*Whether the other one comes back or not. I don't trust him. I don't trust any of the Agaku, they're too cunning. Ordinary orcs would be a pushover. We counted on it being Men, remember?*

Will musingly agreed: 'Mmmm . . . Your deal.' He added in fingerspeech:

—*We don't have long. Four or five days, maximum. And thanks to these knuckleheads, we're severely under-equipped.*

37

—Courage, brother. We won't need long. But let's not tell them that.

'I wonder if it's dark or daylight?' Will played a deuce he had not been dealt. 'It feels like afternoon. We'll have to do some scouting of our own, soon.'

A scuffle in the passage attracted his attention. Zarkingu lurched upright. The candle sent her spiked shadow dancing in a sudden draught.

'Who goes there?'

'I, Ashnak.' The big orc shambled into the cavern. Four fresh heads dripped from his belt, hung by the hair. He threw down the other male orc, unconscious, laughing deep in his chest. 'I found Imhullu unsuspecting – wake up, fool!'

Will huddled unobtrusively into his cloak. The big orc unsnapped the whip from his belt and welted Imhullu across the back and legs until the other orc stirred, muttered something thickly, and then prostrated himself in front of Ashnak, banging his head on the cave floor.

'Captain!'

'I'll *captain* you, you miserable gut-rotted offspring of an elf!' Ashnak threw the severed Man-heads to Zarkingu, who cradled them. He strode over the prostrate Imhullu, towards the halflings. Will got to his feet, dusting himself down, and met the orc's glare with a civil smile.

'Captain Ashnak. We were afraid you wouldn't be rejoining us. No trouble, I hope?'

At the passage mouth, Zarkingu whispered, 'I smell magic, much magic, stinking magic, magic of Light . . .'

Ashnak coughed gutturally. He reached down and picked Will up by the front of his doublet, nails digging in through heavy wool and mailshirt to cringing flesh. 'Now we are in these unchancy mountains, halfling, you tell me – what are you here for?'

The mailshirt, riding up under his arms, pinched Will's skin painfully. He wriggled. Ned Brandiman stood up and tapped the orc's arm, as high as the halfling could reach.

'We're here for the usual,' Ned said. 'To steal a hoard from a dragon.'

3

T HE AIR HAD morning's clarity in the mountains. Barashkukor looked up at the immensity of the rock; the great range of bare crags that ended, to east and west above him, in rock-walls almost vertical. Mountain stone gleamed grey, silver, ochre and gold in the dawn light. He bared small fangs and snarled at the grandeur.

He shuffled down the parapet above the gate-house, sorting out the straps of his helmet and plated brigandine as he went.

In this sole gap in the mountain range, the isolated crag of Nin-Edin rose up cliff-sided, and the small road through the pass ran around the foot of it, under the walls of its ancient fort.

Barashkukor averted his gaze. He scratched at his balls, missing the sleeping warmth of the fifty bodies in his own orc-nest. He spared a glance back across the ruined motte and bailey of Nin-Edin – the bloody wreckage of the previous day's Orcball tournament; several dozen orcs around the thinly smoking night's firepits, sorting out the hunt and rutting in the open air.

'Here, Barashkukor.'

'Thanks, Kusaritku.' He took the wriggling rock-vole the black orc offered, knocked its brains out against his heel, and swallowed it in two gulps without chewing. 'What news of the night?'

'Silent as a throat-slit elf.' Kusaritku passed a small bottle of black spirit.

The air had an unwelcome chill. Barashkukor drank. 'Who's the day-watch?'

'Duranki, Tukurash, Ekurzida. I'll rouse 'em.' The black orc grinned. 'Trust me!'

Barashkukor shambled further down the parapet, staring down the long valley of the pass while he pissed a steaming black jet off the wall.

A voice close at hand shouted, '—and *I* say he will reach it!'

'Never!' Marukka's baritone bellow.

'You arse-licking elf-lover, he *will!*'

Barashkukor started, dribbling piss down his leg. Hastily he stuffed himself back in his ripped breeches and came to what might pass for attention. The largest of the black orcs, Azarluhi, strode past him without even a nod, deep in conversation with Marukka. The big female orc held a tiny orc by one leg.

'Watch!' she demanded.

She raised her arm above her head and whirled the small orc like a slingshot. Barashkukor ducked as its hands clipped his helmet. At the point of maximum velocity she let go, and the orc shot away in a low arc. A diminishing wail followed it down.

Barashkukor leaned over the parapet.

A puff of dust showed where the small orc first struck the steep slope, then another, then three more like a stone skipping across water. The small body bounced and came to rest on the edge of the road, five hundred feet below.

'Aw. It did. But only just,' Marukka grumbled. She leaned over the parapet and yelled at the just-visibly stirring figure: *'Get back up here, Kazadhuron, you're on guard duty!'*

'That's five shillings you owe me,' the black orc pointed out.

Marukka's eye fell on Barashkukor with a gaze speculative as to weight and aerodynamics. She grinned at Azarluhi.

'Wanna make it best out of three?'

In the timeless dark under the mountains, Ashnak squatted alone in a cavern. The light from the amber cube gleamed on his tusked and prick-eared face; shone from his polished vambraces and the rivets of his black armour.

He prodded the cube's indentations delicately with one claw. A lightning-fork of black light sparked to the cave wall. The rough stone turned black with ice, and a searing cold wind began to blow. The blackness became the dark of the tower. The whiteness of the Throne of Bone gleamed; and a shaft of light shot down and illuminated the seated figure.

The nameless necromancer shaded wide-pupilled green eyes with his hand. He glanced up, painfully, and made a magic sign with long, pale fingers. The shaft of light dimmed somewhat.

'What news for me, Ashnak, other than that you are arrived in the mountains?'

Ashnak rumbled, clearing his throat. 'I allowed myself to be taken, for a short time, by the cursed horse riders, and during this time I met one who is called The Named.'

A glacial amusement leaked into the cavern.

'So you have met my sister. That is well. This concerns her, also. Now attend well to what I say, Ashnak.'

Ashnak heard the background clink of bottle and glass.

'The dragon Dagurashibanipal is old, and her hoard collected from many strange places and times. I have reason to know that in that hoard there are strange and magical weapons. Hmm.' The voice took on a thoughtful tone. 'Halfling bones . . . too fragile to be truly creative with . . . no, you need not bring me back the bodies, once you are done. You are to take the weapons to the fortress of Nin-Edin, put them into the hands of the warriors there, and lead them against Guthranc. There you are to kill or take my sister The Named, so that she shall not ride against our Master the Dark Lord on the Last Day. Am I going too fast for you, orc?'

'We are to fight?' Ashnak sprang to his feet, a light in his eyes. Joyously he shook and brandished his warhammer. 'I am to lead a war-band! Master, I thank you!'

'Not so *loud* . . . There must be servants I might have, of more tact and delicacy than orcs – but there again, you have your uses. Hurry to do my bidding, Ashnak.'

The image on the cave wall altered. Ashnak saw factories belching out smoke, the siege-engines of war, the companies marching in from every land to a Lord greater even than the nameless necromancer; the Horde of Darkness gathering, and its numbers hiding the very earth beneath it.

'Soon, *soon*, we ride out to the Last Battle. But,' the soft voice said, 'my sister The Named must not ride against us. See to it, Ashnak. And be aware that, should you die failing to achieve this, my punishments are not limited by your being dead.'

Will Brandiman walked back out of a carven stone tunnel entrance, slipping between the silver-inlaid oaken doors. Its roof was only halfling-high. He brushed black char from the front of his doublet. A few curls of hair fell, crisped, to the rock floor.

'All right?'

'Fine.' Ned Brandiman, following, pulled the door to behind him, and sheathed a substance-tipped stiletto. 'Gets 'em every time. Right. Let's see what we've got . . .'

Zarkingu, a new skull-ornamented standard-pole over her shoulder, sniffed the air with an ecstatic expression on her tusked face.

'Dragon-magic *dies*,' she announced.

The biggest orc rumbled something to Imhullu and Shazgurim, who hefted their jagged war-axes in the narrow cavern and flanked the group. Will held up a small hand.

'Better let us go first, Captain Ashnak. There'll be booby-traps, or I don't know dragons. Even dead dragons. Ned, bring out the detection equipment.'

The older halfling, avoiding Will's eye, dug into the brass-bound chest and brought out a wire-spring-and-glass contraption. It might even *be* a trap-detector, Will thought, for all I know. He took it with nerve-twitching care between his two hands, and studied it with deliberation.

Ned rattled his fingers absently on the chest.

—I'll do the checking for real traps, brother. You just convince them that we're indispensable because we can work that thing. Whatever it is.

Will took a deep breath and turned back to the carved tunnel entrance. Ned pushed the doors open. A breeze blew out, heavy with the spice-scents of decaying magic. In the light of Ned's torch, and with the uncannily silent footsteps of four crouching Agaku behind him, he walked down the short tunnel and out into the great cave.

'Dark Lord's prick!' Ashnak swore, straightening up.

Blue light blazed into Will's eyes, brighter now as the great dragon died. He heard the other orcs exclaim behind him.

Dagurashibanipal's spiky body lay, a glass mountain, in the centre of the cathedral-sized cavern. He stared at the crystal length of her, camouflage-coloured to the vast heap of silver and adamant upon which she sprawled. Even dead, she towered high as fortress walls. The unnatural yellow light died in the slits of her horn-lidded eyes.

One wing twitched.

Horn and bone slid together under torchlight. Metal sinews stretched, gears and cogs whirred; and Dagurashibanipal's one prosthetic wing unfurled in a last mechanical reflex. It reared up into the cavern's heights; curled, split, ribboned, shredded; then fell like a collapsing ship's sail.

'Golem . . .' Will, eyes wide, stared at flesh and blood, at wire and canvas, and neither moved again. The poisoned dragon's diamantine corpse stilled. He began a slow circling of the cavern wall beside Ned, paying a deliberate attention to the wire-spring-and-glass device in his hands.

Ned muttered under his breath, 'It's only another dragon. Dammit. It's only another dragon . . .'

Ashnak of the Agaku marched across to the hoard, kicking silver crowns and diamonds contemptuously aside. 'This isn't what we came to find! Are you sure this is the right dragon?'

Will, soberly, said, 'There is – was – only one Dagurashibanipal, and that is she. *Look out!*'

Ashnak threw himself flat on the stone floor.

'Elfshit!' A claw ripped Imhullu's face and the squat orc swore, ignored the blood streaming from his eye-socket, and swung the great jagged pole-axe in both hands. Something clashed, impacting against the stone wall. 'Agaku! *Agaku!*'

Wings hissed through the blue air. Chittering, their metallic claws outstretched, a flock of tiny dragonet-golem fell from where they roosted in the cavern's ceiling.

'Agaku!' Shazgurim yelled cheerfully, bassinet's hound-visor down, swinging her axe in a figure-of-eight blur. Gear-cogs and glass eyes sprayed away from her.

'Last magic! Last magic!' The smaller female orc waved her hands in the air, attempting to snatch one of the dragonet-golem in flight. Ashnak straight-armed her into the wall, face forwards, spat on his horny hands, and battered the last of the flying machinelets into crumpled horn and hawser.

'Well warned!' he chuckled throatily. 'Good exercise for the Agaku, master halfling. Is there more?'

Will shook his head dumbly.

'*Here!*' Zarkingu hopped from foot to horny foot, wiping the blood from her battered features. 'Ashnak! Here!'

Will carried the wire-spring-and-glass device carefully over to the entrance of a side-cavern, hands still shaking. 'Madam Zarkingu, best be wary. Let the experts check it out first. Ned, what do you think?'

'Mmm . . . could be fine . . .'

'But what *is* it?'

A vast tunnel stretched out before them, lit by the blue light of dying magic. The sides had been squared off, giving a flat floor and ceiling, and the walls and floor were, for as far as Will could see, lined with metal shelving.

He stared down the ranks of metal shelves. There were stacks of clothing of an odd colour and cut; metal-and-wire devices; chunks of solid but obviously forged metal; and all this piled high out of sight.

Beyond this first one, similar chambers stretched off into the underground distance.

'Different magic . . .' Zarkingu whimpered. 'But not here – not *these*.'

'What's this?' The big orc, Ashnak, pushed past her into the first cavern, seizing a big chunk of metal with what looked like a crossbow grip and trigger at one end. He pulled the trigger.

FOOM!

'Arrrgggh!' Imhullu roared. Fire and shrapnel ricocheted off the tunnel wall behind him, pitted now with a line of two-inch-deep cavities. The squat orc grabbed at the severed tops of his long, hairless ears.

'Yaayy-ahh!' Ashnak lifted the weapon and pulled the trigger again.

DAKKA-DAKKA-DAKKA!

Will ducked. A furnace briefly opened beside the left side of his face. The stone floor hit him between the shoulder-blades. The wire-spring-and-glass device went flying. An ear-splitting sound cracked his skull. Stunned, he hitched himself up on to his elbows, yelling, deafened. 'No! *Stop!*'

Flame seared across Will's vision, bright as the sun at midday; jabbing from the weapon's muzzle. An explosion shook the air. Splinters of diamond flew from the adamantine corpse of the dragon, ricocheting back from the vast cave walls, whizzing past him with dull *whup!* sounds.

'*Weapons!*'

'Ashnak! Ashnak!'

'The nameless was right!'

'Fighting Agaku! Fighting Agaku!'

On knees and elbows, Will Brandiman worked his way rapidly back across the dry stone floor to where his brother lay under the bottom-most metal shelf nearest the entrance. The halfling's doublet and trunk hose were thick with dust. He lifted his head slightly as Will pushed in next to him. Orc feet ran past, forward and back, bringing out piles of the metal objects into the main cavern.

'Are those all weapons, do you think?'

'I wouldn't be surprised, Will. I wouldn't be at all surprised.'

Horny feet pounded past, and then plodded back. Shazgurim swore, dumping what sounded like half a ton of scrap metal in the main cavern.

'But what kind – sorcerous weapons?'

'Their magic-sniffer said not.'

The permanent temperature of the caves, chill but not freezing, began to sink into Will's bones. He rested his head down on his short arms, blocking out the blue-white light. 'They're probably going to kill us as soon as they remember we're here.'

Ned whispered, 'Can I bring three things to your attention, brother? One: as far as we could make out, Dagurashibanipal sealed up every entrance to this place, apart from that one rat-hole. Two: outside in the chests there is a small amount of the dwarven rock-blasting powder.'

Will lifted his head from his arms. 'Enough to bring a reasonable chunk of the roof down in that tunnel . . . What's the third thing?'

'And three,' the elder halfling said quietly, 'the mad one just said *different magic*. I don't believe a dragon as old as Dagurashibanipal would leave this place without a curse on it. And my guess is that it's probably one that operates better the longer one is actually kept near the hoard.'

'Mmmm . . . Yes. Let's *go*.'

Sneaking out, keeping in the odd shadows that dying magic casts, Will hugged the cavern wall, edging round towards the tunnel. He passed close by Shazgurim as she lifted a thick metal stick with two stems projecting downwards, one short and straight, the other curved. She pulled the crossbow-type trigger.

DUKKA-DUKKA-DUKKA-DUKKA-DUKKA-*FOOM!*

The blacksmith-foundry noise ripped at Will's ears and stomach. He ducked down into shadow. Hot metal sprayed the opposite walls, splinters of stone filled the cavern, and the orcs cheered. Shazgurim threw the weapon down and seized another, which seemed to require the loading of a metal canister into the muzzle.

Will, sneaking past the first abandoned weapon, noted the sigils *7.62 AVTOMAT KALASHNIKOV OBRAZETS 1947G* imprinted in the metal.

4

BARASHKUKOR DOZED IN the warm sun, and woke when his helmet fell over his eyes.

He grunted and snarled. 'Marukka, go away!'

Another rock bounced off the parapet wall. This one hit his pole-axe, where he had propped it against the crenellations. The weapon slid down with a crash. Barashkukor picked it up, scratching between his long, hairless ears.

'Barashkukor!' the black orc Kusaritku bawled from further down the wall. 'What's all the bleedin' noise about?'

Barashkukor leaned over the parapet.

Thirty feet below, on the foot-trampled earth outside Nin-Edin's main gate, two halflings stood looking up at him. Each wore doublet and trunk hose, very ripped and travel-stained. The halfling with black curly hair wore black and grey garments, and a blackened mailshirt, and had a short-sword buckled to his side. The brown-haired halfling had a heavy crossbow slung across his back, a mailcoat, and stood with a foot up on one of a pair of heavy, brass-bound chests.

Barashkukor stared down at their foreshortened figures, his jaw gaping.

The curly-haired halfling shouted, 'Open! Open in the name of the nameless!'

Forty-three miles away, as sunrise touches the towers of Sarderis, The Named suddenly wakes from sleep with an expression that

46

makes her pale features shocking in their ugliness.

Barashkukor stared down the pass again, between the massive raw-ochre slopes of the mountains. A small plume of dust rose from the road.

'*That's* not our escort . . .' He slitted his eyes against the sunlight blasting back from the dry earth. 'Marukka! You're not going to believe this, Marukka . . .'

The female orc leaned her hairy elbows in the gap in the crenellations. 'What am I not going to . . . Hey! Those aren't the warriors we sent out as the halflings' escort. Dark Lord's arse! *More* travellers? I don't believe it. Turn out the guard!'

Barashkukor tumbled down the steps into the guardroom, knocking an on-going card-game aside, grabbed up a helmet (a size too large) and a spiked mace, and bolted out to the main gate. He peered through the portcullis.

The plume of dust was closer.

Just distinguishable, on a Man-skull ornamented standard, the banner of the nameless fluttered. Barashkukor strained sharp eyes, making out the standard-bearer, and what looked like an immense loaded traverse made by lashing together pine-trunks.

'You! Here!'

He scurried to lend his weight to the winch that lifted the portcullis. Groaning and sweating, ten orcs at last got it lifted up. Barashkukor sat down with a thud in the dust.

'They're coming,' the largest black orc Azarluhi said, 'whoever they are.'

Barashkukor heaved himself to his feet, settling the too-large helmet well back on his skull. It crushed his long hairless ears uncomfortably. He unbuckled his brigandine, sweating in the noon heat and smelling like wet dog, and strolled to the gateway. The party was near enough now to make out detail.

'What . . . ?'

Marukka, beside him, echoed, '*What* the—?'

Nin-Edin's war-band leader, a hulking orc named Belitseri, elbowed his way to the front of the crowd. Orcs lined the parapet, and massed in the bailey compound, yelling and screaming questions. Belitseri rested an elbow on Barashkukor's helmet.

'What's *that?*' he demanded.

'I dunno!' Barashkukor stared. The wooden traverse trailed dust back down the pass. What could be seen of its load glittered metallically in the sun. Two orcs, a one-eyed male and a hulking female, pulled it by brute force.

47

Both were wearing odd round helmets, visorless, with painted designs. He saw they also wore long breeches with the same green-and-brown patterns, but – never before seen – worn tucked into Man-boots.

The standard-bearer wore the same loose belted green-and-brown breeches, but with a similar jerkin from which the sleeves had been ripped off. One of the patterned sleeves had been used to tie up her purple hair in a horse-tail. The other sleeve hung from the nameless standard. Bulky metal ornaments hung at her belt and on bandoliers across her breasts. At thirty yards he could see the brightness of her eyes and the flecks of foam around her fangs.

Barashkukor, gaping, fixed his eyes on the largest orc: surely the leader. This one wore black-and-white patterned breeches tucked into heavy black boots that laced halfway up his muscular calves. The breeches had at least a dozen exterior pockets. Metal objects like fruits dangled from his belt and the straps that crossed his chest. Something very bulky and metallic hung across his back. One of his fangs was broken off short; he wore a strip of scarlet cloth tied around his forehead; and he was chewing a thick black roll of halfling pipe-weed, unlit.

'Erm . . .' Barashkukor stared. 'Those are *Agaku*.'

None of the four Agaku slowed their pace at the gateway. Barashkukor, caught in the crowd of speculating garrison orcs, elbowed back out of the way of the traverse. Leader, standard-bearer and burden-carriers walked through the gate with a peculiar, rhythmic stride.

By that time the whole garrison crowded the compound and the walls surrounding it, staring and jabbering, calling questions, laughing, throwing small rocks. Barashkukor gripped his mace fervently and used it to make him a place in the front rank of the crowd.

The largest Agaku held up a horny hand. '*Halt!*'

Instantly the other three Agaku stopped, slamming their booted feet down on to the earth. Something in Barashkukor began to fizz excitedly. He stood up on his toes to watch.

The big Agaku strolled over to stand beside the standard-bearer. His gaze swept the garrison, the orcs clinging to parapet and ruined buildings. He spat the unlit pipe-weed out on to the ground.

'*Now listen up!*'

Barashkukor's ears rang. He shook his head, and just managed to grab his helmet as it fell off. The big Agaku surveyed the assembly with an expression of utter disdain.

'Do you know what you are?' His words bounced back from the

heat-stricken walls. The orcs – by now several hundred strong – fell silent out of curiosity.

'I'll tell you what you are. You're scum! Call yourselves soldiers? You're the lowest form of life there is – scum who *think* they're soldiers. I'm here to tell you that you're wrong.'

Orcs to either side of Barashkukor began to rumble, tempers rising. Marukka's eyes flashed yellow.

'Who the hell are you?' a voice bawled from the back of the crowd.

The big Agaku grinned, showing more than one broken fang. 'Who am I? Perhaps you'd like us to introduce ourselves?'

'Yeah!' Marukka challenged. 'Who *are* you?'

The big Agaku strolled over until he was looming head-and-shoulders over the orange-haired orc. His voice carrying in the sudden silence, he said, 'That, with the standard, is *Marine First Class* Zarkingu. You, soldier, are not fit to wipe her arse, lowly though she is. Over there is *Corporal* Shazgurim, and beside her *Corporal* Imhullu. You are not fit to even *think* about wiping their arses. And I, soldier, am *Gunnery Sergeant* Ashnak, and you are not fit to even breathe in my presence, *do you understand me?*'

'Wh' . . .' The strange words bemused Marukka.

Barashkukor looked up at Ashnak, eyes shining.

Beside him, Marukka shook herself and narrowed her eyes. '*Why you shit-faced—*'

Ashnak's fist went up, came down on Marukka's head, and the orc fell to her knees, pole-axed. A gasp went through the crowd. Growls and snarls sounded in the noon heat. A few dozen of the garrison orcs began to edge forward with drawn knives.

The big Agaku turned his back and strolled across to the makeshift traverse, at which point he barked: ''TenHUT!'

The two *corporals* and the *marine first class* slammed their heels together, bulging arms hanging at their sides, beetle-browed eyes facing ahead, narrowed against the light. Ashnak lifted his head and looked round the garrison again.

'I'm here to make you balls of shit into soldiers,' he announced. 'You sure as fuck won't ever make the rank of *corporal*. I doubt I'll see any *MFCs*. You're not the Agaku, but by the time I'm finished, I'll make you dumb grunts into Orc *Marines!*'

Jeers and yells echoed off the sides of the mountain pass. The garrison orcs leaped up and down, chanting, foaming at the mouths. Barashkukor fought to keep his balance.

Gunnery Sergeant Ashnak swung the heavy piece of metal off his shoulder, did something to it with his horny hands that made it click and slam, and lifted it to his shoulder. Barashkukor glimpsed something that looked like a crossbow trigger-grip, and flung himself face-down on the earth.

A loud explosion split the air, and a whoosh of heat scalded the compound. Barashkukor lifted his head as a loud *whumph!* sounded. Metal fragments sprayed the crowd of orcs, scything down bodies and slicing limbs from torsos.

The chain of the portcullis flailed, cut cleanly in two. Three masonry blocks fell out of the gatehouse wall. The portcullis itself, falling free, buried its spikes eighteen inches deep in the earth under the gateway, impaling three small orcs.

Silence.

Barashkukor slowly dared to breathe.

'I'm here to make you into marines!' Ashnak bawled. 'And you're going to stay here until you *are* marines! Now *get in ranks.*'

A minute's furious shoving put Barashkukor in the front of the war-band as it straggled into an approximation of rank and file. Excitement burned in his breast. He put on his over-large helmet and pushed it down level with his eyes, sloped his mace across his shoulder, and drew himself up as straight as he could. The gunnery sergeant strolled up to one end of the ranks, and then back down, and heaved a deep sigh.

'Standatt – *ease!*' he barked. The three Agaku relaxed their erect posture slightly. Some of the garrison orcs copied them. Ashnak spun round. 'Not you! You'll stand at attention until I tell you different. Attennn–*shun!*'

Barashkukor thumped his bare heels down into the dirt. The big Agaku caught his eye for a moment, and Barashkukor straightened still further. Ashnak nodded slightly.

'Now listen up!' Ashnak strolled back to the centre of the compound. 'You scum can consider yourselves in training for a mission for the nameless. And since it's an emergency mission, that means emergency training, and *that* means it carries on, day and night, night and day, until you get it right. Right, marines?'

'Erm . . .'

'. . . well . . .'

Ashnak shouldered his metal weapon threateningly. 'Now listen to me, you . . . you . . . *halflings!* You're talking to an officer! From now on, the first word and the last word out of your mouths is gonna be *sir*, you got that?'

Barashkukor led the ragged reply:

'Sir, yes, *sir!*'

Ashnak scowled and bellowed, 'Can't *hear* you!'

Four hundred orc voices bellowed: 'SIR, YES, SIR!'

'That's better. That's better, you halflings, I can almost hear you.' Ashnak fished in his pockets for another roll of pipe-weed and jammed it into the corner of his broken-tusked mouth. 'Now let me hear you say what you are. You're not garrison orcs. You're not whatever poxy tribe littered you. You're *marines*. That flag on the standard is *your* flag, if you're ever worthy of it. Marines are the best. Marines are killing machines. What are you?'

Barashkukor straightened his slouching spine until he thought it would crack. The strange words the big Agaku used were becoming instantly familiar, almost part of his own tongue. No magic-sniffer, he nonetheless felt by orc-instinct that presence of sorcery, geas or curse. But if the marine first class (Magic-Disposal) wasn't complaining . . . He fixed his gaze directly ahead and sang out: 'We are Marines!'

His voice was almost lost in the full-throated chorus.

Ashnak, grinning, snarled, '*Can't hear you!* What are you?'

'SIR, MARINES, SIR!'

Will put his feet up on the brass-bound chests, rocking to the movement of the ox-cart. He drank deeply from the ale bottle and passed it up to his brother, returning to the chickens, half-side of pork, flitch of bacon and four dozen small loaves that the cart had also been carrying.

The quiet farmland slid past them. The ox lowed from time to time, missing its former mistress, but Ned Brandiman flicked it with a carter's whip from time to time, ensuring co-operation.

'I tell you one thing I want,' Ned said through a mouthful of bread and bacon, 'I want an easier way to carry our equipment!'

Will scratched under the arms of his ripped doublet, by practice avoiding both the mail shirt and his store of poisoned needles. 'I'll be happy to stick to city thefts.'

'Brother, you're a fool. Name me a city that isn't going to be sieged and sacked when the war comes.'

'Ha! Name me one that won't grow up like a weed, twice as hardy, afterwards. Merchants never fail to fatten on wars. Even on the Last Battle.'

Evening's golden light shone on the growing fields. No poppies yet to bloody the green corn. Smoke began to curl up from the chimneys of distant towns. Will shifted round, tugging at the crotch of his tattered trunk hose, and staring whimsically back at the mountains.

'Do you think the orc garrison will have worked it out yet – that we fooled them into giving us an armed escort to the edge of the wilderness?'

51

'And transporting our baggage too? Call it part-payment from our nameless employer.' Ned Brandiman reached back. Will placed a cold partridge in the outstretched small hand. His brother added, 'So far all we've had for our work is whippings, beatings, poverty and—'

'—and is it worth attempting to collect payment from an evil wizard, when his guards are dead or worse, and at any rate trapped under a mountain, and what we set out to thieve is still down there with them?' Will paused.

The ox-cart trundled on down roads that became steadily better paved as they came closer to the city of Sarderis.

Will Brandiman bit into the chicken and ripped a wing free. He answered himself thickly, 'Yes. It's worth it. Not our payment – our *revenge*. What was it you overheard, brother? The nameless has a sister who is called The Named, and who wears the armour of Light? I think we should find her, offer our services, and betray what we know to her.'

The vulture lets the wind feather its wings, rising on a hot thermal. The mountains lie below it like wrinkled grey flesh. Its central vision focuses on the parasites that crawl on that skin. A numerous hive of them, cupped in the fort's stone claws . . .

Pickings are good now. The tough-hided beasts are cast out from the walls, bloodied and sometimes dead, in increasing numbers. True, it is commonly the little or the sick ones. And, true, there is a surprising lack of pickable rubbish in the compound.

It wheels, wings fingering the sky. Other vultures flock in from the wilderness's wide skies.

Below, the Orc Marine garrison trains.

Midnight chimed from Sarderis's city bells. Will Brandiman froze until the harsh clangs ceased. He strained his ears to hear movement from the closed doors that presumably – he and Ned had not been able to case more than the lower floor of the clothier's shop in daylight – led to bedrooms.

His night-vision adjusted. He watched Ned Brandiman pad along the upper-floor corridor, stop at the first door on the left-hand side, and listen for some moments. Ned signalled:

– No movement.

Ned reached up, tried the latch, and silently opened the door.

– Child's room. Man-girl asleep.

Will passed him, treading barefoot and silent to the door on the right. Faint sounds came through the wood. He hesitated, signalled

Ned to remain still, and padded down to the end of the corridor. Probably the master bedroom . . .

The latch of its door clicked, horrifically loud.

Will froze, not even daring to look back at his brother. The beamed and low-ceilinged corridor seemed suddenly airless in the summer night's heat. A scuffling sound came from the room on the right, behind him – someone turning over in bed. But nothing from the room at whose door he stood.

He opened the door, and signalled back, exaggerating the finger-movements in the poor light:

– One Man. One female Man. Both asleep.

Ned nodded, fading back into the little Man-girl's bedroom. During the day the clothes shop had seemed to have two Man-girls, one seven or eight, the other sixteen or so, almost grown; and a much older Man and female Man: the family living over the shop. In a shop doing reasonably well, but not well enough to afford protective spells.

Will's nostrils flared. No scent of guard dog. Nothing but the wool-and-herb smell of the clothier's shop, and the warm odour of sleeping Men. He waited no longer. Eyeing the wooden locker at the foot of the bed, he drew his eight-inch knife and approached the side of the mattress on which the middle-aged Man was sleeping. The man had yellow-tinged grey hair, and liver-spotted hands.

Will clamped his hand over the Man's mouth, pinching the nostrils shut; sliced the razor-edged hunting knife through the Man's throat, and then stabbed it up under the ribs into the heart. The body heaved and twitched once, going instantly into shock and then death.

The female Man stirred, rolled a little, and reached out her hand towards the Man.

Will Brandiman got one knee up on to the mattress, heaved his body up on to the Man-sized bed, and lurched over the bleeding body. His left hand flailed down, striking the female Man above the eyes. She grunted. He slid his hand down over her mouth, hooked the knife across her windpipe and pulled it sharply towards him, and still with the same grip lifted the knife and slammed it down between her ribs. The female Man's throat bubbled. Her body relaxed.

Weak and shaking, he slid down off the bed. Blood soaked the sheets and mattress, dripping down to the floor. It would soak through the plaster and drip through the ceiling to the shop, he guessed; but that would only be discovered later. Tonight there would be no nosy neighbours – not unless anything disturbed the silence.

Will trod stickily across the bedroom floor and looked down the corridor. Ned Brandiman stepped out of the small Man-girl's bedroom. He held his knife, and the front of his doublet and trunk hose were stained red. He pointed across to the remaining closed bedroom door, and cupped his hand to his ears.

– Eldest daughter, Will signalled.

He walked down the corridor. A plank gave under his heel. Caught unprepared, he had shifted his weight before he realized; and the wood groaned. He froze.

Ned Brandiman pressed his back to the corridor wall, a foot to the side of the right-hand door. Will crossed swiftly to the far side. Inside the room, flint scraped, and a lantern spluttered. He heard footsteps move – cross the room – a chair-leg scraped. Nothing more.

Somewhere a city clock chimed a quarter past the hour.

Will flexed his shaking hands. The blood dried and flaked off, itching. He pressed his back against the wall, listening until his head felt as though it would burst. The faintest whisking sound might have been pages turning.

– We have to get her out of there.

Will nodded, and signalled back:

– Get her to the open door. Then we can take her.

He let his chin rest down on his chest for a moment, and then raised his head. The starlight shone in through the bedroom's open door opposite, illuminating in that room a bed too small for any Man but a child; a bed full of wet darkness.

Will put out his fist and knocked on the door, low down.

'Lizzey, is that you?'

Knock, knock, knock.

'Go back to bed. I'll get Mum and Dad up.'

Knock, knock.

'Go back to *bed*, Lizzey.'

Knock, knock, knock, knock.

'Lizzey, go *away*. I'll get Mum and Dad up, and they'll give you a hiding.'

Will knocked again, low down on the door. Behind the closed door he heard a chair scrape on floorboards.

'All right, Lizzey, you just wait—'

The latch lifted and the door opened.

'Lizzey?'

The yellow-haired young female Man frowned, caught stooping over to the height of a child. Ned brought his hunting knife up double-handed, slashing across her throat; and buried it in the back of her neck as she pitched forward on to her hands and knees, and slowly slumped on to her side.

Will stabbed up under the ribs and into the heart. The girl's throat gurgled. He straightened up.

Less careful of noise now, Will Brandiman walked through the corridor towards the master bedroom. A faint lamplight streamed out of the older daughter's room, shining on the sprawled dead body. It gave enough light for him to see the lock on the chest.

'Damn.' Ned swapped lock-picks. '*Damn.*'

'Easy . . .' Will put a hand on his brother's arm. 'Take it slow. There's no hurry now. It won't be light for another three hours.'

The lid gave, opening with a creak that made him flinch by reflex. Will stared into the empty chest. He grunted, smiling slightly; reached down and pulled the false bottom out. The distant lamplight glinted on coin – mostly silver, a few copper bits, and a very few pieces of gold.

'Just that?' Ned complained.

'Sarderis is a city. There are such things as banks. This will be today's takings, nothing more.' Will sifted the money between his stained palms, taking the heft of the cold metal. 'It's still what we said it would be: the easiest way to replenish our funds. Anything more profitable would be harder and take more planning.'

Ned Brandiman, counting, grunted.

Will padded back to the eldest daughter's room. The corridor stank of excrement. He stepped over the body. Something about the un-intended eroticism of the way her limbs sprawled reminded him of another female Man, a long time ago, also dead. There was a jug and a basin in the room, in which he washed his face and hands, and sponged down as much of his doublet and trunk-hose as seemed feasible.

'One thousand and seven silver shillings, twelve copper pennies, nine gold pounds,' Ned announced. 'Fifty-nine pounds eight shillings total. It'll buy us new clothes, and a pony and harness, and *maybe* replace some of the equipment . . .'

'And make us fitly dressed visitors to The Named,' Will said.

The smell of blood hung heavily in the air, as sweet and rich as a butcher's slaughterhouse. His gut rumbled. There is nothing a halfling likes so much as a good meal. He had eaten Man, when times were difficult, and found it more or less palatable, but not when raw.

'Mmm.' Will raised his eyebrows. 'See if the fire's banked in, will you, brother? If it is, let's cook some young flesh, it'll be the tenderest.'

His brother nodded. 'I'll go look.'

'And – before the blood dries – I'll write somewhat on the walls.' Will Brandiman surveyed the stained white plaster. 'Let them think, whoever discovers this, that it was a madman's act, or done by worshippers of the Dark. Anything to stop them looking for two honest thieves.'

Ned Brandiman chuckled, walking towards the stairs that led down to the shop and the kitchens. 'I remember the last time we did this – you hacked off the heads and impaled them on the bed posts, to make it look like the work of a maniac, not a thief.'

'It worked, didn't it? Four copy-cat killings before the end of that week, if I recall. Covered our tracks nicely.'

Will squatted beside the body of the yellow-haired Man-girl, dipping his fingers in the splashes and gouts of blood. After a while he smiled at his own ingenuity. He wrote:

I AM ARMURED IN RIGHTUSNES AND MY NAME IS CALLED HIDDEN.

5

THE BELL HU-1 Iroquois helicopter lurched nose-downwards over the compound of Nin-Edin, skittered in circles, its tail wagging to and fro, and finally planted its skids in the dirt with a crunching thud. Twelve orc marines staggered out of it and weaved away across the compound.

Wind from the rotors blasted grit into Barashkukor's face as he leaped from the Huey after them, head down, staggered a few yards away from it and fell on to his knees on the earth.

'Shit!'

On his hands and knees, eyes streaming tears, he proceeded to vomit copiously. Then, lifting his head slightly, he saw that he had thrown up over the (formerly) gleaming toes of a pair of very large combat boots.

'Corporal Barashkukor!'

'Yessir! Sorrysir!' Barashkukor climbed unsteadily to his feet. Ashnak smiled ferociously.

'What's the matter with you, Corporal? I'm a reasonable orc. Just tell your old Sarge what the matter is . . .'

'Well, Sarge, it's—'

'. . . BEFORE I RIP YOUR LOUSY, SCRAWNY, PUS-RIDDEN SKIN OFF, AND NAIL IT TO THE NEAREST WALL!'

Barashkukor, ears drooping, wiped his runny nostrils. His green combat trousers were sagging towards his ankles, and he dragged them up, tightening his web-belt, and shrugged the over-large flak jacket further down his skinny body. He snapped a salute, catching one of his long, hairless ears painfully.

'Sir, sorry, sir. Beg to report, sir,' he said, 'I think we're going to have a problem with the airborne assault, si—BLLLEGGH!'

Company Sergeant Major Ashnak looked down at the new layer of slime covering the toes of his boots.

'Sarge, I . . . that is . . .' Barashkukor squeezed his eyes tightly shut. 'I'll just fetch a hammer and nails, shall I, Sarge?'

'CLEAN THAT UP!'

Barashkukor's ears flattened in the blast of the big orc's wrath. 'Sir, yes, sir!' He fell to his knees and began licking. 'Sir, what about the Huey, sir?'

The company sergeant major planted both horny fists on his hips, glaring downwards. He spat an unlit roll of pipe-weed a good three yards. The early sun shone on his grenade-loaded webbing and bullet-bandoliers, and lit up the regimental sigils painted on his tusked face. He tugged the peak of his forage cap further down over his beetle-browed eyes.

'Corporal, get that vomit rocket grounded for good! We're gonna hafta move out of this position soon. None of you useless bastards can fly the chopper without puking their guts and crashing it – it's losing me soldiers. Ground it! Frag it! I never want to see the fucking thing again!'

'Sir, yes, sir!'

Barashkukor crossed Nin-Edin's compound at the double from a racing start, avoiding the piles of oily machinery, disassembled jeeps, turds, and occasional orc corpses littering the ground. The air was already hot. The compound steamed. The fort's rebuilt stone buildings now bristled with skull-pole insignia, gun emplacements, and orcs in combat gear. He slowed, hearing the sound of squads drilling.

'Marine Kusaritku!'

The small black orc turned smartly and saluted. Sixteen of the larger orcs shuffled to attention, drawn up in what they obviously fondly regarded as parade formation. Barashkukor sighed heavily and showed his minute fangs in a smile.

'Call this drill, marine? These squads need more hard work.'

The orcs shuffled into semi-upright stances. The sun glinted on their practise blunderbusses and muskets, held at the slope, and on the occasional broom also held at slope-arms position. At least two of the big orcs wore buckets for helmets.

'Now, you orcs.' Barashkukor planted his feet widely apart and clasped his hands behind his back. 'I have a mission of vital importance for you. It may be difficult. It may be dangerous! It's a dirty job, but someone has to do it – and it's your lucky day.'

Kusaritku ostentatiously looked up at the dawn sky, picking one hairy nostril. The squad of orcs variously scratched bits of their anatomy, hummed, stared off towards the mountains, and – in the rear rank – continued playing cards. Barashkukor filled his lungs with air.

'I didn't say anything about *volunteers!*' His voice squeaked. He cleared his throat and resumed. 'Assholes and elbows, you halflings! Get some ropes and heave that chunk of useless machinery over the wall. I never want to see a Huey again. Now *move!*'

The horde of fanged and tusked orcs broke ranks, seizing ropes as they went, and charged towards the helicopter. Kusaritku ran in their wake, shouting unheeded orders.

'Someone's going to suffer for that,' Barashkukor murmured, turning smartly on one heel. 'Lack of discipline. MFC Duranki! See that Marine Kusaritku reports to Sergeant Zarkingu after he's carried out my orders . . .'

'Sir, yes, sir!' The shaven-skulled orc saluted as he passed.

Barashkukor drew a deep breath and began to walk back across the compound, taking salutes from MFCs and marines even where it was necessary to detour some yards to do it. He buckled the GI helmet firmly down over his long ears. The morning sun shone on one of the stone buildings, now ornamented with a bullet-scarred square of metal upon which someone had painted *Officers Mess*. He could see, through the window, a fist-fight in progress; which was not at all impeding the darts game also happening. As Barashkukor passed the window he heard a scream from the orc, nailed to the wall, with concentric target rings painted on her stomach.

'Sergeant Major!'

He intercepted Company Sergeant Major Ashnak as the big orc left the Officers Mess. Ashnak surveyed Barashkukor, and hastily moved his boots out of the way.

'What is it, Corporal?'

'Sir, you said we'd be leaving this position, sir, and that must mean we're going to fight; and—' Barashkukor heaved in a breath of hot, foetid air. 'And you said I could have a *real* gun, sir; please sir, can I, sir? Now, sir?'

Company Sergeant Major Ashnak examined his talons. 'Certainly, Corporal, certainly. In fact, I think we might even issue you with an M79. Follow me.'

Barashkukor trotted across the compound beside the large orc, towards the ruined stone building marked out as the armoury. He passed a smoking crater in the earth. A scorched size-three pair of combat boots occupied the hole, and the explosively dismembered corpse of an orc. Ashnak strode over a second crater, and spat his cigar into a third. Barashkukor narrowly avoided the fourth crater where a larger pair of scorched boots rocked gently.

'I see Squad Three's mine-detector is still on the blink,' Ashnak observed. 'Here we are, Corporal. Try this.'

Barashkukor reached up to the armoury issuing-window and grabbed the gun Ashnak offered. He leaned over backwards to counteract the apparent weight; and staggered, finding it unexpectedly light.

'The M79 forty-millimetre grenade-launcher,' Company Sergeant Ashnak announced.

Barashkukor strained to grasp the fore-end and stock of the blunderbuss-like weapon, which seemed twice as long as he was tall. He flipped the catch, broke the gun, dropped the positively enormous shell that Ashnak handed him into it, and closed it down. He tucked the stock into his shoulder, muzzle waving wildly as his helmet slipped down over his eyes, and grabbed for the trigger.

'Testing the weapon now, Sa—'

FOOM!

The sun shone painfully into his eyes. Barashkukor rubbed a hand across his face and brought it away bloody. Stone dust covered his combat trousers, where he sprawled on his back amongst the rubble of the armoury wall. There was a warm, wet patch at his crotch. His helmet was gone. The M79 grenade launcher had landed several yards away. Every bone in his body ached, his ears rang, and his nose bled.

'I should watch the recoil on that one . . .' CSM Ashnak strode away, grinning, and pointed to a scattered orc body on the far side of the compound, the bits still smoking from the grenade impact. 'Get that taken over to the cookhouse. Then get your squad on parade, Corporal, I've got an announcement to make. *Now*, marine!'

By the time the ringing concussion had died out of his ears the marine company was drawn up in serried ranks, filling the compound to capacity. Barashkukor snapped his squad to attention, saluting, as Zarkingu walked down the ranks.

'Mmm – yes – hmm?' The sergeant (Magic-Disposal and Administration) lifted her snout out from a sheaf of papers. Her tilted eyes glittered in the sun, and a slight froth trickled down from her small porcine jaws. One of her ears twitched arhythmically. 'Corporal, your squad needs a colour designation. Call yourself Red Squad, or Blue Squad, or . . .'

'Yessir, ma'am!' Barashkukor slammed a salute. 'Please, ma'am, permission to designate this squad Black Squad?'

'No!' The female orc glared. She rattled the sheaf of papers under Barashkukor's pointed nose. 'We already have fifteen Black Squads, twelve Dark Squads, four Raven Squads, three Midnight Squads, one Sable Squad, one Ebony Squad, and,' she consulted a sheet of paper, 'one Pink Squad. Hmm. Yes. Well . . . We're all a little worried about Pink Squad . . .'

Shaking her head, she moved on past Barashkukor. He watched out of the corners of his long eyes as she halted in front of Marukka's all-female squad with their black unit-tattoos, whose helmets had BADGURLZ stencilled on their camouflage-covers.

The sun beat down on Nin-Edin. The homely stench of ordure and decaying flesh rose up from the compound, comforting Barashkukor. He unobtrusively straightened his cleaned webbing, and eased the strap of the M79 grenade launcher where it cut into his horny shoulder.

'*Officer on deck!*'

Barashkukor came to attention and slapped his hand against the butt of the M79. The big female Agaku, Shazgurim, paced along the ranks of orcs, grinning nastily. She gave a lazy half-salute.

'At ease, orcs. Sergeant Zarkingu will now read you *this* week's promotion list. Zarkingu . . .'

The smaller female orc marched up to the skull-standard pole, snapped an about-turn, and faced the orc company. Her thin, piercing voice echoed in the noon heat.

'Now listen up! The entrails have been consulted, according to the usual procedure, and the results of the promotion-auspices are as follows. MFC Kusaritku is promoted to corporal. MFC Marukka is promoted to corporal. MFCs Azarluhi, Tukurash and Ekurzida are made sergeants. Corporal Barashkukor is promoted to first lieutenant.'

Barashkukor drew himself up, proudly, ignoring the jealous mutters in the ranks. He grinned his fiercest grin.

The small female orc, eyes gleaming, continued: 'Sergeants Imhullu, Shazgurim and myself are promoted to the rank of captain. CSM Ashnak is promoted to major, in command of the company. That is all.'

A voice behind Barashkukor muttered, 'Arse-licker!'

'You!' Barashkukor snarled. 'After parade. The whip: fifty strokes!'

'*Company, tenHUT!*'

Three hundred combat boots hit the packed earth in unison.

61

Barashkukor, facing eyes-front, caught sight of Major Ashnak in his peripheral vision. The big orc walked slowly between the ranks, Sergeant Imhullu behind him, stopping to exchange a word or two here and there.

Noon beat down on ranks of orc grunts, on web-belts hung with grenades, on rocket-launchers, assault rifles, anti-tank weapons and machine-guns. Orc-fangs glinted; squad insignia painted on hunched shoulders shone. Variously coloured combat fatigue trousers blazed back the light, cleaned and pressed after hard training. Boots shone.

'A good turn-out, Sergeant.' Ashnak walked from the rank behind Barashkukor, Imhullu at his side. 'Very good; I'm impressed. Stand the orcs at ease now.'

'Squaaaads, standat—*ease!*'

Again, three hundred boots hit the earth together. Barashkukor clasped his hands behind his back, wondering just where a first lieutenant's insignia should be tattooed.

Ashnak strode to where several ammunition cases had been assembled in a dais, and stepped up on to them. His black-and-white urban camouflage stood out against the blue sky.

'Right, you orcs, listen up!'

The Agaku had a machine-gun and bandoliers slung across his back, and a Desert Eagle automatic pistol in the holster on his web-belt. His broken fangs had been capped with silver, and polished; and a major's insignia painted on his muscular, sloping shoulders. Grenades hung from his belt. He wore a battered urban forage cap.

'You've trained hard.' Ashnak surveyed the ranks. Barashkukor straightened his aching shoulders as the big orc's gaze swept over him.

'And now, your training's over.' The Agaku grinned. 'I'm proud of you. You're marines! You're hot! You are *fucking* hot marines!'

Shrieks and cheers split the air. Barashkukor shook his grenade launcher in the air, taking two hands to do it. The big Agaku held up a hand for silence. He got it.

'Your training's completed, and you're ready for your first big mission. Your officers will brief you fully in a moment, but I want to say this. We know, now, that the date for the Last Battle has been set.'

The breath left Barashkukor's chest as if he had been hit. Fear and adrenalin sparked through his veins, firing him with a fierce joy; and he growled in his throat.

'The Horde of Darkness will march on the night of Samhain. But *before* that, and to ensure its success, *you* are first going to perform your mission.'

The company stood quiet now. No noise in the noon of Nin-Edin but the vultures wheeling about the mountain fort and crying. Barashkukor swallowed with a suddenly dry mouth.

'And succeed in it. I know you can do it – I'm proud of every one of you mean motherfuckers! You're trained marines now.' Ashnak straightened, one taloned hand resting on his pistol. 'Trained and armed. Captain Zarkingu will be instructing you personally later, but I will say this now. These guns are not sorcerous weapons. They are *not* magical. And therefore – therefore the magic of the Light has no defence against them.'

6

THE INTERIOR OF the great Hall of Sarderis's city keep shone white in the afternoon sun. Will Brandiman, comfortably replete, advanced towards the dais at the end of the Hall and bowed. Ned, walking beside him, looked wide-eyed and wondering at the company of elves, dwarves and Men crowding around the dais, and at the female Man sitting on it in the high-backed chair.

'Will and Ned Brandiman.' Will bowed again. 'Halfling brothers, my Lady. Very much at your service.'

He tugged his new silver-embroidered black doublet as if he were straightening it, taking advantage of the movement to check with nimble fingers the position of secret poisoned needles. His short-sword and throwing knives he had handed in at the gatehouse, keeping the mailshirt on pretence of personal danger.

Ned bowed, cloddishly, still gazing up wide-eyed. Will trod on his brother's foot as a warning not to overdo it, unwilling to use the Thieves' Guild fingertalk where it might be recognized and read.

'You two it was who found the family butchered? How is that so?'

The female Man on the dais leaned forward in her chair. The light from the whitewashed walls shone from her plate armour and the dazzling surcoat with the golden Sun embroidered on it. As her face came into the light, Will used every effort to keep from flinching.

Her hair shone yellow as any female Man's, cropped short over pointed grey-white ears. The greyish white of her skin continued across her face, becoming blotched with dark grey and black patches over her jaw and down her neck to where the gorget covered her skin. One misshapen tooth pushed up a corner of her wide, thin-lipped mouth. Thick hairs protruded from her flat nostrils, and her eyes – tilted so that they slanted up from the outer corners towards the bridge of her nose – glinted green.

'Fear me not.' Her soft voice slurred a little, and a drop of saliva ran from under her lip where her tooth lifted it. She wiped her mouth with a gloved hand. 'Fear not, halfling. I am called The Named. I wear another's ugliness of soul upon my body – as he wears the beauty of my virtue, unearned, on his face. But that shall change, also, when we face each other in the final confrontation. For now, believe my heart serves the Light, and speak your answer. You it was who discovered the bodies?'

Will Brandiman spread his hands helplessly. 'My Lady, the very sight was . . . horrific. These were good people of the town with whom we took lodging, and I greatly fear that was their down-fall.'

The Named said sharply, 'How so?'

'It must be that we were followed, Lady, on our way to you; and whoever sought our lives found those good people, and so . . .' Will swallowed. 'We were about our own business that night, not returning until the morning, when we found their bodies.'

A slender elf in green stepped forward from the crowd. 'Some creature of darkness was responsible, Lady. The child's body had been cooked and partially eaten. It is an infallible sign of the orc-filth. None but orcs could be capable of such wickedness.'

'And the writing? Can orcs write?'

The elf bowed her head. 'For that, I know not.'

Ned Brandiman, at Will's elbow, said, 'Our lodging was paid two weeks in advance at the shop. If the Dark has human spies in the city, I suppose they must have found that out, and sent for . . . other creatures to attack us. Perhaps it was spies of the Dark who wrote – but I can't read, Lady. Brother Will told me what filth they wrote.'

'I did.' Will patted his brother's arm. With his hand firmly on Ned's arm he took the opportunity to finger:

– *I said act impressed, not half-witted.*

Will added, 'Lady, there is much that you should know. I fear your brother seeks our life.'

The stunningly ugly face shifted into something that might have been a sad smile. 'Say on, little one.'

'It is to our shame', Will launched himself on his story, 'that we were, in part and as it seems, employed by your brother the name-less . . .'

He wielded ignorance and innocence in a complex web, his eyes on The Named's misshapen face; leaving it to Ned to scan the assembly for armed Men, hostile dwarven-kind, and elvish mages.

'. . . I grew to know something of these orcs. Orcs have no love of magic, Lady – unless it's the sort that requires much torture and sacrifice, and has short and easily pronounced incantations. But their magic-sniffer could tell an absence of magic truly. And so we fled for our lives, concluding that if they should escape, your brother's orcish army now has weapons that are not magical, but are infinitely greater than sword or bow. And these he will put at the disposal of the Dark Lord.'

He paused.

'And so we feared for you, Lady, and for all our sakes, and so came searching for you to tell this tale.'

The green eyes, the only beauty in that face, met his. Her gloved hand beckoned. He walked to the foot of the dais, Ned at his heels, and craned his neck to look her in the face still.

'You have done well to bring this tale to me. What reward would you have?'

Will opened his mouth, and before he could get a word out, Ned said, 'We'd paid our two week's lodging at the house – is there any chance we could have that refunded?'

The female Man's head went back and her wide, loose mouth opened in a bellow of laughter. Will instantly sized up the distance to the guarded exits. He put his heel down crushingly hard on Ned's foot.

'We want no reward,' he said emphatically.

Her laughter stopped. 'A strange quest you tell of, halfling. It seems by it, although you conceal it, that you are thieves. But even thieves may become the instruments of Light.'

Ned muttered, '"Adventurers".'

Will shifted his weight on to the balls of his feet, prepared to grab poison-needles and flee under the feet of the crowd around the dais. 'Thieves it may be – but thieves who hate the Dark as much as you do, Lady.'

'Elinturanbar,' she called. She wiped her mouth again with her soft glove.

A robed elf, taller by a head than any there, walked out of the crowd. Men and dwarves and elven-kind moved aside from the sway of his white robes embroidered with the gold Sun of the Mages. Will stared up into the lean face.

'Elves!' Ned exclaimed. 'I never thought I should see elves, Will.'

Will caught the missed breath in his brother's ingenuous remark, and the imperceptible shift to a combat-stance. Something cold twisted in his gut.

The elf's face showed the faint fine lines of age.

Not half-elven, having none of the signs; nor yet one of the Long-lived come to the finish of his ages and the readiness to take ship to the Eternal Lands. Elinturanbar's lean face, webbed with crow's-feet at the eyes and mouth, shone with a fanatic light – that of those of the elven-kind who, out of the curiosity of the immortal, voluntarily embrace the pain and death that Men and other mortal creatures know.

'Elinturanbar will question you,' The Named said. 'He is my inquisitor. The deceptions of evil are many and legendary – forgive me that I choose to test you, as metal is tested in the forge, before I decide if you are tempered to become a sword of the Light.'

Nimble, Will's hand darted for the needles sewn into his doublet's tabs. Fast as he moved, the ageing elf inquisitor stooped faster and caught his arms, twisting them bone-crackingly hard up behind his back.

Ned Brandiman took his hands out of the loose puffed-and-slashed sleeves of his doublet. Weighed down by the sheer bulk of metal, he nonetheless managed to brace both arms and hold out, muzzle wavering, the 1911 US Army issue Colt .45 autoloading pistol.

The midday sun burned down from a cloudless sky. The orc marines, beetle-browed eyes staring to the front, pounded down the track away from Nin-Edin under four- and five-ton loads of rifles, grenade launchers, machine-guns, machine-pistols, anti-tank weapons and innumerable belts of ammunition.

'*Hut*-two, *hut*-two!' Lieutenant Barashkukor stood with his hands on his hips, on the seat of his jeep. 'Fucking *elves* could move that load faster. You want the major to see you?'

Three hundred pairs of orc boots pounded down the road away from Nin-Edin in unison, the column raising plumes of dust. Barashkukor drew a deep breath and bellowed at the passing rank and file of orc grunts. 'Are you marines? *Move!*'

'Sir, yes, sir!' Corporal Duranki shouted. His jaw set, he pounded on down the track. Like the others, the albino orc staggered under a backpack of weaponry three times his own height.

'Then move your fucking asses!' Barashkukor bellowed happily. 'At the double, orcs!'

A metallic clash sounded.

Harsh, rhythmic; the noise of bells, horns, trumpets, drums and a saxophone split the air. Nine of the smaller orc marines, stepping smartly, bashed out an impromptu military march. They were singing, Barashkukor noted, something to the effect of '*From the halls of Japh-kanduma to the shores of Zithan-dri* . . .'

Captain Zarkingu (Magic-Disposal, Admin., and Band Duties) marched past at the head of the band and the second column, skipping from side to side and tossing her skull-pole standard up in the air, mace-like, in time to the music.

'See you at the Tower, L.t!' Zarkingu yelled.

Barashkukor saluted. He sat down in the jeep's back seat, tilting the GI pot back on his head and letting his long hairless ears spring out from under it.

'Lieutenant Barashkukor!'

Barashkukor jumped up and came smartly to attention, snapping a crisp salute. 'Sir, Major Ashnak, sir! We removed stores of weapons from the mountains, sir. Everything is being transported with the company, sir, including ammunition. The orcs are moving out as requested, *sah!*'

'Thank you, Barashkukor.' Ashnak gave a casual salute. 'Your unit's got flying experience with Hueys, Lieutenant.'

'Sir, yes, sir!' Barashkukor leapt out of the jeep. 'That is . . . sir, no, sir! Incapacitated by illness, sir. The Bell HU-1 Iroquois was disabled according to your orders, sir!'

Major Ashnak took the unlit roll of pipe-weed out of his tusked mouth and threw it down, grinding it under one polished combat boot. He tilted the urban-camo forage cap back on his misshapen skull.

'There were at least two Hueys in Dagurashibanipal's hoard, Lieutenant. Break out another one. Find a pilot and a marine with co-piloting experience and report back to me.'

Ashnak removed his forage cap and buckled on his GI-issue helmet, grinning toothily.

'I have my orders from Dark HQ, Lieutenant. I've got no choice.'

'I have no choice!'

The Named swings up into the saddle of the white war-horse, bright armour clashing. Her destrier lays its ears flat back against its skull. She effortlessly controls it.

'It is my fate to go to the Tower of Guthranc at the appointed time, and use its power to summon the Army of Light to the Fields of Destruction. The time is *now*. The signal is mine alone to give!'

The sun colours her ugly grey-white face with the gold of dawn.

Her breath curls in the summer's-ending chill. Somewhere in Sarderis there is the scent of the sea.

'Follow my orders!' She wipes trailing saliva from the corner of her loose mouth. 'This was prophesied for me when I was in my cradle, and I cannot avoid my destiny. I go now to Guthranc to sound the first war-summons to the Northern Kingdoms – I ride at dawn!'

A gold Harvest moon rose over the distant mountains. The wind felt cold on Ashnak's face. He rested his back up against a trampled earth bank smelling of cow-dung and machine oil.

A scout orc slipped into the cover beside him. 'Sir, nothing, sir.'

The orc's commando knife dripped. Ashnak peered between the hedge's thorn bushes towards the village by the river. It showed even to his eyes as blackness against blackness. No lights, no cock-crows, no hammers in the smithy. He smelled the scent of Man-blood on the air.

'Nothing left but the oldest and youngest of Men, and those were in hiding. All the smithies are empty, all the horseflesh gone.' She saluted. 'No resistance, sir. We can take the columns through the river valley.'

Ashnak's hide twitched in the night's chill.

'This is a land waiting to be at war . . . Their warriors will be riding away to the great musters of the Light.' The wet earth soaked through his combats at knee and elbow. 'Move 'em out, soldier.'

Ashnak rose and walked back from the advance post, radioing for Shazgurim and Zarkingu to move their companies out; and the night became a morass of small noises – muffled boots, the clink of weapons, a snarl, the buzz of a radio transmission. It went on interminably as he walked back; squad after squad of orcs trampling the earth as they passed him. The big Agaku bared his fangs with exhilaration.

The full moon loomed, silver now, patterns of the Dark visibly smirching its face.

Shapes shambled across the fields and resolved themselves into three of the fighting Agaku. The second company of marines began to pass Ashnak, and he saluted the ranking officer at its head. The moonlight cast his shadow heavy and sloping on the wet earth.

Other shadows joined it: squat Imhullu, hulking Shazgurim, and Zarkingu's shadow skipping from foot to foot.

'The artillery are in position!' Zarkingu unfurled a scroll of paper, spreading it out. Her eyes and fangs gleamed in the moonlight. Ashnak and his sub-commanders squatted to study the map.

'This is the Tower of Guthranc. That's cultivated land. This is the edge of the forest, here; and this is the main road from Sarderis,' Ashnak pointed.

Imhullu untied the camouflage neckerchief from his brow, wiped his weeping empty eye-socket, and replaced the cloth. The squat orc punched Ashnak's bandoliers-covered chest. 'Nine platoons – we're taking three whole *companies* in. Practically a small battalion. Against what, less than a hundred of the Man-filth? Armed with swords and bows . . . ?'

'Seven to one,' Ashnak said. 'Reasonable odds.'

'They'll have a few spells. Some damned magic-user or other.' Shazgurim squatted, forearms resting on horny knees, her helmet off; watching the third column begin to pass them. 'But, bullets baffle bullshit. We've got these hard bastards at our backs – no horse-buggering Man is going to kick *our* asses!'

'Brief your squad leaders. It's essential we target the mages, if there are any. Take them out.' Ashnak took the map and rolled it up. 'We can't stop them starting to spellcast – but sorcery will be no defence against these weapons. We'll take a few casualties while we're wasting the mages, but at acceptable casualty levels.'

Zarkingu rubbed her horny hands together. 'No protection! No magic! They'll be cut to pieces . . .'

She paused.

'Are we too good? Will the orc marines worry *him?*'

Above Ashnak the stars are drowned by moonlight. On the horizon, mountains glimmer with early snow.

'The nameless?' Ashnak hawked and spat a gob of phlegm. He felt a laugh building deep in his chest. 'He's like any of the lesser Lords of Evil – jockeying for position among the rest. Hoping that the Dark Lord's going to notice him. He'll do anything for that, rot him. As for *too good* – I tell you exactly what our reward will be for this. We'll get to stand on the right of the line at the Fields of Destruction, and take the brunt of the battle.'

'Fighting Agaku!' Imhullu shook his crop-eared head. '*That's* the war for which we were bred.'

'Poor bastards.' Shazgurim snorted. 'I can even be sorry for the Man-filth in the Tower. They don't know what's going to hit them.'

Zarkingu giggled hysterically.

Ashnak tightened his web-belt, relaced one boot, and straightened his shambling bulk. The RT whispered in his helmet. He bared fangs to the cold moonlight.

'Those Men in the Tower?' Ashnak said. 'They're soldiers, the same as we are – except that they're not marines. Honour them,

70

Agaku. They're close kin to us, although they deny it. And we're going to kill them. All warriors are brothers in arms, whether they fight for the Light or the Dark. We are fated always to make war on our own kind.'

7

T HE NAMED RIDES for Guthranc.

With her ride an ill-assorted company. There are Men in it, who seem uneasy in the brigandines and burgonets they wear. Some are slender enough to be of the Elven-kin. They carry weapons as if they are not used to them. Some of the smaller breeds are there, too, bounced along in the saddles behind the taller riders.

The Dark-touched moon sinks over fields left unharvested, among villages deserted, in a countryside breathing out the relief that comes with the promise of a final accounting with evil.

Under a blue sky, the countryside of the Northern Kingdoms shines red and gold. Heavy-headed golden grain swayed and fell forward, flattened under the metal tracks of a speeding M113 armoured personnel carrier. Spreading poppies among the overripe, unharvested corn blotched the fields with the colour of Man-blood.

Ashnak leaned hairy elbows on the edge of the APC's hatch, holding binos to his eyes. He smelled dusty earth, orc sweat and Man-fear. The machine bucked and dipped under him as it roared along the length of the first orc marine column. Three columns crossed the fields in echelon. He tasted dust in his tusked mouth.

Somewhere the Army of Light will be mustering for the Last Battle. But that is not here, and Samhain is weeks off yet.

The radio buzzed in Ashnak's hairless ear. He thumbed the stud under the rim of his helmet. 'Ashnak receiving, over.'

'*This is Recon 1. Territory is clear, repeat territory is clear. Over.*'
'Recon 1, I copy. Out.'
'*Colonel Ashnak, this is Recon 2. No enemy seen or suspected, over.*'
'I copy, Recon 2. Out.'
'*Recon 3, this is Recon 3. Targets have entered the Tower, sir. Estimate their garrison strength at seventy, repeat, seven-zero. They have closed the gates and are guarding the walls. Over.*'
'Message received, Recon 3. Take no action, repeat, take no action. Out.'

On impulse he had his driver stop the APC at the head of the column. He climbed out of the hatch, avoiding catching grenades and bandoliers on the hatch-rim. His boots hit the furrowed earth. He unslung his M60 general purpose machine-gun, carrying it muzzle-skyward, and fell in beside the marching squads of orcs.

'Yo!' Imhullu loped up to join him. Shazgurim shambled up in the one-eyed orc's wake.

'Like old times, huh, Colonel?' She grinned.

'I smell white magic, Light magic, magic far yonder!' Zarkingu, skulls rattling at her belt, and the marine flag rippling from the standard pole she carried, skipped up to the head of the column. 'We're coming up on them, Colonel Ashnak. Battle before sunset!'

Ashnak heard the word spreading down the columns of marching orcs behind him, and the growls and cheers and yells in its wake.

'*Do we kick ass?*' he bawled.

'*SIR, WE KICK ASS, SIR!*'

Ashnak faced front, marching in the long orc-lope that eats up miles and days. It felt for a moment strange to have Man-boots on his feet, and not to pound the bare earth. Strange to carry the weight of guns, not pole-axe, sword and warhammer. He breathed in the stink of oil and metal and cordite, his chest expanding.

The afternoon air had the first and faintest tinge of autumn in it.

He looked across at Major Shazgurim. The big female orc wore her helmet right down, the rim level with her beetle-brows. Her eyes were shining. She loped heavily along, a hand-held rocket launcher strapped across her shoulders, and an M16 in either hand.

'Nest-sisters,' he acknowledged his three commanders. 'Nest-brother.'

Imhullu growled. 'Nest-brother, this is well.'

Ashnak looked at Zarkingu. 'Little sister?'

Major Zarkingu's tilted eyes gleamed. Bullet-bandoliers clattered as she walked. The sun lit up the dust on her combat trousers and the mud on her boots; she, the only one to march on foot with the companies all the way from Nin-Edin.

'We've come far together. I remember other towers, brother, and other campaigns. I remember other masters. Aren't the Agaku always masters of the battle?' Zarkingu smiled. 'What though one of us falls? There are always the Agaku!'

Imhullu stroked the small orc's horse-tail plume of purple hair. 'Little sister feels her death upon her.'

'We are the fighting Agaku.'

Around the horizon, snow-covered mountains rise up to a blue and purple sky. Ashnak tastes the loneliness of those cold heights on his tongue, here in the deserted lowlands. He looks back at the destroyed countryside, the ravaged fields, and the company marching behind him. Dust and the first fallen leaves rise up, concealing their strength from watching eyes. There are always watching eyes in Guthranc.

But what can any spy do, seeing what approaches now?

Trained, prepared, battle-hardened; there is nonetheless a point where one deliberately abandons fear, abandons the knowledge of victory, abandons the wish to survive. He abandons that professionally and without regret. Ashnak, when he fights, fights as one who knows he is already dead. It makes him deadly: it has given him his life.

'Give me your hands,' he says, 'sisters and brother.'

On the many-towered ramparts of Guthranc a sentry halloos a warning. Inept with their weapons, the newly arrived company nevertheless stands to arms.

The Named emerges in full plate harness that sears the afternoon sun into watching eyes. Her surcoat blazes gold. She raises her sword to cry an order.

An explosion knocks her from her feet. She sprawls on the parapet, armour scratched and dented. Rocks and shrapnel whistle across the still air. The west tower and half its supporting wall collapses into rubble.

'FIRE!'

The artillery barrage boomed, way behind him. The flattened trajectory of the shells took them over Ashnak's head, whipping the air. He stood up in the hatch of the APC, helmet pushed back, chewing an unlit roll of pipe-weed.

'FIRE!'

Smoke rolled up black and orange from Guthranc's walls. Pennants, bright against the blue sky, crisped in flame. Masonry cracked and tumbled, falling slowly outwards, and the whole gate

74

section of the walls slid away, down, and raised gouts of water from the moat. Warriors ran along the parapet like termites. The gate tower collapsed.

'First platoon, go, go, *go!* Now! GO!'

The deep cough of the guns drowned his voice in his own ears, but the headsets obviously carried it. Moving with complete precision the first orc marine platoon began to advance by fire and movement: one squad going into whatever cover the churned-up cornfields and road offered and blazing away at the Tower, while the next squad moved up past them and went down, ready to offer covering fire and then repeat.

On Guthranc's walls a Man threw up his arms and fell. The body wheeled through the sunlit air, mouth open. Ashnak watched until it hit the earth, bones fracturing. The squads had advanced to the foot of the slope. He spoke into his headset:

'Artillery, cease fire; say again: *cease fire.*'

Ashnak looked down from the APC into the bowl of land that held the Tower of Guthranc, nestled in its surroundings of rolling cornfields. The unharvested white grain was mashed down with tyretracks and the marks of marching feet. To the east the Old Forest, massy and green, dreamed under the hot noon. The artillery thudded behind him and stopped firing.

Imhullu's squads of grunts advanced towards the Tower, weapons blazing. Ashnak put the binos to his eyes and caught an intensified image of the squat black orc, Kusaritku, firing a shoulder-held rocket-launcher. Flame belched. Red-and-gold fire bloomed from the foot of Guthranc's east wing.

Gatling-gun fire raked the towers where Men and other filth scrabbled across the fallen rubble. Some threw up their hands and fell. Red drenched the fallen stones, drained into gullies. Ashnak, narrowing his eyes, picked out the cover still remaining, and the tips of longbows raised . . .

'Major Shazgurim, do you copy? Over.'

'I copy, Colonel. Now; over?'

'Take 'em in. Advance at will. *Go, go, go!* Out. Zarkingu; advance your platoon! Keep Imhullu's platoon out of your arc of fire. Go, you motherfuckers, go!'

He slammed a horny-hided fist down on the APC. Its engine roared. He bawled instructions at the driver, shouldered his M60, and braced himself as the vehicle jolted and rocked over the ploughed earth.

Ahead, fire and smoke blazed up in tall columns. The rear walls of Guthranc fragmented and collapsed. Imhullu's orcs scrambled up the long slope towards the foot of the fallen towers in extended line. Cordite choked the air. Smoke hung heavy and low in the stillness.

And from the east, from their concealment in the Old Forest, the two reserve platoons advanced, firing.

'Agaku! *Agaku!*'

His helmet RT deafened him with war-cries. Ashnak yelled wildly, grinning, shoved his GI helmet down over his beetle-brows, and ordered the APC in a wide curve that took him round the western edge of the diversionary attack line and across the Vordenburn road. He raised the M60 and fired, exulting in recoil and noise, screaming over the firefight:

'*Agaku! AGAKU!*'

The APC's nose dipped forward and dug into the soft earth at the moat's edge. Ashnak scrambled up, over and out. His boots hit the wet earth. He ran for the pontoons, craning his neck to see the demolished towers above him; raised the M60 and blazed up at the walls. Combat-clad orcs piled past him, tusked mouths grinning, their guns jabbing flame into the noon sunlight. Smoke and stink began to erase the battlefield. Ashnak hit dirt in the cover of a fallen wall and looked back.

Lines of orcs raced up the slope at the charge, screaming and throwing grenades. The *crump!* of heavy weapons shook the ground. Earth gouted up. It showered Ashnak's face with the smell of cultivated fields.

The helmet RT blared: 'Charge! Chaaaarge!' Shazgurim's voice, tinny over the small amplifier. Satisfied that the main attack was going in, Ashnak shrugged, hefted the M60, and grinned, knowing there was nothing now but to go in at the head of the reinforcing attack. Any hostiles that survived would have no option but to come out to the north – where they would run into the cut-off squad.

He opened his mouth and bawled '*Chaarge!*' at Imhullu's grunts, shoulder-rolled around the fallen masonry and came up the slope with the M60 juddering and wrenching at his grip. Its muzzle rose, stitching the walls of Guthranc from bottom left to top right in one slow curve. An elf and a dwarf broke to run and the rounds spattered their blood and intestines across the stones.

'Chaaaarge—'

He scrambled over smoking rubble into the inner courts, firing the M60 one-handed, and a horse reared up in front of him. The smoke cleared enough to let sun blaze from gold surcoat and white harness. The Named reared above him, one bare hand raised.

Ashnak hit the change lever and dropped another 7.62 mm belt flawlessly into place. 'Die, motherfucker!'

76

All in a splintered second:

DAKKA-DAKKA-*FOOM!*

The rounds track up, beginning to whip through the rainbow shimmer of her protective spell as if it does not exist.

The Named, smiling, sits the white horse's saddle with grace; in her other, armoured, hand is a sword. She has no time to strike, but time to speak.

Ashnak reads her wide, loose lips as they move. The Named mouths: '*Fail weapons.*'

Silence.

Not until then realizing how the metallic shriek and roar of the guns has vibrated through him, numbed his eardrums; how the coughing roar of explosion after explosion has deafened him; not realizing until now when there suddenly falls – silence.

An invisible hand swatted Ashnak to the grass.

Mouth full of dirt, spitting, he shook his head (helmet dented, the air burning on his face) and rolled and came up with the M60 machine-gun tucked into his body. The metal burned his hands with cold blue fire. It seared, cut, sawed at his skin. Ashnak, ignoring the pain, raised the muzzle until he held the armoured female Man in his sights.

'*Die, bitch!*'

He jerked the trigger – useless.

Witch-fire rippled out and over his body, burning his skin.

Every inch of him blazing, Ashnak rolled on the earth. His combat trousers fused, the material sticking to his skin; and the bandoliers of bullets grew warm to the touch, grew hotter—

Ashnak, ripping the bandoliers off, plunged back down the slope. He hit the moat and rolled in the wet mud, quenching witch-flames. The M60 gone: the final disgrace, to lose a weapon. Pain shook him, his sloping shoulders and long arms burned raw; tough hide seared from his legs and torso. He bolted for cover, and crouched shaking and filthy with mud behind a section of the gatehouse wall.

The Men and elves on the ramparts throw down their unaccustomed weapons.

'Yo, marine!' Ashnak pounded across the iron-hard earth towards one of Imhullu's grunts, the black orc Kusaritku, who knelt and fired the rocket-launcher. Witch-fire licked down from the Tower.

The rocket split in the tube and shrapnelled the air.

Deafened by the explosion, Ashnak hit dirt. Warm wet meat draped over his hands and arms. He reached over Kusaritku's body to get the rocket-launcher. The small orc Kusaritku, combats soaked with blood, scooped at the white and green tubes leaking from his

77

belly and then lay back, his eyes on the sky. The camouflage-covered helmet slipped down over his face.

'Rush them!' Ashnak made his voice heard over screams, shouts, and the remnants of firing. '*Target the mages!* Rush them!'

The ruined walls of the Tower loomed above him, white stone blackened with soot. Men and elves stood up on the walls now, behind shimmering guards of magic. They cast off their helmets and threw down their swords, picking up staffs.

'*Charge!*' He raised a discarded M16, squeezing the trigger. Nothing. Feverishly he changed magazines, fired again – the firing-pin fell with a dull click. Nothing. Again, and – nothing. He threw down the gun, ripped the pin from a grenade and hurled it. The green ovoid fell into the rubble with a metallic clink. Nothing more.

Time slipped a gear.

Ashnak became aware that he was running across the inner courtyard of the Tower. He caught his foot and fell. He made to get up and his leg gave way, the bone poking through the flesh. His other leg burned, blistering and pus-filled. Ashnak picked up a dead orc's Kalashnikov and rested it across his seared forearms and began to crawl, using his arms to pull his useless lower body along.

'*Agaku!* I smell magic, *small*-magic, *nothing*-magic!'

Capering, Zarkingu danced on a section of the parapet above him. Her crest, tied up with a DPM sleeve, lashed in the hot air and smoke. Ashnak saw her eyes gleaming. Froth spilled out of her mouth. She cocked her Uzi sub-machine-gun and squeezed the trigger. The gun did not fire. 'Colonel, it's nothing but a simple "fail-weapons" spell—'

'*Incoming!* Take cover!' Ashnak bawled. '*Zarkingu!*'

A shimmering sphere sprang into existence around the orc, where she capered with skulls and M16 magazines swinging from her belt. In the space of a heartbeat the magical sphere convulsed closed, opened, and dropped a compressed ruin of orc-flesh and bone dripping on to the parapet.

Ashnak's bowels let go and he shat himself. He dug his elbows into the rough flagstones, pulling himself up. He detached and slid the Kalashnikov's bayonet into its socket, locking it home; shoulder-slung the assault rifle and pulled himself by the strength of his arms up to the top of the rubble. His broad nostrils flared at his own stink.

He lay and looked down at the battlefield.

Elven mages and human magic-users crowded the remaining battlements of Guthranc. Sixty or seventy strong. There wasn't a warrior among them, only those who wielded the staff, or cast witch-fire from between bare hands, or conjured up arcane death with streams of words. Sporadic firing shook the air and died, drowned out now by the conjurations of magic.

Ashnak watched an extended-line formation of marines go down, scythed like wheat. Orc bodies lay in arcs along the grassy slope that rose up to the tower. Their blood soaked the earth.

Ashnak rolled, with an effort, the Kalashnikov held over his head, hitting every spike of rock on the slope down towards the moat. He came to rest against three dead bodies, stinking and corrupt in the noon sun and magic.

Weakness, pain and fear drained him. The air drummed in his ears. 'Why?' His throat was raw. '*How?*'

A foot stepped delicately over the marine bodies. Ashnak watched it approach, teeth bared. He gripped the Kalashnikov in his burned hands, poising the bayonet to thrust up. An elven voice said, 'It lives, Lady. Shall I end its miserable existence?'

'You,' a slobbery voice said, marvelling.

Ashnak's burned leg had some strength, and he flexed it, gathering it beneath him to spring. His shattered leg trailed like a snake. He watched the approach of The Named.

'Bind him. No, you are not strong enough. I will.' The female Man knelt, plate harness clashing. One of her hands darted out and gripped Ashnak's throat, far too fast for him to avoid, and squeezed.

Breath stopped. His vision went red, black, and then a plain white. He thrust blindly with the bayonet, a belly-cut, and felt her free hand grip the assault rifle's barrel. She wrenched the Kalashnikov from his hands. His limbs were strengthless. Something hummed in his ears. He felt his gullet surge; and then he was released to vomit, and whimper in blindness, and wait for his sight to clear.

Witch-bonds bit into his burnt wrists and ankles.

Ashnak groaned a protest against the binding of his shattered leg. The female Man nodded to the elven mage at her side.

'I am merciful. This one we will keep. He will know much.'

She hefted up the Kalashnikov thoughtfully, testing the weight and length of it in her armoured hand.

The pain of third-degree burns over most of his body loosened his tongue. Ashnak yelled, 'What use can magic be against us? Ours aren't witch-weapons! Why are you using magic!'

The firefight rattled and died to the east, in the Old Forest, where (too far for him to see) the remnants of the orc marine platoons were fighting to a standstill. The helmet RT whispered tinnily in Ashnak's ear:

'—*fall back! Fix bayonets! Use your weapons as clubs! Fall back and re-group at*—'

Shazgurim's voice shrieked and terminated. The distinctive hiss of witch-fire filled the channel, burning it out. Ashnak's head bowed to his chest. He made no movement even when The Named removed his helmet.

'Elinturanbar, this one was my brother's plaything and must be questioned.'

The lisping wet voice ceased. Ashnak raised his head. The Named and the elven mage stared east, to forested cliffs and gorges, and the palls from burning trees.

A Bell HU-1 Iroquois helicopter slanted down across the hill slope.

Flying with unprecedented skill, the Huey feathered between the trees, using them as cover, close enough for the heavy rotors to chop branches. Leaves sprayed up. The shadows of its guns fell on the sunlit trees. Ashnak opened his mouth and hoarsely cheered.

A fork of blue lightning lanced up from the hands of the elvish mage Elinturanbar. Treetops disintegrated. The Huey flared, darted down and pulled around in a tight circle; shot up, and the blue spike intersected its flightpath again with neat economy. One landing-skid fractured and fell.

The Huey lurched in the air, slanting downwards, made a right turn to gain power, and limped the hundred yards of open air between the Old Forest and the foot of the Tower, barely above ground.

The Named's bare hand moved. She whispered, 'Fail-flight . . .'

Ashnak buried his face against the turf. The helicopter dropped, slammed down, bounced up, and hit the earth again no more than thirty feet away from him. He felt the impact through his burned and broken body. Shrapnel sprayed the ground and hummed through the air.

The doors cracked open. Two orcs bailed out, vomiting, and dived into cover amongst the rubble.

A third figure got a slender hand to the hatchway, weaved slightly, and stepped down on to the earth.

A shadow seemed to pass across the sun. Frost fractured the grass, and coated the prone bodies with ice. The earth bit into Ashnak's shattered leg and burned hide. It was so cold that his eyeballs hurt.

The nameless necromancer reached back into the body of the Huey and recovered a spun-silicon bottle. Intact. He shook his midnight-leather robes loose from torn metal, dusted himself down with a flick of spell-fingers, and sauntered across towards the group at the foot of the Tower of Guthranc.

Ashnak stared at the slim, approaching figure. He strained at his bonds. The spell-fraught wires burned into his raw skin and cold tender wounds. The nameless necromancer raised his head and squinted painfully at the sky.

The pale Man dimmed the sunlight with a gesture. 'Ashnak. How pleasant.'

The orc coughed, blood in his throat. 'Sir, beg to report, sir . . .'

The nameless necromancer stepped delicately over Ashnak's body and walked on, the pale hand that was not holding a bottle outstretched.

'Sister,' he said. 'Hail. Well met!'

Ashnak stared in disbelief.

The nameless necromancer let his hand fall, unclasped. He smiled. Somewhere in the curve of his lips, and the shine of his green eyes over high cheekbones, were implied features not his own. 'Sister, you have the victory here, I think.'

The orc-faced woman stepped to one side as others of the company walked out of Guthranc's ruins. Elves, dwarves, Men – and halflings. 'Yes, brother. And I have your thieves to thank for it.'

Ashnak, unshockable now, recognized the two halflings.

The younger had black curls, expensively cut and pomaded. He wore an etched and gold-inlaid breastplate over rich, three-piled velvet doublet and breeches; his ruff was of the finest cloth; and gold and silver rings decorated every one of his ten fingers. Neither his armour nor his expensive silk half-cloak had battle-dirt on them. He smiled.

His brother, standing beside him, wore rich brown velvet; his hair tied back in a tiny horsetail, fixed with a golden ring. He wore no armour, and a heavy gold S-linked chain showed under his silver-embroidered cloak. He appeared rather more plump than when Ashnak had seen him in the wild.

Both halflings wore new swords.

The Named rested a gloved hand on the shoulder of each halfling. 'You see I have rewarded them for their sufferings incurred in coming to me. Though I cannot reward them as they truly deserve.'

'No,' Ashnak growled under his breath.

A kind of exaltation filled The Named's misshapen features. Saliva trailed down unnoticed where a tusk distorted her mouth.

'These two halflings it was who brought me a weapon from Dagurashibanipal's hoard. You did not expect that, brother nameless, but even thieves may turn to the Light.'

Her face shone.

'Master Will Brandiman told me that you had weapons not sorcerous, but more powerful than sword or bow, against which magic was no protection. And Master Ned Brandiman it was who,

81

demonstrating such a weapon, proved that, not being magical weapons, they have no protection *against* magic.'

The Named smiled wetly.

'No protection against magic at all. Not even against the simplest *fail-weapons* spell.'

Ashnak nuzzled his protruding jaw and beetle-browed eyes against the freezing earth. Then he lifted his head, looking down the length of his body – charred webbing and combat trousers fused into open wounds, bloodstained boots – to where his helmet lay on the grass, the RT unreachable. Orc berserker instincts contending with marine training, he muttered under his breath: 'Bug out! Fall back. Fall *back.*'

Ashnak strained the muscles of his hunched shoulders until he thought they would crack. Pain hissed into his skin. The magical bonds bit deep. Green blood trickled down over his webbing, staining combats and boots, slow in the cold air. He raised his head, staring at the nameless necromancer.

'Master . . .' the orc whispered.

'See the recalcitrance of evil,' the brown-haired halfling announced. 'Lady Named, you see what comes of serving the Dark Lord. His creatures are unable to hear your words of virtue.'

Ashnak with difficulty turned his head. 'And I suppose taking payment from the Dark Lord's most loyal servant, the nameless, enables *you* to be virtuous?'

Ned and Will Brandiman looked at each other with extremely pained expressions.

'Such calumny.' The Named shook her head, tutting. 'Never fear, my halflings. Evil cannot trick me. I know your hearts, and they are pure.'

The black-haired halfling squatted, just out of reach of Ashnak's fangs, his round, apple-cheeked face smiling.

'The dragon's curse was powerful indeed, Master Ashnak. The Order of White Mages have detected the curse that Dagurashibanipal laid – it is "*You will become what you steal*". As the dragon collected the terrible weapons of evil, so you have become their user, and one of them. It's tragic, truly tragic. For I am not one to believe even an orc beyond salvation.'

Ashnak spat. The halfling avoided his acidic saliva. Ashnak wrestled himself around, freezing pain searing through his wrecked body. 'Shazgurim was right. Dark Lord, yes! *Tricksy halflings.* She said you'd do for us in the end. And I *do* regret stopping her killing you! Master!'

The nameless necromancer ignored him.

A breath of warm wind blew, smelling of dead leaves, summer's end, cornstalks and the sea. Frost melted.

'Sister . . .'

On thawing, blood-wet grass, in late afternoon sunlight grown suddenly strong, the nameless necromancer fell to his knees. His dark head bowed, and his back bent. He touched his pale forehead to the turf.

His voice came plainly audible:

'Sister, even the darkest may turn towards the Light.'

Disgust and anguish brought a roar from Ashnak. '*Master!*'

'These orcish scum are nothing.' The nameless necromancer spread his pale hands, still kneeling. One hand grasped the neck of the silicon bottle. He drank, waving the bottle in the general direction of the last fighting. 'A few less to battle on the Dark Lord's side when Samhain comes. But if you will have me, sister, the Army of Light shall be increased by one, and my power is not small.'

Silence breathed over the field. Ashnak heard it, despite the screams and shouts of the massacre, the hoarse sound of his own protest, the crack of thawing ice. The silence of destiny.

'I have waited long for this, brother.'

The female Man stripped off her remaining plate gauntlet, dropping it on the turf. She stood in the hot sun, among bodies of fallen orcs and Men, with the miasma of corruption rising from corpses in the moat. Her golden hair blazed.

'Duel me,' she challenged. 'Single combat, brother. Your Dark power against my power of the Light. Come – combat, hand against bare hand. Fight me!'

'She's stronger—' Ashnak's fierce warning cut off as an elven hand clamped across his mouth. Witch-fires singed the horny hide of his face. He opened his mouth to bite.

'I will not.' The nameless necromancer rose gracefully to his feet. There were patches of orc blood on his silver-thread-and-skin robe where he had knelt on it. He flicked a spell-finger and was again spotless. 'I have surrendered to you. To your mercy and honour.'

'I don't trust—'

'And if you will it,' the pale Man said, 'I shall wear my own shape again, sister, and you shall wear yours.'

The Named stared for a moment as if into bright light.

'*Yes.*' Her blotched fingers fumbled at her wet lips. She dragged the back of her grey-and-white-skinned hand across her mouth.

The elven mage demanded, 'Lady, how can you trust him?'

'Has he not humbled himself before us? Knelt, in the humiliation of his defeat? And come defenceless amongst us? You do not know me,' the female Man said, and her surcoat shot back the crimson of the setting sun. 'I am always merciful to those who serve the Light. Brother, be welcome.'

In his last pain, blood soaking into the hot earth, Ashnak made the effort to cry out: 'Master, no! You betray us.'

The nameless necromancer did not even turn his head. 'Be silent, scum!'

The tall elven mage with the much-lined face stepped out from where he stood behind Ashnak, and bowed, and smiled.

'No,' The Named said. 'Elinturanbar, the nameless shall not be subject to the inquisition. I say he shall not. He has proved himself our friend here today. Brother, come.'

One of the tall Men said, 'Lady, you must use Guthranc's power first, to send out the war-summons to the Northern Kingdoms—'

'Later.' Her green, luminous eyes on his beautiful face, The Named held out her hand. 'Come, brother. I would speak with you of the changing of shapes.'

'Let me first instruct this scum.'

Ashnak, the edges of his vision foggy now, watched the pale bare feet of the nameless necromancer treading the grass towards him. He coughed thickly. Pale fingers touched his skull, between his peaked ears.

A blackly warm and resurrecting touch.

He coughed again, more strongly, and showed all his fangs. In the tongue of the Agaku, which is private between themselves and their masters, and in the idiom of Dagurashibanipal's hoard, he said, 'Fuck, man. Even when I'm *dead* I can't get out of this chickenshit outfit.'

'*You*,' the nameless necromancer said, 'my creature Ashnak. Give orders for the fighting to cease. Now, do you hear me!'

His bonds parted. Ashnak studiously failed to catch the eye of any of the company standing near him. He rose to his feet, healed, and looked at the nameless.

'She is merciful,' the nameless explains.

Recalling a village and a church, of which the nameless necromancer has been told, Ashnak searches his pale features. One of the nameless necromancer's eyelids flickers. Ashnak glimpses, very briefly, a hidden laughter.

The nameless necromancer says in that unknown tongue, 'May not I submit myself as you did? *Exactly* as you did – and do – my Ashnak.'

In rueful acknowledgement, and for the last time, Ashnak fell to his knees and prostrated himself, banging his forehead on the trampled grass. Frost-blighted poppies bloomed scarlet in the corners of his vision.

'Yes, master! At once, master!'

Cowering in a practised fashion, head still bent, Ashnak's eyes swivelled up to watch the Men, elves and dwarves depart. The nameless necromancer bowed gracefully, gesturing for his sister to precede him.

In the nameless necromancer's eyes Ashnak sees the look of one who is sizing up yellow hair, grey-white skin, and fresh bones for domestic utility.

A last whistle of incoming fire brought him to his belly, rolling into concealment behind a section of broken wall, and reaching for his helmet RT. 'CEASE FIRE, MARINES! Fall back! Emergency rendezvous at Nin-Edin – *bug out!* NOW!'

'*Acknowledged—*'

'*—I copy—*'

The few voices cease.

Craters steamed in the westering sun. Smoke, cordite and the sparkling fog of magic began to clear. Vapours drifted over slumped bodies, charred DPM combats, abandoned heavy weapons, and minced flesh. The dead lay in clumps and rows.

Because it is our flesh, it seems it should be different. Ashnak shook his head at the thought. Knobs of bone, shining joints, slick muscle tissue; all no different from a shambles or abattoir.

Even looking at the nearest area of the battlefield he can see recognizable corpses. *Three companies: practically a battalion.* The orc marines of Nin-Edin . . . Kusaritku and Azarluhi together, and several with them burned beyond identification. Duranki, Tukurash, Kazadhuron. And, ahead of the rest, as always leading the charge as a commander should, lies Captain Imhullu. The sun shines down on his blind face.

But The Named will not ride at Samhain, Ashnak will bet on it. For whatever her absence is worth.

Not much, as ever, to the dead.

Ashnak stood, the black fire of the necromancer's rough-and-ready healing coursing through him. He wiped pus and blood from his remaining burns and straightened, sniffing, pulling deep breaths down into his broad chest. The air stank of shit and blood.

He took out his forage cap and put it on, pulling down the peak. The charred remnants of his uniform pocket yielded, amazingly, fresh pipe-weed. He stuck a cigar in his mouth and strolled across to the wreck of the helicopter.

A heap of masonry some yards from the Huey collapsed and

disclosed the two orcs who had gone to cover. The larger, a female with her orange hair tied up in a horsetail, shook herself. The smaller, who appeared to have been attempting to hide under his own GI helmet, sat up beside her.

'So what *does* an orc call a halfling?' the small orc inquired.

'Lunch.' The large female orc slapped her DPM-camouflaged thigh. 'Lunch!'

'Damn right,' Ashnak growled.

The smaller orc sprang to his feet and saluted. 'Sir, General Ashnak, sir!'

'At ease, Lieutenant . . . *Captain* Barashkukor,' Ashnak corrected himself.

Marukka saluted. 'The firefight's over.' The orange-haired orc hefted a shoulder-fired missile launcher in one hand. 'I guess we won't be using these any more, will we, sir? I want my pole-axe back.'

Barashkukor folded his small arms over his flak-jacket. 'But I like the armour.'

Ashnak bent down, recovering water bottles and knives from corpses, slinging them from his webbing. He left the guns. He grinned toothily and began to laugh; deep belly-laughs that shook him until his tilted eyes watered.

'It's not important.' Ashnak put his horny arms around the two orcs' shoulders. 'Fuck, man, the weapons aren't important!'

In the Old Forest, now, or in the Man-countryside, there will be orc survivors heading back to Nin-Edin. They've been taught how to fall back and regroup. They'll obey. They're marines. They're *grunts*.

Ashnak of the fighting Agaku grinned an orc grin, and stared into the red light of the setting sun.

'So the hostiles have magic. So what! *Think* about what happened down there, marines. We were disciplined. We fought as units. We were tactical. Orcs fought as a *team*.'

'Yeah,' Marukka said slowly. 'There wasn't just warriors charging off into the fight on their own, or killing each other instead of the enemy. Different orc-tribes fought side by side! My squad kicked ass! If we hadn't had to stop when we did . . .'

Ashnak looked away from the sunset, black dots swimming in his vision. He rubbed the wet corners of his tilted eyes. Beside him, Barashkukor brought one small booted foot down hard, coming smartly to attention.

'Sir, we are marines, sir!'

'That's right . . .'

Ashnak tugged his forage cap down over his hairless skull, between his peaked ears. He shifted the unlit cigar to the corner of his tusked mouth, and thumped Barashkukor between his skinny shoulder-blades. The small orc staggered and sat down hard on the turf.

'That's *right*.' Ashnak grinned ferociously. 'There can be more of us. I promise you. There's always the Last Battle. There's always *after* the Last Battle . . .'

'Sir, yes, sir!'

The crimson sun shines on the three of them, casting their shadows long across the carnage of the battlefield around Guthranc. The forces of Light, badly mauled, limp away from the scene of their victory. Below the Tower, the orc marines are already lighting fires and roasting the wounded.

BOOK 2

FIELDS OF DESTRUCTION

1

IT IS SAMHAIN. The Autumn Solstice, the Day of Dead Souls. The fate of the free world hangs in the balance.

The Last Battle of the Army of Light against the Horde of Darkness seethes backwards and forwards across the vast plain that chroniclers call the Fields of Destruction.

Squadrons of black-armoured orcs and wolverine-riding trolls, battalions of fire-demons and mutant ogres, companies of evil djinni, cacodaemons and dark elves; armies of witch-queens, and the thirteen necromancers of the Horde of Darkness, raven against the outnumbered Army of the Light. Jagged swords, warhammers, and pole-axes bloodily rise and fall. Brigades of mutant monsters lumber into the carnage. Leather-winged beasts swoop down over the pitifully outnumbered forces of Good.

Vast is the Horde. Its sorcery crackles like black lightning around the horizon; it eclipses the sun at noon.

For the third time since midday, the right flank of the Evil Horde began piecemeal to retreat.

A voice yelped, 'Hold the line!'

An evil ogre stood with his spiked helm firmly down over his brows, shield up, his warhammer poised over his head in a fierce attack-posture.

'I said *hold the line*, soldier!' A small and oddly dressed orc loped down the hill from the ridge. The ogre's brows contracted in confusion.

'What the *fuck* do you think you're doing?' the newcomer snarled. He stood hip-high to the evil ogre, who looked down in puzzlement at the mottled green patterns on the orc's round, visorless helmet, and breeches and padded jerkin. The small orc wore boots.

'I *am* holding the line. I'm facing the enemy,' the unwounded ogre explained. He blinked rapidly. 'They won't get past me! I'm holding the line all right.'

The small orc pulled off his helmet and threw it furiously to the ground. It bounced. The orc's spindly, peaked ears began to unkink.

'You're facing the enemy all right – from twenty yards *behind* our lines!' The orc used both hands to wave a snubbed metallic tube at the evil ogre. 'Of course they won't get *past* you, you snivelling excuse for a soldier. They're way over *there!*'

'For the Lady of Light!' a lone heroic voice trumpeted, as a knight in impractically ornamented golden armour charged into a band of Undead, two hundred strong, over *there*. Magic seared the earth. Two hundred Undead fell at the stroke of the enchanted blade. The golden knight charged an even larger band of trolls.

The evil ogre pointed across the Fields of Destruction. 'But, but, but – they got magic!'

'I don't want to hear it! Now *get into the fucking fighting line*. Move it, asshole!'

The small orc reached up, grabbed the ogre by the hem of his mailshirt, and threw him bodily forward. The ogre, terminally startled, lumbered into battle. The small orc recovered his odd helmet, jammed it on his head, and doubled along the back of the line-fight towards the next reluctant warrior.

The ogre heard him mutter as he went, 'I don't know what the Dark Horde is *coming* to . . .'

An Undead barbarian warrior smashed desperately at a dwarf's Virtue-enchanted helmet before speaking to the ogre, now next to him in the fighting line. 'Who was that? *What* was that?'

'I don't know. I do know one thing.' The ogre hacked tentatively at the Army of Light, still outnumbered, but now indisputably advancing. 'I know that the day is not ours.'

On the far side of the wooded ridge, Ashnak, General Officer Commanding the orc marines, shoved his urban-camouflaged GI helmet back on his misshapen skull and focused his binoculars. The eddies and tides of the battle beat against the orc marine company, holding the right of the line.

A halfling Paladin strode up the slope towards him at the head of a band of Men.

'Fear not!' Her smiling confidence echoed across the field. 'My virtue is such that I have never yet even had to draw my sword in anger – see, its peace-threads still bind it into the scabbard! Follow me!'

Further down the line, an orc marine grinned broadly. Ashnak saw her sight the M16 she carried on the halfling's elf-silver mailshirt.

SPLOOM!

Ashnak blinked gold and vermilion sparkles of Light magic out of his vision. A crater smoked where the grunt had been. Overhead, an eagle-mage soared away.

The halfling Paladin strode on up the hill, oblivious. 'Onward!'

'Take her out.' Ashnak glared at the halfling's ostentatiously empty hands. 'Take her *out!*'

An orc mortar team ran forward. The pair of grunts squatted, aimed, dropped in the missile—

SPLOOOOM!

Pieces of mortar rained down around Ashnak's ears. He thoughtfully picked a green, sticky scrap of camouflage material off his boot, and eyed the approaching band of Good warriors.

The halfling took off her helmet, brown curls ruffling in the breeze, and turned her head to gaze back at her followers as she strode on up the hill. 'Follow me, Men! Into the atta—*awk!*'

The armoured figure vanished. Ashnak raised his binoculars. Tracking along a fallen log, he came to where the Paladin sprawled over it, bright leg-harness at an unusual angle.

'Assistance!' the halfling Paladin called. 'My leg is broke! Succour me before the forces of Evil attack!'

One orc marine beside Ashnak started to lift his anti-tank weapon, glanced suspiciously at the sky and the battlefield, and lowered it again. 'Er . . . sir . . .'

There was a sudden burning sensation on Ashnak's chest. He glanced down. Fiery worms of blue light threaded through his combat jacket and kevlar armour. He slapped at them, wincing, and saw a company of the Light's mages moving in towards the foot of the ridge.

'Ashnak,' he radioed. 'Marine standard-bearer to me now; out. Company Sergeant Marukka, get your platoon to pull back to me and regroup in the wood; over.'

'*Marukka to General Ashnak, orders received, sah! Out.*'

Booted orc feet pounded the earth. A tall, skinny orc in green DPM combat trousers and flak jacket loped along the foot of the wooded ridge towards Ashnak. Over one shoulder he carried a tall pole ornamented with Man-skulls, from which flew the tattered and magic-blackened marine flag.

'Ugarit is here, sir, General, sir!'

'Very good, marine.' Ashnak felt in his combat trouser pockets and extracted a roll of pipe-weed, which he jammed in the corner of his tusked mouth, unlit. 'Stick with me, soldier. Right beside me. Or I'll feed you your own fingers, one by one.'

The skinny orc saluted three or four times in rapid, terrified succession. 'Yessir! I will, sir! Count on me, sir!'

'Company Sergeant Marukka to General Ashnak, we're pulling back and letting the witch regiment take the brunt, sir. We are rejoining the main company on the ridge. Out.'

Orcs pounded back up the hill in flawless, disciplined order; falling into cover in the wood. Ashnak glimpsed urban camouflage and a horse-tail plume of orange hair. 'I see you, Sergeant. Hold your position. Out.'

He hitched up his DPM combat trousers, sweating in the autumn chill, and pounded up the hill, Ugarit at his heels. Blood and flesh – none of it orcish – crusted his combat boots and reddened the black-and-grey fabric of his trousers to his bowed knees. Pistol and sheathed sword jolted, hanging heavy from his web-belt. He snatched air into his heaving lungs, and narrowed his beetle-browed eyes.

'Sir, General Ashnak, sir!' A small orc pushed through the undergrowth, tugged his flak jacket straight, and snapped a smart salute, panting. 'I keep putting the Horde back in the line, sir, but they won't stay there.'

'Send another runner to Horde Command, Captain Barashkukor. We need Dark mages on this flank. We must have sorcerous support!'

'Sir, yes, sir!'

'Dumb motherfuckers!' Ashnak snarled. 'If we don't get some magical firepower over here, this flank will *never* hold.'

The lightning strikes of Light's magical discharges coloured the air aquamarine, vermilion and gold. Sorcery went up in black plumes against the blue noonday sky. The shouting, spellcasting and the clash of weapons must echo as far as the coast and Herethlion's deserted streets. Ashnak spat, and thumbed his radio's helmet-stud.

'Marines are never defeated!' he snarled.

A tinny, loud response echoed through from the four hundred orc grunts in the wood:

'SIR, NO, SIR!'

'Barashkukor, did you pass my message on to the other Horde Commanders?'

'Sir, I did. *No one* knows where the nameless necromancer is. Even the Dark Lord doesn't know, and He isn't too pleased about that, sir.'

The big orc shook his tusked head cynically. 'So our nameless commander's gone missing. What a surprise, Captain. Where is the orc marines' fearless patron? Where, indeed.'

'His sister The Named hasn't been seen fighting for the Light, though, sir.'

'I suppose we should be thankful for that. Too much damn magic here as it is.'

In the battle's centre, to Ashnak's left, the infantry line-fight swayed – heroic bright uniforms, white shining armour, the rise and fall of enchanted blades. Trolls crushed skulls, witches cackled and transmuted their enemies to bloody offal, before falling to the Light's magery. Blue fire-worms faded from Ashnak's flesh. He wondered briefly if that meant that the enemy wizard battalions were having problems with the other flank of the battle; and why there was never a magic-sniffer around when you needed one . . .

At the foot of the ridge, a band of elven cavalry wheeled their horned mounts and charged up the slope towards the woods, firing short recurved bows as they came. Sunlight glinted from the unicorns' spiral horns, and from the elven mail.

Ashnak bellowed: 'Heavy weapon fifty yards general targets *fire!*'

An orc squad on the far right opened up, raking the elves with Maxim guns.

'Captain Barashkukor, tell the drummers to signal *fire at will!*'

A ragged cheer went down the line. Ashnak bared his fangs in a smile. He thumbed the RT. 'All marine troops go over to primary weapons, repeat, *all marine troops use primary weapons.*'

He unslung an M60 machine-gun from his back. With his standard-bearer close behind he pushed into a gap between squads at the wood's edge, cocked the weapon, and the stuttering roar of a firefight broke out. Grenades exploded, throwing up showers of dirt and meat. Cordite smoke obscured the battle. The orc squads around him fired on automatic, M16 and AK47 muzzles jabbing flame. The *boom!* and *crack!* of fire hurt his ears until they bled.

'Suck on that, motherfuckers!' Ashnak lifted his machine-gun and fired again, exhausting the belt.

Hooves cut the turf as elvish cavalry pounded up the ridge towards him. Ashnak dropped to one knee, hit the change lever, and dropped a full belt in. The arrow-storm fell around him. Eighty jewelled riders: bright swords raised, banners flying, spurring their unicorns' flanks bloody. He saw their mouths open, could not hear the Light's spells over the firefight.

'Gotta admire them dumbass heroes. *But . . .*'

Ashnak emptied his M60 into the front rank.

Unicorns and elves slammed into the earth. The banners of the Light dropped and fell, trampled. Broken-legged mounts screamed, struggling to rise. One mailshirted elf got to her hands and knees, blonde hair falling over her almond eyes, and Ashnak let off a burst that ripped her into bloody shrapnel.

'Keep firing! We're gonna take 'em!'

As he spoke, an enemy *fail-weapons* spell glanced across the ridge and the wood. All the automatic weapons coughed and fell silent; all the grenades failed to explode. The sudden quiet filled with the screaming of wounded unicorns.

'Where the *fuck* are our mages? Damn it, we could turn the battle here!'

'They've run!' The standard-bearer, Ugarit, fell to his knees and began to giggle hysterically.

Captain Barashkukor hit dirt beside Ashnak. 'Dark magic-users were supposed to be protecting this flank, sir, but they pulled out.'

A rare breath of wind parted the smoke and magical flames. Ashnak stared out from the ridge, across the battlefield. The fight on his left between the Undead and their dwarfish opponents swayed backwards and forwards and broke, the Dark Undead falling back in confusion.

To Ashnak's right, the Dark's trolls turned their backs and ran from Men in full plate harness advancing across the Fields towards the orcs' position, the shimmer of spellfire blazing from their armour.

'If we don't hold 'em now, we've lost it!' Ashnak slapped the butt of his M60. 'Captain, pass the word down to the NCOs: if these weapons fail, the marines are to go over to axe and hammer. We've done it before. We're the fighting Agaku! Drums: signal the advance. Let's go, marines. *Go, go, go!*'

Pounding the earth, boots slipping in blood and intestines, Ashnak loped down over the fallen bodies of the elvish cavalry. Exposed now, on open ground, the orc marines pounded forward.

'Chaarrge!' Ashnak bellowed, deep voice lost in the foundry-racket of fire.

A good part of the right flank of the Horde began suddenly to roll forward with the orcs.

SPLOOOOM!!

Momentum gone, Horde warriors dived for cover in the waving grass and found none.

'How do you like it? The bastards are running out on us!' a voice marvelled in Ashnak's ear. Company Sergeant Marukka swung her shoulder-fired rocket-launcher around and pulled the trigger. The *whump!* of high explosive failed to materialize. 'This ain't no Horde general advance, sah! We're marooned way out in front of the battle! The enemy are going to take us on both flanks!'

The armoured Men closed the distance, screaming into the fight. Ashnak wiped his brows, damp with the fine spray of blood that fills the air above the infantry line. The sky stood empty of all but the eclipsed sun. Black riders grouped on a distant ridge to the east. No sign of his runner; no word from Horde Command.

'*We* can hold without firearms – but the rest of them candy-ass bastards won't!'

The smoke of magic hid the left flank now, and rolled across the centre of the battle, so that all he could hear were screams, battlecries. Longbow arrows began dropping from the sky, scattering the command group around him; and an orc NCO lifted his helmeted head to shout orders and dropped with a steel bolt through GI pot and skull. Another *fail-weapons* spell sparked from field to ridge. The reserve squads' weapons stuttered and died.

'Son of a *bitch!*' Ashnak howled. He pounded his useless M60 into the weapons-strewn, blood-stained, corpse-littered turf. '*Somebody take out the White Mages!*'

'We're going to die!' Corporal Ugarit crouched at the foot of the marine standard pole, skinny shoulders shaking. His wide eyes fixed on the advancing Army of Light. '*I'm* going to die— they're going to get me— I'm outta here— arrggh!'

Ashnak wiped green orc blood from the butt of the M60 as he kicked Ugarit to his feet. Pragmatic and prosaic, he said, 'If anyone's going to die at the Last Battle, trust me, it won't be the orc marines!'

He thumbed his helmet RT.

'OK, *listen up!* Ashnak to all section leaders. Form up on the standard, repeat, form up on my standard. We can't retreat from this position, we'll never make it. We're going to fight *straight through* the enemy lines, and we're not stopping for anything, got that? Once we're past them, *keep going*. We'll regroup at our emergency rendezvous point. Assholes and elbows, you motherfuckers, and remember that you're the Orc Marines!'

There was a momentary silence. Then, amid yells of 'Fix bayonets!', the company seized their secondary weapons and plunged into the advancing line of armoured Men, wielding their spears, halberds, morningstars and flails.

The smoke of battle hid them from sight.

All across the Fields of Destruction, the evil Horde of Darkness broke, ran and routed in utter confusion.

'Ho, Amarynth!'

The squat figure of a dwarf made a black silhouette against the sunset. She plodded across the field, stout-booted feet trampling over the fallen bodies of tribal orcs wearing black plate armour. Her red hair, tightly braided on the crown of her head, shone in the level golden light.

'Amarynth, you elven rogue!'

The elven fighter-mage leaned wearily against a boulder. Trolls and cacodaemons lay at his feet, his white-fletched arrows jutting from their eye sockets and mouths. A great many more of the corpses surrounding the rock showed the burns of magic. 'Kazra— Is that you?'

'Of course it's me,' the dwarf grumbled, wiping the back of her broad hand across her forehead. It came away green with orc blood, black with the ichor of daemons. Similar blood spattered her small broad breastplate and arm defences. She held out the hand.

Amarynth gripped it with slender, brown fingers. He then examined his hand in distaste, wiping it down his silken tunic. 'I never thought I should be glad to see a dwarf! Kazra, well met. Well met, on this day of all great days!'

'It is a great day,' the dwarf said, 'and a great victory, although I suppose I must give some of the credit to elves and Men, but we dwarves! How we fought!'

'Yes. There will be many a sad burning tonight at the funeral pyres. But we have won the great Victory of our Age. Evil is vanquished!'

The elven fighter-mage clapped the dwarf on the back, reaching down low to do it. Picking their way between the dead bodies of orcs, enchantresses and ogres, the two warriors of Light made their way across the Fields of Destruction to a low ridge.

There, beyond the crows flocking down to settle on the field of battle, the countryside of the Northern Kingdoms stretched away in the sunset light. Gold touched the cornfields, the spires of distant villages and quiet winding rivers.

'We shall go to Herethlion,' Amarynth said softly. 'There will be much singing. The heroes shall be honoured. And the greatest of them all shall be rewarded by the High King Kelyos Magorian.'

Kazra snorted, resting on the haft of her axe. 'And the High King Magorian had better appoint some of us to his Council, since who but we who fought for the Northern Kingdoms best know how to govern them? There is much that needs putting right, friend Amarynth. Traitors and Dark-lovers yet remain in hiding. We must search them out – with an inquisition, if need be.'

An unexpected and unaccustomed smile spread over Amarynth's aquiline brown features. His black hair shone in the sun. The last vestiges of magic fractured in gold light in his eyes.

'Fear not, Kazra. We have vermin to root out, I doubt not, but we this day have created a world to last a thousand years! A world for the Light, in which no shadow of Darkness shall trouble us again.'

'And what of the scattered remnants of the defeated Evil Horde?'

'Oh,' Amarynth said, 'they have nowhere to run to. We shall exterminate them over the next few weeks. After all, their Dark Master is dead and their Dark Land invaded. Where can they go, and what help can they hope for? Every good Man's hand is against them.'

The elven fighter-mage and the dwarf began to walk west, into the light of the setting sun. Kazra's boot squelched. She swore an ancient dwarvish oath and bent down to tug her foot free of tangled white intestines spilling from the gutted body of a great orc. She cracked an orc rib and freed her boot, muttering at the stench of decomposing flesh. Two fat crows waddled across the earth towards the corpse.

'To Herethlion!' Amarynth cried.

Kazra echoed him. 'To Herethlion!'

Side by side they strode west, into a world of golden light.

The first beams of dawn shifted down through the branches of the Old Forest. Sunlight fell through ancient beech trees to the leaf-covered forest floor. Under spreading oaks, bracken turned autumnal red. Dew hung grey on spiderwebs.

A bird began to sing.

FOOM!

Amid falling feathers, Company Sergeant Marukka blew a drift of smoke from her Desert Eagle pistol and reholstered it.

'All *right*, you grunts – hands off cocks; on socks!'

Company Sergeant Marukka strolled down the lines of recumbent orc bodies, bellowing, kicking out with her combat boots. Black unit insignia and sergeant's chevrons tattooed her muscular green arms. Over her squat body she wore a camouflage jacket with the sleeves ripped off, and a black undershirt that strained over her large breasts. Knives, grenades and pistols hung from her webbing. Her orange hair was pulled up into a skull-ornamented plume on the crown of her head.

'I can't wait all da-ay . . .' Marukka sang sweetly. 'On your *feet*, marines!'

Marukka turned and stood with her back to the largest beech tree, bowed legs planted wide apart, her gnarled hands clasped behind her back. The many orc grunts who had slept concealed in bracken began to stir, sitting up and rubbing their heads. One green-skinned orc absently stood up to piss. A boot emerged from the bush he had chosen as his target and kicked him across the clearing. There was a clatter of weapons and armour as he landed.

'You're going to hate my guts,' Marukka announced, satisfied. 'I'm here to see you get it *right*, not to wipe your scaly bums! I'll leave that to your mothers – those of you assholes who *had* mothers. Even a mother couldn't love a scurvy, filthy, undisciplined bunch of wankers like you; am I right?'

Half on their feet, partly armoured, each with a weapon to hand, the assembled orcs hastily chorused, 'Yes, Sergeant!'

'Then get your asses in gear, you 'orrible little orcs, or I'll have your bollocks for breakfast! Corporals, get your orcs on parade! At the double! *Now!*' Marukka paced forward, still with her hands behind her back. She kept a wary eye on the broken-down hovel that temporarily housed the company's officers, hearing muttering voices inside. She surveyed the orcs in the slanting sunlight – some pissing up trees, some fastening combat jackets and trousers, some still slumped on the ground.

'You think because you've just been through the Last Battle, that excuses you? You shower of shit! You're *marines*. You there— Your weapons are filthy. You— your kit is incomplete. Smarten it up, you 'orrible little lot!'

'YES, SERGEANT!'

One orc marine sat down again, clutching his bleeding arm. In daylight, a number of marine injuries seemed to be visible.

'*Fit* marines to the right,' Marukka bawled, 'and *wounded* marines to the left. Crawl if you have to.'

The company split raggedly, some three hundred or more orc marines moving to the right-hand side of the clearing, and perhaps thirty (more slowly) to the left.

Marukka's lips curled back in a snarl. She walked up to the dozen marines who still stood in the centre of the clearing.

'*So*. Can't make up our minds, can we? Not fit *or* wounded marines? Just what do you think you lot are, then?'

An albino orc drew himself more smartly to attention. 'Please, Sergeant, dead marines.'

'What?'

Marukka goggled. The twelve orc marines fiddled with their tattered bloody combat fatigues, attempting to conceal gaping gut wounds and various fractures. A chill came off them that was not the chill of dawn.

'To be completely accurate, Undead marines, Sergeant. We was raised, Sergeant, by a necromancer of unknown provenance.'

'Ah. Well. Lugashaldim, isn't it? Very well, Corporal Lugashaldim.'

Marukka nodded to the albino orc briskly. 'Undead Marine Squad – carry on.'

'Yes, Sergeant!' The Undead orc marine saluted. A finger detached itself from his hand and flew across the clearing, striking a female orc lance-corporal under the left ear. She growled.

Marukka about-faced and marched across to the small hovel in time to salute Barashkukor as the captain came out. 'Beg to report the company is ready for General Ashnak's inspection.'

'The general is ready to inspect!'

While Ashnak walked around on inspection, Marukka ordered her lesser NCOs into assigning spare weapons, checking backpacks, correcting the use of camouflage-paint on scabby orc features, and checking the remaining rounds of ammunition. At the end of half an hour she saluted the orc general under the big beech tree.

'Ready to move out, sir. We're low on ammunition until we get back to base. Suggest the marines only use their pole-arms, sir, if we run into opposition.'

'We'll run into opposition, Sergeant. The Light is going to be combing the Northern Kingdom for survivors of *that* battle. And we just made ourselves the number one target.' The big orc general pulled an urban camouflage forage cap down to shade his eyes. He chewed on an unlit cigar. 'Thank you, Sergeant. Captain Barashkukor, get the orcs ready to move out.'

Barashkukor slammed a small booted foot into the leafmould and saluted. 'Sir! Sir, what about the wounded who can't walk?'

The orc general shrugged. 'We've got a long march in front of us. They're history.'

'Yessir!' Sergeant Marukka nodded sagely.

A strained expression made its appearance on the small orc's features. Captain Barashkukor protested, 'Sir, we don't leave our own, sir!'

General Ashnak considered this new concept. After a few moments he nodded.

'You're right, Captain. Of course you're right. See to it. They're not history – they're field rations.'

The halfling Magda sat in her room in Herethlion.

The distant rumble of magic that had sounded all day from the east became sporadic, and finally died down completely around twilight. Mopping up after yesterday's battle. Magda waited. It did not resume.

She got to her feet, continuing to brush her long auburn hair. A stamp of her tiny foot on the floor brought her halfling maid, Safire, running.

'Yes, miss?'

'Help me dress.'

Magda tossed the hairbrush on to her cluttered dressing table. After a moment's thought she recovered it and threw it up on to the Man-sized bed. She tugged the gauze scarf from her full-length mirror.

A halfling, three feet three inches high, with auburn hair falling to her waist . . . Magda surveyed herself for a moment. She irritatedly pulled off the auburn hairpiece and began to fit a blonde wig over her own cropped brown hair.

'Your clothes, miss. Shall I help you with the laces?'

Magda hopped up to sit on the Man-bed and pull on the tight black leather trousers and laced leather bodice. While Safire adjusted the trouser lacings up the outside of her legs, Magda clipped spiked and studded leather bands around her wrists and neck, and put on her chain-belt. She slid off the bed, wriggling her feet into stiletto-heeled black thighboots, and strode across to the mirror.

Slender curves tightly encased, Magda posed for her own satisfaction. She ran her hands over her black-leather-clad breasts and hips. 'I have a girl's figure still, Safire. A girl's figure.'

'Yes, miss.'

Magda peered closely into the mirror, touching the lines around her eyes. 'I shall be wearing the mask. You must give me warning if one of the customers wants me bare-face. I'll need cosmetics.'

She reached up and took the whip from the dressing table, cracking it experimentally. There was a clatter of iron from the bedstead where Safire checked the shackles. Female and male voices echoed excitedly down the House of Joy's upper corridor, and in Herethlion's streets hoofbeats sounded.

'Go on then, girl! Tell them that Mistress Whip is ready for business.'

'Yes, miss.'

The leather-clad halfling wobbled a couple of steps on her high heels, caught her balance, and picked up and put on the leather head-mask that had only eye- and mouth-holes to break its severity.

'Heroes coming back from the wars.' Magda heaved a happy sigh that strained the laces over her diminutive breasts. 'I'll wager the Light is victorious . . . Either way, there's custom enough out there for all of us for a week. No, a month! We're going to be rich, Safire. *Rich!*'

2

E IGHT DAYS' ORC-MARCH away from the Fields of Destruction, the raw November fog rolled across General Ashnak where he stood in the compound of the Nin-Edin Marine Base.

'Our ass is *grass*,' he announced, slapping the barrel of his M60. 'And these are the reason why.'

''Tisn't fair on the grunts, sir,' Company Sergeant Marukka protested. 'All the *other* defeated Dark warbands are going to form themselves into Free Companies and ravage the countryside.'

''Snot fair at all, sir.' Captain Barashkukor wiped his nose. 'All we wanted to be was brigands.'

'We're marines,' Ashnak growled.

'OK, sir – *disciplined* brigands. Aaaaaaashu!' The small orc wiped his nose on his sleeve, trailing mucus over his camouflage combat jacket. He sniffed. 'I bet they're all doing it. Taking towns, refusing to be shifted by threats or bribes, being declared heir when the present ruler dies of completely natural causes . . . I was really looking forward to being a Duke, sir. Aasshu!'

Ashnak glared up through the fog at the walls, and the travel-worn orc marine company hastily repossessing and rebuilding the Nin-Edin fort. 'No. We're prime targets. The marines were the best unit on the Fields of Destruction. The Light will put it down to these weapons. They'll *want* us.'

Watery daytime torchlight illuminated his ugly features and

brass-capped tusks. He scratched at his flea-infested combat fatigues.

'I want this place bristling with weapons! The Light can use magic to find us here. Even after the Last Battle, I'm willing to bet they'll have mages to send against us.'

'*Aascchhhu!*'

CSM Marukka wiped disgustedly at the bowed leg of her combats, and glared at Barashkukor with more than a sergeant's distaste for junior officers. 'Beg to report, General, I checked out our stores of Dagurashibanipal's hoard in the bunkers here – we're up to capacity on ammunition. I found some crates that ain't *matériel*. One's been taken up to your office for your inspection. I also took a tech squad up to the storage-depot caverns. That old wyrm must have had half the mountains hollowed out – there's enough weapons, transport and ammunition in there to equip an orc tribe for a decade!'

Barashkukor wiped his dripping nose. 'And none of it any use to us without mage-protection! They can wipe us out with the simplest *fail-weapons* spell.'

Ashnak slapped his orc captain between the shoulder-blades. Barashkukor rolled head over heels several times, finishing up on his back with his combat boots up against the inner gate-tower's iron portcullis.

'Cheer up! Damn it, Captain, we're marines. We don't take defeat lying down!'

'Sir, no, sir – aaaa*schuu!*'

Marukka said, 'The general's got a plan. Haven't you, General? He's never let us down yet. We're marines. We look after our own.'

Ashnak thought of the wounded and picked his teeth.

The female orc, suspicion fighting with military discipline in her tone, said, 'You *have* got a plan, General?'

How long can Nin-Edin remain untouched by the Dark's cata-strophic defeat? The nameless necromancer – may he burn! – where *is* he? With no mage-support, there's a limit to how long Ashnak can play for time.

'Don't ask questions, Sergeant, obey your orders! I want that standard bearer, Ugarit, and marine Rast— Razzis—'

Captain Barashkukor's mucus-rimmed eyes suddenly lit up. 'Razit-shakra, sir. Marine Razitshakra.'

'Why does the general want them?' Marukka growled, puzzled. 'They're hardly fit to be called *marines*, either one of them.'

'I want them in my office,' Ashnak ordered. '*Now.*'

The rider of the refugee war-beast dug a makeshift thorn quirt behind its sail-like ear. The great animal lifted a long probosis, curling like a python; and ponderously swung to the left, padding up a steep hill slope.

A fresh wind blew from the ship-deserted sea.

The rider shifted blanket and leather strap, endeavouring to make the seat on the animal's back more comfortable. Rough brown hide, thick with bristles, made uneasy riding. Rags of gold and red caparisons clung to its metal-armoured tusks. The animal's tiny black eye swivelled in its socket, gazing up and back.

'Go, thou bastard offspring of a goat and the World Serpent! *Go!*'

The thorn quirt lashed down. The war elephant turned away and inland, scaling the Downs, and trampling hedges, crops and streamlets in the country beyond.

Freezing fog hung in the general's office in Nin-Edin's inner keep. Mists pearled on the Tower's yard-thick masonry walls. Ashnak ambled across to a large crate, fully accustomed to the strength and influence of the geas that radiated from any item of the dragon's hoard.

'Is there anything *useful* in here, Barashkukor?'

'Don't – asshu!' Barashkukor wiped his snot on his sleeve. 'Don't know, sir.'

'*Then open it, you snivelling little rat!*'

Ashnak put his hands behind his back, watching Barashkukor lever at the wood with fangs and talons. The planks splintered. Barashkukor peered down into the crate, his spindly ears shifting from lateral to vertical.

'*Books*, sir?'

'Books?' Ashnak took a tome out of the smaller orc's hand. With one taloned finger he traced the printed letters on the cover. His wide lips moved as he read, literacy not being a prime requirement for a Horde Captain. '*Von . . . Clauswitz. On . . . War . . .*'

He flicked through the pages and laboriously spelled out, '"War is only the continu— continuation of politics, by other means . . ."'

'Nahhh. War's *fun*, sir, that's what war is.' Captain Barashkukor brandished another book he removed from the crate. 'This one's called *Pliny*, sir.' He thumbed through it, eyes widening. '*Sir!* It mentions *orcs*, sir! It says the orc is a marine monster.'

Ashnak raised a bushy eyebrow. 'Wonder how he knew?'

'*Jane's Medieval Small-Arms and Siege Weapons*, sir?'

'Obsolete, soldier.' Ashnak broke off, hearing a heavy multiple tread on the stairs. 'Come!'

'Hut-two, hut-two, hut-two, *halt!* The marines you requested, sir!'

Company Sergeant Marukka saluted smartly. A tall skinny male orc marched into the office beside another orc female, this one scruffy and wearing spectacles.

'—and because they're *all* out to get me! Oh. Lord General!' Ugarit saluted with the wrong hand. His uniform pockets shifted, clinking with the weight of spanners in them.

Marukka howled, 'Ugarit, you candyass marine, keep your mouth shut in front of the general! That's fifty strokes of the lash for you.'

The tall skinny orc began visibly to tremble. The scruffy female orc with him saluted rigidly.

'Dismissed, Sergeant,' Ashnak rumbled. 'I shan't be needing you either, Captain.'

Captain Barashkukor saluted and followed Marukka out. Ashnak stood for several minutes, looking the two marines up and down. He smiled nastily.

'You're pathetic,' he barked. 'Call yourselves marines? I wouldn't wipe my arse with you! I'm going to straighten this company out *now*, and I'm starting by evicerating you two! We've been occupying Nin-Edin for six hours and you *still* haven't come up with a plan to defeat the enemy.'

'P-plan, sir . . . ?' Marine Razitshakra's combats had quill-pens protruding from her every pocket. Her large pointed ears projected laterally from the sides of her head. Fog condensed and dripped from the tips of each. She blinked golden eyes. 'Wh-what plan?'

'*I've* got a plan! *Alternative* firepower! General, it's the only answer!' Ugarit, spluttering, unfolded scribbled-on sheets of paper, diagrams, a folding tape-measure, and small mechanical models. 'Arrows with ceramic heads! Kevlar armour! Carbon-fibre sword-blades! I have all the designs, all the measurements – calculations – stress loads – they'll *never* get me if I have all this!'

Razitshakra muttered something under her breath of which Ashnak could only distinguish the phrase 'several cogwheels short of a clock'.

'Very inventive.' Ashnak drew a breath and bellowed. 'The first blast of mage-fire will *still* shatter them to ashes! Are you telling me the whole Research and Development Unit can't come up with anything better than that?'

Ugarit shook his head, water drops flying. 'I had *everyone* working on it, General, sir.'

'And just how many personnel do you have in R&D?'

The skinny orc counted on his fingers for some minutes before announcing, 'One, General, sir. Me.'

Ashnak walked across to the vast carved wooden chair liberated from some merchant's wagon inadvisedly attempting the Nin-Edin pass, and sat down heavily at his desk. He wiped his hand across his face. He resisted, with difficulty, the impulse to crack Ugarit's skull against the masonry and see if anything oozed out.

'Sir . . .' Razitshakra scribbled on a small piece of paper she extracted from her pocket, ticking off items on a list with her index talon. 'I think I've got it, sir!'

'Please,' Ashnak purred, 'do tell.'

'*Magic*, sir. That's the answer. I don't do it – I'm an orc, and we hate magic! – but I *know* about it. The other grunts avoid me because of that . . .' She met his gaze, narrowing her tilted eyes. 'If you could find the nameless necromancer, or another Dark Mage – there must be *some* who didn't die at the Fields of Destruction – we could survive. But then that person would automatically end up in command of us, sir. Wizards always commanded the Horde because they could use magic and we can't.'

'True,' Ashnak rumbled.

'Only magic can defend against magic. You need someone who can deal with it – but does it have to be a Man? Or any other race? If we had orcs who could deal with magic, General, we'd be our *own* bosses.'

Ashnak, remembering a nest-sister of his own, magic-sniffer and dead now, shook his head. 'Orcs and magic don't mix.'

The female orc stabbed a taloned finger at her list. 'Normally, they don't have to. In battle we're protected by our side's wizards. But we don't *have* that here, sir! I'm not suggesting we *use* magic. Orcs don't do that. We should just make certain no one can use it against us.'

Razitshakra crumpled her list and shoved it deep in her combats pocket, staring intensely up at Ashnak.

'We don't have to look for a new master, sir. Not if we can get some magical talismans or amulets. *Protective* magical talismans that we can carry into battle with us. So that the Light can throw *fail-weapons* magic at us and it won't work.'

'As one of my nest-sisters, Shazgurim, used to say, *I* know Man-tales.' Ashnak's heavy brows lifted. 'Is it possible for orcs to have a Quest?'

'We orcs,' marine Razitshakra said, 'we orc marines *don't* need a master, General, we can do all this ourselves!'

Ashnak considered this revolutionary idea.

'Tell me, orc who is knowledgeable about magic,' he said softly, 'where you come by those golden eyes?'

Razitshakra's wide mouth dropped open. Her fangs and tusks seemed smaller than usual on an orc of her size.

'Well, marine?'

107

Razitshakra removed her spectacles. Her skin turned a deep grass-green over her cheeks, ears, throat, and breasts. She stared down at the toes of her muddy combat boots.

'It's not *true* that I'm a half-elf,' she mumbled. 'Quarter-elven, sir. At most. Grandmother made a mistake on a dark night in the Enchanted Wood. So did her . . . ah . . . involuntary partner, sir, one he didn't survive. I'm only a quarter-elvish, sir. I may know about magic but I'm a real orc, honest, sir!'

'Yes, yes.'

Ashnak was not familiar with the emotion of embarrassment but he felt a strong urge to change the subject.

He stood and went to the window. Nin-Edin's inner and outer walls loomed in the fog, covered with skull-standards and machine-gun emplacements. Ancient masonry, solid as the mountains, but masonry has been brought down before now, neither by siege machines nor storming the walls, but by the Light's filthy magic. Ashnak becomes aware that he is listening, and has been for some time.

Listening.

Waiting.

'These talismans, Marine Razitshakra. *If* such things exist – where would we get them?'

The golden-eyed orc brightened. 'Ah. Yes, sir. Now that's the interesting part.'

Wine had been spilt in the corridor of the House of Joy, and the halfling put his bare, hairy foot in it before he noticed. Making a face, he wiped his leathery sole on the bare boards. A few remaining coins clinked in his trunk-hose pockets.

The door at the end of the hall was ajar, and he pushed it open. Lanterns illuminated a Man-room – or so he first thought, looking at the bed; but the dressing table and washstand were halfling-sized furniture.

A whip snapped the air beside his left ear. 'On to the bed, slave!'

'Yes, mistress!' He fell to his knees, grovelling in front of a pair of very small, high, stiletto-heeled boots. The lantern light gleamed on black leather calves and slender thighs, and a studded belt from which hung shackles.

The whip cracked, stinging him smartly across the buttocks. He abased himself again, and then crawled over to the bed. It was impractical to crawl up on to it, it being Man-furniture. He stood and climbed up on to the rubber sheets.

'You will address me as mistress, scum – Safire, I'm going to need

108

the small shackles; *hurry*, girl! – and you will kiss my boots, and be thankful for the privilege, is that *clear?*'

'Yes, mistress!' He writhed happily. The maid, whom he assumed to be Safire, locked shackles on his wrists and ankles in somewhat too much of a professional manner, but he could forgive that. He was not by any means the first of the Army of Light home from the wars.

'Now, what have we here . . . A helpless victim, is it? Or a bad boy who needs punishing? Is it a bad boy who needs a whipping?'

He whimpered happily. 'Yes. I've been bad.'

The shackles tightened, pulled back and fastened at the four corners of the bedstead. He sprawled face-down on the bed, his small limbs stretched outwards. A leather-gloved hand slid up between his short legs and unbuttoned his trunk hose.

'Now—' the voice of the whore, mock-triumphant, as she pulled down his breeches and exposed his bare buttocks. 'Bad boy! I'll give you a whipping you'll never forget! *Bad* boy!'

A welt of fire lashed his buttocks. He was too startled to enjoy it.

'Wait—'

'You're a bad boy!'

Unmistakable.

He did the best he could to roll on one side, and look up over his shoulder. The female halfling stood on the bed, legs astride him, coiling her whip. He stared up at the black leather head-mask, seeing only an impersonal pair of eyes.

Bad boy.

The voice is unmistakable.

He said, 'Mother – is that *you?*'

The watery autumnal sunlight broke three days of continual fog as Barashkukor marched smartly across the inner compound of the Nin-Edin fort.

Reaching the door of the stone outhouse designated *Research Laboratory No. 1037*, he took off his GI helmet and, after some thought, tucked it under his left arm. His long, hairless ears sprang upright.

'Assschu!'

A voice from behind the closed door called, 'What is it, Captain Barashkukor?'

His small brows indented. He lifted a fist to knock smartly on the wood. Somewhere inside the stone shed a loud explosion sounded. Smoke drifted out of the glassless windows. An orcish scream split the air. Barashkukor ignored it and knocked again. The door creaked open.

109

'We're busy; what—' Marine Razitshakra stopped. *'What?'*

Barashkukor, his back ramrod straight, came to attention. The small orc's combat boots gleamed, his green DPM camouflage trousers had been ironed and pressed, and a display of grenades and .50 calibre ammunition hung on bandoliers across his thin chest.

'Marine Razitshakra.' He thrust out his left hand. His helmet, forgotten, dropped and bounced painfully off his foot. 'For you.'

Razitshakra inspected the posy of autumn wildflowers the small orc captain held out. 'Um . . . That's . . . um . . . sir . . .'

'They're for you!'

Barashkukor stuffed the flowers into the orc marine's hand, the tips of his ears drooping; snapped a salute, about-faced, and marched off back across the compound.

The female orc took off her rimless spectacles and put them in her top pocket. She blinked. In the distance, Captain Barashkukor about-faced again, marched back, and bent to pick up the camouflage-covered GI pot.

'Forgot my helmet,' he explained.

Razitshakra lowered her broad nostrils into the posy and sniffed it. She took a bite. Tentatively at first, she began to chew the dog-roses, holly and nightshade.

Barashkukor's shoulders slumped. He turned his back on her and walked away, feet dragging, his eyes on the beaten earth of the compound.

On the walls above the marine alarm horns rang out, and an urgent drum began to beat.

Barashkukor shrugged skinny shoulders and carried on walking.

Orc squads pounded past him at the double, corporals and NCOs shouted alarmed orders; and somewhere Marukka's bellow split the chill air. Weapons clashed. Up on the parapet, skull-pole standards were hastily raised. The inner iron portcullis clashed down, three yards from Barashkukor's left elbow, burying its spikes several feet deep in the dirt.

'Captain!'

Moodily, Barashkukor glanced up. The rising bulk of Nin-Edin at his back, he gazed through the iron grating at the great mountain ranges rising to either side of the pass. Grey cloud still clung to the impassable peaks. Before him, beyond the outer bailey and outer defensive walls, a desolate valley ran down to the lowlands . . .

The distant road that wound up to this mountain pass glittered.

'Oh *shit*,' Barashkukor said.

Lowland sunshine reflected back from the helms, shields, armour and weapons of the approaching, besieging Army of Light.

3

'**Y**OU'VE CHANGED, SON. I hardly know you.'

The halfling Magda emerged from behind the room's silk screen wearing a crimson-furred velvet gown. She tied its belt firmly around her hourglass waist.

'And I hardly expected to find you wearing *that* uniform.'

She walked across the room and picked up a thin roll of black pipe-weed, fitting it into a long ivory holder. Reaching up to a candle flame, she lit the pipe-weed and drew deeply. She passed her hand through her short, dark hair.

'Mother, everyone knew which was going to be the winning side.'

Magda inhaled another lungful of pipe-weed. She studied her son as he sat in the chair by the window, watching for first light. His black curly hair was thickly streaked with white.

'Besides, I thought that the Army of Light had a better chance of collecting its pay arrears.'

He lounged back, fully clad; black mailshirt glinting in the candle-light below the white of his small ruff. The favour of the Army of Light – a yellow sash – he wore tied about his left arm. His doublet and trunk hose showed signs of wear, and the wood of his short-sword scabbard had split and been badly repaired with wire.

'You wrote that you had become wealthy.'

The halfling's dark eyes flicked in her direction. There were lines

111

bitten into his round face that had not been there eighteen months ago.

'Wealth doesn't last. Gamblers had most of mine.'

'Mmm . . .' A little suspicious still, Magda walked to the window and stood on tiptoe to peer out. 'And your brother, where is he?'

For the first time in an hour, her son smiled.

'Out there in the frost, wondering if he should come in and rescue me; and whether it's danger that delays me, or over-indulgence in pleasure. Tonight was *his* turn to watch *my* back.'

Magda chuckled. 'I'll call Safire. We shall have hot mulled wine, while we wait. I wonder how long it will take him?'

She inhaled pipe-weed smoke, becoming serious.

'I've been thinking. Life in Herethlion won't be Easy Street for much longer. I give it a month before the celebrations and coronations are over – then the purge will begin. Anything with so much as a scent of corruption will be called *the Dark!* and banned. And that'll take this Thieves Quarter with it. Believe me. I've seen it before.'

She breathed out a long plume of smoke.

'Fortuna is a tricky Goddess. I made an offering in her church last month for help. Behold, she sends my two sons back to me.'

Magda stubbed the pipe-weed out against the window frame. She reached down as she crossed the room to call Safire, and squeezed her son's small hard bicep.

'I thought I might travel north. I shall need muscle – if I'm to set up business in a new city.'

The door of Nin-Edin's main hall closed behind the last senior officer to enter. Ashnak leaned his bulging forearms on the podium and grinned, showing all his fangs and brass-capped tusks.

'I suppose you're wondering why I've called you all here . . .'

The whistle of an incoming fireball spell drowned out his next words. The assembled orc officers hit the floorboards. The fireball air-burst, shrapnelling the glassless windows. Sparks of green flame flickered in the high-roofed hall and went out.

'Now—'

'*Fuck, man, you got us into some* deep *shit here!*' A marine corporal with FRAG THE OFFICERS! stencilled on her helmet cover sprang up and screamed, 'What kind of dumb motherfucker gets us shut up in a death-trap like this?'

Another orc yelled up at the podium, 'You ain't got the *balls* to break out of this fort!'

The orc officers snarled, pounding the butts of their assault rifles

112

on the flagstones. Ashnak's lip curled. 'And does anyone *else* hold that opinion?'

Waiting for the focus of trouble to manifest itself, he was at first irritated when Company Sergeant Marukka lumbered to her feet. He started to say, 'Later: let me deal with this first,' and then realized that a silence had fallen on the sixty officers present. Four of the junior lieutenants also got to their feet. The senior captains eyed Ashnak with expressions between speculation and outrage.

'*You?*' Ashnak demanded.

'Me.' Marukka rested a ham-sized fist on her hip. She wore green tiger-stripe camouflage, a strip of which tied up her plume of orange hair; and a black tank-top with BORN TO FIGHT! stencilled on the front. Deliberately, she cocked her M16. 'You failed in your duty, *sir*. You better let someone more competent take over the marines. I've decided. You're not in command here any more.'

'This is mutiny!'

Marukka grinned broadly at his bluster. 'Too fuckin' right, sah!'

Ashnak straightened his shoulders slightly. He looked down from the podium at the crowded hall and tense faces, chewing on his unlit cigar. Two marines behind Marukka got to their feet and flanked her in support, starting to unsling M16s from their shoulders.

FOOM! *FOOM!*

Wood splintered.

Ashnak shot through the podium that concealed the drawn and cocked .44 Magnum pistol in his hand, shredding the black sweatshirt over Marukka's heart, and putting a greenish-brown-rimmed hole between the eyes of the orc marine with FRAG THE OFFICERS! on her helmet. The third marine hit the floor, M16 raised, and a loyal grunt corporal put five rounds into her from behind with an AK47.

'*No one's taking over here except me!*'

The junior officers who had stood up sat down, attempting invisibility. Ashnak strode down from the platform, backhanding the two nearest and catapulting them across the hall. Chairs went flying. He reached Marukka's body and booted the orange-haired orc over on to her back. The wound pumped green blood less strongly now, pooling on the floor. Her eyes were open, unseeing. Tissue from the exit wound spattered the orc marines behind her.

'What do you shit-for-brains dumb motherfuckers expect me to do?' Ashnak snarled. 'Stand there and ask her questions while she shoots me? Siege or no siege, this coup is over before it's started. I'm General of the orc marines and it's going to *stay* that way, is that clear?'

'SIR YES SIR!'

113

Ashnak stomped back to the dais, lighting his cigar.

'Now. *As* I was saying. We find ourselves in a hostile situation, siege-wise . . .'

Ignoring the wall map behind him, he pointed his swagger stick at the table set up below the dais. Orc majors and captains abandoned their folding wooden chairs, kicking and biting to be in the front row around the war-table. Ashnak glared down at the tops of helmets and forage caps and coughed meaningfully. Orc heads lifted, tusks gleaming in heavy lower jaws, piggy eyes glinting. Reluctantly they shuffled back a few inches.

On the table, a scale map of the Demonfest mountains and surrounding area sported a liberal array of different-coloured map pins.

'Recon units report hostile troops on the roads from Sarderis, Herethlion, and some of the minor western towns; which have taken up positions here, here and *here*, surrounding the Nin-Edin hill. As you know, we have our own well. However, our supply lines to the east have been cut, we can't get out to raid the lowlands, and our stores are low.'

A second lieutenant stopped picking her broad hairy nostril long enough to raise her taloned hand. 'Sir, what strength are they, sir?'

'Good question, that orc. Strong enough to keep us bottled up here – they have Light Mages with them.'

Orc officers growled, boots pounding the flagstones. The wintry sun gleamed from the fortress hall's whitewashed walls. It shone on the wooden podium with its bullet holes, orc marine insignia – an odd arrangement of stars and bars, with the Horde's raven superimposed over them – and the inscription *Operation Librarian*.

Ashnak looked down across the tusked faces and assembled weaponry. 'Now, you orcs. I shall be depending on *you* to hold the fort – I shall not be here with you.'

Orcs looked at one another.

The second lieutenant whispered, 'Did he say . . . ?'

'Did I ask any of you dumbfuck marines for an opinion? *An orc general always leads from the front!*'

Several orc marines cheered. Ashnak eyed Barashkukor for support. The small orc captain, seated on a chair, had his elbows on his knees and his pointed chin on his hands, and was gazing dreamily in the direction of marine Razitshakra.

'We orcs have been the servants of others for too long!' Ashnak proclaimed. 'Dark Mages have run the orc marines, because they have control of the thaumatological firepower. I'm going to put a stop to that! The technical specialist marine (thaumatology) will now give us a briefing on my solution to this problem. Marine Razitshakra.'

'I've done intensive research for the general.' Razitshakra took off her spectacles and began to polish them with her desert camo bandanna. 'We need what are technically known as *nullity talismans*. These are new. They're small devices which any marine could carry. They produce a field which nullifies the operation of magical forces in a varyingly wide vicinity. Actually, they create sink-holes of space-time in which thaumatological forces cannot exist. The physics are fascinating . . .'

Ashnak's muscled arms folded across the bullet bandoliers that crossed his barrel chest. The winter sun gleamed on his marine tattoos and Agaku tribal scars. He licked a fang and growled something that might have been 'Never trust an intellectual orc . . .'

'Nullity talismans.' Razitshakra hastily replaced her spectacles. 'They're new, and they're *rare*. I can only come up with one place where they're likely to exist in sufficient quantity for the marines – that's at the Thaumatological University's research and development laboratories in Fourgate. The Visible College.'

Ashnak stepped forward. 'Thank you, marine. Return to your seat. Now listen up! I myself will be taking a commando group and penetrating the installation in Fourgate. For a mission this hazardous, I shall be asking for volunteers.'

'Let my unit do it, sir.'

At the back of the ranked orc officers, Corporal Lugashaldim stood up. His gaunt albino features had an increasingly livid tinge. Ashnak noted the marine corporal now wore black combat trousers and boots, and a tight knitted woollen pullover with epaulets.

'Your unit?'

'The SUS, sir.' Lugashaldim saluted. 'The Special Undead Services.'

Ashnak returned the salute. 'Very well, Corporal. Get your orcs geared up for a dangerous mission.'

'Sir!' Lugashaldim resumed his seat at the back of the hall. The albino marine took out his commando knife, reached up, and trimmed his ears down to short points. He then fitted a black beret smartly on the side of his head, the unit insignia of orc-skull and cross-bones to the fore with its SUS motto, *Death*, Then *Glory*.

'The technical specialist marine will accompany us,' Ashnak continued. 'Captain Barashkukor – Captain!'

The small orc, his chin on his hands, continued to gaze fondly at Razitshakra, who ignored him.

'Captain!'

Barashkukor jumped three inches in his seat, stood up, saluted, and yelled, 'Sir, yes, sir!'

Ashnak sighed. 'You are promoted major, Barashkukor. You will hold Nin-Edin with the orcs until our return. Send out snipers, raiding parties, sallies – harass the enemy, Major, keep them off-balance.'

Barashkukor, his wistfully dreamy gaze returning to the spectacled female orc, murmured, 'Yes, yes, of course. Whatever you think best, General.'

Ashnak of the orc marines rested his elbows on the podium and put his head in his hands. Once only, and very quietly, he whimpered. Straightening up, he glared at Barashkukor.

'You are Acting Commander, Major, until I get back. *Dismiss!*'

The hall cleared with startling rapidity.

Ashnak moved down from the podium, and crouched beside the dead body of the orc who had been with the marines since the discovery of Dagurashibanipal's hoard. He picked up Marukka's limp, dead hand. For several moments he remained in that position.

Ashnak bent his head forward, bit off three of her fingers at the roots, and left the hall, chewing with some relish.

The war elephant, having grazed on the overripe and unharvested corn of the lowlands, paused to drink from a spring in the foothills of the mountains.

Hurried scuffling could be heard among the concealing boulders and gorse bushes. A black-fletched arrow sprouted from the turf at the animal's feet.

'Hai!' The rider unhooked his two-handed axe from his back and brandished it single-handed. 'Come out, vermin, and fight me man to man!'

The beast abandoned the cold water, lifting its trunk and screaming rage to the overcast skies. Bushes rustled again, nearer to the beast's rear leg. Steel flashed. The war elephant reached down with its trunk, seized a concealed orc by the thigh, wrenched the limb loose as a man might break apart a chicken, and beat the screaming orc with the pulverized limb until – after a surprisingly long interval – all noise ceased.

The wind blew shrill amongst the tumbled stones of the tors.

'Come out and fight, you puling cowards!'

An apologetic voice said, 'Mighty mage! We don't wish to fight the keeper of this great beast.'

'Then step out where I can see you, boy!'

A large orc in a black breastplate, with a ragged green-stained bandage over his left eye, stepped out of concealment. A rather larger orc in battered plate moved out from behind her boulder. Two orcs in mail appeared, one still bearing a halberd with a hacked edge to its blade. Three more; two archers; five; a dozen . . .

Something on the order of forty orcs stepped out of concealment among the scattered boulders. The war elephant lifted its trunk and trumpeted. One of the smaller orcs dived back behind a clump of gorse.

The orc in the black breastplate gazed up. A northern barbarian sat high on the elephant's neck; bare armed, bare legged, impervious to the wind that ruffled his wolf-pelt tunic and wolf-fur leggings. The barbarian's bright mailshirt glinted, and the horns on his helmet appeared wickedly sharp. Thick blond braids fell either side of a weathered face, from which piercing blue eyes surveyed the orcs.

Cautiously, the orc demanded, 'Your name, great lord of this magic beast?'

'I hight Blond Wolf!'

The elephant coiled its trunk around the rider and lowered him to the earth.

The orc stared.

''Ere,' the orc said, 'you're not a Man.'

'I'm Great Lord Blond Wolf of the Howlfang Mountains!' the rider snarled. 'Mightiest barbarian warrior of the Dark; and you pig-swivers can call me "Great".'

'You're not as big as a Man.' The orc peered down. 'You're not as big as a dwarf. You're not as big as a *halfling*, even.'

Narrowed blue eyes fixed on the orc from a point some two feet and seven inches above ground-level. The barbarian snarled, inflating his chest. His helmet, whose attached horns jutted out a good armspan to either side, slipped down over his nose. He shoved it to the back of his head.

'*What* did you say?'

The orc guffawed. 'You're pretty short for a barbarian, ain'tcha?'

The northern barbarian clapped his hands. The war elephant lowered its trunk from the makeshift howdah on its back and set a small pair of wooden steps in front of its master. Lord Blond Wolf spat on his hands, unfolded the ladder and set it up in front of the large orc. He drew his axe, plodded up the steps, and swung his weapon.

The blade clanged into the side of the orc's helmet. The orc, catapulted backwards, knocked three of its nest-brothers into the heather.

'I'm riding to *succour* Evil, damn it, after our defeat!' The northern barbarian climbed back down his ladder, waving his axe. 'Will *that* teach you not to insult a warrior, you rat's arseholes?'

The orc looked up hesitantly, rubbing its skull. 'Where are you riding to, master?'

The northern barbarian threw back his head, tendons cording his throat, and laughed richly. With the orc on its hands and knees, he looked it squarely in the eye. 'What damn business is it of yours anyway, wartface?'

The orcs glanced at each other, rapid consultations going on in lowered voices. Scuffles broke out. The armoured and mailed orcs looked up at the war elephant, and the trackless foothills of the mountains.

'Noble Lord Blond Wolf.' The orc banged its forehead experimentally on the earth, watching the barbarian from one upturned eye. 'We'll form your Dark honour guard, if you let us ride with you?'

4

T HE BESIEGING ARMY of Light set
up just in time for the first snow.

Immense and aloof, the monumental rockfaces of the mountains
that loomed above the pass silted up with whiteness. Snow blurred
the lines of tents on the slopes below Nin-Edin, outside firing range.
Snow shrouded the earth siegeworks. Blue and silver banners shone
through the falling flakes.

Major Barashkukor, Commander (Part-Time, Acting, Unpaid) of
Nin-Edin, stared down from the parapet of the outer walls.

'I don't like it, Sergeant. It's too quiet.'

FOOM!

Barashkukor fingered his hairless peaked ear, a pained expression
on his features. '*Cease fire!* Sergeant, what *is* that?'

Sergeant Varimnak chewed gum noisily. A hulking, trim and
broad-shouldered brown orc; she wore her black combat fatigues
ripped, with engineer boots and a spiked black leather belt in place of
her webbing. Her cropped crest had been spiked and bleached white.

The Badgurlz sergeant narrowed her eyes, removed the gum, and
stuck it under one of the crenellations. 'Looks like they want to
parley with us. Fuck knows why.'

Barashkukor waited, vainly. He drew a deep breath, filling his thin
chest to capacity. 'That's "fuck knows why, *sir*," Sergeant!'

'Yes sir, Major, sir!' The stocky orc grinned.

Varimnak's squad, composed of the smaller female orcs, seemed

119

almost lost in their large, ripped, marine-issue black combat fatigues. They leaned into the cover of the crenellations, two of them carrying shoulder-fired grenade-launchers; three, M60 machine-guns; and one a shoulder-fired surface-to-air missile. Barashkukor surveyed the Badgurlz's spiked crests, scars and tattoos, and his chest swelled with pride.

He sprang up to stand in one of the icy stone gaps in the crenellations, ignoring the thirty-feet drop in front of his combat boots. 'Yo, down there!'

The approaching party halted.

A knight in full plate harness bent his head and removed his helmet. His destrier stamped. In his armoured right hand he carried a white standard of truce. 'Orcs of the Horde! I am Amarynth, Commander of the Light, Mage and Warrior both. Listen to my words of wisdom!'

Sergeant Varimnak looked up from where she squatted, bandy legs bent, cradling an AK47.

'Exactly who is that asshole, sir?'

'Some damn hero or other.'

Barashkukor straightened the peak of his green forage cap, and settled his web belt more comfortably around his thin waist.

'You down there! Unauthorized personnel! I give you statutory warning that you are adopting a hostile posture by surrounding Marine Base Nin-Edin, home of the 483rd Airborne, and by the rules of war I am therefore justified in—'

Barashkukor stopped in bewilderment as the elvish knight dismounted from his steed and knelt in the snow outside Nin-Edin's walls.

'Lady of Light!' the elf prayed loudly. 'Hear my vow! Be with me today, as I battle in the name of Good. Grant me the power to speedily end this battle, so that they shall sing of us throughout the generations, and our glory shall be the greater . . .'

The dark-skinned elven warrior pushed his black hair back behind his pointed ears, frowning.

'. . . ah, yes. And so that fewer of the Light's warriors perish. Grant me the strength of steel and magic both, so that I may wipe these orcs, blood and bone, from the earth! Hack their foul heads from their deformed bodies, tear out their intestines! Gouge out their eyes! Rip the fangs from their jaws and the skin from their faces!'

Panting, the elf smoothed down his blue-and-silver livery, that had two crescent moons woven into it. His fluted plate armour shone cream-coloured under the snow-leaking sky.

'Carve the blood eagle on their wretched carcasses,' he concluded, standing up, 'and put to the fire their still-living remains! In the name of your Mercy, Lady, amen!'

The orcs looked at each other.

'Well, sir,' Varimnak said, 'I guess he was the most diplomatic one they could find to talk to us.'

'Orcs of Nin-Edin! Surrender now and we *may* spare your miserable lives.' The elvish knight remounted and reined in his rearing unicorn. Flakes of snow frosted his pointed ears and high cheekbones. 'Throw down your weapons now! You filth will die, like your master the nameless necromancer, unless you make an honest reparation for your crimes. There is much work to be done, rebuilding the world after the Dark Lord's defeat, and it is meet that you should labour in it.'

'Go into slavery, you mean!' Barashkukor turned to speak to Varimnak and found his sergeant missing. He showed small fangs in a scowl.

''S pure ungratefulness, sir,' a Badgurlz MFC complained. 'After we won the Fields of Destruction for them by fucking off . . .'

The Badgurlz marine surreptitiously sighted her shoulder-fired missile launcher.

'No!' the major snarled. 'Not yet. *Bad* orc.'

Ignoring the indignant Light party, Barashkukor climbed down from the crenellation and strode across the parapet. Sergeant Varimnak trotted back up the steps from the bailey.

'Dumb Light fuckers won't attack under a parley flag,' she grunted. 'But, like I guessed, there was someone hanging around to take advantage. Major, I got something you *got* to see.'

The Light's increasingly impatient shouts faded as Barashkukor followed the bleach-haired orc sergeant up across the bailey and the hill, into the inner compound. A thin snow skittered and rolled in waves, powdery as sand, and stung his eyes. The rebuilt parapets and squat towers of Nin-Edin bristled with wires, spikes and dishes.

'Remind me to have a word with Corporal Ugarit, Sergeant, about that new equipment he keeps mounting – *How the fuck did* that *get in here?*'

'This prisoner, sir? Sneaked in while you were at the main gate.' Varimnak showed orc-fangs smugly. 'I'm gonna have those rear-guard squads drilling till they drop.'

A squad of orc marines stood around something, brandishing AK47s and SA80s. Barashkukor marched up, shouldered through, and came to an abrupt halt.

Seated cross-legged on the frost-hardened earth, with her bare hands resting palm-up on her knees, a female elf looked up at him and smiled.

'Another elf!' Barashkukor anguished. 'Have the marines responsible shot!'

'Sure thing, Major, sir.'

Barashkukor strolled closer and snapped, 'On your feet!'

He then gazed up at the six-foot-tall female elf with some misgivings.

Her glossy brown hair was braided from jaw-level down, woven with strips of red cloth; and tied around her brow with a red headband. It showed both her pointed elvish ears and the deep scar that crossed her cheek from outer eye to jaw. She wore a laced brown leather bodice and thonged leather trousers, and high boots, sorcerously oblivious to the cold. Dark lashes shaded her golden eyes.

There were the scabbards of daggers at her belt, boots and back; but no weapons.

'She's obviously a spy for the Light, Sergeant. Why haven't you executed her?'

The slender young elf put one hand up to her bodice and pointed at a silver badge. The insignia was easily recognizable.

'Press,' she said briskly. 'My name is Perdita del Verro. I'm a war correspondent – from *Warrior of Fortune* broadsheet. You've heard of *Warrior of Fortune*.'

'*Warrior of Fortune!*' Barashkukor breathed. 'Wow! That is, I – well, I read it for the advertisements, of course. Military supplies. Very useful. You're – did you say you *write* for them?'

'Chief news reporter.' Perdita del Verro smiled down at him. She produced a small notebook and a pencil. 'Things have been slow since the Last Battle. I really couldn't miss the chance to come along with Amarynth, and interview your boys. No, don't bother with the weapons – I have the usual magical press immunity. So, Commander . . . "Barashkukor", is it? How do you spell that?'

'Assschuu!'

Perdita del Verro smiled dazzlingly down at the orc, warmth infusing her golden eyes.

Thoughts of the siege parley completely slipped his mind. Major Barashkukor wiped his nose and began, starry-eyed, to look around the compound of the Nin-Edin fort for something of sufficient interest to impress the elven journalist.

Far from Sarderis and Herethlion and the sea, north beyond the wilderness that interpenetrates the Demonfest mountain range, lies

The Four-Gated City. The city has many more gates than four – they number in the hundreds, if not in the thousands – but of the original gates there are only four remaining: Tourmaline, Chryso-beryl, Lapis Lazuli and Onyx. The first three are often used, the last never.

Ashnak's Commandos sensibly chose to make their entrance through the Tourmaline Gate. To remove locks and bars, terminate guards, avoid the sunset alarms, and booby-trap the watch-house was no greater task than running the Wilderness for six days and practising marine survival techniques at the unfriendly end of the Demonfest Mountains.

Twenty-four hours' surveillance from the attic of a deserted mansion left Ashnak chewing his talons. Past sundown, he lifted the night-vision sights of his M16 to his eye, watching the last frock-coated and be-wigged Men leave the grounds of the Visible College.

'Not so much as a dwarf down there,' he muttered to Razitshakra. 'Not a halfling, not an elf – certainly none of us. No race but Men. That leaves us with forcible entry.'

Ashnak surveyed the high walls of the Visible College in the curious green illumination of night-sights. He lowered the gun, his own sight being somewhat better. The fifty-foot outer wall gave way inside to parklike spaces with convolutedly trimmed hedges; and buildings with domes, cupolas, columned porticos and very unClassical slit windows.

'OK, marines. We're going in . . .'

Camouflaged, doing a slow leopard-crawl, it took them an hour to cross the empty space between the last mansions and the wall of the Visible College unobserved. Evening's noise faded. Ashnak flexed his broad hands in the cover of the wall, craning his neck to look upward.

The moon rose from the rooftops, gibbous, in its last quarter. Its faint illumination showed him Razitshakra and the other marines crouched against the wall. Ashnak moved silently over to Lugashaldim, looking up at the masonry.

'Corporal, give me a hand.'

'Can't, sir.'

'What?'

'It fell off, sir.' The Undead orc marine shuffled, embarrassed. In his large, horny right hand he held his left hand. 'I'll fix it, sir, it won't take a minute.'

Stuffing the hand in one of his combats pockets, Lugashaldim detached his sewing-kit from his web belt one-handed, and looked a little helplessly at the thread and needles. One of the other Undead grunts grumbled something, threaded the needle in the faint moonlight, and set about sewing the offending limb back on.

'*If* you pussies have quite finished!' Ashnak hissed. 'Are we an élite commando squad or are we a fucking sewing circle?'

There were mutters of 'Sorry, sir,' and the Undead orc marines returned their attention to the Visible College.

'Bound to be guarded with magic,' one SUS marine whispered to his companion.

The other orc shivered. 'Nobody said nothing about *magic*. That's the marine corps for you. We get sent on these missions; nobody knows if they're safe; could have *wizards* here for all we know; and do we get *asked* if we—'

'*Shut the fuck up!*' Ashnak hissed. 'Marine Razitshakra, what are your recommendations?'

The scruffy orc removed her spectacles and gazed for some minutes at the walls surrounding the Visible College. She fixed on the largest dome.

'If we can go in through that we'll probably find something. It smells right.' She shot a shamefaced glance at Ashnak. 'I'm not really a magic-sniffer, honest, sir. It's just that sometimes I can tell . . .'

'Right. Assault team, that is your target. Corporal Lugashaldim, take them in. Support team Razitshakra and myself will maintain watch here. Maintain radio silence until you've scouted the ground thoroughly, then I want to know what's in there.' Ashnak nodded. 'OK, *go*.'

The three marines drew hammers and pitons from their assault vests and, muffling the noise of the strokes, drove staples into the wall up to head height. Lugashaldim swarmed up the wall, and began to drive higher pitons in. The other two marines followed. Slowly, almost silently, they reached the top of the fifty-foot wall.

Razitshakra whimpered.

Barely warned, Ashnak hit the ground, covering the back of his neck with both horn-hided hands. A searing flare of blue light crisped his vision. Heat burned his back, even through his urban camouflage jacket. He heard a scream, that grew louder and cut off; a thud; and then two more solid, bone-crushing impacts, felt through the earth. An unearthly wail split the night.

Ashnak scrambled to his feet.

'Bug out, marine!' He slapped Razitshakra's shoulder. 'Go, go, go! Corporal! Move it!'

The siren blared. Lugashaldim pounded past him. Ashnak sprinted, combat boots ringing on the cobbles, into the safety of the dark alleys. He loped quietly, and almost as fast, for the space of ten minutes. The commando unit slowed and regrouped.

'Magical . . . defences . . . *very* strong . . .' Razitshakra bent double, squat orc body heaving. Her ears drooped from vertical to horizontal. 'I've never run into anything *like* it, General! I never anticipated they'd have something like that.'

Ashnak turned to Lugashaldim. 'Your orcs all right, Corporal?'

'Yessssah!' Lugashaldim brushed lumps of charred flesh from his rotting chest, legs and face. His decomposing fingers smoked. Part of the back of his skull had been smashed in by the fall. The two other marines were in a similar state.

'Undead marines *do* make the best commandos,' Ashnak observed. 'Good command decision, though I say so myself. Marine Razitshakra, what chance is there of getting through those defences with explosives?'

The female orc brushed wretchedly at her spectacles. Shattered glass fell from one frame, where the magical impact had knocked her flying. 'Almost none. Those are Repeating Ring defences. Knock one down and there'll just be another. I didn't think a research establishment . . . We're fucked, General.'

The moon rose higher. Fourgate's houses gleamed with lamplight, and Ashnak could hear the talk and laughter from salons five streets away. Orcs on the streets of Fourgate are not exactly inconspicuous.

'We're in a city. I've been in cities before. *I* know what we need . . .'

The Undead marines and Razitshakra stared at their commanding officer. Ashnak widened his grin, fangs glinting in the starlight.

'General, look out!'

His peaked ears swivelled, catching the noise of footsteps coming down the road. Quite a number of them: casual, non-urgent.

Using silent hand signals, Ashnak directed the orc marine commandos towards the far end of the alley.

Perdita del Verro flicked her glossy brown hair into neatness with the same minor magery that reddened her cold cheeks and lips. The tips of her pointed ears stung with the frost. Her eyes shone, her breath huffed visibly on the air. She about-faced.

Her spellcast pigeon perched on the battlements of Nin-Edin, blank silver eyes fixed. Perdita gave it her sexiest smile.

'This is Perdita del Verro reporting to *you*, the loyal readers of *Warrior of Fortune*. Well, I've fallen on my feet here, quite unexpectedly. I'm in the Nin-Edin fort, in the orc encampment, engaged in a siege that has already lasted a whole week. There's certainly plenty of action – the Light Mage in the besieging camp favours heavy spells from the St Baphomet Cartulary Grimoire, his elves-at-arms have made a dozen attempts to storm the walls, there may also be sappers at work – but still this garrison is holding out!'

Perdita gave her trademark lopsided grin into the silver eyes of the pigeon's magical sound-and-vision memory.

'Readers, this dishonourable encampment is holding up the great Lord Amarynth *himself* as he destroys the last remnants of the Horde. I came here expecting to report his swift, glorious victory. These orc warriors – or orc *marines*, as this strange tribe prefer to be called – don't have a Dark Mage with them, which normally would make this a very short engagement. Of course, you may wonder why *Warrior of Fortune* is bothering with such orcish scum . . .'

The elf put her fists on her leather-clad hips.

'Firstly there is their unorcish courage. I shall be bringing you some orcish-interest stories later on. But, more importantly, these orcs have acquired from somewhere a variety of strange, magical weapons. A detailed report of these follows – right now.'

She snapped her fingers. The pigeon's eyes returned to black-and-gold. It shivered. She picked the bird up, her hands warming its frost-bitten feathers, and threw it high. It scuttered into flight, winging its way unharmed above the snow-covered tents of the Light.

Major Barashkukor abandoned his desk – completely covered in guard rosters, stores allocations, transfers of weapons, itineraries, stock lists, and personnel forms in quadruplicate – and studied his reflection in the fortress office's polished stone mirror. He carefully settled a pair of dark sun-glasses on his snout. He adjusted the holster at his belt so that the .44 Magnum pistol hung more comfortably, and tugged on a pair of tight black leather gloves over his clawed fingers.

His aide hammered on the door. 'Major! She's there!'

Barashkukor picked up a low-crowned black hat, its wide brim rolled up at either side. The hatband was decorated with a small tuft of feathers. After some thought he reluctantly removed the decoration's centrepiece – a dried elf's ear – and tugged the brim down over his forehead. His stetsoned reflection looked back at him through Raybans.

'Yo the marines!' he beamed, and left the tower.

The female elf waited with his junior officers on the inner wall parapet, overlooking the central compound. Barashkukor strolled briskly up to join her, a dazzled smile widening his lipless mouth. He signalled to the assembled marines by the Research and Development sheds. 'Begin the weapons tests, Corporal!'

'Yessir!' Corporal Ugarit, too-large boots crunching through the snow, saluted his superior officer. A new light glinted in his porcine eyes.

'*One!*' Ugarit announced. 'The precision-guided, fully automatic trebuchet, with smart warhead. *Fire!*'

BOOM!

The large orc by the war-catapult heaved a heavy wooden lever down. The catapult arm rose, hurtling a vast chunk of stone and metal into the air; fell back, rose again, and another missile whammed into the air. Another; and another . . .

Barashkukor stood on the parapet beside the *Warrior of Fortune* correspondent, small fists on hips, watching the missiles fall. Snow sifted down from a grey sky, and a wet cold wind seared his exposed flesh. The small orc grinned, unmoved, as the first missile described a lazy parabola that would take it well past the enemy camp.

In mid-air it zigged, zagged, and proceeded to crash through the roof of a concealed sapper's diggings. Distant cries came up through the snowy air. Perdita blinked in amazement. Barashkukor reached up to pat the female elf's arm; his spindly, hairless ears straightening.

'Spectacular, isn't it? We have a superb Research Unit, ma'am. We can match anything Amarynth can throw at us.'

'Two,' Ugarit shouted, 'the repeating crossbow. Radar-guided bolts; fires bursts at three bolts per second. *Fire!*'

One orc held up a bulky crossbow, pointing it over the parapet at the enemy tents. A gunner walked up to it, twisted her forage cap back to front on her forehead, squinted through the sights, and pulled the trigger.

TAKKA-TAKKA-TAKKA-*DUKKA*-FOOM!

Heavy steel-headed crossbow bolts shrapnelled the hundred yards between the fort and the first tents, shredding canvas, collapsing stores, ricocheting through the smith's and barber's tents. Armed Men and elves dived for cover while the useless shimmer of a protective spell shot up into the chill air.

'Yo!' Ugarit's tilted eyes flashed with an unearthly shine. The tall corporal wore a steel helmet well down on his head, and a heavy-duty flak-jacket strapped around his skinny body. Barashkukor glanced down from the parapet at the orc, who stood something over a metre taller than he did, and made a command decision to let the weapons tests go ahead unhindered.

'Three – smart personal weapons! Ready to demonstrate, sir and ma'am!'

Ugarit skittered up and down the line of waiting marines in the

127

compound, handing out pole-axes and warhammers with jutting metallic and cable additions and adjuncts.

'Fire-and-forget hand weaponry! Remember, these weapons are smarter than you are, so just swing them and let them do the rest. No, no; let me get out of the way first!'

Squeaking, the tall corporal loped up the steps and took refuge on the snow-covered parapet beside Barashkukor and the female elf. The orc marine squad below spat on their horny hands, gripped the unfamiliar shafts of adapted polearms, and raised them.

SPLAT!

Barashkukor winced. A casual swipe from one pole-axe hacked off one marine's arm, twisted in mid-air to block another weapon, changed trajectory through one hundred and eighty degrees and smashed an orc skull; described three separate curves in the space of milliseconds, and dragged its wielder back out of the fight by sheer momentum.

A smart warhammer drove into that patch of snow-covered earth two seconds later, rebounded up, and swung again.

Half the squad dragged their visibly unwilling weapons backwards. A squat and solid orc marine giggled, swinging his pole-axe with gusto. The endspike impaled an orc corporal. She swore. The axe blade swung the squat orc in a circle and marines leaped out of range. The pole-axe lifted in its owner's grip, hovered a second—

'*Halt!*' Barashkukor bellowed shrilly.

The pole-axe twisted up and over and whistled in a short arc, severing the squat orc's own head. The trunk collapsed. Orc blood steamed and sizzled viridian in the snow.

The orc marine squad – having carefully put down their weaponry first – slapped each other on the back and set about gathering up severed limbs and the unlucky corpses. The squad leader kicked the bleeding orc head thoughtfully, and raised his head to gaze up at the parapet.

'Permission to hold an Orcball tournament, Major, sir?'

Barashkukor looked into the upside-down eyes of the severed head. 'Not until you go off-duty, marine.'

'Oh, that's all right, sir. It'll keep in this weather anyway.' The Marine First Class picked up the severed orc head by the ears and walked back to his squad, debating in an undertone with his buddy. 'You don't get such a long game when they've gone squishy. They're better good and solid. Maybe we can sell tickets . . .'

'No – I don't want to know.' The female elf sat down a little suddenly on the snow-covered parapet. '"*Orcball*"?'

'Sometimes it's a raffle,' Barashkukor said helpfully. He fussed, getting the tall slender elf to her feet, brushing the caked snow off her leather trousers. He waved at his R&D squad. 'Not entirely successful, Corporal Ugarit . . .'

'Nossir. And fourthly,' Ugarit said, eyes darting feverishly around, 'my state-of-the-art invention. Personal power armour. It's a *motherfucker* of a defence. Just let them try to take me out now! I shall demonstrate this one myself, Major.'

Barashkukor noted the way the elven reporter's mouth hung open. Obviously impressed. He proudly puffed out his thin chest, clasping his hands behind his back.

'Watch this, ma'am.'

The doors of the Research and Development building crashed open. A team of heavily built orcs wheeled a wooden trailer out into the compound. Resting on it was what at first appeared to be a metal-and-glass statue of an orc, or possibly unusually full plate harness.

'Is that armour?' Perdita del Verro queried. 'I don't recognize the country of origin . . .'

Ugarit skipped up to the trailer, waving the other orc marines back. He scrambled up, opened panels in the metal casing, and climbed into the steel exoskeleton. The panels clicked shut.

Barashkukor called, 'Corporal?'

The exoskeleton lay still. A high-pitched whine began to build. Several of the radar and satellite dishes now sprouting from the parapets began to turn. Ugarit, in the full body armour, sat up.

Metal plate and thick glass sheathed him from his skinny ears to his taloned feet. The powered armour whined, servo-mechanisms activating, and put its heavy feet down on the snow-covered earth, and lurched upright. Ugarit's face, where it was visible, was contorted with glee. His hands could be seen manipulating pressure-pads in the heavy glass-and-steel gloves.

His mechanically amplified voice boomed out. '*I'm invincible! I feel like a god! No one can get me now, Major, no one!*'

Ugarit took one step forward.

The exoskeleton's left foot came down on compacted snow and skidded forward. Servo-mechanisms shrieked and gyros whirred, compensating. Ugarit's face, high up and small, could not be seen now, but a wail echoed down from the machine. The power armour's right leg lurched another step, came down in soft ice and lodged. The left leg jerked, attempting to pull the other free. Sparks shot from all the power armour's joints. The left leg crabbed itself around, beginning to circle faster.

'*Help!*'

Ugarit's power-armour suit swayed and began to pivot with increasing rapidity about its trapped right foot. Mechanisms sheared. Sparks flew. Two explosions sent sickly, thick black smoke into the air.

'Aaaiieeee!'

'*Incoming!*' Barashkukor threw himself flat. Fast as he was, the *Warrior of Fortune* reporter hit the dirt before he did. A solid loud *crack!* sounded. Panels of power armour whipped across the compound, slamming into buildings. A choking, acrid smoke spread through the still, snowy air. Barashkukor buried his face in his arms while fragments hissed into the snow around him. Slush soaked through his combat trousers.

BOOM!-taka-taka-taka . . . *click* . . .

tkk!

'Is it safe?' Perdita del Verro whispered.

'Erm . . . Maybe. Yes. Of course!'

Orc marines picked themselves up out of the slush, brushing down green-and-brown combats, and scratching their heads. The powered armour had apparently snapped at the waist, the top now hanging over upside-down. It smoked gently.

'Uhhhnn . . .'

The Research and Development Department (Nin-Edin Marine Base) crawled out from under a collapsed shed. His combats steamed, and green blood dripped from rents in the camouflage cloth. Ugarit wiped his singed crest away from his blackened face, staggered to his feet, and aimed a cross-eyed salute several yards to Barashkukor's left.

'Sorry about that, sir,' the tall orc corporal apologized, dazed. 'I'll take that one back to the planning stage.'

Barashkukor coughed and forced a sickly grin. The back of his neck burned with embarrassment at having the elf witness the failure. 'We have enough weaponry to be going on with, Corporal. Put the rest of the stuff into production immediately.'

'Sir, yes, sir!' Ugarit stared fixedly into the middle distance. 'Permission to report sick, sir?'

'Permission granted,' Barashkukor sighed.

'Thank you, sir.' The tall thin orc saluted, shut his eyes with his hand still raised, fell forward with his body unbending, and smacked face-first into the slush.

Perdita's hand rested on Barashkukor's thin, muscular shoulder; warm in the winter air. 'Major, I see what you're doing! Every strange new weapon you can throw at the besiegers stops them – for a day, or half a day, or a few hours – by sheer surprise. It's a war of the mind. *Psychological* warfare.'

Barashkukor internally debated the wisdom of, in the first flush of his enthusiasm, having let the elf poke around in some of Dagurashibanipal's miscellaneous crates.

The elf added softly, 'But each time it gains you less respite. Major, you can't go on like this for ever. That's a lot of army out there. What are you waiting for?'

5

THE DAWN OF the siege's eighth day coloured the eastern heavens lemon-bright above the Demonfest peaks.

A trebuchet thunked and whirred. A gelatinous sphere hurtled from its catapult-scoop on a rising trajectory, and struck Nin-Edin's walls just below the outer gatehouse. The sticky substance clung and burst into sorcerous blue-and-gold flame, brilliant against the fresh snow.

The dwarvish engineer Kazra, hip-deep in snow, rubbed her small calloused palms together.

'Ah. I love the smell of Greek Fire in the morning . . .'

Another scoop of sorcerous fire sparked trails over the white landscape. Just visible on the walls, orcs scurried with gravel-buckets. The sparks of hammer on steel flew from the armourers' firepits, and their welcome clangour made music in her ears. She drew in a breath of frozen air and the scent of magic.

'My old friend and comrade.' Lord Commander Amarynth reached brown fingers down to touch the shoulder of her padded brigandine. 'With magery's help today we will winkle out these obstinate sinners – *Lady of Light!*'

The gilded ball on the peak of the main command tent dipped and went down as the central pole collapsed. Acres of snow-wet canvas billowed. An unearthly shriek split the morning. Men and elves ran through trampled slush, hurriedly pulling on pieces of armour, shouting. Kazra unshipped her war-axe from her back. A serpent uncoiled against the sky.

'War elephant!' Kazra screamed. Orcs in black breastplates and riding on wild mountain wolves reared up in front of her, out of the breached camp's confusion, and she swung and missed; swung again and dented one breastplate.

'Ho, the dwarves!' Kazra hacked her way down to where Amarynth, blue cloak falling back from his silver armour, fought in the first blaze of dawn to touch the mountain's lower slopes.

'Revenge!' cried the wolf-riding orcs. 'Revenge for Samhain! Kill their commanding officers!'

Amarynth idly gestured a spell, inverting both wolves and riders.

Abruptly, dwarves, Men and elves were all Kazra could see. No orcs that were not writhing masses of intestines. The war elephant trampled out from the ruins of the command tent. High above, the rider coolly gestured and the beast ponderously reared to crush.

Kazra cocked her arm, muttered an incantation, hurled her war-axe, and caught the elephant's rider solidly on the helmet. The rider fell. The elephant, released, rampaged up the slope towards Nin-Edin, the Light's warriors sprinting out of its path.

'*For the Dark!*'

Amarynth stepped past her at that cry, slender sword pointing towards the elephant's rider. The rider scrambled to his feet, glaring out at the surrounding men-at-arms from under a dented horned helmet. His eyes, fiercely blue, glittered like the northern skies. Kazra forced her way into the front rank of the crowd and looked down at him.

'Bit short for a Man, aren't you?' the dwarf enquired.

The diminutive barbarian, feet planted in the ruins of the command tent, stood with his two-handed axe braced over his head, flashing back the dawn's light.

'Who's asking you, you fucking midget? I'm here for the sodding Dark, to relieve Nin-Edin! Single combat, warrior against warrior! Which one of you flea-bitten, whore-mongering, arse-licking goat-fuckers thinks you can take me?'

Kazra looked up at the slender, dark-skinned elf. Amarynth looked down at her. 'How *barbaric*.'

Simultaneously they sheathed sword and put away axe, turned to the surrounding fifty men-at-arms, and directed, 'Take him.'

The northern barbarian vanished under a heap of armoured bodies.

'Prepare that Dark scum for questioning,' Amarynth ordered.

Kazra turned to look back up the slope.

133

A few fleeing orcs, screaming in their own guttural tongue, arrived before the gates of Nin-Edin. Kazra saw how, before her own people could reach the walls, the defenders opened the gates, and the refugee orcs streamed in to join them.

The gate being open, and no orc being about to attempt to prevent it, the war elephant also lumbered inside Nin-Edin.

The gates slammed rapidly shut.

Twelve hours later, at the far end of the Demonfest mountain range, four figures emerged from an alley in Fourgate.

The four tottered on high-heeled red shoes. Piled and powdered white wigs uneasily surmounted their heads, and they swathed themselves in the folds of black silk cloaks to hide the rips in their coats. Ashnak abandoned hope of buttoning his frock coat up to his chin, and adjusted the strings of his black domino-mask.

'Marines?' he hissed.

'Yessir!' Lugashaldim shrugged his cloak over his bulging, muscular shoulders, and rested the ferrule of his amber cane on the cobbles. The two SUS orc marines with him mumbled 'Yo!' and went back to arranging their lace ruffles, and pulling silk gloves on over their bulging, taloned hands.

'Razitshakra!'

The fifth orc emerged from the alleyway, shaking out the immense flounces of a silk brocade gown. Razitshakra tugged the bodice of the ballgown lower, covered her granite-coloured breasts with a lace fichu, and swept the aquamarine silk cloak about her shoulders. A black velvet mask covered most of her features, leaving visible only a somewhat protruding jaw. Her white, feather-spangled wig sat slightly crooked on her head.

'It'll have to do,' Ashnak said firmly. 'Forward, marines!'

The five be-wigged orcs minced out into the street. Lugashaldim flourished his cane with style. Ashnak reached across and grabbed it from him, cracking it down on the cobbles with an equal flourish, and set off down the road, cloak swinging.

'Sir!' Ashnak accosted a passer-by, holding a silk kerchief to his wide mouth; relying on that and the indistinct moonlight. 'We are strangers come to Fourgate for the celebrations. I pray you, sir, where might one find a little – Guild thievery and pleasure?'

The passer-by lifted a minuscule velvet hat from a towering peruke and bowed. 'You need the Abbey Park, brave sir. You will be well advised to take your swords, as I see you do, but there you will find all that you desire.'

Ashnak bowed and twisted his ankle, not used to high-heeled court shoes. He muttered muffled thanks and marched off in the direction indicated. The houses leaned together over the streets here, darkening them still further, with only the linkboys' torches to light the way for Men, elves, halflings, and dwarves. Ashnak's night-vision served him perfectly adequately.

'Here,' Razitshakra objected, 'I haven't got a sword.'

The fourth orc marine fiddled with the butterfly-hilted small-sword at his belt and growled, 'Call *this* a sword?'

Razitshakra replaced one of the Dragon hoard's thin books within her fur muff. 'I don't see why male orcs should have the monopoly of coercive force. It's a politically unsound principle.'

'What?'

'*Why* haven't I got one?'

'Because you're a Lady!' Ashnak snarled. 'Quiet, marine. This must be it.'

A tall temple stood deserted on their right. The road opened into a piazza crowded with all races. Ashnak's wide nostrils flared at the scent of enemies. An elf in a gold-embroidered brocade coat strolling past, talking with a ragged orange-seller . . . Two dwarves in frieze coats and slouch hats muttering about interest rates and then diving into the low door of a dwarf tavern . . . Male and female Men eating at the food-shacks and drinking outside bagnios and public baths . . .

'There.' Ashnak nodded. A bottleglass-windowed coffee house stood on the corner across from the temple. In the last glare of the setting moon, and the new flaring of torches about the piazza, he could spell out its name. *At the Sign of the Dancing Orc.*

The roughly drawn picture was of an orc, its feet waving as it dangled from a noose.

Lugashaldim growled deep in his throat. Ashnak, suddenly scenting the SUS orc marines, waved his silk kerchief in front of his masked nostrils and walked to open the door of the coffee house.

'Stand aside!' A young flaxen-bearded dwarf with a torch straight-armed Ashnak away from the door. He hesitated, wrung his wrist, and stared up at the broad-shouldered, masked figure. ''Ere, you're a strong cove, ain'tcha? No matter. Way for Mistress Betsy Careless! Way for Captain Mad Jack Montague! Make way, I say!'

Ashnak trod back on Lugashaldim's foot. He bowed, getting his balance better this time. The dwarf – a boy hardly more than forty, dressed in ragged blue velvet – cackled, and kicked open the coffee-house door. A sedan-chair creaked as its bearers let it thump to the ground, and Razitshakra and the two masked grunts were forced to step back from the figure seated astride the sedan-chair's roof, wildly waving a broadsword.

'Ho! Little Cazey!'

The dwarf leered and bowed to Ashnak. 'That's me, sir. Laurence Cazey, not at your service, but at his.'

The Man leaped down and flung open the sedan's door. 'My lady! Accompany me, I pray!'

The dwarf filled his lungs and bellowed through the open door: 'My Lord Mad Jack Montague, Earl of Ruxminster! His paramour, the very gay and sprightly Betsy Careless! Make way!'

Ashnak let the noble bully and his cyprian clear the door and then led his orc marines inside, under cover of their noise. The low-ceilinged room hung heavy with pipe-weed smoke, and the fumes of coffee brewing. Ashnak slitted his tilted eyes and gazed around – mostly Men, dwarves, and halflings, in silk breeches and frock coats: some reading broadsheets, all with bottles of arrack or brandy at their elbows; the yellow lamplight gleaming on the exposed breasts of whores; the noise of raucous singing filling the air.

Lugashaldim chuckled. It was not visible behind the domino mask, but Ashnak guessed the albino orc to be grinning. 'This is all right, General. A home from home, you might say.'

'Quiet, marine.' Ashnak pointed to a table, hobbling over and taking a seat in one of the alcoves. The oak settle was hardly comfortable, but the partitions screened him from other patrons. The other four seated themselves along the table.

'An' what would you gentlemen – and *lady* – be wanting?'

Ashnak glanced up, then lowered his vision. A tiny halfling child, no more than knee-height, and dressed in ragged shawl and robe, licked her diminutive finger and poised a pencil over a scrap of paper.

'Bring me the day's broadsheets,' Ashnak ordered, 'and your best Java coffee; a bottle of arrack; no companions, for the meanwhile; and speech with the landlord when it shall be convenient.'

The halfling child bobbed its head and scuttled away. Lugashaldim, half-buried in the flounces of his lace cravat, said in an amazed tone, 'You've done this before, General?'

Ashnak made to draw off his gloves, and thought better of it. 'I know how to behave in polite society.'

Squat and wide-shouldered, Lugashaldim leaned out of the partitioned alcove, peering through the fug to the back rooms. Greasy playing-cards were being slapped down on a stained tabletop; whores in cotton lace took frock-coated Men and dwarves up the back stairs; and Mad Jack Montague had his head buried in the bosoms of Betsy Careless.

A voice said, 'Mighty curious, ain'tcha – gents?'

Ashnak leaned back against the oak partition, removing his

136

masked face from the direct lamplight. His wig wobbled precariously. The big orc looked up through the velvet mask's slits at a broad, black-haired man in leather apron and bag-breeches.

'Mine host?'

'I be Jan Tompkyns, ay. Who might *you* be?'

White wig powder trickled down Ashnak's forehead under the mask, irritating his wide nostrils. Under the table, he prised his cramped feet out of the court shoes, flexing taloned toes. Every muscle tense, about to spring—

'*I* am the Lady Razit— Rasvinniah,' the orc marine Razitshakra said in a bored tone, taking the day's broadsheet from the little halfling bar-girl, flicking it open, and peering over her spectacles. 'Landlord, you will have heard of Rasvinniah, the famous blue-stocking, and her circle of Wits. We are come to view the Abbey Park and your fine establishment.'

Ashnak recovered his dropped jaw in time to nod, firmly, when Jan Tompkyns looked at him.

'Then your ladyship is perhaps composing a poem, dedicated to *The Dancing Orc* and its customers?' The Man's eyes narrowed suspiciously. 'Which you will read, tonight, to yonder other Wits; I mean my journalist friends from the *Spectator* broadsheet.'

'Of course.' Razitshakra inclined her head. The feathers decorating her wig brushed cobwebs from the ceiling.

'Then I bid you good evening, and pray you enjoy my house.' The landlord stomped off.

'Poem?' Ashnak demanded. '*Poem?*'

Razitshakra flourished the bar-girl's pencil and began to scribble on the back of one of the roughly printed broadsheets. 'I've been reading some good books lately. A marine should be fully trained in all skills, General.'

'Poetry! It should take *three* marines for a mission of that nature,' Ashnak grumbled. 'One who can read, one who can write – and one to keep watch over those other two dangerous subversives.'

'I'll allay the landlord's suspicions, sir. Trust me.' Razitshakra thrust the pencil-point up her nose and sniffed. 'Now let me think . . .'

'Dance wiv me, governor?' A female Man, her ears pointed enough to make Ashnak suspect her half-elven, leaned over the table and thrust her breasts into the big orc's masked face. 'Come on! Blind Dick's about to play 'is fiddle. Dance with Poor Meg or be called a coward for ever!'

The whore's hand slipped beneath the tabletop and groped Ashnak's groin. Her eyes widened.

''Ere! You *are* a big boy, ain'tcha? Come upstairs with me, mister. Only two silver shillings. We'll dance the dance you do on yer back.'

Ashnak placed her hand back up on the table. He pitched his voice high, with difficulty making his accent genteel. 'Can't you see I have drink, and companions? I'll call on you when I need you; for now, begone!'

The piping of a whistle and the sawing of a fiddle filled the air of *The Dancing Orc*. A raucous lavatorial song broke out in one corner, soon drowned out by the competition of a dozen Men singing of the skills of one Bet 'Little-Infamy' Davies. Ashnak took a mouthful of the arrack, scowled, and turned his attention to the steaming pot of coffee. There was a silence at the table broken only by Razitshakra's furious scribbling, and one of the other marines scratching through the thick cloth of his frock coat for fleas. Despite this attempt to blend in there was, Ashnak felt, still something unmistakably military about the party.

His tilted eyes narrowed, searching the room. Plenty of patrons with the signs of the Thieves' Guild on them, but which to approach?

'Are you done, my lady?' The black-haired landlord, Jan Tompkyns, loomed over the table. A gaggle of peruked Men in stained velvet coats hung at his elbows.

Razitshakra rustled the broadsheet, peered at her scribble, cleared her throat, and announced modestly: 'An Ode to Jan Tompkyn's Hostelry':

> Behold a House, both fair and Sweet,
> Where all from High to Low do meet.
> The High's laid lowest, with a Whore;
> The Low is rais'd – then *rais'd* once more.
> The Bullys roar, their Cats do scratch,
> Good Tompkyns bawls, 'Beware the Watch!'
> The roof rings with outrageous Noise,
> And louder sing all Roaring Boys,
> And there is drawn full many a Cork,
> In merriment, at *The Dancing Orc*.
> 'Ode to a Coffee-House' I proclaim this still,
> Tho' what I *ode* was commonly – the bill!'

One periwigged Man clapped his hands and the rest began to applaud, more in relief than appreciation.

'' 'Tis well done!'

'Ay, you cannot say it isn't. We are indebted to you, my Lady.'

'If you are inclined to publish,' an elderly, prune-faced Man hung back and addressed Razitshakra as the rest departed, 'I can offer you

138

reasonable terms, and the anonymity due to a Lady of Quality . . .'

'I—' Razitshakra brought her fan up to cover her masked face, wincing. Ashnak, who had clawed her under the table, nodded affably at the Man.

'It is her pastime, only, sir.'

It was unnecessary to show the decorated hilt of his short-sword. At Ashnak's bass-voiced comment, the Man bowed and hurriedly departed to his comrades on the far side of the coffee house. Ashnak drew breath, about to speak, and the landlord returned and leaned over and planted a jug of arrack and five mugs on the table. His black-browed face had cleared.

'Welcome, sirs and madam, welcome. I do apologize for my suspicions, but we have Justices come here in disguises, searching out vice, and then it is myself and my wife who will be whipped at the cart-tail for keeping a bawdy-house, do you see, sir? Please drink this on the house.'

Ashnak, still leaning back out of the lamplight, said confidentially, 'We are not Justices, sir, I warrant you. The very opposite in fact. I hear the *Guild* knows this tavern, landlord. To tell the truth, we need to hire a servant or two – servants who shall know how to thieve, but not from their employers . . .'

Jan Tompkyns straightened, wiping his hands down his leather apron. Tall for a Man, he would have topped Ashnak only by half a head if they had both been standing; and Ashnak huddled into his cloak and coat so as not to have it noticed that he was himself four times as heavily built as the landlord.

'Ah, sir, now I appreciate . . . yes. The custom is for the house to recommend, and a small fee – why thank you, sir. Very kind. Now let me think . . . Do you see her, yonder?'

Ashnak noticed one of his silk gloves had split, showing the granite-coloured skin and talon beneath. He tucked his large hands up into the cuffs of his frock coat. He peered through the smog. A female halfling sat alone in an opposite nook, her crimson cloak hood drawn up shadowing her face.

'She is a thief?'

'What, Magda, sir? Lord, sir, no! But she's the mother of two of the most ingenious thieves in the kingdom, and if you speak with her, I'm sure you can come to terms.'

Ashnak nodded to Razitshakra. 'Write a note for the halfling Magda. Landlord, I would as soon leave this note with you to give to her. Here is silver.'

'Holloa! I've won!'

Captain Mad Jack Montague, Earl of Ruxminster, leaving the back gaming room riding on the shoulders of a stout whore, whipped at her with his crop. His boot swung round and caught the table, knocking arrack and lukewarm coffee into the laps of Ashnak and the orc marines.

'Faith, ye're wet! Baptized ye, ye Lightless dogs!'

Lugashaldim stood, furious, wiping himself down, bandy-legged in silk breeches. Ashnak inclined his wigged head. 'No harm done, sir.'

'Faith, a piss-britches coward!' The Earl Captain swung his hanger above his head, knocking one of the lamps, and galloped his whore around the room, kicking at other tables, and ducking the jugs and shoes flung piecemeal at his head.

Razitshakra finished writing. Ashnak took the letter. He did not read it, it not being a common thing in a Wit to have to spell prose out letter by letter, lips moving. Besides, the marine had her orders. He folded the paper and handed it to the landlord.

'You are to give this to the female halfling's thieves. To the thieves themselves. Will you remember that?'

'To the thieves?' Jan Tompkyns looked puzzled. 'But you may speak with Magda herself now, sir, at your pleasure.'

'No.' Ashnak stood up and moved out of the partition, not bothering to conceal his bulk or his quickness. A number of the patrons glanced over, and he saw how they took in five square-built, hunch-shouldered, supposed Men in frock coats and silk gown; features hidden behind domino masks. At his back he heard the four other orcs scuffling out from the benches. He thrust the letter into the landlord's hand. 'You will remember, sir, I promise you. The thieves *must* have this letter. Do it.'

'Yes, sir. But sir—'

Ashnak casually backhanded the Man across the face, breaking his jaw and rendering him unconscious. The landlord fell across chairs and hit the floor. Ashnak caught Lugashaldim's and Razitshakra's eyes. He nodded.

'Now.'

Wading in swathes of silk, bow-legged and broad-shouldered, Razitshakra kicked over tables and chairs and coffee-drinkers on her way across the room. Lugashaldim shook his head, peruke and domino mask flying off. Someone gasped and swore. In the space of fifteen seconds the two orcs ploughed across the room, snatched up the female halfling, bundled her in a cloak, and bashed their way out, demolishing one of the doorposts as they went.

A dozen or so of the less-drunk patrons drew sword. Ashnak clawed the cloak off his back and unholstered his concealed Uzi automatic sub-machine-gun. The two remaining orc marines dropped cloaks and masks and shifted M16s around into firing positions. Ashnak cocked the gun, shifted the fire-selector to automatic, and let off a series of three-shot bursts.

'*Aaiiiiieee!*'

The M16s opened up. Noise shattered the coffee-house. Ashnak scythed down Captain Mad Jack and his whore, the flaxen-haired dwarf, the table of *Spectator* journalists, and emptied the magazine through the back room. Bodies jerked, staggered, caught half-rising. The halfling bar-girl, picked up by the force of the shots, splattered across the back wall as it collapsed.

The big orc hit the magazine-release catch, snicked a full magazine home, and – firing on semi-auto to conserve ammunition – slewed a burst of fire around the room and fell in behind the remaining two orc marines as they left *The Dancing Orc* by way of the demolished back wall. Human, dwarf and halfling blood painted the walls, spattered the ceilings; Men clutched at guts spilling through burned and tattered frock coats and lace shirts; faces minced, limbs shattered, bone-fragments flying like shrapnel.

In less than thirty seconds, and always firing above waist-level so as to avoid one unconscious body, the orc marines cleared the building and disappeared into the alleyways around the Abbey Park.

Jan Tompkyns, eventually conscious and in great pain, did not think to study the letter until he had had a surgeon to his jaw, fled two streets away before the Justices should investigate the room of bleeding, stinking corpses in *The Dancing Orc*, and wept hysterically for close on four hours.

It was some time after midnight when Magda's sons found him.

'Our mother – she's not among the dead. Damn you,' the elder demanded, 'what *happened?*'

His jaw bound up, the landlord could not speak. He proffered the stained letter. The elder son took it. The younger read over his shoulder.

It was unsigned.

> *Thieves:*
> *We have taken the halfling Magda, who is our hostage for your obedience. Do as is written below and no harm will come to her. Fail to obey and she will be very slowly killed.*
> *Steal from the Visible College those talismans that prevent the operation of magic, in as great a number as you can. Bring them in secrecy to the besieged fort of Nin-Edin. There collect your mother. If you cannot enter a besieged fort, or the Visible College, then you are not the thieves we have been told that you are.*

We will be inconvenienced by this, but it is always possible to obtain more thieves. We believe it is less easy to obtain another mother.

Do this, at the very latest, before the moon passes out of its first quarter.

6

T HE WAR IS over now.

Vultures wheel at heights from which the Demonfest mountains are only rumpled white rock patching the curved earth. The birds' centre-magnified vision sees all:

The northern kingdoms ravaged, fields unharvested rotting in early winter rain. Men and other races huddle in their villages against famine and death, while in Herethlion and Fourgate songs are sung of heroes' victories. Vultures avoid the cities of Men. The dead tossed over the walls stink of plague.

The war is over.

The abandoned Dark strongholds, the magical dead of the east, are desolate now beyond even vultures' picking.

And vultures follow the Last Battle's soldiers in their company-sized refugee bands, waiting as they take forts and castles, hold them for a time, lose them to their lawful owners or (more often) to larger marauding bands: leaving enough behind to glut the vultures so that they can barely fly.

The war is over. This is peace.

Vultures circle at heights where, like the fields of destruction beneath, the only rules are those of hunger.

The unseasonable November snow whitened the porticos of Fourgate's mansions and turned to peach-coloured slush in the cobbled streets. Will Brandiman tipped the carriers of his sedan-chair, got

143

out, and trod cautiously across the slippery flagstones of the courtyard outside the Visible College.

A small girl with brown pigtails hurled a snowball. It burst against Will's tricorn hat. He growled, 'Cut it out, Ned!'

The girl, slightly taller than Will, stuffed one somewhat coarse hand inside a rabbit-fur muff and picked up the hem of her gown and cloak together as she skipped across the street. Close at hand, her hair was a little too short for braiding, and her brows too thick, and her mouth had lines about it that eight years olds do not commonly have . . .

The brown-haired halfling shuffled his large, hirsute feet under the scarlet velvet of his dress. He lowered his head demurely. 'Greetings, brother Will.'

'Brother Ned.'

They both looked at the Visible College.

'Let's set fire to the building,' Ned Brandiman said. 'Then when everyone comes rushing out, we can rush *in* . . .'

'Dark damn it, Ned, that's your answer to everything!'

'It works,' the elder halfling said, miffed. 'Well? I've watched outside this place for two hours. We're not going to get in. I'm not surprised orcs didn't make it. There's magic oozing out of the very stones.'

Will Brandiman raised his hand. Cold wind and flakes of snow brushed his eyes. The monumental walls of the Visible College here gave way to a terraced frontage, lined with Corinthian columns, and a vast set of double doors flanked by stone griffins. Uniformed Wilderness mercenaries patrolled the colonnade in front of the doors.

Ned squatted and began constructing a snowman, singing a child's game-rhyme in a high-pitched voice. The mercenaries' gazes slid away. Will stopped pretending to be digging in his purse for coppers.

They casually walked away from the courtyard to one of the hot chestnut-sellers' braziers in the street, and stood picking the shells off finger-burning nuts and chewing them, and dropping the husks.

Will swallowed thoughtfully. 'It's guarded. Magic and steel. The walls are insurmountable. I don't fancy coming back tonight to pick the lock on *that* door. It'll probably turn you into a hippogriff if you don't have the right magical key.'

'We could set fire—'

'Ned!'

'It was only a suggestion.'

Will stamped his booted feet in the slush. There was no jingle from the mailshirt under his cloak, nor from the bandolier of throwing knives he wore over his doublet, or the daggers at his belt and in his boots. A thin coil of elven rope, wound about his waist, made him the image of a fat, possibly dwarfish, merchant (if not for his feet). The wind blew through his curly black hair, silver at the temples. He narrowed his eyes.

'But there's Mother to be thought of . . .'

'Yes.'

The two halflings exchanged glances.

'If they harm her . . .' Ned scowled.

Will said viciously, 'I'd like to take something else out of the Visible College. Enough experimental magic to make mincemeat out of her kidnappers!'

'No point. Not if we're stealing magic-null talismans for them. I don't think we *dare* cheat.'

'Damn it.'

There was a pause, in the deadened silence that comes with snowfall. A coach crept by, cartwheels skidding, percherons straining to pull it across the icy cobbles. Will nodded absently. He wiped wind-tears from the lined corners of his eyes.

'The Nin-Edin fort,' he asserted, 'we already know. Those are the orcs we bemused into giving us an armed escort out of the wilderness three months ago. Chances are it's the same orcs there now—'

'No way!' Ned shook his head emphatically. One pink ribbon slipped from his braids. Nimble, he picked it up and began plaiting his hair again as he watched the frontage of the Visible College. 'After the Last Battle? There are stray orcs all *over* the place!'

'You'd know about the Last Battle,' Will said sceptically.

'And you'd know too, I suppose?' His brother gave him a look of absolute cynicism. 'Having fought impressively on the side of the Light – as you insist on telling all the gamblers and ruffians and whores in Fourgate?'

'That has nothing to do with anything!'

Snow fell faster from a lowering sky, the flakes black against the clouds, white against the masonry of mansions and arcades. Will flexed his fingers inside embroidered gauntlets. It is never wise to let hands become too cold to act. He eyed the lantern light visible through the windowed dome of the College; a dome accessible only by flight, if then.

'It has to be the same orcs! They lost their leaders at Guthranc, but they weren't all massacred, not by any means. The question is, do they know it's us?' Will shivered in the wind. 'I do wish Mother wouldn't pray to Fortuna. It brings about the most amazing coincidences.'

Ned Brandiman hurled a snowball at the nut-seller. The elderly woman good-naturedly tossed a bag of hot chestnuts back. She turned back to her cash-tray, counted, and began to frown.

Boots stamped and weapon-butts hit the flagstones as the mercenaries changed guard. Will eyed the oiled brilliance of their halberds and the much-worn grips of their swords. Under his breath he murmured, 'No thank you . . .'

'Perhaps you should have told Mother that we still have all that money,' Ned observed.

Will nodded morosely. 'Perhaps I should. But you know what she's like with gold . . . I didn't want to put temptation in her way.'

The snow fell faster, silting up in the creases of Will's cloak. Ned put both hands inside his rabbit-fur muff.

'So how are we going to get in there?'

'You're not,' Will said. He surveyed the crimson velvet gown and grinned. 'You're going to freeze your ass off in the snow, waiting to see if I make it, and if I don't, you're going to come in and rescue me. Right, brother Ned?'

Ned Brandiman groaned. 'Right, brother Will. All right. I'll try that again. How are *you* going to get into the Visible College?'

Will brushed down his cloak, taking advantage of the movement to unobtrusively check the position of throwing-knives, daggers, concealed poison-needles and blackjacks. There were bulges at his belt. He straightened his shoulders and stared through the falling snow at the steps and colonnade and guards outside the Visible College.

'In cases like these,' he said, 'I always find the judicious application of enormous amounts of money works wonders. Excuse me.'

Careful of the ice, he strode across the road and up the steps towards the mercenaries, taking out from under his fashionable cloak a bag of gold as large as a troll's fist.

'Here.' He clapped it into the mercenary captain's hand. About to bellow, she first hefted the bag thoughtfully, opened it, and her eyebrows then attempted to climb through her hairline.

'That's for you,' Will said, 'with another one when I come out. I wish to speak to the director of the Visible College, with a view to making some purchases – a large quantity, wholesale.'

'I must no longer let myself be distracted by their devilish engines!'

The Paladin-Mage stood silhouetted against the racing black clouds that hid the peaks of the Demonfest mountains. A fierce cold wind flapped the white surcoat he wore over his armour, to signify the purity of his intent, and seared into his dark, aquiline face. Amarynth did not so much as blink.

'Lady,' he prayed, 'now send me Grace!'

146

He stared up the Nin-Edin pass at the squat dark fortress, silhouetted with old snow, bristling with guns and flags on the keep and inner walls, and (on the outer, lower walls which Amarynth now faced) crowded with jeering orcs.

A brown orc leaned between the crenellations, starting a chant:

'*You can't beat no orc marines*
When we fire our M16s!'

Amarynth lifted both his dark hands and spoke a word.

'*You c—*'

The orcs ceased to chant. In the sudden silence, a whispering noise sounded. It might have been the wind. It became louder, a rushing roaring and pouring.

Mortar turned to powder and leaked out between the stones of Nin-Edin's outer wall.

Lichen and iron-rot darted up the dank walls. Nitre spidered across the cracking masonry. Within the space of three heartbeats, the stone *aged*.

Aged, crumbled, and fell into ruin.

The outermost of the main gate's towers slid two yards down the hill, tilted, and the masonry blocks showered out into the air, falling down the slope, and fading, before they hit dirt, into the dust of aeons.

The cold, snow-laden wind blew down the pass. Orcs, running, fell with the dissolving walls, tumbling into shale and earth and a rising cloud of putrefaction, as the entire outer wall of the ancient Nin-Edin fort collapsed within the space of thirty heartbeats.

The clouds broke.

Spiked and cusped armour encased Amarynth, each plate bright with pierced gold borders. As the Powers of the Air bowed to his command, the sun struck down through the pass, and he raised his arms, and his gauntlet took white flame.

'Amarynth Firehand!' one of the elvish warriors cried, and the name was taken up through the massed ranks of the Light encampment. A silver trumpet rang out, high and clear, echoing from rockface to rockface, until it seemed a thousand armies stirred in the mountains. Amarynth vaulted, fully armoured, into the saddle of his caparisoned war-unicorn.

'My part is done!' he cried. 'Warriors of the Light, the next glory is yours!'

He walked his horned mount over the broken outer defences, with the charging elves, dwarves and Men. Evil witch-fires blazed and stuttered from the keep and the inner walls of Nin-Edin. Harsh orcish voices shrieked commands.

The Paladin ignored them, staring down.

Among the rubble lay twitching bundles. He dismounted and knelt by one. The orc soldier dribbled feebly, and gazed up with eyes upon which cataracts had already formed. Age withered the bulging muscles, made the palsied claws shake. The mouth drooled, attempting to form words.

'Her Grace did come upon me,' Amarynth said, satisfied.

He remounted and rode on a few paces, picking his way through the rubble and the dozens of orcs dead of old age.

'*Die, motherfucker!*'

Sword in hand, Amarynth leaned down. An orc lay pinned under a masonry block. Obviously too far from the epicentre of magic to be affected, this orc was yet young. It spat through broken tusks and hurled a rock with its unbroken arm.

'Poor creature!' The elf dismounted and, carefully keeping clear of the orc's fangs, laid a gauntleted hand on its sweating brow. 'Do you repent of your sins?'

The uniformed orc coughed. It stared around at the hundreds of elf, dwarf and Men warriors tramping up the hill; their bright swords dripping with the blood of the aged orcs caught in the outer walls' wreckage.

'Hell, yes! I repent, man. I repent! Take me prisoner—'

A great pity welled up in Amarynth's heart. He thrust his sword-blade deep into the orc's throat. The creature's startled eyes dulled as it dribbled green blood.

'I have saved your soul by sending you to a better world while you were in a state of grace. Who knows but that as a prisoner you might have fallen back into evil ways?'

Masonry shards whipped through the air. Amarynth cast a casual *fail-weapons* spell at the prone, firing orcs further up the hill. The orcs – he was close enough now to see their snarling, ugly features, their hunched bodies and vile clothing – cursed and threw down their useless weapons.

An authoritative orc voice shrieked, '*Fall back by fire and movement!*'

The odd incantation meant nothing to Amarynth, skilled as the elf was in arcane lore. He watched the orcs run, led by a smaller orc in black, who limped.

'Now,' he cried. 'They run! Now, *for the Light!*'

The Man infantry cheered, pounding their green-stained blades against their painted shields. Beams of sun shone on their mail-shirts and cloaks as they swarmed up the slope.

Some orcs hid in cover and fired while other bands of orcs

retreated; the retreating orcs would then stop in turn and begin to fire. Incomprehensible. The Paladin-Mage Amarynth cast *fail-weapons* spells to his left and right as he rode up the hill, head bare to the chill of the day.

A skinny orc danced on the battlements of the inner walls. He frothed at the mouth as Amarynth stared up, the feathers and chains that ornamented him shaking and jangling.

'*I don't need no orc wet-dream—
Let me hear an elvish scream!*'

The red-bearded dwarf Kazra appeared suddenly from the rear of Nin-Edin, stomping through the bloody slush. 'Lord Commander, they won't take the bait. They won't leave the inner walls and come out and fight us!'

A slender elf Captain of Archers stepped forward and smiled. 'Impossible, dwarf. Orcs always respond to taunting.'

'They do?' Kazra stared up at the armed, uniformed orcs lining the crenellations. 'Orcs! *Cowardly scum!*'

A battered and bleeding albino-crested orc muttered, 'You called?'

'I believe I begin to comprehend their strange tongue, Lord Commander,' the engineer-mage said. She pointed up at a large orc. '"Your mother wears combat boots, and pisses standing up!"'

An expression of confusion crossed the orc's face. 'Doesn't everyone's?'

The dwarf's face reddened with more than the icy cold. After a moment's silence, the elf archer sang out, 'All orcs are cowardly filth! You have not one true warrior amongst you!'

Rows of silent, motionless orcs lined Nin-Edin's inner walls. Amarynth saw no sign now of the strange witch-weaponry. Instead, the orcs swung axes and maces, gripped jagged swords, and spears and spiked clubs.

A small orc in black leaned over the battlements and met Amarynth's gaze.

'We lost a lot of people down there.' Its voice was guttural as it pointed to the demolished outer walls. 'If you want us, elf, you're gonna have to come in and take us!'

'What is the matter with them, my lord?' the elf Captain of Archers squeaked in frustration. 'These are orc warriors. They should charge out, tormented to fury by our very presence in front of them! Each tribe should seek to outdo the other by flinging themselves hopelessly into the midst of our fighting elves. Why do they not do this?'

'What does it matter?' Amarynth shrugged. 'Take the inner walls.'

The commander of the Man infantry shuffled back, drawing a

ragged breath. 'Don't give that order, my lord. I don't think you'll be obeyed.'

'But we have them completely at our mercy!'

'These aren't *like* other orcs, my lord! They're . . . they're not natural! This isn't what fighting orcs is like. Orcs run. Orcs are stupid. *These* orcs . . .'

The dwarf Kazra, at the head of her halberdiers, grunted. 'Maybe they're right. This is some unnatural evil beyond our comprehension.'

Amarynth Firehand bowed his head for a moment, and then lifted it again. The sun, level through the clouds, sparked back in points of fire from his white harness. He drew a breath that sucked cold mountain air deep into his lungs.

'This is mere foolery.'

Casually, Amarynth gestured. A noise that seemed the earth's own voice shook the world. It avalanched snow down from rockfaces further up the pass.

The inner walls of Nin-Edin, moved by the Powers of Earth, *shifted*. Orcs howled as stone tottered. The inner gate split in two. The masonry arch cracked from top to bottom, the two halves by some freak remaining upright, leaving the portcullis jammed at an angle in the dirt, with space to pass either side.

'Oh, Lady,' Amarynth prayed, 'since I may grow weary in the killing that now follows, send me yet more of your Grace—'

FOOM!

The thunderclap noise of the shot startled the war-unicorn. Amarynth reined it in. No pain came to him. He looked down. Unmarked.

'My lord!'

The Captain of Archers' yell made him look down to where she knelt. The dwarf engineer-mage Kazra lay on the ground. Amarynth dismounted from the unicorn.

'Kazra, fellow-warrior, what do you there?'

The elf archer turned the dwarf over. Most of the dwarf's face and the side of her head had been blown off. Blood and tissue and bone fragments glistened, matting her fiery hair.

'*Yo the snipers!*'

Amarynth fell to his knees, ignoring the orcs.

'Lord Commander.' The Man infantry commander squatted down beside him. 'A healing mage can— Ah. No.'

Amarynth wiped his mouth, catching his lip painfully on the edge of his gauntlet, and fumbled to strip the armour off. The mountain air felt cold on his skin.

150

He picked Kazra up. What remained of the dwarf's head fell back across his arm. She had no mouth or jaw to fall open. Her weight made him stagger. Blood and the last of her sweat cooled on his hands, and the smallness and solidity of her body in her mail-shirt made him open his mouth and bawl like a child.

'My lord!' the archer protested.

Amarynth Firehand turned and picked his way down the hill. He stumbled, his knees giving under him. The sun shone full in his eyes now. Water dripped down his face, ran off his chin, soaked his surcoat. Although nothing short of a miracle would do, he muttered healing charms constantly.

The dwarf did not move as he took her from the wall and laid her down in the rich furnishings of his own bed in his own tent. He sat by her, bent over, watching for the slightest breath, the slightest motion, to tell him he might be wrong, and Kazra be only wounded.

Some time later, when it became apparent even to him that the dwarf was dead, Amarynth Firehand got stiffly up from the bed and left the tent.

His commanders awaited him outside.

'Bury her in stone,' the elf said. 'What was it all for? She was my oldest friend. I shall never say anything more to her. Not even farewell.'

'Lord Commander,' the Captain of Archers ventured, 'what of the fort?'

'Leave me.' Amarynth turned back to his tent. 'I am going to pray until I can find it in my heart to forgive the orcs for Kazra. Then we shall take Nin-Edin and raze it to the ground.'

7

T HE RAVAGED COUNTRYSIDE teems
not only with deserters, but with the Light.

Driven out of the arctic safety of the Demonfest mountains,
Ashnak hooded his eyes against the winter wind. The stench of
corpses made his broad nostrils flare. The SUS marine ahead of him
looked back and signalled thumbs-down: *enemy seen or suspected*.

'That's two wandering Light war-bands we've run into in two days.
Still mopping up after the Last Battle. Lugashaldim, tell the orcs to
exercise all caution, but to make their best speed.'

'Sir, yes, sir!' The Undead marine corporal, black-clad, and
carrying a hefty commando knife in his rotting hand, doubled over
and ran up through the cover of a burned orchard towards the rest of
the unit.

'Are you sure we can trust these orcs, sir?'

Ashnak stopped peering through the fallen, burned tree-trunks
and stared at the female orc beside him. 'Of course you can't trust
them, marine Razitshakra. They're orcs!'

'No, sir. I mean ideologically, sir.' She wrenched a paperback book
from her combats, waving it in an ink-stained hand. 'If we're going to
be the vanguard of the proletariat, and massacre the oppressing
classes – elves and Men, halflings, dwarves; that kind of filth – we
have to be *sure* of everybody, sir, don't we?'

Razitshakra adjusted her rimless spectacles and gave Ashnak a
long, hard stare.

'Vanguard of the *what?*' Ashnak took the dog-eared paperback. 'The *what* Manifesto? I've warned you before about reading, marine. Just take it from me, we're thoroughly – what is it? – ideologically correct.'

Razitshakra gave him a knowing look, a smile, and a deliberately sharp salute. 'Sir, yes, *sir*.'

'And you can take *this* from me, too.'

Ashnak grabbed the orc marine by the back of her combats, swung her bodily around his head and let go. Razitshakra's chunky body flew a short distance and whacked into a tree. She slid to the earth.

'You can free all the oppressed masses you like,' Ashnak grinned, 'provided you remember orcish political ideology. That is – *I'm* in charge. I am a big hard bastard and you take my orders. When I say *Jump!* you don't say *Yessir* and you don't say *How high?* You say *General, when do I come down?* Got that?'

Razitshakra clawed her way up the tree and back on to her feet, muttering, 'Yessir, that's what I said, sir, isn't it, sir?'

'You might defy gravity, but you won't defy me!' He clapped the marine on the back as she attempted to adjust her rimless spectacles. His grip abruptly tightened. 'Take cover! I hear more riders.'

His unit went to ground. The next few minutes spent at a low crawl brought Ashnak, alone, to where he could peer down off the wooded ridge at the crowded countryside of Men. The Demonfest mountains loomed to the east. A whole squad of orcs would undoubtedly be intercepted. A single orc on his own, however . . .

A single orc, travelling alone, might sneak up into the foothills, double back north, make his way round the end of the mountain range, and vanish off into the Dark Lands of the East. Which, although conquered, are doubtless better for an orc's health than being inside a mountain fort surrounded by the Light's finest mages and warriors.

Ashnak crawled down on to the very inviting goat trail that would backtrack up into the mountains.

He bellied up to a hummock and slid over it.

'Going somewhere, were we, sir?'

The sharp whisper came from one of the Undead grunts surrounding Lugashaldim and Razitshakra. The female orc fixed a very chilly gaze on Ashnak. 'Like you said, sir, we'd better make our best speed back to Nin-Edin.

Ashnak fingered his brass-capped tusks. A war-band of wild orcs might easily be persuaded out of returning to the fortress. He momentarily wished for a war-band of wild orcs, not orcs with the glint of *marine* in their eyes.

153

Lugashaldim rasped, 'Wouldn't want to think Marukka had been right, sir, would we?'

A great orc is tough, but a dozen Undead orcs together are conceivably tougher.

When there is no other option, an orc keeps his promises.

'Of course we're going back, soldier.' Ashnak beamed expansively. 'I was just scouting out the best route. OK, marines. *Harch!*'

In a countryside burned and ravaged by the Dark, but still occupied by uncountable Men, elves and other hostile races, Ashnak's Commandos sought desperate and elusive concealment on their way south.

The fifteenth day of the siege dawns cold and clear.

Work parties of Men and elves used picks to rapidly demolish the rubble of the outer walls of Nin-Edin. Winter light flooded the slope. Views of the mountain pass appeared where there had been only masonry. The smell of magic building up stung in the air, making orcs' eyes and nostrils weep a thin mucous.

'They're going to come right over us!' Corporal Ugarit, a flak jacket tied on over his ceramic-and-steel armour, stared down at the devastated inner walls, and the forces of Light behind earth-banks and wooden barricades. 'It's going to be soon! I'm going to die!'

Barashkukor seized the skinny orc's collar, dragged him down squat nostril to nostril, and spat into his face. 'Be an *orc*, Ugarit! We'll hold this fort to the last orc – the last *enlisted* orc, that is.'

'He's right, man . . .' Sergeant Varimnak smoked a thin roll of pipe-weed, the slit pupils of her eyes shrunk to vertical lines. She stood behind Barashkukor, AK47 slung across her back, a ragged strip of black cloth bandaging her shaven skull. 'Fighting Agaku, man! Call in the artillery! Call in an airstrike!'

'Will you *listen?*' the skinny orc corporal whimpered. 'Every so often those guys down there stop waving flags and polishing their armour and realize they only need the simplest magic, and we're wiped out. They only have to stick that Amarynth motherfucker out in front for long enough, and they're gonna come over these walls like a flash flood!'

And at midnight:

A close voice hissed out of the darkness, '*Password Dagurashibanipal!*'

'Adva—' The orc marine sentry, fear and relief searing his nerves, raised the muzzle of his SA80 assault rifle. His finger accidentally closed on the trigger.

A burst of automatic fire cut the darkness. The echo roared back from the keep walls. Muzzle flash strobed, outlining a figure hammered back by bullet impacts. It whirled and fell.

The orc marine sentry whimpered and took a hesitant step forward, looking down at the supine body.

'Dumbfuck!' The body sat up. It got to its feet. Corporal Lugashaldim glared at the hapless orc sentry.

'Sir, sorry, sir! Accidental discharge, sir!' The guard cringed.

'I'll give you *accidental discharge*,' Lugashaldim snarled. The rounds had ripped his black combats to pieces, and shot away most of his stomach and lower torso. He made a vain attempt to stuff his spilling intestines back inside his body cavity. They slid out.

'Shit!' Lugashaldim shoved handfuls of slick white tubes up under his ribs. They slid out again. Muttering, he grabbed his intestines between two gnarled hands, ripped them and the colon off short, and threw the entire mess of tubes over his shoulder. It hit the keep wall and slopped to the flagstones.

'You're on a charge, marine! So's your sentry partner, for being absent from duty.'

The second guard, who had just finished a roll of pipe-weed in the gatehouse, looked out dreamily, remarked, 'Fuck, we've been sussed!' and vanished back inside.

'Any problems, Lugashaldim?' the orc general inquired, strolling out of the darkness beyond the broken walls with the remainder of the Undead marines.

'No, sir, General Ashnak, sir! None that these fuck-witted, shit-stupid excuses for marines won't regret from now until their dying day – and after.' Lugashaldim bared long teeth in a rotting grin, and clapped the guard on the shoulder. 'You know what they say, soldier. Join the marines, and see the world – join the SUS, and see the next . . .'

A few moments later a sweating Barashkukor appeared out of the darkness. The orc major saluted his superior officer.

'The mission, sir?' he inquired anxiously. 'Was it a success? Do we have the talismans, sir?'

Ashnak turned his heavy-jawed head back from surveying the ravaged fort. 'Well,' he said. 'Not exactly . . .'

The morning came white with frost.

Will Brandiman rejoined his brother in the hills below Nin-Edin. He drew his grey-green concealing cloak back from the mail-shirt and helm that had made him a reasonable facsimile of the Light's soldiers.

'Well?' Ned said.

155

'You tell me.' Will shrugged. 'You've seen the elf. Go up to him and say, We have to break siege and go into the fort because they're holding our mother hostage; and *he'll* say, Tough, war is hell, no dealings whatsoever with the forces of Darkness. Or am I wrong?'

Ned shook his head. 'Not if I'm any judge of elves.'

Both halflings returned to their wagons, parked sufficiently far from the siege camp that the Light's scouts had not yet discovered them – which, given the camp's predilection for concentrating on Nin-Edin itself, amounted to about half a mile. Will looked back at the squat, broken fort in the pass.

'We don't have long, Ned. I kept my eyes open going through the Light's camp. If we don't get into the fort today, there isn't going to *be* a fort to get into.'

Ned Brandiman scratched through his greasy brown hair. 'We could always set fire to the besiegers' tents.'

'Why do the orcs any favours?'

'Or we could hire an army of mercenaries. There's plenty of stray soldiers around.'

Will put his fists on his hips. 'And we're going to get them collected, organized, paid and *here* in the next two hours, are we?'

'I'm not totally bereft of practical suggestions.'

Ned, looking injured, moved to the back of one of the wagons and, with some effort, unloaded a wooden chest. He thumped it down on to the snow-covered turf. The icy wind ruffled the curly hair on his feet.

'I knew we'd have to find a way past the besiegers into Nin-Edin, brother Will. So I made plans.'

Late-morning wind blasted out of the blue sky, cold enough to make even an orc shiver.

Ashnak stared out through the portcullis of Nin-Edin's inner gatehouse. The whole arch above his head was cracked, blocks hanging down precariously a yard lower on the southern side.

'Beg me for terms, then.' The elf removed his sallet helm, exposing aquiline brown features. He sneered down from his horse. 'Is that not why you have summoned me? I have suffered a great loss here . . . I do you infinitely more honour than you deserve in speaking to you.'

Inside the taken bailey, warriors of the Light jeered, banging swords against shields. Ashnak scowled, estimating firepower, morale, magic . . .

He bared his fangs in a grin. 'Better listen good, you pointy-eared asshole. Orcs ain't the only personnel on the Nin-Edin Marine Base!'

He removed his clawed hands from behind his back, holding a female halfling up bodily above his head, gripping her by the shoulders of her crimson velvet gown. Her bare heels brushed futilely at his peaked ears as she kicked, and her flailing fingernails failed even to scratch his skin.

Amarynth Firehand gasped. 'An innocent halfling!'

The forces of Good hissed. Ashnak let them have a good look and then lowered her to the earth in front of him, his talons resting on her diminutive shoulders. 'This is a prisoner of war, Commander. Her safety depends solely upon your actions.'

'I . . . I don't understand.'

Ashnak showed sharp, curved fangs. 'I might hold a military tribunal and decide she's not a prisoner of war. She might be a spy. Spies get gutted and eaten, or hung on hooks on the walls. *Think about it, elf.*'

The elven fighter-mage's eyes brimmed with tears. For a moment there was only the huff of the unicorn's breath, and the flapping of its indigo caparisons in the wind.

'We . . . *No*. No! We can never give in to blackmail. We cannot spare a whole fortress of evil for the sake of one innocent creature,' Amarynth Firehand stated proudly. 'We shall kill you all – the Lady will know her own.'

Ashnak shrugged. 'Then the halfling gets it.'

He began to tighten his hands, getting a solid grip on the small and muscular shoulders, preparing to rip the halfling's arms from their sockets.

Faster even than orc-reflexes, nimble halfling fingers groped at the front of his combat trousers, undid the buttons, and slipped inside. A small hand gripped him firmly by the testicles. Sharp halfling nails pricked tender skin.

'On the other hand,' Ashnak hastily added, 'I'm not in any way an *unreasonable* orc . . .'

The nails retracted fractionally.

Ashnak looked down. The female halfling stared absently out through the portcullis at the besieging army. Apparently resting back against her captor, both hands behind her back. A small hand grasped his member. Another pricked his balls. Ashnak very carefully loosened his grip on her shoulders, that rested against him at belt-buckle height. He swallowed hard.

'I'm always open to the concept of negotiations . . .'

Both hands kept a firm, chilly grip.

Barashkukor, behind him, gasped. 'Sir, are you out of your mind, sir?'

Ashnak snarled dramatically at the elf. 'I'm going to give you one last chance.'

'And *I* shall give you one hour to give her up. Then, orc, you shall pay for *all* your atrocities.' Outside the gate, the dark elf reined in his destrier and rode back down the hill.

The forces of Light began to mass, preparing to attack.

Small hands began most professionally to squeeze and stroke.

'Mmm . . . Major, I . . . ahhhm . . .' Ashnak's hands fell to his sides. He muttered, 'Stop it! That's an order!' under his breath, and glanced back over his shoulder at Barashkukor.

'Delaying tactics, Major. We must . . . must buy time. Go and see if the scouts report anyone approaching. If we can hold out until the talismans arrive – *urk!*'

Ashnak coughed. Barashkukor and the other officers' departing boots echoed under the gate arch. The cold wind ruffled the female halfling's fur-short hair.

She leaned her body back against him, hands still hidden behind her, and the halfling and the orc stood under the arch, gazing out through the portcullis, unseeing of the warriors' preparations, for quite some time.

A sudden silver trumpet rang a clarion call across the siegeworks of the Light.

'*Monks* would have been bad enough!' Will Brandiman whispered.

The road cut deeper into the defile as it approached Nin-Edin. The sun, overhead at midday, illuminated blackened slush and deep cart ruts. The covered wagon jolted and rocked. He grabbed at Ned and the backboard to steady his balance.

'Patience, sister. We must put up with discomfort to bring succour to poor sinners.' Ned whacked his cartwhip down on the mules' quarters with unmaidenly strength. Will wondered momentarily if the skill was genetically inherited.

'Maybe we *should* have fired the camp . . .' Will adjusted his gown, hiding his large booted feet. The faded red homespun wool itched across his shoulders and under his arms. He tightened his burr-lined mortification belt. A Talisman of the Light lay heavy on his padded but still somewhat flat chest.

'I'm going on your judgement of his character.' Ned Brandiman ran a thumb around the edge of his wimple, making sure no coarse hair showed. 'This is the only thing I can think of that will get us inside Nin-Edin.'

Will Brandiman stroked his beardless chin. A smear of rouge marked his hand when he lowered it, and he scrubbed it fiercely against his dress, staring all the while up at the broken fortress. The cart slowed, creaking uphill on the main road, and he began to hear the shouts and hammering of the besieging camp, the bawled orders, the clash of warriors scrambling into armour.

'If he's that good a mage,' he said unhappily, 'he's going to *know*, isn't he? And then what?'

'A good mage is not necessarily a clever mage, nor,' Ned observed sententiously, 'better at looking under the surface than the next elf. You can always sing to him, sister. Elves like songs.'

Will rumbled under his breath as the heavily laden covered cart ground up between the tents and earthworks, a verse of which the first lines seemed to be *There was a maid whose vast capacity / Was only equalled by her rapacity* . . . He studied the faces of the thronging warriors they passed – elves with gilded bows, Men in thonged leggings and carrying painted shields, dwarves with axes and hastily braided beards, a few halflings running errands for the cooks.

'That looks like the final attack. You're right, brother. Sister, I mean. If anything's to be done, it's to be done now. And there he is.' Will squeezed Ned's shoulder.

The cartwheels slipped on the shale as Ned reined the mules in. Will got down with restrained speed and picked his way between tent guy-ropes in Ned's wake. Lord Commander Amarynth Firehand stood with a group of Men and dwarves in front of an over-embroidered and somewhat battered command tent, and turned his dark aquiline face as the two halflings approached.

'The Lady of Light greets you,' Ned said in a flawless contralto, 'through her humble servants, Sister Hope and Sister Faith.'

Will watched his brother, hands clasped at the buckle of his mortification belt, bow his head humbly. He followed suit. Ned straightened, interlocked his fingers, gazed around wide-eyed at the warriors, and exclaimed, 'Glory! To see the power and right arm of the Light, her heroes assembled; it moves my poor heart. All the Little Sisters of Mortification shall pray for you, be assured of that!'

Politeness made Amarynth incline his head. Seeing him on the point of turning back to his companions and ordering the attack, Will pitched his voice high and quavery and spoke. 'Sister, do you not recognize him? This is that mighty elven warrior-mage spoken of in Herethlion, and in all the cities of the south. It is Lord Amarynth Firehand himself! The Lady of Light has steered us to you, my great Lord. Her grace shines upon us.'

'Do not let it be said that Amarynth Firehand was ungracious to age.' The elf preened his blue surcoat. 'Speak, aged one. What has the Lady of Light to say to her holy knight before I enter into battle?'

Now that's a Dark-damned good question! Will looked under his lashes at Ned. His brother's eyes widened fractionally. No help there. Will drew an unobtrusive deep breath.

'We have travelled far,' he began, 'and with great privation have we come to you, although great sustenance lies within our wagon. Not mortal food and wine, but spiritual food – the words of the Lady of Light, which feed beyond measure and satisfy beyond pleasure.'

'We thank you—'

'Do not thank me so soon.' Will held up his gloved hand. He put it down by his side again quickly: the stubby fingers being broad and unfeminine. 'The Lady of Light tries you, my great Lord. She knows that you are great in her service, a mighty warrior before Her chalcedony throne; and that you have slain your thousands and your tens of thousands . . .'

Very occasionally, Will thought, I have cause to thank Mother for leaving us in the care of a convent school.

'. . . and that you are a warrior and a mage unparalleled. Now, she tries your mercy.'

Ned Brandiman clapped his hands together, turned his eyes up to the blue midday sky, and exclaimed, 'Glory, glory!' Two or three of the elves in the group by the tent echoed his words.

Amarynth Firehand knelt in the churned snow, bringing his dark features on a level with Will's face. Will lowered paint-thickened lashes. The elf's slender, steel-shod knees reflected the tents, fires, and weapons of the camp in curved miniature.

'Speak. What will the Light bid me? I will do it.'

Best in public, Will rejoiced. If there's an ideal place for making theatrical gestures, it has to be in front of his command tent, under the eyes of half his army.

'You must send us up yonder hill. Sister Faith and myself must go, alone and with no armed guard, up into the fortress. There we must give the Light's word to the poor sinners within. And you must give us time in which to perform this holy act.'

Silence.

Will Brandiman raised his eyes and stared the dark elf in the face. Black-lashed eyes narrowed momentarily, and the fine elven nostrils flared. A sick feeling churned in the halfling's gut.

Amarynth declaimed, 'Let Holy Sisters go unguarded into a nest of orcs? No! No, it cannot be! It shall not be said that I sent two most gallant ladies to their deaths. Never! If you may have no other of my army, then I myself, with my trusty blade, shall walk with you and defend you single-handed against a whole host of orcs.'

Relief robbed Will of words. Ned Brandiman cut in swiftly.

'You must let us go alone, my great Lord. It is your test. It is *our* test. Our faith must be great enough that we enter even into the citadels of evil to bring Light, and I am named for that Faith. I must live as I am named. Or else how are we better than those who grovel in Darkness? You cannot deny us, great elven Lord!'

Will, his hand fisting his robe, stared right into the face of the elven fighter-mage. 'And I am named for hope, my Lord; the holy Hope that we shall prevail against the Darkness in the souls of those poor transgressors. What does it matter if our bodies are violated, torn, dismembered, dissected—'

He heard Ned make a small noise of distress.

'—or even *eaten*, so long as we give our souls into the hands of the Light? We are called. You must let us go.'

Amarynth sprang to his feet. The midday sun seared back from his mirror-plate armour and the silver moons embroidered into his blue surcoat. He gestured with one armoured hand.

'You have—' Amarynth's voice broke. 'You have great courage. I will delay my assault on the walls! I could wish that the Lady had called me, as She has so clearly called you, no matter how hard the task. Willingly would I be scourged, whipped, burned and broken, for Her sake. Oh that She would cast me naked into the snow, humiliated before mine enemies, if that would mean I might serve Her! I would cast myself wounded, torn, and bleeding at Her feet—'

The elven warrior-mage broke off, choking. Men and dwarves rattled their swords against their shields in applause. Will murmured, 'Remind me, sometime, to introduce you to my mother.'

'What saith thou, good nun?' Amarynth queried.

'I said, the Light is a mother to us all, and no mother will let her children come to lasting harm.' Will bared his teeth. It passed for a smile.

Wiping tears from his dark cheeks, the elf snapped his fingers. An aide ran into the command tent and emerged seconds later with a furled flag.

'Take this white ensign. It is an acknowledged sign of peace. It is all I can do. Yet know that you go with Amarynth Firehand's blessing – and regrets.'

Two hands seized his shoulders. Will found himself smearily kissed, first on one shaven cheek and then on the other. He reached up and took the furled flag, bowed speechlessly, and tottered back towards the wagon. He heard Ned behind him adding felicitous farewells; then his brother was at his side, climbing up on to the front of the cart.

'Haai-yah!' Ned Brandiman whispered, cracking the reins against the mules' flanks.

161

'They didn't even bother to search the cart,' Will grumbled under his breath. 'You've been hauling that load of scrolls around for nothing. Dark damn it, if I'd known it was going to be *that* easy . . .'

A silver clarion call echoed around the military camp, reverberating back from the high mountain walls. His brother shoved the reins into Will's hands, stripping off his gloves and worrying at the fastenings of the white flag. He shot a glance ahead and upwards as he worked.

Nin-Edin's outer bailey was a mess of snow, slush, dried blood, mud, trampled bodies, broken weapons and cast-off dented armour. None of the siege army crossed it, except behind new and hastily thrown up earthworks from which stiffening orc limbs protruded. Nin-Edin's inner walls glowered down; blackened with sorcerous fire, lined with silent watching orcs.

'*That* was the easy part,' Ned said.

Will brushed his robes, holding the reins single-handed, and checked the positions of poisoned darts, throwing knives, short-sword, and small cases of the secret dwarven rock-blasting powder. The bitter wind brought tears to his eyes. He grinned fiercely.

'Sister, where's your faith?'

8

ASHNAK OF THE orc marines stood in the great hall of Nin-Edin's keep.

'When they attack, we *can* break out.'

Barashkukor, standing to attention, touched the brim of his black stetson. 'Yessir!'

'I want *all* the spare weaponry got out of the stores. Each orc is to carry as many weapons as he or she can. If we're lucky, a *fail-weapons* spell will only affect the weapon it's directly cast at – have the marines carry spares, and use them one after another. That should give us just enough of a surprise element to break out. We'll then regroup and take up positions in the mountain caverns, with Dagurashibanipal's hoard. We can set traps and ambushes, and take prisoners, and I', Ashnak observed, 'have never refused to eat elf or Man in my life. And dwarves are only stringy when the meat isn't well-bruised.'

'But sir, the caverns can be taken by magic, just as easily as the fort.'

Ashnak growled deep in his throat. Barashkukor swallowed audibly, but continued:

'Sir, there's nowhere to run to, sir! Not if we don't have anti-magic capability. Maybe we could find another Dark Mage in time—'

Ashnak drew his jackhammer fist back. He was interrupted by a Badgurlz marine, AK47 held loosely over her shoulder, who stuck her spiked and crested head around the doorway. 'Two non-identified

163

non-combatants approaching main gate from the east! They appear to be halflings, sir, in a vehicle. Sir, Varimnak's squad subjecting them to fire, sir!'

'Halflings?' Barashkukor abruptly sat down on one of the hall's wooden chairs.

'*Halflings!*' Ashnak hit his fist into his palm. His eyes blazed. 'Major, get your orcs under control! Stop the firing, take the non-combatants prisoner, bring them to me in my office in ten minutes, alert Corporal Ugarit and Marine Razitshakra; *move it, marines!*'

Ashnak strode out through the cold and wet stone corridors of Nin-Edin. Old snow crusted the floor. Orc marines snapped to attention as he passed. The two SUS marines forming the honour guard at his door saluted carefully, with the less detachable of their limbs.

Five minutes later Ashnak sat behind the vast desk in his command post, chewing an unlit cigar and sorting through piles of paperwork. With his back to the slit window he was a black silhouette of immense bulk and invisible expression. From time to time the sunlight glinted off one of his fangs as he turned his head.

A hand rapped on the door, and Ashnak buried his attention in a sheaf of papers. 'Enter!'

His eyes on the difficult print, he did not bother to look up. His ears swivelled slightly, hearing two sets of footsteps; one heavy and one light. His nostrils flared to the scent of halfling. And something familiar . . .

'Sir, General Ashnak, sir!' Barashkukor's heeled cowboy boot hit the flagstones. His voice throbbed with military enthusiasm. 'Prisoner present, sir! Beg to report that the other prisoner refuses to leave her vehicle, to wit, one mule-drawn covered wagon, on threat of firing charges of dwarven rock-blasting powder that are aboard it. We are unable to establish this as true without—'

Ashnak swivelled his eyes up in their sockets. Major Barashkukor, still wearing his Raybans inside the fort, was addressing his remarks rather to the right of Ashnak's desk. Beside the small orc, a robed halfling stood with her head bowed. Ashnak's nostrils flared widely and he frowned.

'Hhhrmmmnnn . . . surely not.'

The halfling lifted her head.

'*YOU?*'

Ashnak instantly backhanded piles of paperwork into the air. The whirling files deflected two panic-thrown daggers. Before the halfling could move again Ashnak stood, thrusting the desk bodily back three yards. He sprang, seized the Little Sister of Mortification by her metal-burred belt, and yanked the halfling into the air until they were eye to eye. His free hand chopped palm-edge against each of the halfling's arms in turn.

Shaken off, the pinned wimple fell to the floor, disclosing curly black hair with streaks of white in it.

'It's a male!' Barashkukor exclaimed. 'Sir, I *know* this halfling, sir!'

'*So do I.*' Ashnak tightened his claws on the halfling's belt and stared into Will Brandiman's wide-eyed face. Both the halfling's arms hung paralysed or broken. The faded red wool gown pulled up, disclosing enormous booted feet. Ashnak growled, the corner of his lip lifting over one sharp fang.

'Thief,' he snarled, 'how is it with you now? Are you rich from betraying us to The Named, the great captain of the Light who is not heard of now? Did *she* suffer for trusting you and your weasel brother?'

He put one calloused hand over the halfling's mouth and nostrils as he laid the kicking, struggling body flat on the office desk. Exultant, Ashnak grated, 'Did you think *I* was dead too? Asshole, it ain't your lucky day!'

With one dextrous claw he slit Will Brandiman's robe from neck to hem, tore it off, broke the belt and threw it aside, and picked knives, needles, and small weapons from the holding straps on the tiny body. Barashkukor, an expression of distaste on his small features, dropped them into the office wastebasket.

When Will Brandiman lay squirming and naked on his back, Ashnak raised his hand briefly and then closed it again about the halfling's throat.

'I'll eat your heart raw,' Ashnak promised, poising a claw over the tiny rib-cage, 'and you'll live just long enough to see me doing it.'

'. . . *talismans* . . .'

Ashnak batted the halfling irritably, quarter-strength. The naked body smacked against the stone wall and slid down, bleeding a little, to the floor. Ashnak waited until Will Brandiman collected himself and got unsteadily to his hairy feet.

'You are Magda's sons?'

'Yes.'

'You have the nullity talismans?'

'Yes.'

'A brief conversation. That pleases me. It argues some respect.' Ashnak chuckled deep in his throat. He sat on one corner of the desk, looking down at the halfling, and slapped his camouflage-trousered thigh, remembering Guthranc. 'Ha!'

Will Brandiman wiped his bloody face against his shoulder. Both arms hung useless. His lip and cheek were swelling darkly. The halfling drew himself up to his full three feet six, attempting dignity. 'The bargain, Ashnak. I wish to see our mother alive and unharmed. I wish for safe conduct for myself and my brother.'

Major Barashkukor gave a high-pitched giggle. 'Son, you have got yourself a whole *world* of grief . . .'

Ashnak beamed. His tusks flashed in the winter sun. Without a word he got up, seized the halfling by one leg, and slung the small body across his shoulder. He strode out of his office and through the stone corridors of Nin-Edin. Barashkukor marched smartly at his heels.

'Sir, permission to remove the other halfling from the vehicle, sir?'

'Leave that to me!'

Down three levels, where the walls were running with damp and white with nitre, Ashnak paused outside a heavily barred door. He pulled it open, threw the halfling bodily into the unlit cell beyond it, slammed the door, and twisted the key in the lock. He stood for some seconds in the torchlight looking at the key. No rats squeaked in the cells, which was to be regretted. All eaten days ago.

Ashnak dropped the key into the filth-brimming gutter that paralleled the corridor. It glinted and vanished into the excrement. His grin widened.

'Now the other one,' he promised.

Ignoring the surprisingly loud protests from behind the locked and barred cell door, Ashnak strode up from the lower levels of the keep and out into the inner compound. He squinted against the blue sky and bright sunlight. Those platoons on guard lined the parapets, weapons pointed towards the siegeworks of the enemy. Most of the off-duty marines formed a wide circle around a mule-driven cart that stood just inside the broken portcullis.

Seeing their general, the orc marines leaped up and down, banging their weapons on the frozen earth and flagstones, their cheers reverberating from the keep's walls:

'Ash-nak! Ash-nak!'

'Fighting Agaku!'

'Yo, Ashnak!'

'Are we marines?'

'*WE ARE MARINES, SIR!*'

He elbowed his way to the front rank of marines surrounding the wagon and stood, fists on hips, chewing his unlit cigar. A swift glance found him Ugarit and Razitshakra. The orc technical specialist shivered continuously, his broad hairy nostrils running with mucus, and his eyes flicked around every corner of the inner keep's defences.

166

His combats, armour and flak jacket were smeared with oil and less identifiable substances.

Eyes narrowed to slits in the sun, Razitshakra watched him, her pencil poised eagerly over a small notepad. She scribbled occasional words when Ugarit's terrified muttering reached clarity: 'Ideological instability . . . Un-orcish sentiments . . .'

Barashkukor watched her with dewy-eyed admiration. Ashnak growled in his throat. All became silent. He stared at the wagon.

'Yo, halfling! Mistress nun!' He paused a calculated moment. '*Ned Brandiman!*'

The ragged curtain at the front of the wagon twitched aside. Ashnak looked at the dishevelled figure of a male halfling wearing the red habit of one of the Little Sisters of Mortification. The brown-haired halfling, his skirt hiked up to his knees and disclosing hirsute feet, sat astride a wooden barrel. With one hand he rested a cocked heavy crossbow across his lap, finger on the trigger. In the other hand a fuse burned and sputtered, audible over the noise of the orc marines.

The halfling's face paled. The orc saw the small lips soundlessly form the name *Ashnak*. He stepped two paces forward of the front rank.

'A bargain!' The halfling's voice came shrilly across the compound. 'My mother and brother for these talismans. Else they're blown to pieces before your eyes, orc!'

'I remember you and dwarvish blasting powder – if you'd had your way, boy, I'd be buried under half a mountain!' He began to walk towards Ned Brandiman, combat boots loud on the flagstones.

'I wouldn't put it past you, *boy*, to come here with nothing more in that wagon than empty boxes, and try and trick your way out again with your mother – if that cut-price whore *is* your mother.' Ashnak registered the halfling's snarl, and grinned. 'What did you expect? Dumbfuck wild orcs, that's what you expected. What you get is orc *marines*, boy. What you get is *me*.'

The heavy crossbow shifted, the point of the bolt following Ashnak. He walked steadily forward. The halfling, in a scurry, shoved the sputtering fuse between his teeth, dug into a barrel behind him, and held up a handful of tiny metallic objects. Strung on wire, they clattered together.

Razitshakra loped across the compound, nostrils flaring. 'That's them, General, sir! Nullity talismans. I smell them true! And – I smell dwarven sorcery too.'

Ned Brandiman smiled around the fuse clasped between his teeth. He dropped the handful of talismans, removed the fuse from his mouth, and said, 'Better listen to her, big guy.'

The big orc, close enough now to rest one taloned hand on the mule's neck, stared directly into the eyes of Ned Brandiman where the halfling sat in the front of the wagon. The mule shifted, bothered by orc smell. Ashnak abruptly closed his hand, wrenching a gobbet of living flesh from the beast; he put it in his mouth, and chewed bloodily. The orc grunts cheered. The beast sank to its knees and tipped over in the shafts.

'*Put that fuse down!*' Ashnak snapped.

He held the halfling's gaze, seeing in those brown eyes a concealed desperation. He edged a step forward.

Ned Brandiman cried, 'You'll die with me, orc!'

The halfling's tensing muscles prepared him, the speech gave him the second in which to act. Ashnak grabbed the front of the wagon with both hands, his powerful arms projecting him forward, and his jaws slammed shut – not on Ned Brandiman's hand, the halfling was a fraction too fast in drawing back – but on the lit fuse, dowsing it in a mouthful of mucus and orc saliva.

Ashnak spat, sore-mouthed. His taloned hand seized the heavy crossbow in time to send the bolt through the roof of the wagon. He closed his hand, crumpling the metal firing mechanism. With his other hand he batted the halfling bodily out over the tailboard, where it vanished, biting and kicking, under a gang of marines.

'Major, escort my prisoner to the cells. *Alive.*' Ashnak put his finger in his mouth, wiggled it around, touched a raw-burned spot and winced.

'Marine Razitshakra, start dishing out these marine-issue anti-thaumatergy talismans to the grunts! Corporal Ugarit, your tech orcs are going to incorporate nullity talismans into every weapons casing you can find. Move your asses, marines!'

Ashnak got down from the wagon and walked untouched through the furious, orderly confusion of the inner compound. The sun, just beginning to wester, was a faint warmth on the back of his head.

Wide-winged ravens soared down from the mountains, haunting the churned earth of the outer compound; and he stared across it at the enemy camp, willing them to inactivity, willing them to desire the advantages of a night attack or a dawn attack, or any attack at all so long as it didn't come within the next few precious hours.

'The only reason we're alive is that he wants to kill us painfully and slowly.' Ned Brandiman shivered. 'What that orc considers a painful death, I don't want to think about.'

Will Brandiman chuckled, a small sound that slipped into a sob and a hard intake of breath. He looked down at his yellow-and-black

168

bruised arms, then stared up at the ceiling with wet eyes.

'Why did it have to be *that* son of a bitch? With anyone else it would have worked. Anyone else would have cared more about damage to the goods than damage to us. *Shit!*'

The torches in the corridor outside the cells dipped and flared. To Will, the air had the scent of night about it. But no attack on the fort yet. He fumbled tenderly at his bare arms and naked body, fingers feathering the cuts and contusions on his legs. He pressed the taut drum of his stomach and winced.

'Internal bleeding. I need a medic-mage. So do you.'

Ned Brandiman grunted. It was a weak sound. Will squinted at his brother in the yellow light from burning oil torches. The brown-haired halfling's face was crusted with blood, one eye blue and squeezed shut by swelling; at least three teeth down to jagged stumps. Naked, he still shivered in the chill of the dungeons. Will watched for when that shivering would cease.

'You didn't . . . keep lockpicks . . . ?' Ned coughed, hugging his bruised arms across his bare chest to restrain the racking movement. He glimmered white in the dim cell.

Will winced, laying on his side, recalling the penetrating orc fingers that searched every orifice. 'They took them all. We shouldn't have come without backup.'

'Who could we trust?'

At a question that ingenuous, Will snorted. He winced at the pain that followed. Determined, he shifted up on to his knees, on to his feet, and staggered the few steps over to the cell door. The barred grille was two feet above his head.

'I hear something!' Will waved Ned to silence. 'One. Maybe two. Make a noise! Get them in here!'

The elder halfling, propped up against the dank wall, raised his glinting eye to Will. 'Will . . . *why?*'

Will flexed his bruised hands. Breathing evenly, concentrating to ignore the pain, ignore the two broken fingers; the wrist and elbow fractures; think of nothing now except escape, nothing about medic-mages or temple healing; think only that even naked one has teeth, nails, and strength, one is not weaponless—

Ned began wordlessly to howl. The sound made even the hairs on the back of Will's neck stand up. He poised himself to one side of the cell door.

The metal covering on the grill slid back. An orc hand was briefly visible. Something metallic clinked against the bars. A small metal ovoid hit the cell floor, rolled across the flagstones, and came to rest a yard from Ned.

169

Before either halfling could speak or move, there was a flat *crack!*, frighteningly loud in the enclosed space. White fog billowed up, pouring rapidly into every corner of the cell. Will choked, coughed, ground his fists into his suddenly streaming eyes; bent double and began to retch helplessly. In pain, through tears and convulsions, he heard Ned whimpering, an ululation of pain broken by racking coughs.

At some point an altercation between orc voices resulted in a silence, after which a key was turned in the lock. The cell door opened, clanged shut; bars and bolts were settled again. The booted footsteps departed.

Three people coughed, retched; lay choking on the damp cell floor.

Some while afterwards, his eyes still swollen shut and his lungs raw, Will Brandiman whispered, 'Ned?'

His brother groaned.

A new voice said, 'Son, is that you?'

Will Brandiman began to weep, with a sound not too far removed from laughter. At last he crawled across the flagstones until he encountered a soft bulk. A hand rumpled his hair. He seized it. In torchlight through the grille, with the foul mist gone, he made out the calm features of Magda Brandiman.

He wept in her lap for some while, and after that Ned was discovered to have stopped shivering, so between the two of them they chafed feeling back into his body and hypothermia out of it, and Magda wrapped her crimson velvet cloak around her sons' bodies. They sat huddled together, arms around each other, in the least damp corner of the Nin-Edin cell; brief mutters and whispers passing information on capture.

'You *paid* the Visible College . . . ?' Breath failed Magda Brandiman. Will felt her small body tense. 'That must have cost – you could have set me up in my own House – a chain of Houses – *you told me you were poor!*'

Embarrassed, Will murmured, 'Mother, you know what you're like with gold.'

'My *sons!*' She began to weep, small sounds of surprise and outrage rather than grief.

'Mother, we've come to rescue you!' Ned stopped, and glanced around the dim, dank cell. 'Look, don't worry, we'll think of something.'

The halfling raised her head, her dark cropped hair spiked up into cat's-fur tufts, the lines prominent around her eyes and mouth. Her eyes glittered. 'That big *orc* treats me better than my own boys! And who said I needed a rescue? Who *asked* you to come here? He and I— Oh, you could be killed!'

She wept again, softly this time, hugging Will and Ned to her prominent bosom; and neither of her sons winced against the pain of their injuries.

The air began to smell of deep night.

Will broke the long silence.

'I think I see a way. It isn't easy. All of us will have to do things we don't like. You most of all, Mother.'

Magda Brandiman's voice came neutrally. 'What must I do?'

Aching, the weakness of internal bleeding filling him with dread, Will schooled his voice to confidence.

'Simple enough, Mother. Come out of hiding, abandon your false name – come forward and be recognized as who you really are.'

Standing on the parapet, Ashnak spared a glance for the winter stars above Nin-Edin. Three hours till daybreak. *And is the Light planning a pre-dawn attack too?*

His broad, hairy nostrils suddenly flared.

'Sir!'

Ashnak took a salute from a rotting, albinoid figure in black combats that materialized out of the night. 'Yes, Corporal?'

'Reports from the scouts, sir. One recon team got back,' Corporal Lugashaldim announced. 'They advise that in the last hour dozens of messengers have been coming into the enemy camp.'

Ashnak wiped his hairy nostrils on his sleeve, his eyes watering at the proximity of the SUS marine. '*Reinforcements*, dammit! They're getting reinforcements.'

'Nothing else it can be, sir. We think there are more Light forces in the general area.' The Undead marine grinned rather more widely than Ashnak found comfortable. 'Guess they didn't want Amarynth Fartarse to have all the glory of doing for us, sir.'

'Well done, marine. Keep me advised of any further reports. You!' He snapped his fingers at an orc marine aide, whose helmet slipped down over her eyes as she saluted. 'Send the halfling prisoners to my quarters for interrogation. Start with the female. While I'm there, see that I receive regular situation reports on military developments.' Ashnak showed his fangs. 'You know how involved I get in interrogations.'

'Sir, yes, sir!' The orc marine left at the double.

Ashnak loped slope-shouldered through the chill night. Inside the keep it was colder with the damp of ancient stones. The chambers and corridors echoed to the shouts of orc marines gearing up, NCOs bawling out their grunts, officers shouting for reconnaissance and situation reports. He walked through it all, grumbling under his

171

breath about the burdens of command, and shrugged his flak jacket tighter across his muscled, hairless chest.

Approaching Nin-Edin's largest tower, and his Command Post, a noise attracted his attention. He paused by the closed door of the guardroom, hearing the whistle of a whip.

'Ah. Interrogating prisoners. Well done, marines.' Ashnak, cheered, opened the door and beamed. 'Possibly a *little* in advance of ourselves . . .'

Chained face to the wall, stripped of everything but leather underwear, Perdita del Verro winced and arched her back as the lash struck. Ashnak glimpsed her between the six or seven orcs surrounding her chained body – grunts in a somewhat unorthodox Battle Dress Uniform of black leather, with studded belts and wristbands; female orcs with spiked white hair.

The Badgurlz marines jeered their helpless victim. Sergeant Varimnak, sleeves rolled up, black cloth headband tied around her brows, wielded the heavy whip. 'Take that, bitch!'

'Mercy!'

Ashnak beamed sentimentally to himself at the traditional sight of orcs inflicting pain.

A petite Badgurlz marine with silver studs through her hairless ears, nostrils, and nipples elbowed Varimnak in the ribs. 'She's had *ages*, Sarge. What about the rest of us?'

Perdita del Verro turned her head, chin resting on her striped, bleeding shoulder. 'You *stopped* . . .' she complained.

'Take her down,' Varimnak ordered. 'Hey, Tukurash, get up there; I'm gonna make hamburger of your pretty ass! Unless our guest . . . ?'

Ashnak witnessed the *Warrior of Fortune* correspondent climb down from the stone bench, and grin painfully and widely at Varimnak. The elf's glossy braids had come half-undone, her red ribbons were sweat-stained. She took Varimnak's black leather whip.

'Take that, bitch!' The elf cracked the tip of it accurately across the orc marine's back. Tukurash whimpered. Varimnak nodded admiringly.

'*You're* supposed to torture the prisoners!' Ashnak exclaimed, affronted. 'Damn it, they're not supposed to torture *you!*'

Varimnak put her muscular arm around the female elf's sweating shoulders. 'You do it your way, General. We'll do it ours.'

Ashnak opened his mouth, and after some thought closed it again, and shut the guardroom door behind him as he left. Shaking his head, he strode back up through the tower towards the command post. He gathered himself together enough to order further preparations for

172

the pre-dawn attack, speak with his sub-commanders, and set basic strategy and tactics, before entering his inner office.

The female halfling sat waiting for him in a torn robe.

'Now, my prisoner . . .'

Ashnak reached down and took Magda Brandiman's hand, drawing her through into the inner chamber. He closed the door. Starlight illuminated the bare room and his camp bed.

Her hand, tiny in his, felt hot and dry. Ashnak seated himself on the edge of the camp bed and drew her to him between his thighs. She freed her hand. The starlight profiled her sharp face, easing the lines of age, gleaming from her short hair.

She cupped the orc's face in her hands, drawing her fingers across his rough, horny cheeks; catching the lobes of his pointed ears between fingers and thumbs and nipping. She drew his head forward, kissing the corner of his mouth, darting her tongue between his wide, thin lips.

Ashnak made a sound, half groan and half sigh, and fell back on the bed. It creaked. Magda Brandiman sprawled across his chest and body, small legs straddling him, muttering under her breath as she winced, bruising her hands against webbing, water bottle, and flak jacket. She stripped him impatiently until they lay in a bed full of military equipment, bruising knees and elbows.

He put his hands around her body, so small that he could encompass her waist with ease. Her skin like finest chamois leather rippled under his fingers, and the soft hair on her feet tickled his thighs. She grunted, at first sitting up, and then easing herself down on his erection, gradually taking more than seemed possible; and rocking in the starlight, silver-limned, her eyes half shut, her face smiling.

This time he worked until she arched her back and cried out: a sound sufficiently like pain to satisfy any orc who might be listening. Ashnak groaned, his hands clamping her hips tightly down, his body jackhammering up; and when the world came back to him he sprawled on his back, grinning so that all his tusks showed.

The female halfling ferreted in his combats pocket and brought out a thin roll of pipe-weed.

Magda struck flint against Nin-Edin's walls, lit the pipe-weed, and drew deeply. The flare of light illuminated her lined face.

'I've been thinking about retiring.'

Ashnak made a small, querulous noise of protest.

'Going into management.' She blew out a plume of pipe-weed smoke, and wriggled further up into the odorous crook of Ashnak's armpit. Her feet brushed his hip. 'You could set me up in a nice little business. Some girls, some boys – some fabulous beasts.'

173

Ashnak unkinked the tips of his hairless ears and leered. 'I got other things on my mind right now . . .'

Magda ignored him. 'I said I *had* been thinking about retiring. But now I can only see one way to ensure the safety of my sons.'

'No way! They're dogmeat!'

The halfling leaned back in the rough marine-issue blankets, the red eye of the pipe-weed roll swelling and dying. The night sky gloomed outside the window, stars covered in cloud. She said nothing more.

Cooling sweat slicked Ashnak's hide. 'Halfling, you expect me to—'

Magda exhaled, utter confidence in her voice. 'You're going to win the battle tomorrow.'

'I am? I mean: I am!'

'But what happens after that, my orc?'

There was a very long silence.

'So what', Ashnak rumbled, 'are you suggesting?'

Magda Brandiman rolled over, feline, and drew a finger down the centre of the orc's broad, hairless chest.

'I'll tell you later.'

'You'll *what?*'

Ashnak glared, watching her with orcish night-vision. The female halfling rummaged in the tumbled bed. One of her hands seized his wrist, not able to encompass it with her own, and she swiftly knotted his trouser-belt about it, and then tied it to the bed's post.

'*Oi!*'

Searching among miscellaneous military equipment for another leather belt, the female halfling looked up directly into Ashnak's eyes.

'I don't believe in instant gratification. Let me show you. In a while I'll tell you about my plan.'

Her tongue darted out to lick her lower lip. She smiled.

'You'll like it. Trust me, you'll like it.'

9

MAJOR BARASHKUKOR SQUINTED through the pre-dawn darkness.

With some reluctance he folded his Raybans and put them carefully in a pouch on his web belt. 'All right, you orcs. Check your weapons.'

FOOM!

A red-crested orc in desert combats looked down the smoking muzzle of her Kalashnikov. 'I think mine was loaded, sir.'

'Quiet!' Barashkukor snarled.

Chill slid down from the heights of the mountains on just-stirring breezes. Orc-vision alone could glimpse the east growing light. Stars still clustered in the arch of the sky; no birds sang. Barashkukor lifted his head and squinted up at Nin-Edin's magic-blackened and battered inner walls. Hundreds of orcs lined the parapets, scaling ladders ready; orcs clustered in dozens of squads in the inner compound, receiving their last briefings.

Barashkukor shook out and re-tied a white silk scarf around his thin neck. The small orc's long hairless ears whivvered in the dawn wind, and he crammed his stetson down over them. Drawing his Desert Eagle pistol from its belt holster, muzzle skyward, he tucked one black-gloved thumb under his web belt, and leaned into the cover of the broken gateway.

Nothing stirred in the enemy siegeworks, a scant thirty yards away.

'We must be alert, orcs,' Barashkukor whispered. 'We must think on our feet— Not you, Corporal.'

Corporal Lugashaldim of the SUS looked up briefly from his marine-issue survival sewing-kit, murmured 'Yezzer!', and went back to threading a needle and more securely sewing on the toes of his left foot.

'Any minute now—'

'Sir!'

'What is it?' Barashkukor took his gaze off the enemy siege-works. Sergeant Varimnak saluted him lazily. She nodded at the nearest squad of orcs: newcomer refugees in plate armour, carrying axes.

'We got a problem, sir.'

'Not *now*, Sergeant!'

'Sorry 'bout that. It's those refugees we took in. Dumb mother-fuckers say they ain't going in on no front wave, Major.' Varimnak shrugged leather-clad shoulders. She shifted her chewing gum to the other side of her heavy jaws. 'Guess we haven't had 'em in here long enough. Funny thing, Major, they don't seem to be able to work the weapons when they first get 'em – have to drill the dumb shits into the ground, make real marines out of 'em, *then* the guns start firing. Guess that's the Dragon's Curse. But they say they're not going in with inferior weapons.'

Barashkukor fumed, tapping the toe of one tooled cowboy boot on the cold earth. 'Don't worry, Sergeant, *I'll* handle this.'

The small orc marched smartly up to the band of orc warriors who, in the growing half-light, leaned disconsolately on a selection of obsolete polearms.

'New recruits, ten*HUT!* We gave you refuge in here – so you can damn well fight for us.'

The orc warriors muttered recalcitrantly.

Barashkukor glared at them. 'You're marines now and that means you obey orders!'

''Oo's orders?' A bow-legged, grey-skinned orc grinned, showing a jaw full of broken fangs. He towered over Barashkukor by a metre or more. '*Your* orders, you little runt?'

The grey-skinned orc snarled menacingly, hefting a pole-axe.

Barashkukor gripped his massive Desert Eagle pistol two-handed, drew himself up to his full three feet six inches, and faced the leader of the refugee orcs.

'One wrong move', Barashkukor announced, 'and you're history!'

The looming orc paused, scratching his head. 'What's *hist'ry?*'

FOOM!

'Anyone *else* want an academic education?' Barashkukor demanded.

Thirty different squad leaders hissed, 'Sssssshhh!'

'You, marine!' Barashkukor whispered, blowing the smoke from the muzzle of the pistol. 'Clear up that mess. As for the rest of you new guys, get down to the gate, you're going in with the forward units!'

He watched the refugee orcs run, with some satisfaction. He thumbed the RT. 'Forward unit Bravo to command, forward unit to command.'

General Ashnak's voice crackled: *'Command post to forward unit Bravo. Artillery barrage going in. Standby; over.'*

'Forward unit, message received, standing by.'

Without warning the pre-dawn split apart and lit up like noon.

DUKKA-DUKKA-DUKKA-*FOOM!*

Missile emplacements on the walls and towers opened up simultaneously with the precision-guided trebuchets and heat-seeker crossbows. Tracer fire seared the lightening sky. Great gouts of earth shot up from the siegeworks. Flashes of fire strobed the outer compound's wreckage. Barashkukor shaded his eyes with his gloved hand, small fangs gleaming in the glare.

'Major!'

He barely heard Ugarit's yell. Turning, he saw the tall, skinny orc straighten up from tightening a leather strap harness around the body of one of the smaller orcs.

'My latest military development, Major!'

The tiny orc, bandy legs bowing even further, puffed under the weight of a heavy metal casing now attached to her back. She took the goggles Ugarit handed to her, putting them over her wide-set tilted eyes, and staggered off into the gloom.

Barashkukor said, *'What?'*

'It's quite simple, Major.'

The squads in the compound moved back in orderly formation, letting something through. Barashkukor gazed up at a great black bulk.

The war elephant clanked to a halt.

Kevlar and steel armour covered its limbs and body, and a fine metal mesh shielded its trunk and eyes. Spikes jutted from the armour, and flags with marine unit insignia, and the Raven with stars-and-bars.

A steel howdah sprouting wires, spindles, nozzles, dishes and heavy-duty power packs had been attached to the beast's back. The inside of the howdah was lined with orc marines.

'Yo, Major!' Varimnak climbed up to sit with her muscular legs either side of the elephant's ears. She pulled on a sheepskin-lined black leather jacket with the Marine flag painted on the back.

Barashkukor coughed, blushing as he noted Perdita del Verro slip out of the gloom with elvish quietness to stand gaping up at the war elephant. 'I think you'd better explain what it is you're doing here, Corporal Ugarit.'

Ugarit chuckled and rubbed his knobbly knuckles. He beamed at the elf correspondent. 'A simple scratch-built antigravity device, sir and ma'am. This is its maiden flight! I'll demonstrate. Sergeant Varimnak, ma'am! Prepare for takeoff.'

The peroxide-haired orc removed her chewing gum and stuck it under the elephant's right ear. She pulled goggles down over her eyes, zipped up her jacket, and held a metal quirt up in the air. Radar dishes on Nin-Edin's walls swivelled. The quirt radiated infra-spectral colours, bright against the pre-dawn indigo sky. She turned her head to address the orcs seated in rows down each side of the howdah. 'Flight check one! Sound off, marines.'

'Squad one all present, Sergeant.'

'Squad two, present and correct!'

Sergeant Varimnak grinned and wiped her splayed nostrils, streaming in the cold air. The RT built into her helmet crackled. Barashkukor heard her call, *This is Flight One to Control. Yo! Ready for takeoff, man!*'

Ugarit skipped up and down on the spot, clicking his heels together, slavering over the walkie-talkie he held. 'You have mission clearance, Flight One – go, go, go!'

The elephant lifted its trunk and trumpeted. Barashkukor grabbed his stetson with both hands. Perdita del Verro scribbled furiously in her notebook. Powdery snow blasted back as the war elephant beat its ears, rearing its front legs an inch or two above the earth. The ground shook under Barashkukor's boots. Varimnak brandished the quirt. The whine of a highly powered para-electrical field rose beyond even orc-hearing.

'—*achieved takeoff!*' the RT squawked.

The war elephant's ears beat strongly and rhythmically. Clouds of dirt and snow whirled across the compound. Barashkukor slitted his eyes. The beast reared.

Up out of the dirt and darkness, into the new light of dawn. The sparkling quirt appeared, and the great crowded howdah, and Varimnak banged her studded boots in behind the war elephant's ears, triggering the cybernetic flight-guidance systems. A blast of warm air shook Barashkukor. He craned his neck to look up, look up higher . . .

Ears beating, cradled in the sparkling discharges of a para-gravitational field, the great war elephant gradually lifting above the compound. Grunts cheered. Gaining height rapidly, legs trailing, the war elephant narrowly cleared the walls of Nin-Edin and soared up into the dawn air.

Perdita del Verro lifted her patrician chin, glossy braids gleaming, and breathed, 'Now I think I've seen about *every*thing . . .'

Her gold eyes widened. 'What a scoop! What an exclusive!'

'I've done it! I'm safe at last!' Ugarit jumped up and down, shaking spanners and soldering irons out of the crevices of his flak jacket. 'The unbeatable weapon! *Bomber Flight One away!*'

Barashkukor ran for the gate. He hit the portcullis some seconds after Perdita del Verro, grabbing at the stone-chilled metal and staring out into the vast air of the mountain pass. The war elephant's lights made a tiny speck high above, circling over the enemy positions.

'*Varimnak to base, man. About to commence first strategic bombing run, over.*'

'Sergeant, this is Major Barashkukor. Proceed with experimental bombing run. Over.'

'*Ya got it, man! Out.*'

The war elephant circled high above the pass of Nin-Edin, illuminated by the sunrise while the world below was yet dark. A small speck fell from the back of the elephant. Then a second, a third, a fourth . . .

Barashkukor lifted armoured binoculars and focused. 'Corporal Ugarit . . .'

The binos brought Barashkukor the image of one orc marine hanging on to the straps of his pack harness, face contorted against the cold wind as he fell. The great mass of the bomb strapped to his back made him plummet towards the earth. As Barashkukor watched, the orc pulled a tag. A small drogue chute opened – not large enough to arrest his fall, but strong enough to slow the rate of descent.

The orc grunt reached up, grabbed the straps, and began to pull them one way and another, guiding his plummeting descent towards the position of the besieger's main tents and the impact.

'There you are, sir!' Ugarit yelled triumphantly as the first explosion rocked the cold air, and a ball of black and orange smoke went up. 'Terminally guided munitions!'

Another explosion rocked the ground. Barashkukor clutched the female elf's elbow. Her mouth hung open. There was a light in her eyes. Black ash and fragments of wood rained down across the snowbound fort.

179

'Have to ask you to move to the rear now, ma'am.' Barashkukor thumbed the RT. 'This is Bravo to Command. Am going in now, sir!'

'*OK, marines, let's rock and roll!*'

The artillery barrage cut out. Orc voices bellowed commands. The noise of ladders sounded strangely loud as the squads went over the top, down the walls, and fanned out to cross the outer compound. Grenades cracked; heavy weapons bellowed. The earth shook.

Barashkukor sprinted behind his squad, clear across the outer compound, over the ruined walls and into the main enemy camp. Ahead of the forward squads, ahead of heavy weapons—

'*Yee-hah!*' Barashkukor fired the Desert Eagle pistol.

DUKKA-DUKKA-*KER*-FOOM!

'Bravo to Command, repeat Bravo to Command, we are encountering minimal resistance. We did it, sir! We've taken them completely by surprise! Move the troops up on my position; over.'

'*Wilco, Bravo. Out.*'

Cloud cleared. The dawn sun's light swept across the siegeworks and the enemy camp.

Barashkukor lowered his pistol. He reholstered it.

The sun shone on long-dead camp fires from which the cooking gear had been removed, abandoned tents with a few broken weapons scattered outside, and a vast pattern of circles of dead turf where panoplied tents had once stood. The beams shone on piles of horse dung, but no horses. Cart-ruts, but no baggage carts. Holes where flagpoles had been sited, but no Colours or Ensigns of the Light.

Barashkukor stared. He tipped the stetson back on his head. One long ear drooped. Still staring, he used his radio to direct Varimnak's armoured war elephant to overfly the whole length of the Light's camp.

'*Nothing, man! No warriors. No surprise ambush. No traps or pits. Nothing!*'

A stray shell from the creeping barrage ahead dropped short, fragments whistling past Barashkukor's ears.

Barashkukor fumbled for the RT and screamed: 'Abort attack! Bravo unit to Command, abort the attack, repeat, *abort the attack!* We have no hostiles. I repeat, we have no hostiles. Send out recon. Sir, they've *gone*, sir!'

The noise of suppressive and speculative fire died away.

'*Command to Bravo.*' Ashnak's voice came loud and distorted over the channel. '*What do you* mean, *you have no hostiles! It must be a trap!*'

The rising sun shone full into the valley of the Nin-Edin pass. In its light Barashkukor looked back and saw the devastated fort, the swarms of orc marines going into cover and holding the outer bailey. He stared forward at the abandoned siegeworks and the completely deserted enemy camp.

'It's not a trap. Come out and look for yourself, sir,' Barashkukor whimpered. 'They've all gone away.'

10

A SHNAK LEANED HIS horny elbow on the side of his jeep, camouflage sleeve rolled up, bare orc-hide resting against metal biting cold in the morning frost.

'Someone must have yelled for help,' Ashnak switched the chewed roll of pipe-weed to the other side of his wide mouth, 'and Amarynth Arselicker got orders to pull out. Elfshit! Just when we could have done with a fight to knock the new marines into shape.'

Since this was not wholly bravado, he was pleased to see his subordinate orc salute smartly and with every appearance of regret. Major Barashkukor stood beside the jeep, thumbs hooked under his belt, small booted feet planted widely apart. His Raybans reflected Ashnak's camouflage-creamed features.

'They must've moved out stealthily after midnight. Sorry, sir!'

'You will be,' General Ashnak promised. 'And so will my reconnaissance teams.'

Ashnak sprang down from the jeep, boots crunching the trodden slush and black embers of the abandoned enemy camp. Squads of orc marines combed the slopes of Nin-Edin in disciplined order. He narrowed his eyes against the knife-wind and early sun.

East, the foothills ran down into empty country, the farmlands of Sarderis too far away to be properly seen. White frost covered the hills, white mist blurred the sunrise. Vultures wheeled in the high sky. Ashnak drew in breath cold enough to freeze a Northlands orc.

'Wonder how long a start they got?'

Barashkukor looked nervous. 'There are still whole armies of Light out there, sir.'

A SUS marine scrambled up the slope towards Ashnak, halted, and snapped a bony salute. About to reprimand the orc for grinning at a superior officer, Ashnak concluded that he might be mistaken in this when it came to the Undead.

'What is it, marine?'

'Sir, report from Corporal Lugashaldim's Special Services recon group. Amarynth's main force is six hours away from us, and closing on Sarderis; armed and ready for battle with the rogue mercenary units down there. The SUS report we can't catch them up, sir.'

Ashnak nodded morosely. The Undead orc marine continued:

'Sir, Corporal Lugashaldim also reports that the enemy baggage train is only *two* hours away, down the main Sarderis road. It's moving very slowly. And it's unguarded, except for one mage.'

This time there was no mistaking the orc marine's grin, Undead or otherwise.

'The Light's "rules of war", sir. Since the baggage train's sacred, they've only bothered to put a couple of crossbowmen with it, at the van and the rear. We could intercept it in the Red Gullies, sir. What are your orders?'

'Tell Lugashaldim we're on our way!' Ashnak hit his fist into his palm. 'Major Barashkukor, get your platoons together and move out to the gullies. I'll follow with mine!'

'*Sir, yes, sir!*'

Galvanized into action, two platoons of orc marines loaded themselves into four-tracks and jeeps. Ashnak, beaming, swung himself up into a jeep, jammed shoulder-to-shoulder with Varimnak's Badgurlz, their M16s and grenade-launchers jutting into the air. Sergeant Varimnak stood her booted feet down on the pedals and the jeep roared away down the hillslope, rocking and juddering.

'*Go, marines!*' the peroxide-haired orc bellowed, overtaking the assembling column of vehicles. Ashnak saw her hit a control on the dashboard. Loud music blared out into the snowy silent dawn.

'Marine, give me an assault weapon,' he demanded.

A hulking orc in woodland camouflage combats proudly handed over an XM18 grenade launcher. 'Eighteen rounds in five seconds, sir, four hundred metres range. Loaded with alternate smoke, flares, gas, frag, and anti-personnel shells.'

Ashnak checked the drum magazine. The weapon smelled beautifully of grease and metal and wax. 'OK, you marines, *listen up!* No need for a stealth approach. This is a baggage train, it moves at the speed of the slowest horse-and-cart, it isn't going anywhere.

Those pointy-eared mothers cut us up in Nin-Edin – now it's *our* turn!'

'YAYYY *ASHNAK!*'

A short time later the jeep crested the hill above the Red Gullies. The road, almost past the foothills and into the lowlands, here split into a dozen narrow tracks between outcrops of red sandstone.

Wagons blocked all the narrow tracks.

Ashnak took it in at a glance: seventy or eighty heavy wagons weighed down with tents, chests, cooking gear, spare armour, cord, anvils, hammers, saws, bottles, benches, chairs and beds, candles, flagpoles, haybales – everything that heroic warriors need but cannot carry on their backs.

Elves barely of an age to walk sat on the wagons and sang. Scurrying around the draught horses' heads, young Men and dwarves fought with the recalcitrant beasts. Ashnak spotted the crossbow guards. He raised the XM18.

CRACK!

Two mailed bodies tore apart, splattering the sandstone walls of the Gullies.

'*Chaaarge!*' Ashnak bawled over the RT's open channel; pounding Varimnak's back. The jeep dipped, rolled, and drove down on the rear of the column, music blaring, horn sounding; and, over all else, the Badgurlz ripping off rounds of suppressive fire:

TAKA-TAKA-TAKA-TAKA-FOOM!

The young elves, dwarves and Men ran in panic. Ashnak stood, steady, bracing the grenade launcher and firing. An anti-tank grenade coughed, soared and impacted on a tent-carrying wagon. Fingernail-sized scraps of canvas and cord spattered the Gullies.

The lone mage – a dwarf young enough that his beard had barely grown past his belt – raised hands flaming with the Powers of Earth. 'Fail weapons!'

Ashnak grinned, holding his breath.

A bolt of Earth power enveloped the jeep. A shrill cheer rose from the Light youngsters. Ashnak, one taloned hand gripping the side of the vehicle, and the other his XM18, shook his head. The talismans around his neck stung.

The green dazzles in his vision faded, harmlessly.

The jeep's engine raced and roared, intact.

'Eat *this!*' Ashnak lifted the XM18 and fired, looking directly into the dwarf's terror-stricken eyes.

FOOOM!

The mage and the Earth power aura vanished together, tough flesh not so much blown apart as vaporized.

'Close weapons!' Ashnak made himself heard over the RT. 'No projectiles. Hand-to-hand!'

The orc marines bayed.

The sun rose higher, slanting into the slush-ridden Red Gullies. Something over a hundred and fifty elves and Men – none of them more than children or adolescents, and kept safe with the baggage train for that very reason – ran about, their screams piercing the morning. Ashnak abandoned the vehicle. He swept a green-robed young female elf off her feet and tucked her, scrabbling and weeping, under one muscular arm. With the other hand he wielded a commando knife, rejoicing (as all orcs do) in close-quarters combat. The knife, dripping, rose and fell as he loped up the line of jammed wagons.

An older elf sprang down from a sandstone outcrop, swinging a mace, screaming. Ashnak batted her aside. She hit the earth and slumped, sack-like. Fifteen or so adolescent Men and dwarves – spawn-herds, Ashnak assumed – recovered enough to attack as a group.

He stunned the elf-child and dropped her between his feet, wielding the knife and his free, taloned hand. Varimnak, using the bayonet and butt of her assault rifle to strike, came up and stood back to back with him.

Most of the jeeps were empty now, disgruntled marine drivers gunning the motors. The squads of grunts rampaged over the wagons, tearing bundles free, ripping chests open, scattering the tools and gear and keepsakes of the Army of the Light all through the Gullies' trodden red slush.

The first killing done, the sound of elf-shrieks rose into the air: prisoners kept alive to provide amusement.

Ashnak rolled the semi-conscious female elf on to her back, unbuckled his webbing and trouser-belt and knelt down.

Varimnak licked red blood from the butt of her assault rifle with a rasping tongue. 'Hey man, we got 'em! The whole fucking baggage train! No survivors!'

A grunt on top of one of the red sandstone outcrops stared down into the deep crevass on the far side of it.

'Sarge,' she called down to Varimnak, 'you want to know something about elves?'

'What's that, Shakmash?'

'They don't bounce.' The orc marine shrugged. ''Ere, Sarge, can I have a doggy-bag?'

Varimnak grinned.

Ashnak saw a Badgurlz marine run past, dragging a semi-conscious elf by the ankle. The elf's skull cracked and jolted against rocks on the path. Another marine humped a dwarf with a slit throat.

From the gullies Ashnak heard shrieks and the butcher's-shop sound of blows.

'Hhnff!' Ashnak braced his elbows and toes, his blood-rimmed palms in the icy slush. Head hanging down, body pumping; his spittle draped the elf-girl's face. 'Good. My grunts need R&R. Post scouts. Just— in— *hhnf!*— case . . .'

He smelled Varimnak lighting up another of the thin, black, oddly scented rolls of pipe-weed that she affected. Her voice above him agreed, 'You got it, man.'

Ashnak stopped moving.

'And pass me another elf, sergeant. This one's split.'

The noon sun penetrated the depths of Nin-Edin's dungeons at several removes and faintly, but clear enough for Will to see Perdita del Verro.

'Of course I'm a minor healer-mage,' the elf confirmed. 'It's a necessity in my line of work.'

'What *is* your line of work, mistress?' Will beamed politely.

'War correspondent.'

Ned Brandiman groaned and made some attempt to cover his filth-caked, naked body with bruised hands; his haemorrhage-tight stomach tender. 'No kidding. An investigative mage-reporter.'

Magda Brandiman's face appeared outside the bars as the elf lifted her like a child. The halfling was, Will noted, wearing what appeared to be an over-large combat jacket.

'Boys, *I* think we can do business with Mistress del Verro.'

'What kind of business, Mother?' Will asked.

Magda smiled.

'Firstly,' she said, 'there's the matter of Perdita's pigeons.'

A fist hammered on his door. 'General Ashnak, sir!'

Ashnak snapped the wrist-bonds tying him to the bedposts and sat up. He kissed Magda Brandiman, passionately, scrambled into his combat trousers, and flung open the door.

'What do you *want*, Major?'

Major Barashkukor's ears flattened tightly down on his skull. He hastily took off his Raybans and put them in his combats pocket, cringed, and squeezed his eyes tight shut. 'Sir, it's time, sir!'

Ashnak backhanded the small orc, who impacted against the oak door frame and bounced back off, shaking his ringing head.

'It's bad timing, marine. And I do mean "marine".' Ashnak shut the door behind him, clipping his web-belt and pistol holster around his muscular body. 'Because if you interrupt any more of my interrogations, Major, you're busted down to marine, and on permanent latrine duty!'

'Sir, yes, sir!' Barashkukor swallowed audibly. 'But it's one of the new halflings, sir. Cornelius Scroop – the Chancellor of Graagryk. He wants some cushions.'

'Whaddya mean, cushions?' Ashnak demanded. 'This is an armed camp, for fuck's sake; where does he expect me to find *cushions!*'

Major Barashkukor ceased punching the dents out of his formal marine flat hat. 'Sir, both the halflings say they can't see over the conference table. They're right, sir. They can't.'

Ashnak groaned. Dangerously quietly, he said, 'Find some blankets. Fold them. Use those as cushions. Dismiss.'

'*Sir, yes, sir!*'

Barashkukor precipitously fled.

'I'm surrounded by idiots!' Ashnak strode off down the tower stairs. Tech-Corporal Ugarit joined him on the way to the main hall.

'*Magic!*' the skinny orc muttered disgustedly.

'Instantaneous trans-location spell, Corporal,' Ashnak said expansively. 'High-level, very expensive Southern Kingdoms magic. Has everyone that I want here for the conference arrived?'

'Yes, General! Had to site the transfer point outside the fort, because of the nullity talisman influence, but they're here. All the way from the Southern Continent.'

Ashnak strode through the doors of the main hall. Commissar Razitshakra saluted him from behind a table. She tore off a small piece of paper.

'Ticket for the Orc Ball, sir?'

'I've already got one!' Ashnak regarded the big hall. 'This your idea of a high-level conference, is it?'

Marine flags were pinned up all around the walls of the bright, war-battered hall. One squad had sacrificed marine-issue sheets and a pot of khaki paint. The resultant banner read NIN-EDIN ANNUAL MARINE DINNER-DANCE. A bar, set up at the opposite end of the hall to the dais, was crowded with orc marines in off-duty fatigues. Above Ashnak's head, among the spell-blackened beams and slit windows, a multi-faceted glass ball began to spin. Small lights chased over the off-duty grunts.

'Wouldn't want a high-level conference to look conspicuous, sir,' Commissar Razitshakra remarked. 'This way it blends into the general victory festivities.'

Ashnak grinned.

A voice spoke from approximately the height of the great orc's belt buckle.

'Lord General, I really must protest! You cannot expect us to sit on these greasy, smelly blankets. I demand that you find us either higher chairs, or a lower table best becoming a Graagryk halfling's dignity!'

Ashnak looked down at Cornelius Scroop. The halfling from the Southern city of Graagryk wore a full-length fur gown, upon which rested his S-linked gold chain of office, and a velvet cap on his long, barbered red curls.

'Those are marine-issue blankets, Chancellor Cornelius, and marines get nothing but the best.'

'They're *dirty!*'

'Oh, I wouldn't say that. Unwashed, perhaps. Oh, you mean the *blankets*.'

'Things are not done like this in the South!'

Ashnak, who had been hearing that refrain for some hours now, merely rested a clawed hand on Scroop's shoulder and pointed the halfling towards a long table standing by one wall. Corporal Ugarit clanked his way back carrying a tray of beer glasses.

Eight marines from the Badgurlz squad marched smartly up to the dais at the end of the hall, Major Barashkukor at their head. The small orc saluted Ashnak, then snapped his fingers. One marine set up a pot of greenery, hiding the wall-map. The others unpacked what Ashnak took to be musical instruments of varying descriptions.

Barashkukor drew himself up to attention in polished and brushed brown dress uniform, surmounted by silver-surfaced spectacles and flat hat. 'Sir, entertainment detail present and correct, sir!'

'Carry on, Major.'

The Badgurlz band launched into something with a deal of rhythm and spark. Marines moved out into the cleared centre of the hall and began enthusiastically to jitterbug.

A soberly clad halfling in black silk doublet, breeches, half-cloak and sword, already sat over a plate at the long table, jingling her spurs. She nodded cheerfully to Ashnak, and offered her hand to the body-armoured Ugarit.

'Simone Vanderghast. Captain of the Graagryk city civilian militia.'

Ugarit inspected the small calloused hand. 'General, it says it's a civilian, General.'

'It's an honorary marine for this evening, Corporal, and you are *not* to eat it, do you understand?'

Ugarit muttered, 'Yes, General!' in a dispirited manner and clanked off to find the bar steward.

188

Ashnak seated himself at the head of the conference table. 'Now, gentlemen.'

Chancellor Scroop sniffed. 'This blanket is dirty. This mug has not been washed. Admittedly this is an orc encampment, and has just suffered siege warfare, but nevertheless one has standards!'

Simone Vanderghast chuckled in her bluff, soldierly manner. 'Come, Chancellor, these are times of war, rough times, one must make the best of it. *You!* One has just found a cockroach on one's plate. Take it away!'

Commissar Razitshakra removed the offending insect in passing, her eyes gleaming avidly.

'We marines—' Ashnak slurped beer and wiped his tusked mouth with his sleeve. 'We marines want to come to a business arrangement with Graagryk.'

'At last we get to it!' Cornelius Scroop spread his hands, upon the pudgy fingers of which rings glinted. 'There is a problem. With all due respect, General, look at you. You're orcs.'

Ashnak sat back in his chair. It creaked. His muscled bulk overspread it considerably, and the wooden legs bowed. He glanced across Nin-Edin's hall at the orc marines standing by the bar. Two hunch-shouldered grunts were engaging each other in a belching contest.

'You're not meant to throw up when you do that!' Ashnak called. 'Wipe the bar-orc down and order another drink. And *you*, orc. Stop picking your nose!'

'Yessir!' The third grunt cheerfully turned to picking the nostril of the orc next to her.

The Southern halfling groaned. 'No one will trust you enough to deal with you, General. And if it were known we had dealings with orcs, then no one would trade with *us*.'

The music screeched to a halt. Ashnak glanced up as Major Barashkukor rapped the microphone. It squealed. Barashkukor beamed out at the hall full of orcs, tapping his baton to call the band to order.

'And now!' the small orc cried. 'A song I've dedicated to Quartermaster Zaruk. He tells me he's been getting a lot of requests from you orcs for those camouflage cloth squares you can roll up and tie around your head. Unfortunately there aren't any left in the stores.'

'That right?' a grunt drawled from the floor.

'Oh, yes.' Major Barashkukor lifted his baton and launched into song. '*Yes, we have no bandannas . . .*'

Ashnak, who had opened his mouth, shut it again and shook his head. A movement caught his eye at the hall door.

189

'Gentlemen,' he said, 'allow me to introduce another of the delegates to this conference.'

Magda Brandiman swept into the hall, her expression serene. She wore a full-length court gown which showed no signs of its having been cobbled together from reject parachute silk. She inclined her head to Ashnak and his guests.

'General. Chancellor Scroop. Captain Vanderghast.'

'Magda Brandiman, gentlemen.'

Ashnak, with extreme satisfaction, watched the halflings' jaws drop.

'But—' Simone Vanderghast sprang to her feet, toppling off the chair and blankets in the process. She stared up from the floor, booted ankles tangled round her sword-scabbard, and shifted with difficulty on to her knees. '*Your Grace!*'

Chancellor Scroop slid until his heeled court shoes touched the flagstones. He stood and stared.

'Cornelius,' Magda Brandiman said gently, 'is this manners?'

Scroop sank to one knee. 'Your Grace . . . is it really you?'

She rubbed her hand ruefully across her fur-short hair as she seated herself at the conference table, leaving Scroop and Vanderghast kneeling on the floor.

'Has it been so long? I flattered myself I was still recognizable.' She turned graciously to Ashnak. 'I apologize, sir. Magda is not my name. At least, not all my name. I am Magdelene Amaryllis Judith Brechie van Nassau.'

'Magdelene of Nassau!' Cornelius Scroop breathed. 'The Duchess of Graagryk!'

Ashnak guffawed in mock surprise. 'Graagryk! All those scrubbed streets and polished doorsteps. No wonder you left.'

Magda fixed the orc with a steely eye. 'I *left*, sir orc, because I was thought unsuitable to be a Duchess. Fortunately not all of my courtiers thought so. This is why I asked you to invite Master Scroop and Captain Vanderghast here for this conference. Ah, it has been so long since I saw any of my own people!'

'Ten years or more.' Simone Vanderghast regained her seat, still gazing in a dazzled fashion at Magda. 'Your Grace, what have you been doing all these years? How have you lived?'

'There will be time for such discussions later,' Magda said smoothly. 'After our business talks.'

'Smile for the camera!' a voice chirruped.

Light flashed.

Perdita del Verro had exchanged her pigeons, Ashnak saw, for some of the more complex reconnaissance equipment out of

190

Dagurashibanipal's caverns, and was busy pointing a zoom-lens at him. He preened himself, adjusting bullet-bandoliers, combat-stained trousers and combat jacket with the sleeves rolled up over his tattooed muscles, to best advantage.

'General, may I have full technical details of your new range of weapons? *Warrior of Fortune* would like to buy exclusive rights to details of weight, bore, stock-length, magazine capacity, fire-rate—'

Ashnak eyed Ugarit. The Tech-Corporal shrugged in an embarrassed manner.

'She was interested, Lord General. What could I do?'

The words *elf stew* went through Ashnak's mind every time he looked into the elf's warm golden eyes, but it is never entirely wise to offend the Press.

'You can have an exclusive on any details cleared for general release,' he said pointedly. 'We shall be issuing a conference statement *later on.*'

The elf reluctantly left the table.

'That', Ashnak said, 'brings me to the subject of these negotiations. We've won a victory here at Nin-Edin. That's why my orcs are celebrating. But I think ahead, gentlemen. I think about the next few years. As you say, orcs are not well-respected.'

Cornelius Scroop, re-seating himself on the greasy blanket, snorted.

Ashnak continued. 'The marines want to come to a business arrangement with Graagryk. We have a problem, gentlemen. Namely – arms manufacture.'

Vanderghast took her eyes off Magda and gaped. '*What?*'

'We have a limited supply of the new weapons you've seen. At some point soon, we're going to need to make more. However, gentlemen, you will have noticed that we have very little in the way of an industrial base up here in the Demonfest mountains – which is why my Corporal Ugarit has done a great deal more experimental weapons *development* than manufacture. We need an ally who *does* have a substantial economic base.'

Ashnak flexed his talons.

'The economics of the problem are simple. It's Dark-damned expensive to manufacture arms, because they're complex – so we'll have to make more than we ourselves need, purely to keep the price down to something economic. We will then have a surplus to sell.'

Simone Vanderghast looked at Cornelius Scroop. Then both of them looked at Magda van Nassau. She, in the process of lighting a long and slender roll of pipe-weed, glanced up. 'The general is not the sort of orc you're used to dealing with, Chancellor. Do try to bear that in mind.'

'A recent but Classified development means that the orc marines are no longer seriously challenged by forces such as Amarynth's. We would have very little trouble in coming south and taking over a kingdom, or a duchy. But I find,' Ashnak said reflectively, 'that warfare tends to wreck a country's economy. We don't have time to rebuild it if we're going to get a decent arms trade up and running in the next few months.'

The Chancellor and the Captain stared, the glazed shock on their faces giving way to something Ashnak had no trouble in identifying. Greed.

'This needs thought,' Captain Vanderghast said.

'Have some more food while you're thinking.' Ashnak snapped his fingers, and Ugarit's stewards replenished the plates. The halflings dug into the traditional mountain dishes of blackbirds, thrushes and snails.

Ashnak pondered the advisibility of eating raw food and decided against it. Even if it were dead raw food, it would probably not be tactful.

'I'll leave you gentlemen to discuss matters.' He beamed at Magda. 'And catch up on old times.'

Ashnak headed between the orc marines fox trotting across the dance floor, making for the bar. His grunts greeted him with shouts and cheers. The wooden boards echoed to the stomp of combat boots. Witch-ball lights flashed. The Badgurlz ripped into keyboard, strings and horn with vigour.

Perdita del Verro passed him, swaying to some ancient unheard ancestral music of her elvish blood. Major Barashkukor wheeled around on the podium, baton still keeping the rhythm, fixed his eyes on her, and began to sing:

'Yes sir, that's my baby;
No sir, don't mean maybe—'

Ashnak fixed Barashkukor with a baleful glare. The band clattered and screeched into silence. The milling throng on the dance floor slowed to a halt, gazing apprehensively at their general.

Barashkukor audibly swallowed. He tapped his baton on the edge of the podium.

'Ta-ta, ta-*ta*-ta, TAH!' he murmured, and as the music restarted, launched into:

'Sir, yes, sir! that's my baby;
Sir, no, sir, don't mean maybe;
Sir, yes, sir! That's my baby now . . .'

'Better,' Ashnak grunted, reaching the bar. 'Ah. There you are.'

Both Will and Ned Brandiman slitted their eyes against light brilliant after Nin-Edin's dungeons, wearing their cut-down, borrowed DPM combat trousers and jackets over their bruises with some dignity.

'You wanted another damn fur-jockstrap villain,' Ned Brandiman said, flicking back straggling brown hair that Ashnak only marginally resisted bellowing at him to get cut. 'We've got you one.'

A northern barbarian peered up at the bar, his wolf-pelts cleaned of campaign dirt, and his wide-horned helmet balanced precariously on the back of his head. He glared up at Ashnak and bawled, 'Warriors of the North cannot live within walls! Our honour lives with us under the sky, not in amongst the stink of elves and halflings and orcs. Could we at least have *one* frigging window open?'

'See what I can do,' Ashnak promised as he steered the three of them back to the conference table.

'Lord Blond Wolf,' he introduced, as the barbarian scrambled up a pair of steps on to his seat.

'My sons,' Magda added. 'Wilhelm and Edvard van Nassau, Princes of Graagryk.'

'We prefer to think of ourselves as defence analysts,' Will said sourly, sitting down on his cushions with some care.

Simone Vanderghast glanced up from her plate and said shrewdly, 'General, why are you so anxious to let marine weapons out of your own hands? Given how orcs are regarded, it's foolhardy.'

'The Dragon's geas on these weapons involves certain conditions. Training, gentlemen. *Training*.' Ashnak gestured expansively as he resumed his seat. 'These weapons just don't work for untrained personnel. What is going to have to happen, gentlemen, is that the orc marines get used as cadre troops, sent out to whoever buys the surplus weapons, to train that country's troops in their use. Make them into marines. And – once a marine, always a marine. Loyal to *other* marines.'

Grunts crowded past the conference table, queuing for the buffet the stewards set out on the bar. One orc returned, balancing a glass and digging into a loaded paper plate. 'Why do I always get the bit with the boot in it?' she complained.

Chancellor Scroop put down his knife and fork. He swallowed greenly. 'Your firepower demonstrations earlier today were . . . interesting. As was the tour of Corporal Ugarit's workshops. But . . . How could this arrangement possibly work? We couldn't sell these arms to just anyone.'

Ashnak nodded to Magda.

193

'It's necessary to legitimately sell surplus arms to fund manufacture.' Magda leaned her small muscular arms on the table top. 'I say legitimately, because – as we all know – the High King and his Council are clamping down on anything that looks remotely dodgy. What the marines can do for Graagryk in that respect is simple. They can provide end-user certificates, certificates to show that we've sold our arms to a good, Light-fearing land that needs them to defend itself against the left-over Horde.'

Simone Vanderghast fingered her sword-hilt. '*End-user certificate.* I like it.'

Ashnak drank his beer down in one swallow, belched and wiped his wide, lipless mouth.

'Lord Blond Wolf here, perhaps,' the orc rumbled, 'comes from a small northern Light-loving kingdom which needs to defend itself against evil neighbours?'

Magda's eyes danced. 'They do have a troublesome border, yes.'

'Probably a poor kingdom,' Cornelius Scroop speculated. 'Most of the northern ones are – a bit of mining, if the dwarves don't get it; bit of forestry; nothing much for export.'

He paused.

'Be honoured to extend a loan, Lord Wolf.'

The northern barbarian picked up a dish, stuck his finger in it, licked it and remarked, 'Fish eggs.' He then fixed his ice-pale eyes on Ashnak.

'I'll lend you frigging orcs my *name*, like the lady here explained to me, and that's all you swiving sons of goats will get from me! I wouldn't touch your arms with a shit-pole. Honest iron's for me! Honour of the north!' He slurped a beer tankard dry. 'Couldn't afford 'em anyway. Ship 'em where the fuck you please, just not to us. Bugger our economy if you did. But for the right price you can use our name.'

'Ah . . . yes.' Cornelius Scroop blinked at Vanderghast.

The Badgurlz marines reached the end of a number and screeched into silence, dropping their instruments and ploughing through the startled dancers in a flying wedge aimed at the bar. Major Barashkukor left the podium and approached a corner table where Commissar Razitshakra sat, the peak of her cap pulled down, taking surreptitious notes.

'Razzi . . .'

The commissar turned her back. 'Suspect little creep! Fraternizing with civilians. *Elvish* civilians, at that.'

The major moped back towards the bandstand and the returning Badgurlz.

'Won't speak to me since she came back from the commando

194

mission,' he muttered. 'Isn't *my* fault I didn't go on a commando mission. I'd *like* to go on a commando mission. Mistress del Verro knows how to appreciate a soldier, even if she is a civilian . . .'

A light came into the small orc's eyes, and he marched out on to the dance floor, and tapped Perdita del Verro's orc partner on the back.

Sergeant Varimnak glanced over her shoulder. She freed one hand and pushed her talons through her cropped white crest in a soldierly manner. 'Just doing my bit to cement interspecies relations, sir.'

Perdita, standing head and shoulders taller than her partner's muscular bulk, rested in the orc's arms, dancing with her golden eyes half shut.

'May I have the —erm —the pleasure of this dance?' Barashkukor asked the elf.

She ignored him.

Varimnak looked down lazily. 'Sir —fuck off, sir.'

Left standing, the major plodded dispiritedly towards the bar. The Badgurlz band, with a certain amount of schadenfreude, began to play *He Was Her Orc, But She Done Him Wrong*.

'General.' Cornelius Scroop recalled Ashnak's attention. 'This has a promise of being profitable, true – you orcs will be developing and making arms, ostensibly for your own defence, and for the defence of certain minor kingdoms; while being funded by us and using our industries.'

Ashnak nodded. 'We'll make arms for any mercenary band, enemy country, or overseas force who'll pay. They'll have to hire marine instructors, or the weapons will remain deactivated. The price of Dagurashibanipal, gentlemen, the moral of which is: never unnecessarily kill a dragon, they have graveyard tempers.'

'But,' Scroop went on doggedly, '*you're an orc.*'

Commissar Razitshakra shouldered past the long table. Ashnak overheard her spit, 'Fraternizing with civilians!' as Sergeant Varimnak left the dance floor, the elf journalist on her arm.

The Badgurlz sergeant stopped, grinned, polished the studs on her black leathers, and remarked, 'Hey, man! I hear *some* of us have done more than fraternize . . .'

Varimnak's gaze deliberately shifted to the band podium.

Commissar Razitshakra stomped off.

Magda Brandiman slid to the floor in a flurry of silk. 'You'll have to excuse me, sirs. Powder my nose.'

Ashnak grunted an absent-minded acknowledgement. He prodded his disappointingly immobile meal, and glared at Cornelius Scroop and Simone Vanderghast. 'Of course I'm an orc!'

Tech-Corporal Ugarit stared across the dance floor. 'The tuba's a musical instrument, isn't it, General?'

'*What?* Yes, Corporal. It is. Why do you ask?'

'It's just that Major Barashkukor appears to be wearing one.' Ugarit pointed. 'You can see his boots sticking out of the bell-end.'

Ashnak's eyebrow lifted as he watched Commissar Razitshakra stalk back across the dance floor with a highly satisfied expression.

'Orcish high spirits. Victory celebrations,' he said confidently to the two influential halflings. 'Now, as we were saying . . .'

Some minutes later, Magda Brandiman emerged back into the main hall. She tapped an orc's shoulder where he leaned morosely on the bar.

Barashkukor leaped six inches into the air and regarded the female halfling with wild eyes. 'I didn't do it! It wasn't me!'

'Woman-trouble, soldier?'

The battered orc major sighed. His shoulders relaxed. 'Sure thing, ma'am – I mean, your Grace.'

'News gets around.' Magda gathered her silk petticoats and turned, regarding the dance floor, and the oblivious great orc at the conference table. The corner of her mouth twitched up.

The female halfling proffered her arm.

Barashkukor glanced to either side, then over his shoulder, and finally back at Magdelene van Nassau. He pressed one spindly finger to his chest. 'Me, ma'am?'

'A little jealousy,' Magda Brandiman said, 'never hurt anyone.'

Barashkukor tugged his tunic straight, stuck his small snout in the air, gripped Magda's hand and waist, and waltzed off past a startled orc commissar and elf journalist. The Badgurlz band played *It Takes Three To Tango*.

When Magda returned, the great orc was tapping his talons on the tablecloth.

'But you're an orc!' Chancellor Scroop wailed, in the tones of a halfling seeing an opportunity for profit vanishing. 'No one will *ever* trust an orc!'

Simone Vanderghast agreed. 'The High King would have an army in Graagryk in days!'

Corporal Ugarit chuckled; a thin, high sound. 'Let 'em send an army! We're not afraid of magic now, not even Southern magic, no we're not, let 'em come, I'll have 'em, I'll take 'em all—'

Ashnak lifted his fist and brought it down on the top of Ugarit's head. The kevlar helmet cracked. Ugarit beamed daffily, fell off his chair, rolled over on the floorboards and began to snore.

'There is some truth in what my corporal says,' Ashnak confirmed.

'However, my strategy at the moment doesn't involve fighting the High King and all his many, many allies. As I said, it involves peaceful trade.'

'But *how?*'

Ashnak eyed the two halflings. They did not seem anything like as convinced as he had imagined they would at this point. He scowled.

'As to how,' Magda Brandiman said, 'firstly, I am an accredited Southern Kingdom Duchess. Magda Brandiman can vanish, and Magdelene of Nassau return with no stain on her reputation. She could make the orcs and their general welcome in Graagryk . . .'

Ashnak beamed and nodded.

'. . . but of course, that would still give the High King and Council great excuse for suspicion. So that won't work.'

Ashnak's heavy jaw dropped.

'But that was our plan!' he spluttered.

'That won't work *alone,*' Magda emphasized. 'However. I have the perfect answer. It will turn the orc marines into Graagryk's trusted allies; and by that move, make them the Light and the High King's allies too.'

'What is it, your Grace?' Cornelius Scroop queried.

Simone Vanderghast said, 'Your Grace, the city would welcome your return. How we would welcome it! Only I don't understand what you can do about this political problem of orcs being unacceptable in the Southern kingdoms . . .'

'I can make the orc marines respectable,' Magda Brandiman said.

She rested her diminutive chin on her interlinked fingers, and met Ashnak's bemused gaze. She smiled.

'I can make the *general* of the orc marines respectable,' the Duchess Magdelene said. 'Ashnak. Will you marry me?'

'*No!* Listen up: I'm telling you for the last time! I won't do it!'

'Yes you will.'

'It isn't what we planned! It's nothing like it!'

'I know.'

'Dark damn it, halfling, I am *not* going to marry you!'

'Yes, you are.'

'*Fuck off and die!*'

'If that's what you want. But let me hear you tell me twice.'

'I'm *not* getting *married!* No way!'

'No industry. No arms trade.'

'I don't care!'

'No Magda Brandiman.'

'So what!'

'You'll do it. When you get to my age, you know these things.'

'And how old *are* you, exactly?'

'Let's just say I don't look as though I have two sons in their late forties, do I?'

'I won't do it! I'm a marine, and I'm an orc; and when an orc marine says something, he means it, and I'm saying it now: we are *not* getting married!'

11

FOUR HUNDRED MILES to the south
of the Demonfest mountains, the Duchy of Graagryk lies on the flat
lands bordering the southern coast of the Inland Sea. Snow perches
pristine white on roofs and leafless trees, as it properly should, and
does not clog the boots of the Graagryk halflings as they hurry
towards the city's great cathedral.

Chimneys belch smoke at the edges of the frozen salt flats: smoke
that by magery is made to vanish even as the factories produce it. The
warm winter sun shines down on a clean land. Even the poorest
halfling housewife has the use of cleansing magery, and the very
cobbles in the streets gleam, cleaned of slush.

Baroque horns ring out. Graagryk's thronging citizens fall silent
entering the great halfling cathedral – which by orc standards is a
largish church. The pews being too small to take his bulk, Ashnak,
General of the orc marines, remains standing.

'—but I must talk to you *immediately* after the ceremony!'
Chancellor-Mage Cornelius Scroop protested. 'The political situation
is becoming urgent!'

Ashnak peered down at the flowing red tresses of the Chancellor-
Mage of Graagryk, at last making out a pair of mournful halfling eyes
regarding him from amongst swathes of haberdashery.

'See me later, stumpy,' the orc snarled, tugging the lapels of his
brown formal marine uniform straight. For some reason the tunic
collar seemed more than usually tight around his bull neck.

The holly decorations of Yule Solstice made the interior of the white cathedral bright with red and green. Candles burned in sconces. Outside the high, pointed windows the sky glowed a fierce winter blue.

'Ash-nak! *Ash-nak!* ASH-NAK!'

Orc marines, unmagicked snow crusting their boots, crowded the pews behind Ashnak. Uniformed, armed grunts sat up in the window embrasures, hung off candlestands, stood on the bases of pillars and the backs of pews, and sat hip to bony hip along the edge of the lectern. They chanted:

'I don' know but I been told
Orcs is vicious, mean and bold!'

There were probably a lot fewer marines present than there were halfling citizens of Graagryk, it was just, Ashnak reflected, that orc marines seem to take up more room.

Halflings in aprons, carrying mundane brushes and buckets, scurried from nave to aisle and back, hopelessly scrubbing and wiping in the orcs' wake. Ashnak resignedly lifted his combat boots, one at a time, as a Graagryk cleaner mopped under them. The nullity talisman around his leathery bull neck tingled. Breath fluttered under his breastbone.

'Urgency?' he queried.

The halfling Chancellor waved his lace-cuffed hands. 'The news is that companions-in-arms from the disbanded Dark and Light armies are ravaging the kingdoms from the South to the sea! They take towns and fortresses, are driven out again, take others; take good men for ransom and are paid, or kill their prisoners out of hand; it's terrible!'

Ashnak raised beetling brows in surprise. 'It is?'

Cornelius's round face sharpened. 'We have orders for arms flooding in from every kingdom for leagues around – contracts to be signed, they stipulate, only *after* this ceremony.'

'Civilians!' Ashnak showed his carious fangs. 'Don't worry. Your percentage is safe . . .'

Major Barashkukor trotted smartly down the aisle from the cathedral entrance. The small orc wore parade dress: black uniform brushed and belt buckle shining. His thin crest had been combed and watered flat to his misshapen skull, and he wore a new black stetson.

'Yo, sir!' He saluted, taking off his mirrorshades. 'She's coming, sir!'

Ashnak glanced down at his own polished black boots, worried by their unorcishly pristine splendour. 'The ring?'

'Sir, got it, sir! Here, sir.' Barashkukor patted the top pocket of his black tunic. His spindly, clawed fingers groped at the cloth. Suddenly panic-stricken, he dug his hand into the pocket, and brought it out with a sigh of relief, clasped around a small gold ring, plain except for some script engraved around the inside.

'One size fits all, they said. Nice piece of goods, sir.'

'Should be. I had enough trouble to get hold of it.'

'*Ash-nak! Ash-nak!*'

The orc marines cheered, their voices echoing up into the low cathedral roof, and abruptly fell silent. The organ sonorously blasted out a few bars of something Ashnak charitably recognized as the orc marine march. A Badgurlz marine added her saxophone to the cacophony. Ashnak turned his head, looking back down the aisle.

Magda stood in the doorway, silhouetted against bright snow and blue sky and the crowds in Graagryk's main square. Her satin and white lace dress trailed in the trodden slush from the orc marines' boots. A maid in a pink satin farthingale, her brown hair braided up on her head, picked up the train and walked down the aisle behind Magda.

'Erm.' Barashkukor spoke *sotto voce*. 'Isn't that *Ned* Brandiman carrying her train? Sir, I mean Edvard van Nassau, sir.'

Ashnak nodded his great tusked head ponderously. 'Yes, Major. That's him.'

'Is this what he does, sir?'

Ashnak sighed. 'I don't think it's *all* he does. Scroop mentioned something about him building a fireworks display for the celebrations afterwards . . .'

Magda walked sedately forward between lines of orc marines and the burghers of Graagryk, all of them cheering so loud that the music of the organ was drowned out. A veil of white lace and diamonds covered her delicate face, flowing back over her hair that today was long and blonde and curly. Plain white silk cupped her small breasts, hugged her narrow hips, and foamed in lace and frills around her tiny white-booted feet. Ashnak recognized Archipelago mulberry silk, the purchase of a single bolt of which can beggar a ducal household.

A shaven-headed halfling priest walked out on to the steps before the altar, his purple robe sweeping the marble. 'People of Graagryk! Merchants, militia, and great Duchess! We are gathered together at this Yuletide Solstice to perform a solemn ceremony . . .'

Out of the side of his wide mouth Ashnak muttered, 'Ought I to be doing this?'

Barashkukor patted his elbow in a fatherly manner. 'Yes, sir, you should, sir. Think of how popular it's going to make you. And the rest of us. And besides, sir, she's . . .'

Ashnak's heavy brows lowered. '*Yes,* Major?'

The small orc spread his hands widely. 'The boys love her, sir. She's – erm – been like a mother to us.'

Ashnak had no more time to speak. Magda Brandiman arrived at his side, her train-bearer in her wake; and the great cathedral full of orcs, citizens, vagabonds, burghers, deserters, merchants and mercenaries became hushed. He looked down, and further down, and gazed at the bright blue eyes he could see through the thin veil.

Magda Brandiman winked.

The priest cleared his throat. 'Who giveth away this halfling?'

Will Brandiman took his mother's arm. Spruce, clean, scrubbed and polished, his greying black hair newly cut and his doublet and hose banished in favour of viridian silk coat and breeches, he still bore the traces of his beating. He regarded the large orc marine with a look that plainly denoted neither forgiveness nor finished business. 'I do.'

Wilhelm van Nassau looked for a moment at the manicured, muscular hand in his; glanced up at Ashnak, and somewhat unceremoniously shoved his mother's appendage at the orc. Ashnak took the small, hot hand in his own. His granite fist enclosed it entirely.

The priest coughed and adjusted his half-moon spectacles. 'We are gathered here on this auspicious occasion to join together in matrimony this orc and this halfling. If anyone knows of any reason why this marriage should not happen, let them speak now, or for ever remain silent.'

Ashnak glanced over his broad shoulder. The church was silent enough to hear a sergeant's stripes drop. Ranked orc marines looked back at him, quite a number grinning rather more broadly than he appreciated.

The priest's voice echoed sonorously:

'Do you, Ashnak of the Horde of Darkness, General Officer Commanding the Orc Marines, betrothed of the Duchess of this great city of Graagryk, take the halfling Magdelene Amaryllis Judith Brechie van Nassau to be your lawful wedded spouse?'

Ashnak looked huntedly from side to side. The bride's train-bearer chuckled in an unexpected baritone. Will Brandiman folded his arms; rather more purses at his belt than could be accounted for by his changing into the dress of a Graagryk prince.

Major Barashkukor, starry-eyed, nudged his commanding officer in the ribs. '*Sir!*'

'I suppose so,' Ashnak rumbled.

'Do you, Magdelene Amaryllis Judith Brechie van Nassau, Duchess of Graagryk, hereditary Holder of the Golden Cobble, Six

202

Hundred and Seventh Admiral of the Inland Sea, take this – this *orc marine* to be your lawfully wedded consort?'

'I'll think about it,' Magda said. 'Oh, all right then.'

'I hereby pronounce you heir and consort, orc-husband and halfling-wife,' the priest finished, 'and may the Lady have mercy on your souls!'

With a curious delicacy Ashnak fitted the ring to the halfling's largest finger. Scant seconds later, it seemed to him, Ashnak stood in the snow and trodden slush outside Graagryk's cathedral. The press of the crowd prevented him moving forward.

'Well, my love, we—'

Bells drowned out his words.

Wild in the snowy air, shaking ice down from the cathedral's gargoyles, the deep bells clanged out across the city. The citizen militia, in velvet and lace, brandished their halberds, leaning back in a cordon against the front rank of the crowd as the cathedral doors were thrown wide open.

'*What?*' Magda bawled.

'*We may have lost— I SAID WE MAY HAVE LOST—*'

Magda waved him to silence in the clangour of the bells. A dozen squads of orc marines clumped out at the double into the snow, shouting, cheering, and throwing snowballs. Company Sergeant Varimnak, her black leather uniform dark against the whiteness, bellowed orders.

The orc marines formed two smart lines leading out from the cathedral's entrance, unslung their AK47s, and on command let off a blast of automatic fire over the heads of the crowd. Halflings, Men, and the few elves present screamed, ducking. The orcs bellowed with laughter and fired the next volley lower.

'Marines, *tenHUT!*'

Ninety booted feet slammed into the snow as the honour guard came to attention. The orc marines nearest the cathedral doors held up an arch of pole-axes, warhammers and M60s.

'Here we go.' The halfling squeezed his hand with a surprisingly strong grip. Ashnak looked down at her and grinned.

'Yo!' He scooped her up, long-trained wedding dress and all, and sat her firmly on his shoulders. The female halfling, resplendent in white satin, silk and lace, turned her unveiled face up to the bright blue sky. She kicked her legs free of the skirts, her booted feet resting on his barrel chest; snatched off his peaked cap and waved it joyously at the crowd.

Major Barashkukor inflated his small chest and bellowed, 'Three cheers for Duke Ashnak and Duchess Magda! Hip, hip—'

'HOORAY!'

TAKKA-TAKKA-TAKKA-FOOM!

A volley of automatic fire ricocheted off the cathedral frontage. Stone chips spanged, and a gargoyle toppled over and fell with a dull thud into a snowdrift. Orc marines, drinking from water bottles that patently obviously did not contain water, began to sing raucously and fire at random. Major Barashkukor beamed at them tearfully.

'I do so love a wedding,' he observed.

Magda Brandiman wriggled, sitting on Ashnak's shoulder, and threw her bouquet of winter blossoms into the crowd. A stocky figure in pink silk straight-armed a burgher out of the way, snatched the bouquet out of the air, and in a gruff voice bellowed, 'Me next!'

'Your stepsons,' Magda said demurely, 'they really *do* need a father's hand . . .'

'"Stepsons"!' Ashnak groaned.

Magda reached down a hand upon which the veins were beginning to stand up. She took Ashnak's horny hand in her own. Her ring caught fire from the sun. He slitted tilted eyes against the light, and his talons spiked her expensive silk bodice, drawing her down to where he could plant a kiss squarely on her mouth.

'You can't keep a bad orc down.'

The orc Duke surveyed the halfling city of Graagryk and looked up at Magda van Nassau. He belched and grinned.

'We may have lost the Last Battle – but we definitely won the war!'

BOOK 3

WAR CRIMES

PROLOGUE

THE AMERICAN MARINE walked through the open door into the bar of *The Goat and Compasses*, ducking his head to enter.

Amy, behind the bar, registered him first as a shadow against the light. She put on her professional smile. 'What can I get you?'

'Whiskey. Please.'

An American accent, with a slight Middle European edge. Thirty, maybe thirty-five; carrying himself with a tensile spring in his step. Amy read the brown identification tapes sewn above the breast pockets of the crisp brown-and-ochre camouflage jacket: STRYKER, one read, and the other, US MARINES.

Conscious of the stir among the pub's regular clientele, she had time to study the sturdy American, register camouflage colours made recognizable by weeks of TV Gulf War news broadcasts, and then the darts match in the snug broke up, and one of the older men from up on the housing estate said, 'What are you having, mate? Bloody good job you did out there. That's what I say. Bleedin' good job. C'mon, what're you having?'

The American marine rested his elbows on the polished bar. Under a forage cap his blond hair, shaved down almost to the scalp, gleamed under the pub lights.

'Whiskey,' he repeated quietly.

'Good for you, mate. Amy!'

'I'm here.' She poured a measure, watching the marine drink while she served others. There were lines about his eyes, as if he had spent time squinting into Arabian sunlight. She recalled news videos of similar men loaded with seventy-pound packs, piling out into rocky wastes blasted by aircraft and sown with mines. You could not tell, under the camouflage jacket, if his heavy arms and shoulders were tanned, but she thought they might be. She tried to make more eye-contact.

'So what was it like out there, mate?' an old man persisted. 'I saw it on the telly. Kill any wogs, did you?'

The American drank off half the whiskey. He leaned on the bar, in a position from which he could see both the public and the saloon bar door. Amy waited, almost holding her breath.

The brief roar of Tornado fighter jets flying back to RAF Chicksands vibrated through the building. The marine did not flinch. The regulars were turning back to their conversations, or watching the TV above the bar; the younger lads were playing the video machines, and Amy, flustered, wiped her hands on the bar-cloth. 'Sorry about that. Sorry.'

The American raised his eyes from his glass.

'No harm, ma'am.' The quiet, accented voice did not alter.

Outside the lounge-bar window, Darren – somewhere between the ages of seventeen and nineteen, wearing engineer boots, and civilian copies of military-issue combat trousers, and a ripped Megadeath T-shirt – took out his black-bladed, serrated, guaranteed SAS Commando (style) knife and scored long lines on the bodywork of the parked US Army military jeep. He pressed the knife's point into the valves, deflating the tyres, and slashed at the rubber.

'You're fucked!' The older youth, Mark, wiped his acne-ridden upper lip. His words slurred. He leaned too close over Darren and his breath was hot and beery. 'You're fuckin' fucked! When he comes out.' He made the motions and noises of cocking a bolt-action rifle. '*Kchaa!*'

'I'm not bloody scared of him!' Darren wiped his streaming nose. He cast wary glances at the saloon-bar door.

Two crowded, rusty vehicles swung into the car park in a skirl of gravel, shouts, and thrown beer cans. Mark elbowed him.

'*Yes!* Mike and Billy're back!'

The American marine stepped out of the pub at that moment. Darren took him in from combat boots to the width of his shoulders. The man's pale eyes flicked over him, registering his presence but not giving it any importance.

'Fucking squaddie!' Darren grunted.

Mark leaned on Darren and raised his voice belligerently. 'Who the fuck do you think you are?'

Amy, collecting beer glasses from the pub garden's tables, had paused to let her eyes travel across the countryside visible from the small village. There, under rolling English downs, a radio-farm marking the presence of a NATO bunker. There, across farmland and towards the much-patrolled North Sea, the white spheres of golfball-transmitters . . .

She spun around as brakes squealed in the car park, followed by the hollow *bang!* of crunched metal. She ran to the wall, aware of drinkers looking out of the open windows and coming to the pub door.

A large Ford Escort slewed caterwise across the car park, its crumpled hood buried against the US Army jeep. Another car blocked the entrance. Ten or twelve youths that Amy recognized from the housing estate piled out of the cars and stood in a spread-out line between the crashed vehicle and the pub door, blocking the American's path to the jeep.

''Ere, you, you hit my fucking car!' Aggressive, daring a denial of the blatant lie, a tall and heavy-shouldered young man faced off against the American. 'There I was an' you ran right into me. S'right. What you going to do about it?'

The marine said levelly, with that slightly Germanic accent, 'Drive away.'

'No, you bloody ain't, my son. No fuckin' way!'

Six of the young men began banging their fists and the flats of their hands on the jeep, laughing, rocking it on its wheelbase. Amy snapped her fingers at the assistant barman peering through the pub window and mouthed *Phone, Police*. The barman nodded and vanished.

Caught without being able to cross the car park and get back into the pub, Amy stood and watched as the large American soldier came to a halt. He surveyed the shouting, raucous young men with a weary acceptance.

'I don't want any trouble,' he stated.

The jeep failed to turn over. The dark-haired youth she vaguely recognized as Darren bawled, 'Bleeding camel shaggers. Think you're so bloody hot, don't you? Well, come *on* then. *Do* something. Unless you're chicken!'

The marine's eyes fixed on the middle distance, a stare that was not cold or angry or anything very much. Amy felt her stomach twist, abruptly afraid, not for this calm man, but for the half-drunk, violent children facing him. The American had moved with an economic

209

grace, no energy wasted; and now he merely stood, nothing to prove, waiting until their voices died away.

'If I were you,' he said, 'I'd get out of here before the cops arrive.'

'Chicken! Faggot!' The dark-haired youth jabbed his middle finger in the air. 'Fuck *you*, asshole!'

Amy twisted the bar cloth between her suddenly cold hands. She stepped towards them whispering 'Stop,' just as the gang of youths shouldered forward together. The American's feet moved. His eyes widened.

Without any warning, the earth turned suddenly sideways.

Behind the American the air curdled and *opened*.

Amy fell and barked her knuckles against the car-park wall. Her fingernails broke as she dug her fingers into the brickwork, grinding her heels into the dirt to stop herself skidding across the car park towards the sprawling youths and the American. The earth swivelled up and sideways, so that it seemed she hung against the gravel, pulled towards the vast dark hole in the air that opened near the main door of *The Goat and Compasses*.

The American vanished into it.

'*Nooooooo . . . !*'

Screams, cries, a young man weeping; air sucked as if from a depressurizing cockpit; the crunch of metal as parked cars slid across the gravel and into each other; a sharp crack of snapping wood as the pub sign broke and fell *across* the air—

Her bloodied fingers lost their hold on the wall. Amy screamed and plummeted towards the void.

Pressure vanished. She fell to earth in a sliding curve that raked gravel across her arms and thighs, banging her head against the bumper of a car. The bodies of young men, breath sucked from their lungs, sprawled across the tarmac like the aftermath of a battle.

There were sirens, after that, and a fire engine, and crowds came out from the houses in the village street, and arrests for disorderly behaviour. A police sergeant came and put his coat around Amy while the ambulancemen checked her for shock and bandaged her hands.

'It was like a hole!' She looked up, eyes red-rimmed. A coal of fear burned in them that would not go out, but would remain an ember in her for the future. 'A *hole*. In the air. Like a door opening behind him. I saw it – he *fell*. Into nowhere. There wasn't anywhere to go, but he just vanished. I . . . I saw what it looked like, where he went. I saw the other side. *And it didn't look like here at all*.'

This was before the TV or newspaper reporters or military police arrived. She told her story only once, then, and another quiet, dangerous man in marine uniform ordered her to be silent, to admit it all the product of concussion, a hallucination, female nonsense . . . and could she please give them any *real* information as to the whereabouts of the missing man, Sergeant John H. Stryker of the US Marine Corps?

1

THE SUMMER SUN blazes down on the final of Graagryk's first annual Orcball League.

Stands full of halfling workers watch the game, cheering; in their shirtsleeves, with knotted hankies on their heads.

'Of course,' Chancellor Cornelius Scroop remarked distastefully, 'this game is nothing but a crowd-pleaser.'

'URP!' The great orc Ashnak, granite-skinned, Man-tall, and wide, sprawled in his chair, towering over the halflings in the Ducal box. He dug into the hamper by his seat, snared half a boar, and chomped his steel-strong jaws into it.

'General!' Scroop reproachfully wiped boar-grease from his court dress.

'Master Cornelius, I'm particular about my food these days.' Ashnak belched and threw the stripped bone over his shoulder. 'As befits a Ducal Consort, I refuse to eat anything that hasn't stopped moving yet.'

Out in the exposed arena, sweating orc marines plunged their heads into water barrels and loped back into the game, shaking sprays of water from their pointed ears. Clouds of dust rose up into the still air.

Ashnak lumbered to his combat-booted feet, his bulk shadowing the box, farting with a crack as resonant as a grenade launch. 'COME ON YOU ORCS!'

The stadium hummed. A breeze brought the rank scent of the

Inland Sea. In the Ducal box, Graagryk's respectable halflings sweltered in their best finery: baggy silk breeches and bucket-top boots, steel gorgets and rapiers, long barbered curls, and occasional velvet face-masks. Down in the stands, halfling workers bought pies and wine and exchanged betting slips.

'GOAL!'

The dust began to clear. It disclosed a dozen grunts leaping up and down and cheering; and thirteen tall, slender bodies slumped motionless on the worn turf.

Halfling helpers rushed to remove the Dark Elf team's bodies.

A halfling mother in the Ducal box covered her child's eyes with her hand and tutted furiously, with an expression on her small features as if she were smelling something even more distasteful than sweaty orc.

'*That's* better.' Dew had long since burned off the field. Even under the thatched stands, the air seared. Ashnak reached into the hamper for a magnum of champagne and emptied half down his throat and the remainder over his head. Sticky courtiers glared at him.

The halfling cheerleaders on the far side of the arena chanted, 'Yaaay, Graagryk! G-R-DOUBLE-A, G-R-Y-KAY: Graaaaaagryk!'

At the near edge of the arena, Sergeant Varimnak lounged on the grass and chewed gum, conducting the orcish cheerleaders. Each of her small, spike-haired orcs wore studded leather boots, and filigree steel basques, and juggled maces and morningstars as if they were pompoms. The stand seats behind them were curiously empty.

'Two, four, six, eight,
Who do we annihiliate!
E-L, V-E-S: squeakies!'

'Half time!' the troll referee called from the field. 'New players!'

A brawny orc, stripped to the waist and wearing combat trousers and brightly polished boots, marched up and saluted Ashnak in the Duchess's box.

'General Ashnak, sah. Further representatives of the 'Orde's orc marines reporting to play orcball, *sah!* Permission to pound these 'ere hairy-footed bastards into the turf, sah?'

Ashnak lazily returned the salute. 'Permission granted, Sergeant Major Guzrak. Carry on.'

'Sah, yes, *sah!*'

Walking away, Sergeant Major Guzrak put his arm around one of the large orc marine's shoulders, and spoke to him in a fatherly fashion. 'Soldier, I has some good news and some bad news. The good news is, you've made the orcball team. The bad news is – as the ball . . .'

Captain Simone Vanderghast slammed a purse of gold down. 'That says your marines lose to us, General!'

Ashnak regarded the civilian militia captain's money. 'That's right, it *is* the home team next. You're on!'

He spat on his horny palm and held it out. The halfling looked at it, swallowed, shut her eyes, and shook his hand gingerly. She then wiped her palm repeatedly against the wooden walls of the box.

From the tunnel at the far end of the stadium, twenty halflings rode out into the arena on well-groomed ponies. Bridles and stirrups flashed in the sun.

Ashnak's eyebrows raised. 'They're mounted!'

Simone Vanderghast, smugly, said, 'Nothing in the rules, General, about how one gets around the field of play.'

A pony whinnied.

The halfling leader buckled a black, peaked helmet over his curls, brandished his crop, and galloped up to the centre line. Like all his fellow stout, hairy-footed riders, he wore white breeches, riding boots, and a bright scarlet doublet; and carried over his shoulder a long-handled mallet.

'One is ready to play!' he called.

A rumble went through the stands.

One of Ashnak's aides, a black orc second lieutenant, leaned back from his seat in front of the general.

'Little fellas really take to this game, sir, don't they?'

'So it seems,' Ashnak growled.

'I suppose a Kalashnikov *is* a missile weapon,' the lanky orc lieutenant reflected wistfully. 'It's a pity we're not allowed to use them, sir. But I suppose it makes it more sportin'. Pole-axes and warhammers, well, it really takes you back, sir, doesn't it?'

His head with its widely jutting ears and woodland camouflage forage cap bobbed in Ashnak's field of vision. The tiered seats were hardly orc-sized. Ashnak reached forward, grabbed the lieutenant's ears, slammed the orc's head forward on to the guard rail, and resumed watching the field over the orc's prone body.

'That's better, Chahkamnit.' Ashnak leaned back comfortably. 'I can see the game now.'

'Oh, jolly good, sir . . .' a weak voice whispered.

Cornelius Scroop waved his printed broadsheet-programme in front of Chahkamnit's lugubrious orcish features. It did not noticeably revive him.

The troll referee brushed the field's dust from his knees without having to bend down. He adjusted his loincloth and bellowed, in a voice loud enough to penetrate to the highest back row of the stadium:

'Final half! These are the *rules*. The object of the game is to get the orc's head in the bucket. *That* bucket for you orc marines, and *this* bucket for the halfling team. Those are *all* the rules. There will be a new ball in just a moment!'

Somewhere in back of the stands there was a scream, a swish of metal, and a sticky thud.

'And now—'

The grunts in the lower stands cheered as a linesman returned with the new ball. It dripped a green trail behind it, and the tusks shone in the sun.

'*—play on!*'

The troll referee hurled the severed orc's head towards the middle of the arena, lumbered into a sprint towards the far stands, and dived over a plank barrier. A few seconds later an optical device of metal and lenses appeared over the edge of the bunker.

'I must say, General,' Cornelius Scroop remarked disapprovingly, 'the referee doesn't seem to exercise much control over the game.'

'"Control"?' Ashnak said blankly.

Simone Vanderghast chuckled, pointing at the halfling leader who raised his mallet, swung it forward, and whacked the orc's head towards the marine end of the arena. 'Your team isn't even on the field yet, General.'

HHHHHHHHHHHRRRRRRRMMMM!!!

Sergeant Major Guzrak, at the head of a squad of fifteen grunts, gunned the motor of his Harley Davidson and zoomed out on to the field. His orc squad fanned out, steering their motorbikes casually with one hand, and brandishing polo mallets with the other. The sun glinted on swords and maces slung across their backs.

'But,' Cornelius Scroop protested, 'but— but—'

Guzrak skidded his Harley in a half-circle and saluted.

'I say, sir,' Second Lieutenant Chahkamnit remarked dazedly. 'The sergeant major's got a mascot on his handlebars. How nice.'

Ashnak's brows drew down in a massive frown. He glared at the pink fluffy toy orc adorning Guzrak's Harley Davidson. The marine sergeant sweated and shuffled.

' 'S lucky, sah. Honest, sah.'

'I think,' Ashnak purred, 'we'd better win. Don't you?'

Sweat trickled down Guzrak's green face. 'Yessah!'

The cloudless sky seared. Halfling linesmen sprayed water to damp down the dust. The crowd roared, chanting.

'One has the ball!' a pudgy halfling in a red coat called, leaning off

215

her pony to whack the orc's head. 'One has the— *urk!*'

Sergeant Major Guzrak hooked his mallet under the halfling's, expertly flicked her off her pony, and rode off down the field in pursuit of the bouncing orc's head.

The halfling sat up dizzily. 'One *had* the ball . . .'

Simone Vanderghast cricked her neck glaring up at Ashnak. 'General, have you ever considered playing this game fairly?'

'Yes.'

Halflings rose to their feet, cheering, as four of the red-coated riders charged back to the sidelines, dropped their mallets, picked up stout spears, and galloped across to form an escort for the halfling with the ball. A biker orc zoomed to a halt just too late.

'Body detail!' Sergeant Major Guzrak bawled. 'Body bag! Prepare to recover marine corpse. Corpse . . . wait for it, wait for it . . . corpse: recovered! Prepare to make substitution.'

The halfling riders galloped down the field, one slinging her spear between the spokes of a biker's wheel. The Harley flipped. The orc rider sat wide-legged on the ground, shaking her head.

The pudgy halfling dismounted from her pony, mounted the bike, and opened the throttle wide, mallet swinging. 'One has the ball! One *has* the b—'

The grunt whose Harley had been downed lowered her shoulder. She butted the halfling's bike head-on. The halfling hurtled over the handlebars and thudded into the turf. The orc marine expertly swung the bike round, remounted it, and gunned it into action. Mace in one hand, mallet in the other, she charged the halfling team.

The halfling leader couched his mallet under his arm, pointed end forward. He dug his spurs into his pony's barrel-sides, and galloped towards her from the opposite direction. 'I say, tally-ho!'

SPLAT!

'Better than huntin' peasants, what?' the scarlet-doubleted halfling called back gaily over his shoulder, trotting off.

Ashnak heard a low growl go around the stadium. Several of the rows began to boo.

'Well, *really!*' Cornelius Scroop said. 'How can they boo their own side? Ungrateful *plebs*.'

'*I've* got the ball!' the pudgy halfling shrieked, still dismounted, emerging on foot from the scrum. The ball dripped green down her scarlet jacket. She waved it triumphantly. Ashnak glimpsed her startled expression as twenty halflings on ponies and fourteen orcs on Harley Davidsons converged on the spot where she stood.

The resulting dust cloud hid threequarters of the field. Chancellor Scroop fanned his hand before his face, pale with exhaust fumes.

216

'We got the ball, sah!' Guzrak cried, emerging out of the ruck on his battered bike.

'*We* have the ball,' the halfling leader contradicted, galloping out of the enveloping cloud of dust. 'We have the . . . er . . .'

The halfling held up an unmistakable curly haired head.

'Oh dear . . .'

'That's more like it!' Ashnak enthused. '*Come on you orcs!* My money's safe,' he added to the ashen-faced Simone Vanderghast, and turned back to the field, slitting his eyes against the white sunlight, cheering along with the stands full of halfling workers.

The halfling leader galloped furiously back towards the entrance tunnel and reined in his pony.

'You there!' he shouted. 'Bring one's reserve mount!'

A huge shape loomed out of the heat and dust.

'Oh, *what!*' Ashnak slammed his fist down on the side of his chair, cracking the wood. 'Foul! The referee must be blind! At least,' the orc general added, 'he *will* be. Chahkamnit, make a note of that.'

The lanky black orc, now sitting well to one side of Ashnak's field of view, murmured, 'Very lenient of you, sir. Very sportin'.'

Ashnak leaned his elbow on the seat in front and, as Simone Vanderghast chuckled in his ear, watched the scarlet-coated halfling leader ride a huge, shaggy war-mammoth into the arena. It trumpeted, and pounded towards the marine end of the field.

'Never fear, you orcs!' Sergeant Major Guzrak dismounted from his Harley, standing at a smart parade rest. 'I has an infallible method of dealin' with such a fiendish war device, what I learned on the eastern frontier. A chargin' mammoth will never trample a fallen orc! Lay down, and stab upwards as it passes over you!'

The brawny orc sergeant flung himself to the turf, rolling on to his back and unsheathing his bayonet.

SPLATTT!

'So that's why we had so much trouble on the eastern frontier,' a mounted orc corporal remarked. She stopped her Harley, leaned down, and released something tiny that appeared to be armoured in minute links of mail.

'What's that?' Ashnak bellowed down.

'War-mouse, sir,' the orc corporal shouted, over the terrified trumpeting of the fleeing mammoth.

Ashnak got to his feet.

'Right, marines! In the absence of Sergeant Major Guzrak— *I'm* coming down to take over the team!'

The orc marines cheered. The halflings in the stands cheered. Simone Vanderghast scowled.

'Husband and Consort,' a new voice said.

Ashnak hitched up the urban camouflage trousers that he wore tucked into laced high-ankle boots. He removed the peaked cap jammed between his ears, revealing the tribal scarring of the fighting Agaku, and assorted marine tattoos.

'Magda!'

Ashnak whooped, slipped his hand between the female halfling's legs, and lifted her up bodily in a whirl of black leather skirts. The city's dignitaries tutted. He took her chin in his hand and planted a wet kiss squarely on her mouth. Her tongue probed his, darting.

'I've just arrived back from the arms factories.' Magdelene van Nassau, Duchess of Graagryk, seated herself, rearranging the flounces and layers of a skin-tight and full-length leather gown. Her hand dropped into the lap of Ashnak's combat trousers, groping and squeezing. As the assembled Councillors averted their gazes, her hand moved in thieves' fingerspeech.

Ashnak, his mind at first on other things, deciphered:

—*Urgent news! I must not speak of it in public. Even this fingertalk may be over-read!*

'With you in a moment, my love!' Ashnak vaulted over the front of the box and dropped down to the field, loping across towards the scrum of bikes, ponies, halflings and marines.

Magda described orcish sexual failings under her breath in fifteen languages. She snapped her fingers for her maid Safire to fan her in the summer heat; clapped formally, applauding the game; and addressed Cornelius Scroop.

'Our sales force abroad are doing *extremely* well . . . I rode back with the treasurer. He reports many interesting titbits – the price of saltpetre in Shazmanar; rumours from further up the coast that the Kraken is being a danger to commercial shipping; Queen Shula's lovers . . . But there, I mustn't bore you with gossip. COME ON YOU MOTHERFUCKER ORCS!'

Down on the field, Ashnak bestrode a Harley Davidson with a line of stickers on the engine casing, the most recent being a dark elf's head with a line diagonally through it. He gunned the motor. The stuttering concussion beat at his ears. In the stands, tiers of halfling workers rose to their feet, ten thousand mouths showing like wide Os.

'That halfling,' Ashnak pointed at the fastest rider, a stout curly haired fellow almost four feet tall. 'Termination with extreme prejudice!'

'Yessir!' The orc corporal gunned her Harley, unslung a mace off her back, skidded in a circle that brought her speeding up behind the pony and rider, and swung the weapon.

The riderless pony galloped off the field.

The corporal tripped a second rider off his mount and wielded her mace in one hand and a warhammer in the other; pounding the remains of both into the turf.

'Bit excessive, Corporal.' Ashnak, motor idling, glanced down at what was left.

'Yeah, well . . .' The grunt grinned. 'You know how it is at this time of the moon, sir.'

The squad of orc bikers formed up into an extended line, Ashnak at the centre, and roared down the field. Five of the ponies reared and ran away with their riders. The halfling leader, on foot, crimson coat stained with dust and blood, waved his polo mallet furiously.

'One is not going to be beaten by a miserable pack of greenies!'

An anonymous voice from the stands called, ''Oo you kiddin', guvner!'

The biker line hit.

'YO THE MARINES!'

Ashnak squelched the orc's severed head down into the opposing team's bucket. The halflings in the stands leaped to their feet, screaming applause. On Magda's right, the halfling mother held her child up for a better view of the field, spittle flying from her mouth as she howled, *'Are they marines?'*

The halfling tot lisped, 'They are mawines, Mama!'

Plumed hats soared up into the sunny air. Drums beat. The disposal teams wheeled their carts and shovels on to the field as the Badgurlz cheerleaders changed the scoreboards to the final 1–Nil result.

The surviving grunts drew themselves up and saluted in unison as Ashnak ambled back to the Ducal box. Magda leaned down and gave him her hand to kiss.

'I need to speak with you!' she hissed.

The orc licked the sweat from her palm. He reached up and pocketed Vanderghast's purse. 'Sure thing . . .'

'Ahem!' A large marine trotted up to the Duchess's box, coughing discreetly for an orc. She wore green DPM camouflage fatigues, her crest was shaved down to the regulation quarter-inch, and her boots gleamed. Magda deduced garrison rather than field troops.

'Sir, excuse me, sir! Message from the barracks. They need you back there immediately, sir.'

Ashnak wiped sputum from the thigh of his urban combat trousers. 'I'm busy! Tell Lugashaldim to handle it himself. Or I'll rip your head off and you can carry *that* back to him for an answer!'

'Sir, yes, sir!' Her leathery brow shone in the Southern Kingdoms'

heat, green skin pearled with sweat. 'Sorry, sir, *no*, sir. Need *you*, sir.'

Ashnak kissed Magda's hand. 'You'll have to excuse me, my little one. Present the Orcball League cup and make the relevant posthumous awards.'

'Hurry back, honey-cake!' Magda blew him a kiss. Her waving fingers moved in the signs for:

—*Damn it, marine, I need to talk to you* now!

Outside Graagryk Stadium, Ashnak glowered at his marine corporal. The orc saluted several times in succession and looked ready to continue it indefinitely. Ashnak picked the large orc up by her webbing and threw her head-first against the stadium wall. The masonry held.

'Pull yourself together!' he snarled.

The corporal staggered upright, weaving. She made as if to salute again and thought better of it. 'Confidential message for the general from Lieutenant Lugashaldim, sir. Please to report, the general has a visitor waiting for him back at the barracks.'

At that same hour, four thousand miles to the south-west of Graagryk and the Inland Sea, on the far side of all the Southern Kingdoms' vast civilization, and beyond the Deserts of Endless Sand, an orc marine mounted a podium in the main square of Gyzrathrani.

Two marines flanked him: hulking granite-skinned orcs stripped down to brown-and-ochre desert camouflage fatigue trousers, belt-magazines of .50 calibre ammunition draped across their brawny chests. The equatorial sun of Gyzrathrani beat down on their kevlar helmets and M16s.

Between them, standing some three feet six inches tall, the orc with spindly ears crammed down under a black stetson tugged on his black leather gloves, flicked the last grain of desert sand from his dress-issue black combats, and adjusted a pair of mirrorshade Raybans more firmly on his small snout.

He stepped up on to an ammunition crate placed on top of the podium.

'Gentlemen: good morning!'

He tapped the stand-microphone mounted on the podium with one neatly trimmed talon. The microphone squealed. The sound echoed around the palm trees, honey-glazed bricks and beehive-buildings of Gyzrathrani. Several of the assembled warlords – Mannish warriors with plumed head-dresses and long robes – drew back, their tasselled spears raised, until one called, 'It's only magic!' and another added, 'And not strong magic neither!'

220

From slit windows in the tall beehive-shaped buildings, the eyes of Gyzrathrani's sequestered male Men watched. Distant giggles were just audible.

'I am your sales-orc, marine Major Barashkukor,' the short orc announced. 'The demonstration you ordered will begin in just one moment.'

Barashkukor hastily checked his squad, assembled on the cobbles below the podium. Noon's shadows pooled under the soft-top army lorry; light and heat slammed up from the earth. The twelve orc marines in brown-and-ochre desert camouflage fatigues rapidly unloaded a vast heap of crates, boxes and steel cases from the truck.

'We here from Marine Sales and Services,' Major Barashkukor continued pleasantly, 'are pleased to welcome the warriors of— of the fine city of— of the excellent city of—'

'Gyzrathrani!' the orc corporal beside him hissed.

'—Gyzrathrani,' Barashkukor finished, 'to one of our private sales demonstrations. All right you orcs, move it!'

The two orc corporals left the podium and descended into the crowd. The tall, brightly robed warriors, bored, barely moved aside to let the marines pass.

'My assistants', the major continued, pulling at one ear and twisting it into corkscrews around his skinny finger, 'will demonstrate the weaponry available. But first let me tell you a little about ourselves.'

In the square, a team of four orcs held up Kalashnikovs over their heads, then held up the curved magazines, and, in unison, fitted the one to the other.

'We are the Orc Marine Armaments Co.' Barashkukor drew himself up proudly. 'Orc marines have been providing the most sophisticated infantry, tank and air-war systems and services to discerning customers for, oh, it must be . . . over six months, now. *We* counter threats to *your* security.'

'Fully automatic – *fire!*' the orc corporal shouted. The fire team raised their Kalashnikovs to leathery, brawny shoulders and squeezed the triggers.

DAKKA-DAKKA-DAKKA-FOOM!

Shrapnelled brick flew across the main square, causing Gyzrathrani's warriors to throw up their hands and mutter spells of protection. Screams sounded as these failed. The warriors stared up at the craters gouged across the glazed brick walls of their beehive-shaped buildings.

'Our reputation', Major Barashkukor continued obliviously, 'comes from our inventive product line, and superb engineering. The orc marines are the recognized leaders in the field of anti-terrorism, security protection, and general all-out firepower.'

The orc marines around the truck bustled and came up with what appeared to be clusters of steel tubes on their shoulders. The corporal swivelled his heavy-jawed head, surveying the square, and pointed a gnarled finger at the tallest of the beehive-buildings. 'Target thirty metres, ten o'clock, high, one round, fire!'

FOOOMMM!

'We are particularly proud—' Barashkukor absently brushed brick-dust from the sleeve of his combats '—of our infantry-fired missile systems. We are fully aware of all of our clients' varied needs, and our experience in serving kingdoms, duchies, war-bands, empires and independent city-states makes us ideally suited to inform you about our multiple enforcement-systems.'

The two veteran orc corporals below the podium exchanged glances, mouthed '*What's* 'e say?', and shrugged.

Smoke and dust blanketed the main square, obscuring the blue sky. A heap of rubble now blocked the narrow streets on the west side, cascading down from the shattered building. The warriors of Gyzrathrani, retreating to the striped awnings and palm trees at the sides of the square, began to stamp their feet and chant a rhythmical desert magic.

'Should you purchase our systems,' the orc major continued, 'they come complete with orc marine cadre troops who will train you in their use, advise you on tactics and strategy, provide a secondary command-structure, and—'

KER-FOOM!

'We are also proud . . .' Barashkukor removed his hat and took off his Raybans. He surveyed the shrapnel fragment embedded through the stetson's crown, shrugged, and put his hat back on. He slitted his tilted eyes against the towering column of black smoke and orange flame that now blocked the eastern streets of Gyzrathrani. 'Also proud, I may say, of our anti-tank weaponry. Gentlemen, our weapons systems have the advantage of being entirely impervious to hostile acts of magery—'

Spear raised, screaming, a warrior-mage of Gyzrathrani charged the podium. Her face contorting, she screamed powerful spells and curses. The orc corporal raised his M16, sighted, and shot her between the eyes. The body's momentum carried it forward to thud against the portable podium, just under the banner that read *Orc Marine Arms Co. – Our Business Is Killing People*.

'Entirely impervious to magery— Where was I? Ah, yes.' Barashkukor beamed across the square in the general direction of those warriors who had taken cover inside buildings. He turned the volume of the microphone up.

'Our weaponry has a further advantage over magic, gentlemen, in that magic, while doubtless superior, takes decades of training; and our weaponry, while possibly inferior to planetary-level strategic magery, can be used after the standard twelve-week marine training course. I'm sure you can see the advantages when it comes to mounting a snap-decision campaign or responding to unprovoked retaliation.'

The orc marine squad, at the double, produced a small metal trailer upon which sat a pointed steel cylinder. Seeing this, the robed and spear-carrying warriors of Gyzrathrani frantically increased their mage-chants.

'That building *there!*' the corporal cried, with the expression of an orc who enjoys his work. 'Take it out!'

BOOOOOMM!

'Way to go!'

Barashkukor coughed brick-dust from his throat. In the silence, warriors crept out from under fallen palm trees and from behind walls, their exit cut off by the collapsed buildings to the north of the square, and the orc marine podium in the south.

'Warriors of Gyzrathrani!' Barashkukor pointed expansively at the crates still on the truck. 'Having seen some of our top-of-the-line equipment, let me introduce you to some of the less budget-straining second-hand equipment we can provide. Now, this job-lot of M16 assault rifles with M203 grenade-launchers, we ourselves bought back from the Syannis – as you know, the Syannis tribe campaign only one month in every twenty-five, for religious reasons, so I think I can safely say that we are offering this bargain lot in as-new condition . . . What am I bid?'

Bidding was brisk.

Later, with the truck and support vehicles on the road to the next settlement, Major Barashkukor relaxed in his staff car as they jolted south. The steel lock-box was heavy with silver ingots and copper bangles. His wide nostrils flared to the smell of hot metal and oil, and he sighed with pleasure.

'Only two more settlements. Be good to finish this tour of duty,' he remarked. 'Don't you think so, Corporal?'

Orc Corporal Uzkaddit, his regular driver, shrugged shoulders muscled like boulders and grinned. 'It has its good points, sir.'

'I suppose it does.' The small orc sighed. 'But I miss the dear old barracks back home in Graagryk . . .'

*   *   *

223

Outpacing the three marine guards at his heels, Ashnak ploughed through the door into the anteroom of his office.

Suddenly, the sweetness of decomposing flesh filled Ashnak's hairy nostrils. A sickly chill shivered across his leathery hide. With a creaking squelch, a tall figure lurched up from behind the office desk.

Its rotting uniform might once have belonged to an orc marine. The black combat trousers and woollen pullover with epaulets were white with mould, and hung in tatters. Albino flesh, dried and mummified, still clung to the skeletal figure looming up over Ashnak. Two mucus-white eyeballs swivelled in their sockets. The sun glinted on its bare ribs and flesh-stripped arm as the partly decomposed orc corpse saluted.

'Ssssir . . .'

'Lieutenant Lugashaldim.' Ashnak ignored the salute and seized his Undead officer by the front of his rotting Special Forces pullover. 'We get a visitor you can't handle, so you haul me out of the goddamn Orcball *finals* to deal with it – your ass is grass, soldier!'

It is always tempting to reprimand the Special Undead Services marines for insolence; Lugashaldim's grin, however, was probably entirely inadvertent.

'Sssir, the SUS can't act against him; we need you here!'

Ashnak dropped Lugashaldim, hitched up his webbing that strained to encompass his huge orc's body, and drew his sidearm. The Desert Eagle pistol all but vanished in his gnarled hand. He snapped his talons at the three M16-carrying marines. 'That door, forcible entry, *now.*'

The first marine rapidly crossed to the far side of the inner office door. His partner flattened herself against the wall on the nearside, weapon raised. At a nod from the other two marines, the first orc kicked the door open, the third charged in, M16 aimed, and his hoarse voice bawled, *'Freeze, motherfucker!'*

Ashnak, still holding the pistol, shouldered his way into the inner office. The hot Graagryk sun shone in on wall-maps, partly disassembled weapons, manuals and textbooks of strategy, map-tables, field-telephones, a heavy typewriter, and the vast stone desk transported down (with no little difficulty) over the four hundred miles of terrain called The Spine that lies between the Nin-Edin Marine Base in the Demonfest mountains and Graagryk.

A figure sat behind the desk.

'Shall I blow the mother away, sir?' The orc marine who had been acting as first doorman raised the M16 to his shoulder.

The temperature in the room plummeted. It grew so cold that the moisture covering Ashnak's eyeballs froze. He rumbled a deep

224

chuckle down in his chest, threw one camouflage-covered leg up on the corner of his desk, sat, took out a thick pipe-weed cigar, and shoved it in the corner of his tusked mouth.

'Out!' he growled. 'Lugashaldim, you too. Stay on guard outside. Move it, fuckheads!'

'Sir, yes, sir!'

The clatter of orc marine boots was punctuated by the slam of the office door. Ashnak shifted his huge bulk to a more comfortable position, struck his talon against the stone desk to create a spark, and sucked deeply on the glowing cigar.

Rime-frost dripped from window-ledges, the edge of the desk, and the chair in which the seated figure sprawled. Ashnak slitted his long eyes against the window's sunlight.

'*We* were at the Last Battle,' he growled. 'Where the fuck were *you?*'

The nameless necromancer laughed.

He lounged in the carved chair, a tall Man with black hair fastened in a silver ring at the nape of his neck. Through the sash of his long robe was stuck a flute, the brown colour of old bone, about the length of a halfling's thigh. The nameless necromancer fanned himself languidly with a war-fan, the struts of which had the sheen of dragonbone, and the folds the suspicious fineness of tanned Man skin.

'My creature grows insolent.' His voice set up echoes in the bones of Ashnak's skull, and his green-eyed gaze bored into the orc's eyes. 'My creature will be punished, unless he submits and pays me the proper respect.'

His patchwork robe of fine multicoloured leather was sewn with silver thread. The shapes of the patches were not, to anyone with a field-knowledge of anatomy, reassuring.

Ashnak drew deep on his pipe-weed and blew a plume of smoke towards the nameless necromancer. With his free hand he thumbed back the hammer of the Desert Eagle pistol.

'*Respect my ass!*'

The nameless necromancer's aquiline features tautened. A red spark burned deep in his black pupils. 'You will feel, slave, the wrath of the necromancer. Is that your wish?'

Ashnak bared his brass-capped fangs. 'Whaddaya want me to do, bang my head on the floor and beg for mercy? Things have *changed* around here.'

It became obvious that, wherever the nameless necromancer had spent the intervening twelve months since the Last Battle, it had not been far enough away that rumours of the orc marines had not reached him. His chin and his fine-featured face lifted as he brayed a laugh.

'Oh, very good. Very good! You must forgive me if I attempt to put our relationship back on its old footing. But I think very fondly of old times. Don't you?'

'Can't say as how I do,' Ashnak rumbled. He switched the cigar to the other corner of his heavy-jawed mouth. 'Dammit, you deserted the orc marines at the Last Battle!'

'But my sister The Named did not ride against you.'

'Thought you'd have robes made out of grey-and-white skin if you ever turned up again – maybe with yellow hair fringes. The Named never stood much chance against you.' Ashnak kept the pistol's muzzle steadily on the nameless's chest.

'You may spare yourself the trouble, Captain – and the ammunition.' The temperature in the office continued to drop. Sun glinted off icicles hanging from the cupboards and from Ashnak's boots. From the anteroom came the ululating howl of an Undead orc marine officer in pain.

Across Graagryk, dogs began to wail. The noonday brilliance dimmed, and the smell of fresh frost haunted the streets. The stench of an opened charnel house, sour-sweet and dizzying, crept under the doors of halfling houses, muddying the sun as far away as the arena, where the Duchess Magda looked up at the sky and shivered. Inside the barracks the orc marines stopped their various tasks and stood, ears pricked, heavy jaws hanging open, the seductive flute notes of an old slavery filling their ears.

Ashnak shook his heavy head and lumbered to his feet, boots apart, both hands gripping the pistol. The marine-issue dogtag talisman on its chain around his bull-neck thrummed with its nullification of sorcery. 'Fuck you, man! You're outta here. You're history!'

'So it *is* true.' Abruptly, the level of magic in the room increased. The nameless necromancer added smoothly, 'Now we shall be a great presence, the nucleus of a new Horde of Darkness. My creature Ashnak, little orc, little captain: you have been a good steward in my absence. Now – before I snap that silly talisman like a sugar-stick – *bow down and make your submission to me!'*

FOOM!

Ashnak's knees creaked. He caught himself with one hand against the desk. The Desert Eagle had bucked as it fired, and a shower of wood and plaster sprayed out of the wall behind the nameless necromancer's head, missing the target by a yard.

'It's like this.' Ashnak's bandy legs shook. He kept a strong grip on the edge of the stone desk. 'My orc marines are running the world's number one arms dealing and marine training business. You make one move against us, and all the kingdoms from the Northern Waste to the Antarctic Icelands will land on your neck, and how do you like *that*, you lich-humping, skinny little fuck?'

The sun dimmed. The clamminess of long-buried flesh crept across Ashnak's leathery hide. The nullity talisman whined. He sighted the pistol again, grip steady.

The room thawed.

'Consider yourself lucky', the nameless necromancer purred, 'that I have a sense of humour.'

The slender Man closed his war-fan and thrust it through his sash, reaching up to free his waist-length, fine black hair, smooth it, and then clasp it again in its silver ring. The summer sun warmed the office. Only the scent of old death remained from the power of moments ago.

'Riiiight . . .' The orc general stepped somewhat unsteadily round the desk and sank down into his chair. He rested the heavy pistol across his lap. He looked up at the ancient, youthful sorcerer, and picked meat from behind a cracked orc-fang.

'Lucky also,' the nameless necromancer added, smoothing the tanned Man-skin robes about his slender body, 'that this is nothing to me. A game, merely.'

'Game?' Ashnak sat back and put his combat boots up on the desk, re-lit his pipe-weed cigar, and tugged the urban-camo forage cap down over his neanderthal brows. 'You came all the way from Dark-knows-where to Graagryk for a game? *Suuure* you did.'

Deep in the nameless's black pupils, fire glinted. The thin-lipped mouth drew back in a smile.

'No,' the nameless necromancer corrected. 'I came all this way to bring you a message from my master – who wishes to see you. Now.'

Ashnak choked on pipe-weed smoke. '*Your* master?'

The nameless necromancer folded his arms. Feet apart, the slender curved eastern blade thrust through his sash, he might have been any young Man warrior fighting on the side of the Dark. Only the face, only the eyes, only the strong stench of carrion gave him away.

He reached for the door-handle.

'Oh,' the nameless necromancer said. 'Haven't you heard? The Dark Lord's back. And this time He's *really* pissed off.'

2

AT THAT SAME hour, but six thousand miles to the south-east of Graagryk, on the other side of the continent, a black orc crouched in the bush in the Forest of Thyrion.

Even with his keen elvish eyes it took Gilmuriel several minutes to discover her. When he finally spotted her, the elf strolled across the clearing and stood over her.

'I'm not at *all* convinced this is going to work.' Gilmuriel, elf Hunt-Lord and now marine lieutenant, frowned down at his sergeant. 'When the Forest-King of the Elves bought this equipment from your sales people, I *said* he was mistaken. We should never have given up the elven bow.'

Gilmuriel's previous dealings with orcs – filthy brutish creatures scuttling in darkness – had not prepared him for an orc who tucked sprays of creepers into her mottled uniform through loops sewn on for the purpose. Brown and green paint blotched her fanged orcish features. She had tied a red strip of cloth around her brow. Only the stink of orc was totally familiar. That and the coiled orc-whip hanging off her belt.

The orc sergeant looked up from cleaning her mud-splattered M16 assault rifle, lazily surveying the twelve elves who lounged in the bushes at the edges of the clearing, wearing their camouflage fatigues unwillingly. As usual, chores and tasks (such as cleaning weapons) had been abandoned when something more interesting presented itself. Four of the smaller female elves were singing a roundelay. The nominal Marine First Class was writing what appeared to be poetry on the back of his area map.

'Marine Belluriel Starharp!' the black orc snarled, wiping the sweat that shimmered in her quarter-inch unnaturally white crest. 'Get those elves into cover, dammit!'

'This is only a – what is your word? An *exercise*.' Gilmuriel smiled. 'We shall do it for as long it amuses us.'

Dakashnit, he thought, was a strange sergeant even for an orc. In between drilling the Elf King's reluctant conscripts she had a habit of smoking pipe-weed from her own private store, after which she was prone to develop a several-thousand-yard stare, and declaim, 'Don't bother me, man,' even when there was no representative of the Man race for miles.

'This *exercise* is under your command,' Gunnery Sergeant Dakashnit of the orc marines reminded Gilmuriel. 'What are your orders, L.t.?'

'Obviously we shall wait here until the craft returns to fly us back to the City of the Trees.'

A chugging noise sounded from above the jungle canopy. Gilmuriel stepped out into the clearing. A whirling blur emerged over the edge of the trees. Rotors whipping, pistons chugging, and vapour spurting from every joint, the steam Chinook helicopter hovered above the clearing.

Gilmuriel's arched brows curved, dipping into a frown. 'I don't care what you say, Sergeant – that thing will never replace the milk-white elven steed.'

'Not one of Ugarit's more successful efforts,' the orc admitted.

The helicopter's curved windows shone like the faceted eyes of giant insects. Sun slid down the olive-drab bodywork, shone in through the doors-off cargo bay. Gilmuriel took off his peaked forage cap, disclosing his pointed ears, and waved at the invisible pilot. The sunlight shone on his high cheekbones and the sleek braids decorating his shaggy golden hair.

TAKKA-TAKKA-TAKKA-FOOM!

A line of craters stitched across the clearing, spraying dirt high into the air. Gilmuriel threw himself flat, his arms over his head. He heard the screams of the other elves, and the crashing of bushes as they fled into the jungle, all hunt-lore forgotten in panic.

Engines roaring, the twin-rotored, steam-powered helicopter sank down into the landing zone. It touched, settled; and the motors cut to tickover. Pistons hissed. The smell of hot steam and coal drenched the evening jungle heat.

'Just orcish high spirits, sir!' Sergeant Dakashnit stepped over Gilmuriel on her way to the helicopter. She swung herself up, exchanged a few inaudible words with the pilot, and began throwing sacks out of the back of the flying machine.

'See you got the idea of taking cover,' she called. 'Works better when you're behind something, Lieutenant.'

Gilmuriel stood up and dusted himself down. His high cheekbones burned red. Swearing under his breath, he bawled into the jungle for the return of his squad. They slipped from the shadows and reassembled.

Dakashnit tossed him one of the sacks, single-handed. He caught it with a *whoof* of breath. It was a pack, dangling straps, and whatever was inside it was soft.

'Today,' the orc sergeant said, 'you elf marines get to do your first parachute jump. Those of you who survive until tomorrow get to do a *second* parachute jump. In the unlikely event that there are any of the squad left by the third day, we'll do a number of jumps into different terrain. And when we have landed, we will conceal ourselves in cover, and we will not stand in the middle of the dropzone where everyone can see us – will we, sir?'

Gilmuriel put his hand to his hip, wishing for his slender elven knife, but encountered only his water-bottle. He unscrewed the cap and took a long drink of water. 'Any special instructions for us on this drop?'

Dakashnit nodded her heavy-jawed head. 'Sure are, L.t. In the unhappy event that your 'chute fails to open, always remember one thing – take up the proper marine emergency landing position. Stick your elbows out, and cross your right leg over your left leg.'

Gilmuriel frowned. A number of the elf marines on the ready line were vaguely crossing their legs and lifting their elbows in a puzzled manner.

'And why should we do that, Gunnery Sergeant?'

Dakashnit showed all her fangs and tusks in a grin. 'So that we can unscrew you out of the ground after you land . . .'

The orc uncoiled her whip and cracked it.

'Right you elves, into the chopper, on the double, move it! Go, go, go!'

Once seated in the cockpit of the helicopter, Lieutenant Gilmuriel eased the unaccustomed headphones down over his pointed elven ears and stared at the jungle canopy receding beneath his feet. Pistons sliding with smooth precision, the steam helicopter wheeled around and chugged into a vast orange sunset.

'Plenty of time for a first drop.' Dakashnit's voice came crackling over the headset. The uniformed orc gave him a gnarled thumbs-up, and grinned toothily from under her mirror-visored flying helmet.

Don't know how elves and parachutes will get along, L.t. You may not all make it. But hey, there's always drop-outs from every course . . .'

'You don't like elves, do you, orc – I mean, Gunnery Sergeant?'

'Me?' The orc grinned and shrugged, massive shoulders rising almost to her pricked ears. 'Man, I just *love* elf! You can't beat roast and basted elf-haunch. Unless it's breast-of-elf with chilli peppers.'

Gilmuriel stared at the slavering creature, appalled. 'This is impossible! Elves cannot serve with *orcs*! I shall inform the Lord of the Forest Elves of my resignation this very night!'

A fluting chorus of support came from the main body of the helicopter.

Dakashnit's voice came back over the RT: 'Fine by me. Let's just say I've seen better marines than you lot, L.t.'

A third voice crackled in the headset, faint and breaking up. Gilmuriel frowned. The orc pilot fiddled with the receiver. Suddenly Dakashnit's arm reached over his shoulder and tuned the signal in.

'*—to any unit! Sergeant Moondream to any unit! We are taking hostile fire in sector seven bravo, repeat, sector seven bravo. This is not an exercise! We are coming under hostile fire, targets not visible. Sergeant Moondream to any unit—*'

'Signal's breaking up.' Dakashnit tried unsuccessfully for several moments. 'Pilot, contact base! Tell them we're altering course for Seven Bravo – if that's all right with you, *sir*.'

She shoved the mirrored sun visor up. Her deep-set piggy eyes glinted in a way that disturbed Gilmuriel. 'I guess your Forest-King wouldn't need trained troops if he wasn't expecting battle, huh?'

'Well, I . . . Sergeant, perhaps we shouldn't . . .'

'Who else is there, man? L.t., ask yourself how *I* feel about going into combat with *this* lot? We're talking last-ditch emergency here!'

The lieutenant looked over his shoulder into the body of the steam-helicopter and surveyed the rows of reluctant uniformed elves. Pointed ears darkened with camouflage cream, long-fingered musical hands stained with the green of jungle plants, slender bodies web-belted into uniforms that hung on them like sacks . . . Their ascetic, high-boned faces stared back at him sullenly.

'On the whole,' Gilmuriel agreed, 'I'd rather be singing.'

In Graagryk, in the fortress of Graagryk's ancient nobility, the stonework shows old. Unicorn tapestries cover the rough walls. Bear-pelts from the fabulous Antarctic Icelands are flung down on the flagstones. A fire burns in the great hearth, despite the summer, to take the edge off the room's chill.

Ashnak strode across to the fireplace and stood, bowed legs

231

planted widely apart, and pissed into the flames. He sighed with pleasure and re-buttoned his trousers; web-belt and bandoliers of 7.62 calibre ammunition shifting on his brawny frame.

'Anyone can see why you need the authority of a Dark Lord.' The big orc clasped his taloned hands behind him. 'But the Dark Lord died at Samhain, at the Fields of Destruction, and some impersonator won't fool anyone.'

The nameless necromancer spat, '*You* are the fool!'

Ashnak's hairy nostrils flared. No corpse-stink here; the nameless necromancer muted his power – one could only suppose, out of assumed respect.

'The orc is here,' the black-haired Man announced, not to Ashnak; his skin robes whipping about his ankles as he strode towards the great arched window. Ashnak had not noticed the figure seated there, against the light, until now.

'So *that's* it!' Ashnak guffawed. He planted huge fists on his hips, threw his tusked jaw up, and bellowed orcish laughter. '*That's* what you did with her!'

He prowled closer, outsize combat boots making no noise on the flagstones.

A female Man sat on the window seat, head bowed, the light shining on her sleek, bobbed yellow hair. The hands that rested in her lap were smooth, their skin patched black, grey and fish-belly white. She was not wearing the full plate armour of her last encounter with him. A dress forged from silver links so fine they ran like water clung to her form, shimmering with black light at every breath lifting her breasts.

'Lost out,' Ashnak commented. 'Well, lady, that's what you get for having a bastard like the nameless for your brother.'

Her head bowed. The window light illuminated her face. The lashes of her long eyes (that tilted *up* from the outer corners) rested on her piebald cheeks. Small tusks drew her lips up and apart, so that a thin thread of saliva ran down from the exposed corner of her mouth, across her pugnacious jaw.

Ashnak had always thought her orcishly handsome for one of the Man race.

'So you've destroyed The Named's mind. So what? She still isn't—' Turning his head to speak to the nameless, reaching one talon out to lift the female's chin, Ashnak froze.

The ugly Man rose to her feet with a grace The Named had never possessed. Light sparked from her metal-mesh robe that chimed with the soft resonance of bells. A heavy perfume moved with her as she moved; throat-filling, musky and ancient. She lifted her head.

Her eyes were without iris, pupil or white. As her lashes lifted, her

232

eye-sockets showed featureless orange. And even in full sunlight, they perceptibly glowed.

'Orc . . .'

A cloud lifted from Ashnak's mind. Previously unnoticed figures of halfling servants in lace and linen became apparent to him, bringing choice Ducal food and drink from the fortress's cellars, their manner that of sleepwalkers. Guards drowsed with their halberds at attention. Graagryk's fortress dreamed a daymare, not even able to be restless in its sleep; and the city on the Inland Sea, oblivious to the presence which cloaked Itself in their midst, continued with the commerce of a normal life.

The orc's hide shivered. As if he had looked down to find himself standing on a pressure mine. *'Dark Lord?'*

'Yes.' She reached out and grasped his heavily muscled arm. Her touch made his skin wrinkle like rotten fruit.

The dogtag talisman about his neck burned to a degree that gave an orc pain, and then, with a high note, shattered.

'I am calling you to account for your life.' She paused. 'After the defeat of Samhain, none of My Horde Commanders should remain living. But you do. What is your excuse, little orc?'

Ashnak, looking up from under his beetling brows, met that blind, all-seeing gaze.

The nameless necromancer said, 'It pains me to admit it, but it was something more useful than cowardice.' Helping himself from a flagon of yellow wine at the table, he downed one tiny cup and then a second. 'Great Lord of the Nightmare Dark.'

Ashnak had not previously witnessed the nameless necromancer afraid.

'Lord!' the big orc cried, suddenly falling to his knees on the flagstones before Her. Ashnak threw himself forward, arms outstretched, and banged his forehead on the stone.

'Lord, You live! Darkness be praised!'

A naked foot planted itself on his exposed neck. He controlled a shudder of relief and continued:

'Dread Lord, we nearly *won* the Samhain Battle for You – if I'd had support from the Horde Mages we could have turned the tide of the war. The orc marines are shit-hot! And we're Your loyal servants. Servants such as no Dark Lord ever had before.'

'That,' Her contralto voice remarked, 'I can well believe.'

The foot (small only by orc standards) removed itself from his neck. Ashnak's eyes rolled up in their sockets while he remained abased before Her. He squinted hopefully in Her direction, seeing the wet-lipped mouth curve into a smile.

233

'You have bullied My necromancer and grovelled to Me.' Amusement sounded richly in Her voice. 'Admirable. You had plans for his return, I think. Perhaps even for Mine. But not together, and not on the same day!'

There was a silence.

Ashnak climbed awkwardly to his feet, brushing dust from the knees of his combat trousers. He picked up his forage cap and jammed it down between his ears. The hypnotized halfling servants walked around his bulk on their way to serve more wine, and he looked down at them, but they showed no awareness of his presence.

'Er,' the orc general said. 'Yes. Well. Erm . . .'

Splinters of the Visible College's anti-magic talisman stood embedded in the hide of his chest. He brushed them out. At last looking at his Dark Master, he was startled to recognize green-irised eyes before Her gaze burned again the colour of fire.

'Yes. She lives within Me. I allow The Named to witness what she has become; the Paladin of the Light, whom I inhabit.'

The Dark Lord stepped closer to Ashnak.

'It was in a church, was it not? A little temple somewhere in the northern countryside, and you grovelled to the Light's paladin, and she said, *All you need to know of me is, I am merciful*, and, like a stupid fool, did not kill you. Orc, all you need to know of Me is, I am *not* merciful. Nor am I stupid. I am the Lord of Darkness, and you have failed Me, and you will answer for it here and now!'

Shadows hovered in the corners of the stone tower room, undiminished by sunlight. Not a presence of darkness so much as an absence of everything. The Man walked until She stood facing the window again, looking out over the halfling city to the Inland Sea. Towering thunderheads crept across the sun, lightning cracked and split the sky into jagged pieces, and hail lashed down on the summer streets. Visible only as a silhouette in the dim light, She languidly lifted one piebald finger.

'Great Lord!' Ashnak sensibly kept his hand away from the pistol holstered at his belt. 'I have a force almost at brigade strength. I can train raw levies. When the new war against the Light begins, you'll need the orc marines.'

The nameless necromancer muttered, 'Need traitors and cowards!' as he put down the empty wine flagon.

'The loyal and the brave didn't do so well at the Fields of Destruction,' Ashnak noted drily. He advanced a step, coming to a smart parade rest on the flagstones. 'Great Lord of the Ebon Abyss, put no faith in his magic. You need superior firepower. Mages *take* territory, marines *hold* it. You need us for the post-Samhain campaign.'

The Dark Lord turned Her head, looking at him over Her slightly too-wide shoulders. The Named's tall, raw-framed body carried the metal-mesh robe with a hint of awkwardness not yet tamed by the Dark Lord's possession of her; she moved sometimes still as if she would rather have carried a sword in her hand than magery. A sooty darkness hovered in the corners of Ashnak's vision. Recalling the briefing before the Last Battle, in the Dark Lord's great towering keep in the far east, a kind of orcish homesickness attacked him.

'I remember', he said wistfully, 'the legions of the Horde marching out of the Dark Land, descending on the west. Our warriors covered the earth, and our Dark beasts the skies, and You rode out to war on the back of a frostdrake, against the outnumbered small companies of the Light . . .'

The orange glow of Her eyes dimmed.

'The Horde of Darkness', Ashnak concluded, bass-baritone voice roughening, 'got its ass kicked. Great Sable Lord, I don't want that to happen again. You need us. We're loyal. And if we failed You once, we won't fail again.'

Abruptly, the normal summer chill of the tower room returned. There was a strain in the air as if from the working of invisible great engines, familiar to Ashnak from the days when he wore black steel armour in place of combat fatigues, and his weapon was the fighting Agaku's traditional pole-axe. He came to attention, boots slamming down on the flagstones.

'Awaiting your orders, Lord! When do I muster the troops?'

The nameless necromancer giggled.

Ashnak's vision of a return to the old days faded with the glare in Her eyes. Her eyeballs shone momentarily like grey glass, and the dust of destroyed aeons whispered past Ashnak on no earthly wind. Death reaching so swiftly made him grab, automatically, for the pistol at his belt, although even without the loss of the talisman he would have doubted an automatic pistol's validity against the Lord of Night and Silence.

'Be still.'

The orc, after some minutes, opened his eyes. Finding himself corporeal, and undamaged, he looked to the Dark Lord where She sat, now, on the window-seat, Her bare feet swinging.

'Be still and attend to Me,' the Dark Lord said. 'Did I have you brought here to Me to play games? Orc, your thuggery is of no use to Me. Domination by force of arms in this world is useless.'

The nameless necromancer's finely chiselled lips curved into a patrician smile.

The Dark Lord added, 'So is magic.'

235

Ashnak looked at the nameless necromancer. The nameless necromancer, his pale-lipped mouth falling slightly open, stared at Ashnak.

'What?' the orc general said.

The nameless necromancer added, 'I beg your pardon?'

The Dark Lord sat, to all appearances a female Man of startling ugliness, the sun spotlighting Her piebald grey-and-white skin, shining back from Her burnished hair, but not dismissing the darknesses that hung in the folds of Her clinging robe. She lifted Her wrist and wiped saliva from the corners of Her mouth.

'I have returned. My ambition is undimmed. I *will* rule.' Her inhuman eyes glowed orange.

Ashnak for the second time in the space of half an hour took his life in his talons. He interrupted Her. 'But you said—'

'There will be no military conquest,' She stated. 'I have decided that conquering with Dark Armies is . . . outmoded. Old-fashioned. *Passé.*'

3

A ND AT THAT very hour, twelve thousand miles to the south of the Inland Sea, in the fabled Antarctic Icelands, Razitshakra strode between the rows of huts that made up the tundra bootcamp. Snow crusted the squat female orc's heavy military greatcoat as she stomped, bandy-legged, across the icefield. She rebuckled her webbing, pistol-holsters, and stick-grenades over her coat, looking up to check that the marine striped-and-starred Raven flag still proudly flew. It did.

The ideology class waited, drawn up to attention outside her command hut, in front of the wooden table that stood out in the snow. The orc seated herself at the table, placed her elbows on the wood, and rested her pugnacious chin on her talons.

'Recruit Balan Orcsbane,' she purred, eyes gleaming. 'You of the unfortunate surname – perhaps you would be kind enough to state basic orc marine ideology.'

The dwarf drew himself stiffly to attention, his forked orange beard jutting horizontally. Like the rest of the twelve-dwarf recruit squad, he wore olive-drab fatigues rolled up at the ankles and elbows. His orange braids had been shaved down to a bare fuzz of hair on his scalp. He carried a much-abused Kalashnikov assault rifle, and a steel helmet from which the sharp horns had been forcibly removed.

'Ma'am, politically correct orcish ideology is as follows.' Balan Orcsbane pointed at his fellow bootcamp trainees. 'If you're smaller than me, I'm in charge here. If you're bigger than me – you're in charge. And if something's gone wrong, *he's* in charge!'

'Very good!' The Endless Sun glinted from Razitshakra's round, wire-rimmed spectacles, and from the peaked brim of her cap. Her lateral-pointing ears twitched. She removed a small notepad from her greatcoat pocket and scribbled a few words. 'Tell me more about command responsibility.'

The dwarf rapped out, 'The commander is always right!'

'And?'

'The commander is *always* right,' Balan Orcsbane added smartly. 'Even when he's wrong.'

'Well done.' Razitshakra pointed at the next dwarf in the line. 'You. Owaine Elfhunter. Name a test to determine whether a recruit is fit to become a marine.'

The dwarf scratched her trimmed beard. 'The recruit is tied—' she hastily corrected herself '—the recruit *volunteers* to be tied to a sabre-toothed tiger, and shut up in its cave. If the recruit comes out, she passed. If the tiger comes out, she failed. If she comes out riding the sabre-toothed tiger, make her a corporal.'

'Excellent.' Razitshakra's unorcishly golden eyes gleamed. 'Now—'

'Commissar, ma'am!' The centaur Coms officer galloped up, ice and snow spraying from his hooves, and thrust the radio handset towards Razitshakra. 'It's Alpha Squad. Commissar, you have to hear this!'

'That is not approved radio procedure. Barzoi! Take over the dwarf squad.' Razitshakra stepped aside, in the shadow of the glossy-coated centaur's heaving flanks. The rasp of distant gunfire was plainly audible over the radio link. 'Bootcamp Base to Squad Alpha – who authorized a live ammo exercise in that area!'

The reply crackled back:

'*Squad Alpha to Bootcamp, this is not an exercise. Repeat, this is not an exercise.*' Orc Corporal Zakkad's gruff voice shook with urgency. '*Ma'am, order all your recruits on full armed alert. There are hostiles coming out of the walls here! Species not seen. Weapons not recognized. Numbers unknown. They're not stopping to talk, they're just piling into us!*'

'Zakkad!' Razitshakra barked resonantly into the mouthpiece. 'Don't lose your grip, orc! What weapons are you facing?'

'*Unknown, ma'am. Could be mage-work – but it's getting through to us! I'm out here with a squad of untrained dickheads, ma'am; it's all I can do to manage a fighting retreat; we need urgent support—*'

The line hissed. No further voice sounded.

'Sierra and Foxtrot squads reinforce the perimeter guard,' the orc commissar yelled, shambling through the camp at the double.

238

'Barzoi, get the 483rd and the cold-drake to overfly map reference 098-756! Tango Platoon gear up, you're coming out with me. *Move, move, move!*'

The cyclopean ruins of an ancient city lay half-buried in a glacier two miles to the south, at 098–756; its spires and ramps and towers long gone, leaving only a maze of broken masonry walls. Razitshakra had been in the habit of using it for a training ground for Fighting In Built-Up Areas.

The 483rd Airborne Division took off to fly air support.

'Hai-yaaaahh, yo!'

'Hai-yahhhh, *yo!*'

Winged white horses took off and wheeled in the air above the jagged mountain peaks. The brilliant antarctic sun gleamed through the pinions of the tactical pegasi, shining on the heat-seeker fire-and-forget missiles carried under each wing.

'Hai-yah, yo!'

The airborne riders whooped and yelled. Frost sparkled on their mailshirts, cinched in tight over their swelling breasts with wide leather swordbelts. Their long braids hung down. Fur leggings protected the riders' shapely limbs; fur wristbands hugged their otherwise-bare hands. Their horned steel helms glinted in the Endless Day.

One Valkyrie marine reined her winged horse's head up. 'Missile away!'

BOOOMM!

The Hellfire missile zipped into the icefield several miles away, throwing up debris and steam.

'Damn you!' Razitshakra bawled over the com. 'I want reconnaissance, not fire support! There are some of our own out there!'

The Valkyrie marines wheeled their winged mounts above the plain, soaring through the sky. Passing close, one rider held out her hand, palm-up; the other slapped it with her own palm, and gave soprano voice to the marine recognition signal:

'YO!'

'No movement visible at map reference 098-756, ma'am,' an advance Valkyrie marine radioed back. 'Nothing at *all* . . .'

The advance by bounds on Alpha Squad's last position took time. Commissar Razitshakra cuffed and kicked and bit, where necessary, to spur the raw recruits into battle. Pondering the wisdom of taking a recruit platoon into an attack (and indeed of leaving two-thirds of another recruit platoon to guard the base), the orc commissar cursed volubly.

'If it's magery, you've got nothing to fear!' she snarled. 'If it's conventional weapons, remember you're *marines* now. Are we marines?'

The dwarf squad, advancing almost tactically towards the cyclopean ruins marking the beginning of the antarctic's true Icelands, muttered in their braided beards.

'I said, *are we marines?*, you political subversives!' Razitshakra raised her fist and brought it down on the back of one of the dwarf grunts. The dwarf fell to its knees, staggered up as Razitshakra booted him, and moved reluctantly on under the weight of a 70lb infantry pack.

The platoon determinedly continued to treat the orc commissar's question as rhetorical.

'There'll be an inquiry held after this,' Razitshakra promised. 'Now clear the area through. *Go!* There may be some of our lads still alive in there.'

The dwarf recruit squads advanced more in a cluster than by fire-and-movement. Razitshakra, in the rear with the reserve ursoid squad for command and control, bellowed orders. No shot, no spell, no hostile sound broke the silence.

'Area clear!' the dwarf recruit Balan Orcsbane called.

'It had better be, marine. Secure the perimeter!'

The snow-covered glacier was dotted with prone lumps, leaking fluids. Even in the antarctic chill, the area stank. Razitshakra's orcish nostrils flared, identifying the blood and faeces and urine of dwarves and orcs; all of it stinking of the fear, rather than the joy, of combat. Alpha Squad being least trained, and least exposed to Dagurashibanipal's geas, she was not surprised to find that most of their weapons had not fired.

She prowled among the bodies for quite a while, under the Endless Sun's radiance, tossing aside severed dwarf limbs ragged with blood, and heads from which the eyes had been sucked. A wind began to blow from the Icelands. The cold-drake, patrolling the skies, reported no hostile movement of any kind. The Endless Day wore on.

When she found him – his dead eyes staring up at her – orc corporal Zakkad of the marine training cadre lay in two parts; his arms, head and torso in the cover of an ancient masonry wall, and his lower torso, legs and genitalia in the open ground beyond.

One gnarled fist still grasped his rifle and exhausted magazine. Rags of his combat fatigues, stained with stiffening green blood, dotted the ground. Pale intestines shrivelled in the sun. Judging by the recruits around him, he had been trying to assault his way out through the enemy's position. It is not an infallible technique, merely the least worst of options.

Nullity talismans on body and weapon were intact.

Squatting over the half-body, Razitshakra prised the powerful, low-slung jaws open. The fangs and tusks of the orc corporal were blackly discoloured. A black, cone-like object blocked his throat, with teeth-marks where the orc had bitten it off. Razitshakra poked at it with one talon. It echoed with a metallic sound.

After a while it began to stink.

Later, back at the antarctic-warfare bootcamp, the dwarf recruit Balan Orcsbane approached Commissar Razitshakra where she stood, handset to her ear, cursing her Coms officer and her communications equipment. He plucked the sleeve of her greatcoat.

'*Please*, Commissar, ma'am. The recruits want permission to pack for immediate embarkation.'

'Nonsense!' Razitshakra, spectacles glinting, clapped the dwarf on the back with her free hand. 'I've just officially re-named this training base "Camp Zakkad". Zakkad, our first Hero of the Orc Marines! Corporal Barzoi, make a note: recruits' contributions to the Memorial Fund will be compulsory.'

The dwarf corporal saluted. The squat orc commissar stood, her hulking shoulders broad as five dwarves.

'Corporal Barzoi, *you* will proceed with the bootcamp training in my absence. Find a pilot for the cold-drake; I'll fly back.'

'Absence? You're deserting us!' recruit Balan Orcsbane gasped. 'Retreating!'

Razitshakra slammed the handset of the RT back down, making the centaur Coms officer stagger. The orc glared up at the Endless Sky. Even had there been a night, the communications satellite would not have been visible.

'Orc marines never retreat!' Commissar Razitshakra snarled. 'I'm flying back in person because there seems to be a complete communications breakdown with Marine HQ, Graagryk.'

'*No* military conquest?'

Incredulous, the orc general Ashnak showed all his bronze-capped tusks in a grin of ferocious *bonhomie*.

'Dread Lord, are You aware of what's been happening during Your . . . unavoidable absence?'

Outside, the sluggishness of nightmare drifted through Graagryk's streets, dimming the shine of cleansing magic on the cobbles, and poisoning the afternoon naps of halfling children and halfling elderly. The whistling of lizard-beasts quietened, barely audible here in this ancient tower room.

Her voice whispered, 'My servant the nameless necromancer has

241

informed Me of your new weaponry. I shall not need it.'

Ashnak, orcishly bow-legged, paced down the tapestry-hung hall; about-faced; and paced back towards the mullioned window. Overhead, the strange birds and beasts carved on the beams writhed, making obseisance to the female Man who sat with Her back to the sunlight.

'The South has just spent a year putting down the flood of Horde survivors and their own deserters fleeing the Fields of Destruction. They think it's over, now. They think this is peace.' Ashnak came to attention. 'Dread Lord, as you're the *de facto* Commander-in-Chief of what remains of the Horde of Darkness, let me officially inform you: my troops are proven magic-resistant to the highest degree. If you were to send the orc marines against these Southern Kingdoms – man, those guys'd have themselves a whole *world* of shit!'

The nameless necromancer downed another cup of straw-coloured wine, his gaze pitted with crimson.

'Dread Lord, pay no attention to this creature. His battles have all been in the north. Magic', the Man said, his voice blurring, 'is proportional to *civitas*, and derives therefrom. The north has no proper cities, its magic is therefore rare and weak. The cities of the south are great, and they have great magics like . . . like dogs have fleas. You would need ten thousand warriors of his sort, and he has not a tenth of that number!'

Ashnak glared, deep-set orc eyes staring into the sea-green, crimson-flecked gaze. His granite bulk loomed over the Man by several inches. The fingers of the nameless necromancer began to move.

The Dark Lord's voice whispered, *'No.'*

The necromancer rubbed his fingertips together as if to expunge something barely begun.

Ashnak turned his heavy head to face the window. 'Strategically this is the perfect time to attack! We should immediately mobilize—'

The Man straightened Her shoulders. Shadows chased themselves in the ultrafine chainmail of Her garment, and its soft chiming rang like the bells of drowned cities. 'I have spoken. There will be no domination of the world by Dark Armies.'

Ashnak scratched at his peaked ears and settled his urban camouflage forage cap more securely on his bald head. 'If you say not.'

Strands of yellow hair lay against Her piebald, black-and-grey cheek. Yellow lashes opened, and behind Her eyelids Her eyeballs were orange glass.

'I will travel to Ferenzia, that greatest of southern cities,' the Lord

242

of Night and Silence announced. 'You, orc Ashnak, shall choose a number of your *marine* warriors to form my honour guard.'

She ceased to speak. It might be that She smiled, the yellowing tusks pulled Her lip into such ambiguous shapes that Ashnak could not be sure. The yellow hair swung as She shook Her head. Gently, She added, 'You are thinking, quite suddenly, that if I need a guard, I must therefore be vulnerable. You wonder if My defeat at Samhain has weakened Me. You ponder in your mind that I may be a bluff, a pretence, a pale copy of what I was in the heyday of My power.'

'Thought never crossed my mind,' Ashnak said.

'I choose your warriors for the honour of it,' She said. 'For I will not go to Ferenzia without the ceremony and attendance that I am properly owed. And it may be that I shall make you one of My major-generals, or field marshals; some rank befitting My status. Orc Ashnak, you are thinking now that I will not try conquest by force of arms because I fear certain defeat. You think therefore that I can be tricked, used and manipulated into a figurehead for your plans.'

Ashnak shot a sideways glance at Her out of his tilted eyes. His gnarled thumbs lodged under his web belt, pulling the pistol holster closer to his fist. His thin lips drew back from his fangs.

'Nobody fucks over the orc marines,' he growled. 'Not even the Dark Lord. If You want the marines for Your protection, there's a price. We want *Your* support when we attack Ferenzia and the other Southern Kingdoms. Otherwise no deal!'

It being a calculated bluff, Ashnak was not completely surprised to find himself, at the flick of Her finger, immobilized. Held at attention, the heels of his combat boots together, staring eyes-front, he could just see the nameless necromancer retrieve from his table a whip braided from some strangely dubious skin.

Ashnak admitted gruffly, 'Dread Lord, I erred in thinking you powerless.'

'But you will continue to test Me, I fear.'

Clicks marked the passage of Her bare feet across the flagstones, as if the soles of Her feet were sometimes chitinous. Her swaying blond hair did not come higher than Ashnak's chin. Ashnak tensed his bull-muscled shoulders. There came a smell of rotten fruit: his skin began to soften, the colours of decay chasing themselves across his leathery hide. As soon as he relaxed it faded.

'Not torture!' Ashnak roughened his bass-baritone voice. 'No, Dread Lord! Please, no! I beg you! Not that!'

'I have no intention of resorting to the question.' The Dark Lord lifted Her face. Her orange eyes in the sunlight did, quite visibly,

243

glow. 'I well know the amount of physical punishment an orc can take. And I know your general resistance to pain.'

Out of the corner of his long eye Ashnak witnessed the nameless necromancer, with scowling regret, replacing the metal-fanged whip on the table.

'But you must know Me, and My power.' The Lord of Night smiled and wiped a trail of saliva from Her lip. 'I can reach into your soul, orc.'

'Illusions!' the orc sneered.

The Dark Lord cried, 'I see into you! I know what you once most feared, living through night after night in the hierarchy of the Pits; inflicting and suffering abuse, proving your right to live and become adult. I know what hides, unacknowledged, in your memory; and from it I create soul-pictures, pains more powerful than the severing of limbs. *Ashnak, I touch your soul!*'

The big orc's body stiffened: ramrod-straight from his combat boots to the tips of his pointed ears. His eyes rolled up in their deep sockets and showed the whites. Stiff as a board, pivoting from the heels, the orc's body tipped over backwards. His skull impacted on the floor with such force that two tiles cracked. Lying unconscious, it could be seen that the General of the Orc Marines had wet himself.

The nameless necromancer stepped carefully over the orc's supine body on his way to pour himself another drink, and stepped back over the body on his return, pausing only to spit in the orc's face.

'You will not defy Me more than once,' She promised. 'Ashnak, you may wake.'

The orc groaned, sat up, opened his mouth, and shut it again. He wiped his face and rubbed the back of his skull, and at last got to his feet. Dusting his filthy fatigues down with his forage cap, he regarded the Lord of Evil with the air of one unfairly tricked.

'My warrior-orc Ashnak, do you like what I have showed you?'

Ashnak said blankly, 'What?'

'You do not remember the terror created from your past?'

Ashnak's leathery brows furrowed. He shook his head. 'Negative, ma'am.'

'Amazing,' the Dark Lord commented. 'Finesse is wasted on orcs. Next time I shall merely kill you. Now . . .'

Her voice, soft from that command-roughened throat, soaked into the summer afternoon air of Graagryk. Nothing stirred in the tower room while She spoke.

'. . . I have no wish for easy victories. I am weary of war. There are only so many new ways to shed blood. I could take the souls of those fools of the Light and make them Mine. But I am weary of sucking souls: the little races of this world are tedious to the heart. It pleases Me now to do things otherwise.'

Ashnak slurred an orcish curse under his breath, unadmitted shock chilling his ox-body. He raised his voice again to audibility. 'Lord . . . If not armies . . . or soul-magic . . . then *how* will you conquer?'

Her hair like sunlight, Her metal robe hiding all darknesses within its folds, the ugly Man stands against the light. The splotched patchwork of Her skin blends Her into the dazzle. She smells of dead cities that breathe perfumed dust on to the world's winds.

'This time,' the Dark Lord said, 'I think it will please Me to win an election.'

Ashnak could not move, his muscles still shook and trembled. It took him all his strength of will to stay upright. He became aware of the nameless necromancer only as the black-haired Man strode forward to face the Dark Lord.

Simultaneously, both the orc general and the nameless necromancer demanded, 'What's an "election"?'

A ducal carriage rattled past the orc marine sentries and into the barracks compound, steel-shod wheels striking sparks from the cobbles under the archway.

As Lieutenant Lugashaldim of the Special Undead Services watched, Magdelene Amaryllis Judith Brechie van Nassau, Duchess of Graagryk, descended from the carriage in a flurry of aides, nursemaids, outriders and guards. Her young children scurried about her feet, playing with a pack of wolfhounds twice their height; and tame parrots fluttered above her in scarlet and green. Magda snapped her fingers. Her chief lady-in-waiting, Safire, extended a parasol to protect the ducal head both from the late afternoon sun, Lugashaldim imagined, and from the birds.

'You may let the children play here,' Magda announced to her entourage in a clear, carrying voice. She waved away the orc gate guards clattering across the cobbles towards her. 'You! Lugashaldim! *You* may fetch me my Ashnak. *Now.*'

Behind the fortified walls that faced Graagryk city, sunlight slanted into the Orc Marine HQ and illuminated brick walls, machinery-cluttered sheds, gutted barracks, and deserted armoured vehicles. The off-duty orc marines sprawled on the grass of the compound, drinking Graagryk's fine wines, roasting something of worrying dimensions on a spit, and fornicating energetically around the firepit and under the lime trees. Upon sighting an approaching Undead orc lieutenant there was a concerted effort to button uniforms and shuffle the worst of the debris out of sight.

'Ma'am.' Lugashaldim, sun shining through his mummified flesh and bones, looked down and saluted the female halfling. 'I'm afraid the present whereabouts of General Ashnak are Classified.'

The Duchess Magda stared down her halfling nose and replied in fluent marine. 'I'm his *wife*, you dickhead!'

Her entourage snickered. The rotting orc marine shifted from combat boot to combat boot uneasily. 'But, ma'am—'

'He is my Ducal Consort and I will speak with him *now*.'

The Undead officer blinked ragged eyelids over curdled eyeballs. The stripped bone of his skull gleamed, and he cast an elongated skeletal shadow on the grass. Magda's nostrils flared.

'You may as well let the hounds off their leashes,' she remarked. 'They need to relieve themselves, I think.'

Her servants obeyed. Five wolfhounds, two parrots, and the Duchess's children ran across the parade ground. Orc marines started to their feet, hauling automatic weapons out of the way of clutching hands and dogpiss. Childish shrieks of glee drowned out an orc sergeant's orders. A wolfhound stole the roast from the spit. Two marines pursued it as it dragged the meat off, snarling.

Lugashaldim wiped a parrot-dropping from his decaying uniform.

'I guess you can wait in his office, ma'am,' the lieutenant conceded weakly.

Calm amid the chaos of children, dogs and orc marines trying to retrieve their belongings without being caught disposing of any intruders, Magda said, 'I do not wish to wait at all. If I do, I shall wait right here.'

Lugashaldim gazed across the compound. Dormitories – long brick barracks that had stood just high enough to house halfling warriors – lay gutted. Marine ponchos had been fixed between their broken walls, and under these were the offal-strewn, refuse-ridden, rubble-buttressed lairs of siblings known as *orc-nests*. Brown, black, green and albino limbs stirred frowstily as the chaos spread, and he heard the familiar rumble of orc snores.

The Duchess Magda remarked loudly, 'How unlike the home life of my own dear Ashnak!'

'Sorry, ma'am—' He paused as young orcs just out of the Pit shrieked and gibbered past Magda's people, their orcish spawn-herd in close pursuit. Magda's eyes followed their compact, long-armed bodies; pointed ears; and crimson-glaring eyes under beetling brows. The young orcs were herded back past the planks spiked with broken glass that covered the tops of brick-lined Pits. Grunts, snuffles, screeches and wails echoed up from the depths.

'Ma'am, I'm sorry. He didn't notify us of his departure, destination, or time of return.'

The Duchess Magda swore with a fluency gained in the brothels of two dozen kingdoms. 'Then find him! Search!'

The Undead orc stood with his skeletal shoulders hunched, trying not to tower over her. 'Ma'am, we don't know where to look—'

'*Magda!*' a voice bawled.

Ashnak strode in under the barracks archway, his forage cap tugged well down over his eyes and a pipe-weed cigar jutting from one corner of his tusked mouth. Both he and his uniform looked somewhat the worse for wear, although with orcs it is difficult to tell. He drop-kicked a couple of slow-moving marines out of his path, and acknowledged Lugashaldim's salute. 'Magda, my dear . . .'

Gallantly, the large orc reached down and took her hand between two of his fingers, lifted it to his lips, and kissed it.

'Husband.' Magda drew herself up to her full three feet two inches. Gloveleather flounces frothed around her. She arranged her sleek petticoats more decorously. 'Safire, you and the others may wait for me back at the carriage.'

She took Ashnak's muscular arm, reaching up high. Amid the panic of a garrison that has realized it has just incurred a snap inspection, she led him to stroll in the dappled shade of the compound's lime trees.

The big orc lowered his heavy head, gazing down at her. A shadow of Darkness still lingered in his eyes. 'You brought the children to the barracks?'

'It's time they saw where their father works. I don't wish them to remain in ignorance. I myself', Magda said, 'am often uninformed.'

One corner of his lip lifted over a tusk in unwilling amusement.

'Things you did not tell me, for example,' Magda continued levelly, 'include just how many offspring orcs spawn at one time. *And* how quickly they mature. There are six of my little half-orcs running around back there – and one of them is already talking. I can only assume she heard *that* kind of language from her father!'

Ashnak side-stepped the broken brick hurled by an approaching ducal offspring.

'Really, my sweetheart, the old ways are the best. Ah, the good old days in the Pit,' Ashnak remarked with nostalgia. 'The shit-slinging contests . . . gangbangs . . . Eat-the-Runt . . . Finest days of your life, the Pits. Really make an *orc* out of you.'

Magda glared up at him. 'Half-orc though they may be, I am not bringing our children up in any Pit! Although I have to admit, what

247

they're doing to the other halfling children in nursery school doesn't bear thinking about.'

She scooped the running toddler up on to her hip. Already the size of a two year old, the half-orc halfling infant beamed, showing its first tiny tusks. Magda stroked the thatch of brown hair that fell over its prominent brow-ridge.

'My heart, what have you done with your tutor *this* time?'

'BURP!'

'You see?' Magda complained. 'I'm beginning to have difficulty getting nursing staff. I hear you're making deals with the Dark Lord.'

'Y—' Ashnak halted, put his huge fists on his hips, and glared down at her. 'Where the fuck did you hear that?'

'Be serious. I know you.'

Magda wiped their child's wide mouth with the silk hem of her farthingale and set it down. It scuttled off to join its brothers and sisters in tormenting the off-duty marines. Rather than damage their general's offspring – or, rather than explain such damage to him afterwards – the helpless grunts found themselves constrained into allowing the halfling half-breeds to climb over military equipment and personnel irrespective. Magda noted one orc surreptitiously wiping scarlet and green feathers from the corner of his mouth.

'I've not seen Wilhelm or Edvard of late,' she remarked inconsequentially. 'I think my older sons have fled Graagryk.'

'Good!' the big orc grunted.

'That is no way to speak of your step-children, Ashnak! I want us all to be one big happy family.'

The orc seated himself on the turf, tucking one BDU combat-trousered leg under the other. He reached out and drew Magda into a powerful embrace. The pungent musk of orc filled her nostrils. The Duchess squeaked. Eventually, seated in his lap, his back to a lime tree trunk, she heard him say:

'That was your news at the Orcball game? The Dark Lord's return?'

'I wished to prepare you for any possible meeting. Little passes in Graagryk that isn't my business – my contacts brought me word of His return. Why has He come to my city?'

'Why?' Ashnak's voice vibrated through their flesh where she leaned against him. 'Because He's gone absolutely bugfuck, that's why! He's out of His fucking tree!'

The orc marine rested his elbows on the scuffed knees of his urban camouflage combat trousers, and leaned his heavy jaw against her neck. Watching Lugashaldim do his best to discipline the Graagryk HQ, the orc said, 'Have you ever heard of a thing called an *election?*'

The Duchess Magda, whose experience spanned several continents and a number of species, frowned. The crow's-feet deepened around her eyes. 'No. What manner of beast is it?'

Ashnak coughed. If he had not been the General of the Orc Marines, she might have thought him embarrassed.

'His Sable Eminence explained it to me. Apparently it's a method of ruling a kingdom. You give everyone what they call a *vote*. Then, when you have commands, the people cast these *votes* to decide whether they'll obey. The Lord of Night and Terror says they also get to cast these *votes* to decide who'll be the kingdom's ruler. And that's called an *election*.'

Magdelene Amaryllis Judith Brechie van Nassau thought about it. '"Casting" *votes*. A *vote* will be a kind of stone, then? Certainly a missile of some sort . . .'

She stood up abruptly, removing herself from Ashnak's embrace, and began to brush down her dress. Cheeks heated, she snapped, 'The whole thing's ridiculous! Think about it, you dumb orc. Give *everyone* one of these *votes*, and where are you? With every dirty peasant thinking she has as great a right as me to decide what is best for Graagryk! It's . . . it's immoral! Why— Why, a Duchess might even *lose an election!*'

She paced up and down rapidly, heels indenting the leaf-scattered turf. Over the noise and bustle of the orc HQ making itself minimally tidy, she said, 'His Sable Eminence's mind must have snapped completely! Samhain was such a blow, it's driven Him into insanity! This is no way to bring about the Dark Domination!'

'The information is Classified,' Ashnak said gloomily. 'I'm not telling the marines about *votes*. It will only give them ideas.'

The halfling and the orc stared at each other for some minutes. A sergeant-major bawled orders across the compound and squads of marines doubled in all directions, parking the APCs in straight lines and removing the bodies from the assault course. Sunset coloured the sky above the Inland Sea salmon pink and violet. Evening lizards called.

Magda narrowed her eyes against the levelling light.

'Orcs,' she said. Ashnak raised his head, teeth and eyes gleaming.

Magda continued, 'Orcs are tolerated in the Southern Kingdoms only on sufferance. My dear, yours is a very small company, and its presence here is totally dependent on your ability to run an arms industry. Come to think of it, His Nightmare Excellence may be a very good person to have on our side.'

The orc marine got to his feet, belts of ammunition shifting with his muscles. He removed the pipe-weed cigar from his mouth, looked at it, and threw it away. He removed his cap and scratched at his bald, leathery skull.

'He's going to the capital of the South to talk to the Light Council – about *elections*.' The orc bared brass-capped fangs incredulously. 'Why He thinks they won't call down every battery of Light magic they've got on His head beats me.'

For the first time, Ashnak's brass-baritone voice altered.

'I don't consider disobeying the Dark Lord an acceptable level of risk. He could wipe out every orc in the marines just by snapping His fingers . . . His orders are, I'm to bring a platoon and escort Him to the capital, Ferenzia. We leave tomorrow.'

Magda stepped forward and threw her arms around Ashnak's hips, burying her face against his web-belt and hard-muscled gut. Taloned hands gently stroked her fur-short hair.

She heard footsteps approaching and did not move. A creaking, deathly voice spoke.

'General Ashnak, sir. Satellite communications are back on-line. Sir, I really think you ought to listen to the situation reports that are coming in.'

4

THE FORT SWELTERED under the equatorial sun.

'Excuse me, sir.' A polite orcish voice spoke in Barashkukor's ear. 'The second recce patrol's overdue, sir. What shall we do?'

Patrols are nothing more than habit on peacetime trips. Especially with a squad of sales-orcs. The major rested his skinny elbows on the deserted fort's parapet and gazed out at rock and sand. Even wearing Raybans, the gusting yellow and white sand of the Endless Desert reflected the light back painfully. Hot now, and only an hour after dawn.

'Get back to HQ on the radio. Post them officially missing.'

The Marine First Class saluted Barashkukor with a hand upon which the talons were trimmed. Her uniform showed signs of being ironed, her combat boots shone, her tusks were polished. Of her M16, however, there was no sign. Barashkukor regarded his squad of twelve sales-orcs with despair.

'Sir,' she added, 'Corporal Uzkaddit didn't come back *either*. What are we going to do, sir?'

Under any other circumstances Barashkukor would have said *Act like an orc!* Appreciating that it might be futile in this case, he refrained. Having only two combat veterans in his sales-force, it *might* have been an error to send them both out on recce . . .

'We're not even *fighting* anyone,' the large orc, Arakingu, whimpered. 'Sir, we aren't at war here, sir, are we? We're here to *sell* things—'

251

Patience expired. Major Barashkukor climbed up on to the step of the parapet, drew back his black-gloved fist, and punched the orc squarely in the face. When she got to her feet, combat fatigues dusty, there was a glint of red in her eyes.

'You're a marine, orc! I don't care if you're support services, you're a marine!'

'*Sir, yes, sir!*'

The rear echelon marine retired to the other end of the parapet to tinker with radio equipment, muttering something about a slur on a fine body of orcs. Major Barashkukor, adjusting his black stetson, strode bandy-legged down into the compound and went around his orcs at the walls' murder-holes, checking weapons and boosting morale. The fort, little more than a square of walls around a tiny courtyard and well, was small enough that Barashkukor could cross it in five strides.

'Sir.' The MFC, Arakingu, appeared at his elbow. 'Sorry, sir, satellite link's down again.'

'That does it. Get Graagryk back,' the small orc major said fiercely. 'I don't care how you do it, but *contact* them. Tell them we've got trouble here, and we're under strength. Either we get reinforcements or they pull us out – I want an airlift, and I want it today!'

At the same moment a marine called from the walls, 'Sir— it's out there again, sir!'

'Give me distance and direction, you snivelling ball of orc-dung!' Major Barashkukor loped over to the walls, black cowboy boots kicking up sand. He squinted through the slit in the masonry. 'Where is it?'

Dredging up some memory of basic training, the grunt muttered, 'Those rocks at two o'clock, sir. Movement. Number of hostiles unknown.'

'Well done, Luzdrak.' Barashkukor shoved up the brim of his stetson and wiped sweat from his leathery forehead. His thin, long ears wavered; drooping in the heat. 'Remember, orcs, we have the demo ammunition from the trucks. We outgun everything for miles. Keep your heads and we'll dogmeat this sucker! Are we marines?'

The marine major pointed up at the striped-and-starred Marine flag, with the Horde's raven superimposed, flying bravely from the ruined fort's flagpole. The dozen sales-orcs grinned, showing tusks and fangs, and rumbled, 'We are marines!' with a certain bloodthirsty gleam in their deepset eyes.

'It doesn't matter if there are *hundreds* of Desert Riders out there!'

252

Major Barashkukor enthused. 'We have the firepower. More importantly, we are trained and disciplined soldiers.'

'*Oh, my god!*' Luzdrak shrieked, clutching his superior officer. '*It's horrible! It's out there! It's coming for us!*'

Barashkukor shoved the orc bodily out of the way and crouched down at the wall-slit. A hot wind blew. Squinting into the eastern light, he made out movement in the rocks a hundred yards away.

'Shit . . .' Luzdrak crooned. 'Oh, shit, man, we are some unhappy mothers! What *is* that thing?'

'Don't worry, marine. I am completely familiar with the native indigenous life-forms of the desert terrain . . .' Barashkukor's voice trailed off.

Segments of chitin hauled themselves up over the rocks on jointed black legs – and then it stood upright. Desert sunlight shone on a black carapace.

Barashkukor registered a shiny, elongated Man-like body, with clawed hind limbs, half as tall again as an orc. A scorpion-like tail curved up and hung above its long, domed chitinous skull. Spines lined the clawed forelimbs. Soft clusters of rubbery black objects hung on its underbelly.

The orc stared. 'Man, that fucker's *big!*'

Arakingu called, 'Sir, I'm through to Graagryk!'

'Call in air support. *Now!*' Barashkukor showed small fangs in a satisfied smile. 'That's got to be the mother who took the recce patrols. Marine, I want you to put one aimed round into that piece of shit – encourage it to lose our trail!'

Luzdrak raised his AK47 assault rifle and settled the wooden stock into his brawny shoulder. One tilted eye squeezed almost shut. Barashkukor caught the moment when the orc marine held his breath. The trigger pulled. The muzzle jerked fire.

FOOM!

Tensed against the noise, like a hammer banging steel an inch from his ear, Barashkukor peered through binoculars at the rocks. The insectoid beast shambled up into the open on jointed hind legs, claws jutting from its shiny, hard forelimbs. It jerked. A spray of black substance punched out from the soft underside of its body and spattered the rocks.

Beside him, orc marines cheered.

'Let's see if it's got sense enough to run from that.' Barashkukor held the binoculars steady. 'Holy *shit.*'

Seven more of the creatures appeared. The first insectoid monstrosity hesitated, shiny black against the white rocks and sand, its sectioned tubular body shimmering in heat distortion. Segmented claws dipped down behind the rock. When they came into sight again, a green and dripping mess hung between them.

The orc's body leaked blood darkly on to the sand. His head and body had a curiously chewed appearance. Both arms and one leg had been bitten off. His jaw, wrenched loose from its sockets, flapped as the insect brandished the body high in the hot desert air. A scent of carrion travelled on the wind. The cloth of combat fatigues, belts of bullets, and twisted metal that might have been an M16 assault rifle, were embedded in the rib-cage of the dead orc marine.

'That's Corporal Uzkaddit . . .' Barashkukor breathed. 'Right! Fireteam one, hold your position. Fireteam two, withdraw to the trucks. Luzdrak, when you hear the engines, pull out. Use mortars. We're going to make a fighting withdrawal. Arakingu, give HQ our position, let 'em bomb the fuck out of here as soon as we're gone.'

'Yessir.' Luzdrak blanched a very pale grey. 'Sir, what *are* those things, sir?'

'I've told you. Just native wildlife,' Major Barashkukor said firmly. 'OK, marines, let's bug out. Move it!'

The silent desert echoed to the shouts of orc marines. Barashkukor led the run for the trucks, the Coms marine Arakingu at his heels, an M16 a comfortable weight in his arms. Hitting cover behind the Bedford vans, he ducked down as the remaining two orcs in his team jumped for the cabins and ferociously gunned the engines.

'In!' the small orc snarled.

Clinging to the truck door, Barashkukor glanced back towards the tiny fort.

The first insectoid horror, out-distancing the rest, galloped over rock on segmented, clawed legs. It held two limbs outstretched before it. The thin tail jutted high over its head, spike or sting catching the sun. Metallic flashes shone from the body-segment. A thin whistling jetted from the clashing mandibles that dripped a black substance on the desert sand.

'Yo!' Luzdrak's team broke for the trucks at the sound of engines.

'Fire at will!' Barashkukor leaned from one window of the lead truck with Arakingu, firing, the metal of the gun hot against his leathery hands. Rounds impacted on the insect's chitinous shell and ricocheted off, leaving only silver metal smears: no damage apparent. He wrenched a taloned finger off the trigger, pulled a grenade, and hurled it towards the insect-monsters – *that* close? *that* large? – and ducked his head.

At the fort, mortars coughed.

FOOOOM!

Fragments of black carapace bowled along the rocks, end over end.

Soft tissue spattered the truck. Barashkukor raised his head and glimpsed the insectoid thing rearing over the back of the truck, one forelimb missing, mandibles slavering.

The forelimb, even as it twitched, began to re-form. To grow. *Fast.*

'Hit it!' Barashkukor yelled at the orc marine driver. 'Go, go, go!'

The truck's wheels dug deep into sand, hit rock, and the vehicle lurched forward and away. Screams echoed from the morning behind them. The engine growled and roared.

'Sir!' Arakingu shook him by his black uniform collar. 'Sir, what about Luzdrak and the rest!'

Barashkukor cuffed her across the side of her head, skinning his knuckles on her kevlar helmet. 'Get through to HQ, marine! That's your job.'

The small orc clung to the open window of the truck as it dipped and weaved across the desert. No mortar fire now. Sunlight flashed from shiny black shells. The hammer of automatic fire rang out across the desert. The second truck had not moved. Stalled.

'One thing they teach you in officer training.' Barashkukor looked at his radio operator, eyes hard, haunted, sad. 'It doesn't matter if *none* of the grunts get out, so long as the officer does. I'm command and control. I have to make it back out and report. Marine, get into the back of the truck and start slinging crates out; I want us lightened for speed!'

Barashkukor stared back. The heavy-shouldered forms of orc marines ran and scattered across the desert, going into cover behind rocks, firing. The hollow, unimpressive *whuck!* of grenades sounded. From the rear of the stalled truck, flame jetted. The shoulder-fired anti-tank missile impacted on one of the insectoids.

BOOOMM!

'Sales Force Alpha to Graagryk Headquarters!' He shoved the headset on and yelled over the engine's roar, spraying automatic fire back towards the racing giant insects. The truck jounced wildly. 'HQ, are you receiving? Acknowledge! We got us a fucking *bug-hunt* here, man! Are you—'

The front of the truck rose up at an angle of forty-five degrees.

The orc had one glimpse through the shattering windscreen of a rearing black carapace, frothing mandibles, and faceted eyes.

The truck flipped.

Barashkukor opened his eyes to see a truncated orc foot. All green with blood, the boot still on it, black leather covered in dust. It rested on rock a yard from his face. He rolled over, skin stinging from the sun. A stink of oil and petrol made him gag. There was the smell of faeces. He looked down at his ragged, green-bloodstained, filthy combats. Shock chilled him; he could not feel what his eyes saw. A chunk of muscle tissue blown out of his thigh, large enough to put a fist through, and bone gleaming in the depths. And the foot was obviously his, too.

'Marine Arakingu . . . ?'

The truck's wheels still spun. Something hissed.

The Bug loomed over him, black against the bright blue of the desert sky. Its segmented body convulsed, twitching, and the clawed forelimbs went under its body, into the clusters of rubbery black organs that hung down between the powerful hind legs. Barashkukor registered that some of the shine about its body-segments was black metal, not chitin. Devices, not organs.

Between him and the fort, nothing else moved but Bugs.

A cold sensation flooded his back. The orc raised his head again. A Kalashnikov lay beside him, magazine still in place. Blood covered the bolt, wet and sticky. Arakingu lay on her back two yards away, helmet fallen from her bald head, her brains hanging out in a green glob. Barashkukor began to reach for the rifle.

The hissing came from the headset, still jammed into his spindly long ears.

The Bug's shadow fell across him.

'This is . . . Major Barashkukor . . . calling Graagryk. Over.'

'Graagryk receiving. Your signal's breaking up, Major. What's the situation on the ground? Over.'

The insectoid thing's clawed forelimbs rummaged in the rubbery organs under its body. They came out clasping an angular, long shape. Barashkukor squinted sand-blasted eyes. Stock, receiver, barrel . . .

The insectoid being stood over him, a chitin-and-metal replica of an M16 held in its claws. The orc in shocked amazement gazed up at alien organs that might replicate weapons, his small heavy jaw hanging open. Dizzily, he thought, *But I suppose they had Corporal Uzkaddit to copy from.*

It raised its forelimbs and pointed the organic weapon into the desert, pulling the replica trigger.

FOOM!

Shrapnel ricocheted.

'Graagryk calling Barashkukor! Major, give me a sit. rep., now!'

A different voice, Ashnak's familiar bass rumble, fading with the satellite's struggle to keep the link open. Barashkukor's mouth widened and he showed small fangs in a tired grin.

'General, I am receiving you . . . Foreign hostiles; eight seen; no mage-power; chameleon technology possible . . .' He breathed harshly. 'Some kind of giant Bugs, General. They followed us last night, took the patrols this morning. We couldn't pull out . . . Man, we just got our asses kicked . . . !'

The muzzle of the organic weapon swept down, turning, aiming towards Barashkukor.

The coldness flooding his back, soaking his marine uniform jacket, was petrol.

'Barashkukor are you receiving me? We have target-acquisition. ETA bombers twenty-five minutes. Vacate the area!' And then, lost in static, *'Barashkukor, for fuck's sake get your skinny little ass out of there!'*

Heat shimmered up from the rock of the Endless Desert, evaporating the fuel. Silence hung over the fort. From that distance Barashkukor could hear the chewing of mandibles over the unanswered hissing of the radio. The Bug stood with its hindlegs straddling him. He could move nothing but his arms.

While he could still feel the chill of petrol soaking through to his skinny back, and before the cold of shock wore off to let him feel the pain of amputation, Major Barashkukor of the Orc Marines took the Kalashnikov in a two-handed grip, pointed the muzzle up at the belly of the Bug, flipped the fire-selector to fully automatic, and squeezed the trigger.

'Bugging out, General!'

The muzzle flash ignited the spilled fuel.

Graagryk's military airfield sweated under midsummer sun.

Ashnak flattened his peaked ears against the blast of the cold-drake's wings as the beast took off, heading back south at a considerable rate.

'Working for the *Dark Lord* again?' Behind her round wire-rimmed spectacles, the newly arrived Commissar Razitshakra's eyes narrowed. 'But, sir – are you certain He's ideologically sound? After all, He's a civilian.'

The orc general made no reply to this impertinence. City living can make an orc soft. Marine Commissar Razitshakra began to eye the married Ducal Ashnak with suspicion as he examined closely the fragment of black substance enclosed in a plastic envelope that she handed to him.

'I wonder, sir,' she ventured, 'if *that* has anything to do with what the late Major Barashkukor reported?'

Without looking up, Ashnak absently drew back his fist and drove it forward.

The orc commissar picked herself up off the hard earth and wiped a trickle of green from her jaw. She spoke approvingly, if somewhat indistinctly. 'Good to see you're still a marine, General Ashnak!'

'That's "Field Marshal Ashnak" to you,' Ashnak snarled.

The heavy *whup-whup!* of a Chinook sounded. The big orc looked up as the troop-carrier touched down. Beyond the airfield the candy-bright colours of Graagryk city gleamed, scoured clean by magery, with never a plume of smoke from the factories lining the Inland Sea coast. Three APCs also approached, crossing the field.

An Mi-24 Hind D touched down fifty yards away, rotors whipping over its two stubby wings and missiles and rocket pods.

Ashnak thumbed the RT stud in his kevlar helmet. 'Chahkamnit, I'm gonna want a rapid dust-off. On my word: count of five: *mark.*'

The twin-rotored troop-carrier thundered, standing on the flattened grass. A platoon of orc marines left the APCs and doubled across the field towards it.

Two figures followed them, more slowly, and where those walked, shadow haunted the grass. Graagryk did not question their going. Could not notice it, save as the withdrawal of a nightmare not remembered on waking.

'Have your report complete by the time we land at Ferenzia, Commissar,' Ashnak ordered. 'I'll listen to it there.'

The orc, sweating in her heavy greatcoat, stared across the Graagryk landing field at the approaching figures.

'Sir, I can't approve the presence of civilians in military transport! It isn't wise during the present crisis. Orc lips make slips—'

Ashnak swung his head around and displayed a grin so full of teeth that the Marine Commissar saluted twice and made for the Chinook at the double. Ashnak waited, the Hind's rotor-blast whipping the material of his camouflage trousers, GI pot pulled down over his beetling brows, pipe-weed cigar in one corner of his mouth. The heavy flak jacket made him sweat.

'Field Marshal.' The nameless necromancer greeted Ashnak silkily. The slender handsome Man wrinkled his ascetic features at the peculiarly pungent smell of hot orc, and fanned himself with his Man-skin fan. 'You *are* ready to transport the Dark Lord to Ferenzia, I trust?'

The sashed leather robes of the necromancer and his waist-length black hair fluttered in the rotor blast from the helicopter gunship. The Dark Lord's fine mesh robe did not stir. The winds did not disturb Her glossy yellow hair. The heat did not spring sweat from Her piebald skin.

'We go to Ferenzia in peace,' She said clearly. 'I will have no fighting, Field Marshal Ashnak. Neither there nor here. My servant the nameless necromancer will remain here as My regent. Your marines are to obey him as they would obey Me.'

Ashnak saluted. 'Of course, Dread Lord, Ma'am. Naturally.'

She turned her back on the nameless necromancer and walked towards the Hind, barefoot on grass that withered under Her feet. Ashnak followed, webbing clanking with grenades, magazines, and his shoulder-slung M16.

'Diplomacy, little Ashnak. Peace.' Her upward-tilting, rheumy eye-sockets glowed with a certain fiery amusement. Her small tusks lifted Her turned-back lip, and a trickle of saliva slid down Her chin. Without bothering to wipe it, She said, 'There is one thing more before I leave.'

She did not raise Her voice, but it carried over the mechanized roar of the Chinook's takeoff as they approached the Hind. The smell of hot metal and oil filled the air. Ashnak chewed his cigar, and tightened his webbing. RT-traffic whispered in his headset.

'I think your orc marines will trouble My creature the nameless.'

'No, great Sable Lord,' Ashnak protested.

'I will make him a more suitable commander for them.' Her eyes laughed, and momentarily flashed green: the Paladin of the Light looking out from Her face in panic. The glimpse of the trapped soul vanished. 'When this body was otherwise, it once said, "He wears my virtue, unearned, on his face, as I wear the ugliness of his sin on my body".'

The Lord of Night and Silence held out Her arms, gazing down at Her borrowed body as they came to the Hind. Looking up into the belly of the machine, She asked, 'Am I ugly, as Men conceive it? Possibly. I will not be laughed at, Ashnak, in Ferenzia.'

'Think you're a damned handsome woman, myself, Dread Lord,' Ashnak said gallantly. 'We're cleared for takeoff, so if—'

'Brother, take your shape again!'

She raised Her blank orange gaze. Piebald black and grey withdrew, tidally, leaving skin of a pinkish-cream. Soft blond lashes lay over down-softened cheeks. Her long eyes were now level and wide-set, under gull-wing brows, and Her lips curved lusciously bronze over small, even teeth.

'Very nice, Ma'am,' Ashnak said unenthusiastically.

A high, wavering, and prolonged shriek sounded from the far side of the airfield.

'Come!' The Dark Lord clapped Ashnak on the shoulder with that Virtue-augmented strength that had staggered the orc in a small

259

church in a northern village. Ashnak glanced up at the bubble-glass cabin and Lieutenant Chahkamnit.

'Cleared to go!' Ashnak handed the Dark Lord a helmet and headset, handing her into the armoured body of the machine.

She buckled the helmet down over Her blond hair. Lieutenant Chahkamnit, glancing across, took the full benefit of glowing orange eye sockets, sat rigidly forward in his pilot's seat, and began flight-checks with a concentration that nothing short of air-to-air missile fire could have disturbed.

'I'll ride gunner.' Ashnak climbed in behind the lanky black orc lieutenant, who was wearing a bomber jacket, and a close-fitting leather flying helmet and goggles. Chahkamnit pushed foot-pedals and pulled levers, and the troop-carrier lifted with an ear-splitting roar.

'*My creature Ashnak.*' The Sable Lord's voice sounded over the headset.

'*Yes, Dark Lord?*' Ashnak watched Graagryk dwindle to toy houses; agricultural patterns; pastel shapes on the Inland Sea's coast. The Hind drove nose-down, due south.

'*I will not have My peace negotiations disturbed. There must be no brushfire wars on the Southern Kingdoms' borders. What has happened to your major who reported from Gyzrathrani?*'

Chahkamnit glanced at his superior officer, who remained silent.

'*The last we heard, Dread Lord, he'd got a little hot under the collar,*' the second lieutenant transmitted. '*Jolly rotten show, I say. But he was a marine – at least he went out with a bang.*'

The solid vibration of 'copter flight reverberated through Ashnak. The big orc waited until the Dark Lord either slept or (more likely) achieved some interior trance of Her own; and flicked to a separate wavelength.

'*Lieutenant Chahkamnit, you heard the Dark Lord. No fighting around Ferenzia. There are no orc marine units giving unofficial fire support to the deserters, mercenaries and bandits on the Ferenzi borders – are there? Especially not where Herself is going to land. See to it, Chahkamnit.*'

'*Oh, I say, sir! How am I supposed to do that?*'

'*Contact our ground forces there and tell them to move the battle!*'

'*Move a battle, sir?*' the orc lieutenant demanded. '*How do you move a* battle?'

'*I don't care; just do it!*'

Chahkamnit raised the ground forces north of Ferenzia. '*Right, lads,*' he directed lugubriously. '*Shoot faster . . .*'

Sun reflected from the curving glass canopy. Ashnak pulled the visor of his flight helmet down over his porcine eyes, polarizing light. When he woke, the country below stretched out widely; much wider than the northern kingdoms' mountain-ridden patches of fertile land. Forested hills rolled out to a distant horizon, interspersed with strip-fields, grazing lands, castles built on high peaks, and wide, slow rivers. A blazing sun bleached the colour from the ripening corn.

Due south, the sprawling suburbs of Ferenzia stretched towards the great Lakes.

'I say, sir, contact ahead – the Ferenzi must have spotted us coming. Pretty good for them, isn't it, what?'

Ashnak cast a disillusioned eye at the sky. Circling dots, higher than the Hind, were vultures. Lower, on the helicopter's flight level, twin giant eagles flew figure-of-eights over the spires and towers of the mighty city.

'Door gunners,' Ashnak checked.

'Yo, sir!'

The Dark Lord's voice said, *'I have been watching them for some time now. They are two of Ferenzia's most potent Mages of the Light.'*

Chahkamnit squinted into the sun. *'Really, ma'am? How can you tell?'*

The Dark Lord said, *'The vultures are – have always been – My eyes.'*

Ashnak winced.

The soft voice in his helmet continued, *'It is quite like the old days, watching orcs scurry about. I found that mountain siege quite gripping to watch. And I will not blame you for beginning wars when you did not know of My survival, and therefore could not know My wishes in the matter, and I have been most amused to watch you try to conceal your actions. However, the joke is over. Nothing must interfere with what I do now.'*

It took the orc Field Marshal two fumbled attempts before he reached the commander of the ground forces on the Ferenzi border and convince them both of his authority and his orders.

The Mages of the Light circled above the city.

'Speak with them, Ashnak,' the Dark Lord commanded. *'I will ensure, by My power, that you are heard.'*

The orc cleared his throat and spat between his feet. Phlegm spattered the foot pedals. Five hundred feet below his boots, Ferenzia's blue-tiled roofs cast mid-afternoon shadows into the streets, clear and precise.

'This is Field Marshal Ashnak, Orc Marine Command, calling Mages of the Light.'

Thin magical voices whispered in the hot cabin, vibrating through the talisman-protected metal. 'Vile creature of Darkness! Your hideous engine does not hide our Great Enemy from our eyes. Surrender yourself. Give Him up to our justice, and we may spare you!'

The Hind ceased forward motion and hung, thrumming.

Ashnak leaned forward, taloned hands resting flat on his massive thighs, sweating odorously under the weight of flak jacket, webbing and arms; but not the sweat of fear.

'Well now,' he remarked cheerfully, 'I'm carrying 57mm rockets, wire-guided anti-tank missiles, 23mm cannon, and an electrically powered Gatling gun in the chin-mounted gun turret. I suppose that might put a hole in your precious city. And I wouldn't count on those moth-eaten eagles outflying an attack helicopter with a crack pilot, either.'

Chahkamnit blushed light brown. 'Jolly decent of you, sir. Wouldn't have said that myself, you know.'

The Mage-voices sharpened, echoing through the Hind's metal frame. 'We will perish gladly, knowing that we take with us the Blight of the Earth, the Evil Emperor, the Lord of Darkness Himself!'

The eagles broke their flight-patterns, wings beating as they gained height to strike. Ashnak regretfully abandoned his taunts.

'The Lord of Darkness Himself is with us, but I formally advise you now that He's not making any threat against your ground establishment or personnel. You'll be making a completely unprovoked attack on us!'

There was a puzzled silence, after which one of the voices, somewhat petulantly, said, 'We cannot let you pass unhindered! You have the Dark Lord with you!'

The second Mage-voice cut in. 'It's a trick! If the Dark Lord is here, with these few troops, then He must have an army hidden from our sight, about to descend on our city! Why else would He come here but to make hideous war on us?'

'Actually,' Ashnak rumbled, 'He just wants to talk to you.'

There was a pause.

'"Talk"?' inquired the first voice.

'"Talk"!' spat the second.

'He wants to talk,' Ashnak said, 'but I've got no objection to blowing you dumb-ass fly-boys out of the sky if I have to. I'm putting this chopper down. You go talk to whoever commands in Ferenzia. If they ain't outside the town in under fifteen minutes, I'm gonna take and strafe the fuck outta you, do I make myself clear?'

In his headphones, the Dark Lord sighed.

'Diplomacy,' She reminded him. 'Tact.'

'Highly over-rated virtues, Ma'am. Ah. There they go. Chahkamnit, take us down.'

'Roger, sir. Going down.'

Making no overtly hostile moves, the Hind sank down with the beauty of machinery defying gravity, escorted by one of the vast-pinioned eagles. A preying yellow eye stared in through the Hind's canopy with infinite amusement and weariness in it; tolerating the mage that rode its feathered back.

Lieutenant Chahkamnit brought the helicopter down in a textbook landing on the hard shore between the lake and the city wall. As the wheels touched, the orc marine squad disembarked to secure the perimeter.

Chahkamnit took off his flying helmet and peered out at the Chinook, two squads of orc marines belly-down behind cover, and the third squad forming up as the Lord of Midnight's bodyguard.

'I say, sir, does the Dark Lord consider this hostile territory? I didn't think we were actually at war yet.'

Ashnak fastened the chin-strap of his marine-issue helmet. 'We're not, son. The question is, does Herself consider anywhere *not* hostile territory? And then there's the Ferenzi.'

'Ah. Yes, sir, I take your point.'

Ashnak unbuckled the seat's crotch-straps. Built for a race that certainly was not orcish, they constricted rather more than his circulation. Rubbing his groin, the orc Field Marshal muttered, 'Keep the rotors turning!' and disembarked from the helicopter.

In the deserts of Gyzrathrani, in the jungles of Thyrion, in the tundras of the Antarctic Icelands; there is movement of a kind which has not existed before.

And in other places, too, now.

The animals scent it as if it were a forest fire.

Those beasts that are most magical flee first.

The dwarvish band struck up a waltz. The barbarian swordswoman – persuaded for this official Ferenzi 'Heroes of the Last Battle' reception to drape a selection of shawls, at least, over her curvaceous form and chainmail groin-covering – ceased to sing. The warrior guests in their evening dress took their partners and moved out on to the dance floor, under the magic-fuelled crystalline chandeliers.

Oderic, High Wizard of Ferenzia, eased through the crowd, his long yellow teeth bared in an official smile of welcome.

'Gandoran!' Oderic shot his cuffs, and shook hands with the Hero of Spine Gap. The tall blond warrior nodded uncomfortably and muttered something appreciative. Oderic added, 'Varella will take care of you. Won't you, Madam Varella?'

The jungle swordswoman, sweaty from the bandstand, flashed her eyes at Gandoran and took his hand, beaming. The Hero of Spine Gap cheered up. Oderic bowed and retreated.

Summer's late evening light coloured the sky butterfly-wing blue. Multiple voices rose over the thumping dwarf-music and the clink of magically replenished wine glasses. Oderic proceeded through the ballroom crowd, under the light of spellcast gas-lamps, pausing for a word here, a smile there.

'The reception is a success, so far,' a voice said below his elbow.

One veined hand went up to smooth back the white hair that flowed down over Oderic's cravat and the shoulders of his tweed jacket. The elderly wizard beamed. 'Corinna Halfelven!'

You would not know, to look at her, that she had been one of the greatest mages at the Fields of Destruction; second only to Oderic himself. Here in the great Assembly Rooms of the Ferenzi palace, the nobles of Ferenzia wore formal long-tailed black coats and stiff high collars, with the sashes of knightly Orders across their chests. The women (with the exception of a few; including one fighter who continued to wear full plate harness, and stood red-faced and sweating alone by a potted palm) wore multi-petticoated silken ballgowns, and precious stones in their braided hair.

Corinna Halfelven wore a lavender-and-lace gown that hugged her three-feet-tall form and swept the floor over her diminutively slippered feet. The ostrich plume in her tiara was tall enough to come level with Oderic's shoulder.

'We have waited three seasons to honour these heroes,' the half-elven halfling remarked. 'It should be a joyous occasion, and yet . . . I have a dire premonition of evil, Magus Oderic.'

Oderic felt in his jacket pockets for a foul-smelling black pipe, took it out, lit it with a tiny ball of fire from one thumb, and drew deeply. Corinna wrinkled her sensitive elven nostrils at the stench of pipe-weed that always accompanied the famous wizard. She moved a pace away.

'These are those who fought against the vilest corruption in the Last Battle.' Oderic blew a perfect smoke ring. 'Is it to be wondered at if those who have touched pitch smell a little of defilement?'

Her small golden eyes narrowed under her fair brows. 'You sense it too!'

Leaning on the white oak staff that he carried, Oderic gestured at the thronging hall.

'Here are the greatest nobles of Ferenzia – and mark me well, a

264

lord in Ferenzia is worth a king in a smaller kingdom. Here are the heroes of last Samhain's Battle, warriors and mages from across the Known World. The heroes of the greatest victory the world will ever see.' Oderic gave a dry, old man's cough. 'Some have journeyed for months to arrive here for this night. I told the High King Magorian, if we cancel this celebration, we shall look fools, and the other kingdoms will lose all confidence in the economy of Ferenzia. So, if there *is* evil . . . we must simply be prepared to deal with it. I can count on you, Lady Corinna?'

The half-elven halfling glanced towards the canopied throne at the far end of the ballroom. 'Of course. But King Magorian—'

'Wait.' Oderic threw back his head, sniffing through equine nostrils. '*Ah.* I fear, gracious lady, that we were both correct in our premonitions!'

The High Wizard turned and walked as briskly as was possible through the crowd. Corinna Halfelven scurried at his heels, plume bobbing over her pointed ears. The old wizard, his yellow waistcoat and flowing hair marking him out in that formal gathering, leaned heavily on his white oak staff as he approached the great double doors of the Assembly Rooms.

Before he could reach them, the double doors burst open.

The dwarvish band clattered and thumped to a halt, trailing off in a scatter of tuba-notes. Dancers slowed their whirling steps. Heads turned towards the door; conversation dropped to shocked whispers; and over the sudden silence Oderic heard a plaintive voice from the canopied throne:

'What is it *now?* No one ever tells me anything. Where's Oderic? Where's my wizard?'

'Here, High King.' Oderic's venerable voice was resonant. He did not bother to look back at the king. The open door now filled with a scurry of red-coated soldiers carrying ceremonial halberds. One of the eagle-rider mages appeared, rushed up to Oderic, and whispered frantically in the wizard's ear. Oderic's bushy eyebrows lifted. A further whisper, and the wizard's features went completely blank.

Recovering himself, he called, 'Ladies and gentlemen, I must beg you not to be alarmed by anything you see or hear—'

Squat figures appeared in the doorway.

Oderic muttered a protective ward, only to have his fingertips flash blue sparks as it flew back at him.

'My magic will not bite on them!' Corinna whispered, panic-stricken.

'Nor mine. Wait,' Oderic counselled, hand shaking. 'Do you realize what these horrors must be, elven lady? We are witnessing a new legend of evil!'

The squat figures marched into the hall in close formation. Their muscular brown, green and black forms proclaimed them orcs, and the tusked mouths and deep-set glinting eyes were familiar enough to the veteran warriors there. Oderic heard shouts for weapons from the crowd behind him. He held up a commanding hand.

'Wait!'

Large boots rang out on the parquet flooring. In smooth order the uniformed orcs marched into the hall, raised metallic tubes to their shoulders, and each pointed them at a different sector of the hall. One barked something in orcish.

'These must be those strange Dark warriors of whom Amarynth Firehand spoke,' Oderic said loudly. 'Orcs! What do you in Ferenzia?'

A very large orc indeed stomped through the doorway. His shrewd, tiny eyes swept the Ferenzi nobility and their guests.

'Freeze, motherfucker!' the orc grated.

Corinna Halfelven stilled her fingers, that had begun to weave the Powers of the Air.

'Awriiight! That's better. Now, where's this High King Magorian?'

Behind Oderic, the sea of faces parted. The High King Kelyos Magorian, Lord of the South and North Domains, Defender Against the East, limped forward on the arm of a young squire.

Magorian, almost lost in a crimson, ermine-trimmed robe, halted under the glittering brilliance of the magical chandeliers, surrounded by the nobles of the greatest of the Southern Kingdoms. His golden hair had thinned to the point of invisibility. The hands that once wielded enchanted sword and shield now shook, veins prominent on their backs; and he lifted cataracted eyes to the orc.

'What *is* that?' he quavered peevishly. 'It doesn't matter. Say the usual thing, I suppose. You enter our court with a show of force: vile creature, we are not afraid of you!'

Beside Oderic, Corinna whispered, 'But you, wizard. You are afraid of something, and it is not orcs!'

The High King demanded plaintively, 'This *thing* defiles the air of Ferenzia. Why is it allowed to remain here?'

Some of the visiting warriors were already making for the weapons-cache in the cloakroom. Men in sashed waistcoats tutted and glared, and Oderic overheard one be-medalled general mutter, 'damned green scum!'

The orc tipped his round helmet back on his bald head, scratched his ears, and caught Oderic's eye.

'You.' The orcish voice grated the common tongue. 'Wizard. The old guy's obviously lost his marbles. Get me someone who can count beyond five without using their fingers and I'll say what I have to say to them.'

'I— Ah— I am not familiar with your idiom, sir.' Oderic kept his piercing blue eyes fixed on the squat creature. The eagle-mage's warning echoed in his ears. He leaned heavily on his staff. 'But to spare His Majesty the undue strain of addressing a . . . ah . . . an *orc*, perhaps it would be better if you spoke with me. I am Oderic, High Wizard of Ferenzia.'

With surprising formality, the great orc touched its helmet with the talons of its free hand. 'Ashnak. Field Marshal of the Horde, and General Officer Commanding the Orc Marines.'

Oderic raised his voice. 'The hall will now be cleared of all but the members of the High Council!'

The High Wizard rested his hands on the pommel of his staff, knuckles white, fearing greatly the resurgence of Evil with only one humble old man to stand between it and the Good Peoples. The crowd began to move towards the doors. All of the be-gowned women shuffled that way, accompanied by men with campaign medals on their dress suits, and some with the sashes of Knightly Orders. Clerks, merchant princes and lesser mages began to move, reluctantly. Those who did not stir were those who wore thick robes of state, ornamented gorgets and dress swords; Ferenzi men of middle age with closed, shrewd faces.

The orc barked an unfamiliar word. The other orcs raised their metal sticks.

DUKKA-DUKKA-DUKKA-*FOOM!*

Oderic instantly whipped his staff up, casting a Shield of Protection as the room's chandeliers shattered into crystal splinters. Women screamed. The crowd milled about. The glowing blue fire of the ward brushed the crystal fragments harmlessly away.

The High Wizard had just time to notice that metal shrapnel passed through the magic unharmed.

'Quiet!' The orc did not speak much above a conversational tone, but the great assembly hall became silent and still. The orc flipped open one of the many pouches on his complicated belt, extracted a pipe-weed cigar, and stuck it in his tusked mouth. Looking at Oderic, he jerked a taloned thumb at the warriors and mages in their evening dress.

'They're staying right here,' the big orc said. 'Nobody leaves. *We* got no secrets. C'mon, wizard, get your ass in gear! And by the way – have you got a light?'

Oderic caused the orc's cigar to bloom a small ember of flame. 'Well? What can you have to say to us?'

267

The orc ambled forward into the room, bandy-legged, grinning as only an orc can. 'As Marine military ambassador, may I present to you – the Death of Empires, the Blight of Man, the Heresy of Elvenkind, the One Who Lays Waste to Worlds . . . the Dark Lord of the East!'

Someone screamed.

A hubbub of voices rose, sound flattened by the draped walls. Corinna's elvishly musical tones sounded clearly:

'It can't be! He's dead. I was there at the Fields of Destruction when we slew Him!' The small half-breed leaned up to whisper to Oderic, 'Was that the warning they brought you? It can't *be*, I tell you!'

'Peace,' Oderic commanded sternly. 'It will be an imposter, of course.'

He witnessed Corinna's elf-gold eyes widen. *'No . . .'*

The High Wizard Oderic turned to face the double doors, his last hope gone.

A young female stood there, of a stature tall among Men. Shadows clung to Her yellow hair that was bobbed level with Her chin. Shadows haunted the folds of Her fine metal-ring robe. Her smooth face held a porcelain calm. She did not raise Her head.

Oderic's bones chilled.

Eight orc marines surrounded her, green bulging muscles gleaming in the remaining candlelight; bald heads and ears shining. They stood shoulder to shoulder, facing outwards. The large orc, Ashnak, snarled the incomprehensible phrase, 'Muzzle sweep!', and the orc warriors immediately lifted the metal sticks to point away from him. They pointed them at the crowd of Ferenzi nobility instead.

'Odo, send them away!' Magorian protested, tugging the wizard's sleeve. 'Can't have my royal hall full of damned spear-chuckin' greenies from bongo-bongo land. Get rid of 'em! Don't know what the world's coming to; greenies starting getting above themselves. And who's that damned fine woman? Nice filly, but she's hardly dressed for my royal court.'

The elderly wizard snapped testily, 'That is the Dark Lord, whom we thought to be dead!'

'Really?' Uninterested, Magorian clutched the arm of his squire and began limping back towards his canopied throne. 'Wasn't like this at the Battle of Moonheart. Mowed 'em down in ranks, we did. *Hordes* of spear-chucking greenies . . .'

Before Oderic could restrain her, Corinna Halfelven strode out of the crowd. She glared up – and up – at the tall shape of the female Man. *'Die, vile creature of Darkness!'*

268

All the windows along the assembly hall shattered inwards. A wind icy as the heights above mountains soared in. Oderic felt the Powers of the Air, which are vast as the world, press into the palace; masonry groaning at the pressure.

Corinna Halfelven, at the centre of the power vortex, threw out one elbow-gloved hand and pointed her finger at the heart of the Dark Lord. Her other hand held up the petticoats of her ball-gown. Wood-ash pale hair floated about her tiny aquiline face. She cried out in the elvish tongue an incantation older than the glaciers. The Powers of the Air poised at her command.

The Dark Lord, Her voice gentle, said, 'No, I don't think so.'

A smear of grease smoked on the marble floor tiles of the Royal Assembly Hall of Ferenzia – all that remained of the halfling mage.

The Dark Lord stepped delicately over it on bare feet, light from the remaining candles sliding down Her metalmesh robe. Glints of black light flashed. She raised Her chin, bobbed yellow hair swinging.

'A mage-assassin. The Light has grown hypocritical of late. No matter. It does not harm me. Being dead has, I think, been good for My evil magic.'

Oderic broke the shocked, impressed silence by snapping his fingers. Halfling servants in brown waistcoats, with their shirtsleeves rolled up, pushed through the crowd with mops and cloths, and cleared what remained of Corinna Halfelven from the floor.

'Be swift,' he directed, 'but reverent.'

A chill walked down the knobs of Oderic's spine. He recognized the Dark Lord's impatience. Battle-hardened, he took his time in turning.

Four orcs clustered tightly around the Dark Lord, blocking the crowd's sight of Her. The other four split into pairs, heavy metal sticks slung across their backs; shoving between frock-coated Men, tearing down the few remaining drapes and lace curtains to expose the night-view of Ferenzia beyond the Palace windows, and secreting abandoned champagne bottles about their persons. The Ferenzi nobility complained in precise, hysterical accents about 'green barbarians!' Oderic kept the same disgust, icy and strong, from showing on his lined features.

'Dark Master.' The big orc knelt formally. 'The Royal Assembly of Ferenzia hears you.'

The four orcs with Her knelt, covering the crowd.

Formless Darkness coalesced in Her eyes. The tall, straight young woman raised Her head. A dryness, as of ancient dust, caught in the throats of Men; and those nearest Her grew age-lines in their faces that they never, from that day forwards, lost.

She rested Her hands, lightly, on the shoulders of two armed, kneeling orcs. The assembled nobility of the Light shaded their eyes from Her darkness. Her voice spoke into the silence.

'You thought you had defeated Me at the Fields of Destruction. Poor warriors! Poor mages! Instead you have made Me more strong. For I have died and lived, and what is more strong than that which can overcome death? You think that you have the world in your hands, after that battle. You think the Ages of the World have turned.'

Now laughter, so quiet that Oderic shuddered. To win so great a victory against such hopeless odds, with such sacrifice, and now to see it all to do again . . . In the crowd, Men wept.

'If I wish, I am strong enough to take the world from you. If I wish, there will be a battle that is truly the last, for after it no Man, no beast, no blade of grass will stir on this unbreathing world. If I wish, I can still the heart in your breast and the breath in your body, merely by My wishing it. If I wish.'

Oderic swayed. Of the heroes of the Light assembled together in the halls of Ferenzia, only he remained on his feet. Sweat rolled down his old Man's face.

'It was not *meant* that you should come here and throw this filth in our faces,' the wizard snapped. His bony hand fluttered at his throat and his lips turned blue.

'Was it not?' The Dark Lord seemed unmoved. 'But I do not wish to destroy the world in gaining it. It will be more entertaining for Me if it is whole. And therefore . . . I will step down into the world and compete with you all, upon your terms, in equal contest for election to the Throne of the World.'

Oderic, in the silence that followed, could *feel* the puzzlement of four hundred and fifty Men.

'"Election"?' The High Wizard got his breath. 'That heresy! I might have expected *that* from the Lord of Darkness! Who can you say is qualified to elect a candidate to the Throne of the World?'

The Dark Lord, an ancient smile on Her lips, merely inclined Her head slightly. Her big orc got to his feet. Fists on hips, he grinned at Oderic.

'Who qualifies? The same "who" that would have fought at the next Last Battle, that's who! That means *everybody*, sucker. Everybody from Men to elves; from hill-giants to halflings!'

The wizard stared testily at the orc.

'Some of my best friends are halflings,' Oderic said, appalled

270

beyond belief, 'but really: *no*. If you once allow halflings – good people though they may be – a say in the councils of the wise, then the next thing you know, we'll be asked to consult trolls, witches, werewolves . . . Lady save us, even orcs and necromancers! It just won't do, I say.'

The halfling servants paused in mopping the tiles, looked at each other, and murmured, ''E's right, you know, that there wizard. We know our place, see if we don't.'

Oderic finished, 'We can never agree to it! You're mad!'

'I ain't mad.' The orc switched the pipe-weed cigar to the other corner of his tusked mouth, and blew a lopsided smoke-ring. 'You wouldn't like me when I'm mad. *OK, you guys, listen up!* You heard the Dark Lord. That's the way it's going to be!'

Oderic lifted his head, white hair flowing back over his tweed collar. He caught the eye of others in the crowd – the Lords of Goistan, Lalgrenda and Istan; Shugbar, Vendivil, Kaanistad and Hurost. Old companions, who had been carefree soldiers of fortune or wandering mages, and who now ruled the estates they had been rewarded with in Ferenzia. Their waists were thickening, they might be more intent on politics now than drinking or questing, but he saw agreement in their eyes.

'I suppose it was already too late for us', Oderic said, 'when You survived Samhain. I am an old and foolish man, and I should have guessed. I failed. But this remains to me: I will die before I obey one order of the Dark Lord! I speak for every Man here. We can yet go into the afterlife with honour. Do Your worst!'

Cheers rang in the shattered room. Those few Men who had got to the weapons in the cloakroom clashed spear against shield and loosened their tight evening collars.

The Dark Lord's long-lashed eyelids lifted. Her eyes glowed orange. The hall quieted. Wrapped in a pride as cold as the tiles upon which Corinna Halfelven had died, the Dark Lord of the East regarded Her ancient foes. Oderic saw that She would no longer condescend to explain, much less beg.

'Gentlemen . . .' The orc, Ashnak, stepped a few paces closer to the crowd. He put his short metal stick in a holster on his belt, and stretched out his open hands.

The sight of an orc willingly disarming itself, rather than bloodily flinging itself into the defenceless crowd, axe-blade swinging, got the assembled dignitaries', ambassadors', and ministers' attention.

'Gentlemen. Ladies. I know I am an orc,' he said gruffly, 'but I appeal to you to hear me. Most of you may already know – we have another enemy on our borders. A terrible enemy. We must unite to

271

fight! We're facing a geopolitical conflict that makes nonsense of distinctions between Light and Dark. I assure you, gentlemen, we're all on the same side now.'

A babble of curiosity rose in the Assembly Hall. The orc Field Marshal reached up and pulled off his helmet, and scratched at his ears. Seeming curiously unprotected, standing between the nobility of Ferenzia and the silent Dark Lord, the orc spoke again.

'I am a plain soldier,' Ashnak said, 'and I have always respected the Light as a brave opponent. Now we face a force which is vicious, unstoppable and vile. Men of the Light, your virtues are well known. Trust me when I say they'll slow you down and weaken you in the face of an enemy who doesn't know what mercy or kindness means.'

'What enemy?' a Ferenzi lord demanded.

The hall full of Men in evening dress clutched at their hastily recovered weapons and pressed forward in shouting groups. Orc warriors lowered their fire-sticks. The big orc struck one warrior's fire-stick up to point at the chandeliers.

'*This* enemy!' The big orc felt in a large pouch attached to his jacket. He lifted something out, raised his arm, and threw it down on the floor. It cracked. People flinched away, then crowded near.

'Recognize that?' The orc bared brass-capped tusks. 'Lost any outlying settlements recently? Mysterious disappearances? Parties of adventurers gone missing?'

Oderic hitched up the knees of his tweed trousers before squatting to see exactly what was encased in the transparent envelope the orc had thrown down. When he recognized the chitinous fragments, he had to use his staff purely as a stick to help him rise.

'The . . . the Black Claw! It is a true token,' the High Wizard admitted brokenly. 'The Light's mages have been secretly combating this menace for *days*. But we are not of sufficient strength to defeat it!'

The orc grinned.

'If you good guys can't handle it, then let us bad-ass orc bastards do it for you! If you elect my Dark Master as War Leader – purely for the duration of this emergency – then I can mobilize the entire forces of the Orc Marines, élite corps and reserves, on your side. Without a War Leader, you'll fall into confusion, quarrel among yourselves, while these monsters ravage your homes. We must have this election, and we must have it soon!'

A voice from the back of the wrecked hall cheered, 'Yes!'

'Preposterous!' a fat woman in satin snarled; and a silken-cloaked man beside her protested, 'How can we trust them?'

Another voice called, 'It's our only chance!'

The hall of Ferenzi nobility squabbled among themselves. A number gathered around the canopied throne, harassing the half-asleep High King Magorian. And as is the way with half-breed mages, no matter how they may seem to be accepted into polite society, Corinna Halfelven's murder was not officially protested. The High Wizard Oderic felt suddenly bent with age.

'The plans of evil are cunning,' he whispered, watching the hall full of milling people: how they forgot and turned their backs on the strange orc warriors, how they tolerated in that smashed audience chamber the presence of Darkness Incarnate.

'You think *you* got problems.' The orc Field Marshal dropped his pipe-weed cigar and crushed it under one heavy boot. His pit-deep eyes gleamed at Oderic.

'*I* got two of them on my back. Not that *he's* much, compared to Her. I can hack it. And She may be well out to lunch; but yours is out to lunch, dinner and breakfast the following day . . .'

Oderic brushed pipe-weed ash from his tweed jacket, his piercing blue gaze searching out the High King Magorian. Ashnak and the High Wizard Oderic exchanged the kind of glance that ensues between the servants of masters who are, for one reason or another, somewhat unpredictable.

Ashnak added, '*And* I got you Light guys on my back, and my marines getting chewed up in the boonies. Bitchin', ain't it?'

The emergency back-up magical spells cut in and the Assembly Rooms' lights whirred into action. Small magics began to mend the drapes, re-glaze the windows and replenish the buffet table. Halfling servants brought ladies their fans, gloves and cantrips from the cloakrooms.

Oderic took a deep breath. All certainties gone, he ventured to say, 'Sir orc, you have some plan for combating this monstrous menace that we face?'

'Oh, sure.' The orc buffed a brass-capped tusk with his gnarled knuckle. His eyes gleamed. 'But, plans later. First – we've got an election to hold. Chahkamnit, we're all done here, bring her in.'

A strange *whup-whup-whup!* sounded beyond the windows. The High Wizard Oderic walked forward to see what devilish engine was settling down outside the palace.

'An election,' the wizard mused. 'Elections can be won, sir orc. But they can also be lost. What chance can the Lord of Evil possibly stand of winning the hearts and minds of the free peoples of the south?'

5

THE INLAND SEA and the Western
Ocean are kept from joining, at their most adjacent point, by a
ribbon of land and the mountain chain known as The Spine. The road
through The Spine's magnificent peaks runs from Herethlion to the
south, with only one settlement of any consequence at which to break
a journey or hold a battle.

Towards the end of an afternoon, a sizeable crowd in woollen
tunics and fur leggings surrounded a covered wagon parked in the
main square of Spine Gap. Those inhabitants of the town who did not
hear the thumping drums and tinkling bells were swiftly informed by
their neighbours; and arrived hurriedly, panting, in case they should
miss it. A large number of the town's motley population, mostly
composed of poor labourers and elderly females, herded themselves
into the space between the town hall and the tavern.

'Keep an eye on the town hall,' the halfling Will Brandiman
whispered from inside the wagon. 'We don't want the Councillors
over here.'

'They're richer,' Ned Brandiman pointed out.

'They're smarter. That's how they got to be rich in the first place.
What I always say', Will remarked, 'is that robbing the poor is *easier.*'

'It's the Holy One's mission!' a female dwarf cried, wiping the
remains of her tea from her beard.

'My brethren!' Will Brandiman let down the backboard at the rear
of the wagon and emerged on to the platform it made. Above him a

274

banner read *Mission of Light – Souls Saved – A Refusal of Credit Often Offends.*

The assembled dwarves, frost giants, half-elves, and Men of the town of Spine Gap gazed up at him. A frost giant rumbled, 'Amen!'

'My sisters!' The Reverend William Brandiman threw out his arms in benevolent, all-embracing gesture; smiling with gleaming white teeth. He wore a tightly buttoned black doublet and breeches, a small white collar devoid of lace, and his dyed black hair was slicked back from his brow. His eyes blazed down upon the crowd. 'You poor sinners! I truly believe you do not *know* how you suffer. My heart goes out to you!'

Another halfling stomped out from behind the curtain that closed off the covered part of the wagon. She hitched up the skirts of her red robe. The nun's habit, whip and spiked belt marked her as one of the Little Sisters of Mortification. A red wimple covered her hair, disclosing only a round face to which lip-paint, eye-paint and rouge had been added with a hand more enthusiastic than skilful.

'Brother, brother,' Ned Brandiman rebuked in a rich contralto, adjusting his wimple. 'You have not yet told these good people who we are.'

Will swept his oiled hair back from his brow with his fingers, and then brought his hands palms-together in front of him. 'True, Mother Edwina, true. Know then, you good people of Spine Gap – for I know, despite everything, that you must be *good* people – who it is that speaks to you. I am the Reverend William Aloysius Brandiman, of the Mission of the Holy One. This, my sister, is the good Abbess Edwina. We have come to bring you the Light!'

'Don't need no light,' a somewhat obtuse hill troll remarked from the front row of the crowd. 'Sun's still up.'

A number of heads turned to the west to confirm that the sun was, indeed, still visible. The peaks and high flanks of the Spine Mountains themselves blocked the view to north and south.

'I mean the Light of Virtue.' The Reverend William Brandiman bared his teeth in a dazzling smile. 'I mean that Light without which we are all lost!'

Several mailshirted dwarves in the crowd cried, 'Amen, brother!'

'Oh, I feel the sin!' the good Abbess Edwina cried. She took a tambourine from behind her back and struck it to emphasize her words. 'I feel the sin!'

TING!

'I feel the misery of those sunk in depravity, striving to escape, yet not knowing which way to turn!'

CLASH!

275

Two or three female Men in woollen gowns clapped their hands to the tambourine.

'I hear the voices of souls crying out, *save me! save me!* Crying *save me before it is too late!'*

TING! CLANG!

A raffish-looking male Man wiped his beard on his sleeve. 'If it's too late already, I'm going back in the tavern before Old Joss closes up for the night.'

A half-elf shushed him.

'Ah, my son, you may wish to do so.' The Reverend Brandiman oiled his way across the small platform and stood beaming down at the Man. 'But your soul says, "that tavern is a place of sin and depravity, where Men gamble and lose the honest money they make at their labour, where the drink is served watered, the bar-maids have foul diseases, and no one dare complain for fear of violent retaliation."'

The man scratched his lice-ridden hair.

'No it isn't,' he contradicted.

Will frowned. At his elbow, the Abbess Ned pointed a dramatic hand at the frontage of the town hall, where a group of worthies in fur-lined gowns stood watching the wagon from the steps.

'There is the sink of corruption, brother!'

TING!

'*There* is the source of misery. What chance have souls to see the Light, when the grasping councillors throw single mothers on to the streets when they cannot pay their rent?'

CLASH!

'When the taxes that should go to repairing the roads, rebuilding a hostelry after the war, and feeding the children of the poor—'

TING!

'—instead go to line the pockets of the villains who sent strong yokels from Spine Gap to the Last Battle, and yet remained at home themselves to batten and grow rich?'

CLASH-TING! CLANG!

One of a number of raggedly dressed labourers waved from the back of the crowd, yelling, 'No they didn't. They went off and fought, same as the rest of us. And what's *taxes?'*

The Reverend William Brandiman shook his head in sorrow. 'Ah, the power of Darkness to deceive! We here at the Holy Mission often find this. You good people do not *know* how much you need us. You do not know what the Light can do for your lives.'

CLASH-TING!

Will shot a look at Ned, who put his somewhat large and

276

roughened hands behind his back, stilling the tambourine.

'You, sir, for example.' The Reverend William Brandiman pointed at a half-elf who stood, arms folded, to one side. 'That wound of yours, sir, was taken from a Dark-corrupted weapon, am I right?'

The half-elf fingered his saturnine jaw, letting the crowd see the unhealed cut that wept a pale fluid. He called harmoniously, 'From an orcish blade, at the Battle of Sarderis.'

'And you – and you – and you, mistress!' Will pointed in turn to a Man with an amputated arm, another hill troll with a patch over one eye, and a female elf on crutches. 'All wounds of Darkness, if I am not mistaken? Yes! Ah, how you need our Mission of Light! Though healer-mages fail, and have given you up as lost, yet a prayer to the Lady, through our Holy Master, is never in vain!'

A one-legged dwarf began to weep and cry, 'Heal us poor sinners!'

TING! CLASH-TING! TING!

Under cover of the enthusiastic tambourine the good Abbess Edwina, in a somewhat deeper voice than she had used to address the crowd, muttered, 'I thought we were never going to hit it!'

The Reverend slicked back his short oiled locks. 'Never fear, brother Ned. Look at them. The cannon-fodder of the battle, by the looks of it – I *thought* the Spine Gap levies were locally raised.'

Will reached into the back of the wagon and brought out a crate.

'These relics and devices have been blessed by our Master, the Holy One, the favoured of the Lady. Come forward, brother.' Will Brandiman beckoned the half-elf. 'Let me see . . . prayer shawls . . . beads . . . ah, the Holy One's sacred elixir. It is very scarce and precious, brother, but let us see if it will answer your case.'

Taking a cloth and wetting it with the liquid from the tiny green bottle, he wiped the half-elf's face. The weeping scar came away. It left, Will was glad to see, no trace of Ned's face-paint. A great gasp went up from the crowd.

The female dwarf bawled, 'It's a miracle!'

CLASH-TING!

Under cover of bringing out another crate, Ned growled, 'Think the half-breed'll keep his mouth shut?'

Will put the special green bottle into the back of the covered wagon. Before straightening, he murmured, 'The half-elf will be out of Spine Gap in an hour; I told him we'd run this same scam down the road. We may, but he won't be with us. I never trust convenient rogues found in taverns. Mind that bottle, and remind me to burn that rag afterwards. It's a contact poison.'

'Well thought of, brother!' Ned Brandiman stepped forward, holding his hands out to the beings that crowded closely round the back of the wagon. 'You good people! Oh, how it warms my heart to be able to help you!'

TING-CLASH! CLASH-TING-*CLANG!*

Ned glared back at Will, who gave the tambourine another enthusiastic shake. Continuing in a light contralto, Ned cried, 'And I know that *you'll* want to help *us*.'

Several people in the crowd called, 'How?' and 'Yes!'

'You all know that our Holy Master is building a prayer-wheel,' Ned said piously. 'When it is complete, it will send prayers from him to the Lady of Light every day and every night, and then we can heal all the wounds the Dark dealt out in the last war, we can save each and every one of you, we can do it, yes, we can *do* it!'

The hill troll in the front row bellowed, 'Hallelujah!'

'Oh, yes!' Ned swayed hypnotically. 'As you take these prayer rugs – and prayer beads – and bottles of elixir, please give your contributions *generously*. No amount is too small. Or too big. Give us your money so that the great prayer-wheel can be built! Give us your money for the Holy One!'

'HALLELUJAH!'

Some thirty minutes later the Mission wagon rolled up out of the Spine Gap pass, the draught-manticore pulling with all the strength in its scarlet lion-scorpion body. Will counted copper, silver, and even the occasional gold piece into a small wooden chest.

'Hallelujah!' Edvard Ragald Rupert Brechie van Nassau wrapped the wagon's reins around his ankle, hitching up his nun's robe and disclosing hirsute halfling feet. He dove into a hamper of food. Through a mouthful of roast bear and thrush-in-aspic, he remarked, 'Let's go and give the Holy One the good news.'

'About 10 per cent of it.' Wilhelm Hieronymus Cornelius Mikhail Brechie van Nassau pushed the lid of the wooden chest down and grinned at his brother. 'Now. About that *other* idea we were discussing . . .'

Shortly after dawn the next day, with the mountain vultures whistling and crying in the pale air, the Mission wagon creaked up the winding road and under the archway of the Mission Citadel. The air tasted thin in the halflings' mouths, and cold chilled their fingertips and hairy toes. Will automatically tucked one hand up into his armpit, keeping the muscles warm for use, and simultaneously checking the position of one heavy throwing-dagger.

The Holy One saw their arrival from his place on the Citadel's parapet, where the mountain wind blew across his shaved elven head. The air was, after all, no colder than camp sentry duty or a knight's vigil in a stone chapel. The tall elf locked the fingers of his dark-skinned hands together, banishing the military thoughts and the panic that began to attend them.

'Send them to my cell.' He gestured his attendant priests to obedience. They instantly scurried away. The Mission of Light kept a soldierly discipline in its priestly ranks.

The elf wrapped his ragged white habit more firmly around his dark-skinned body. The high altitude bit into his thin fingers and the tips of his pointed ears. His long golden eyes filled with tears of mortification. When he could avoid comfort no longer, he went inside the chill stone corridors of the monastery. The black-haired halfling priest and his plain (but doubtless good-hearted) abbess sister were already waiting in the bare cell that was the Holy One's abode.

'Sir paladin!' The Reverend Brandiman knelt on the bare flagstones. His sister curtsyed low.

'Do not call me that! It is a title of shame!' The Holy One clasped one fine-fingered hand to his brow. His other hand twitched. He no longer carried weapons, not even a knife; but his hands sometimes searched for knightly accoutrements without his knowledge.

Abashed, the male halfling lowered his gaze. 'I beg forgiveness, Holy One. Your Holiness, there is news. Terrible news!'

The Holy One sank down on the bare planks that served as his bed, a hand plucking at his monk's habit where the hair shirt under it chafed at his brown skin.

'There *can* be no news more terrible than that the Dark Lord yet lives.' The elf reached across to the whip rack, selected a short thong, and began absently to scourge himself. 'And that, when they ride out against Him, I cannot ride with them!'

Elvish blood spattered the masonry. The Holy One stared at the walls of the dank cell as if he could see through them to all the great kingdoms of the south.

'One tiny fort,' he whispered. '*One* stronghold that I could not take. And so I am disgraced.' The elf lord's thin, ascetic features twisted, eyes squeezed shut. Sweat inched down his brown face. The whip drooped in his hand. 'When I held a sword in my hand, and could not defeat mine enemies, the southern cities *laughed* at me. My name was made a mockery at Nin-Edin! How can I live with such disgrace? Orcs, orcs, *orcs—*'

'Funny you should mention them.' The deep-voiced Abbess got to her hairy feet. 'For those orcs are once again at the right hand of Darkness. Your Holiness, the news we have is that there is a terrible task to be done, and no one can be found who is humble enough to submit to it.'

279

The Holy One's sunken golden eyes brightened. 'What is that, my child? And what of the – *ssss!* – orcs?'

The Reverend Brandiman said smoothly, 'Your Holiness has heard of the insidious evil plan of Darkness; how the Dread Lord of the East refuses to go to arms, and instead challenges the free world to a contest of *votes*.'

'Yes, I have heard.' The elf found his slender hand moving as if it would clutch a blade. 'That Great Heretic!'

'Just so,' the halfling priest continued. 'Now the free world must choose its own candidate – someone who will submit to the utter humiliation of contesting with the Dark Lord on His own terms. That person, whoever they may be, must endure the shame of condoning the actions of Evil by setting themselves up as equal candidate for War Leader in the coming holocaust, and afterwards for the Throne of the World.'

The Abbess added, 'Holy One, where can such a person be found, who will descend into the mire, and besmirch themselves, so that the Dark Lord will not run uncontested into high office?'

'But the *orcs*?' the Holy One persisted.

The Reverend Brandiman smoothed his slick hair back from his brow. 'Those same orcs of Nin-Edin once again serve their Dark Master, your Holiness. They are running what they term His "election campaign".'

'Now I see!'

A light burst in the Holy One's mind. The elf sprang to his feet. He seized the shoulders of his faithful halfling priest and nun, and gazed down into their trusting eyes.

'I have had a revelation!'

Laughing, easy tears ran down the elf's high-boned cheeks.

'In my torment, the Lady speaks to me! She tells me that my disgrace and humiliation was all for her sake, and only for a short time. Nin-Edin was my dark night of the soul, but now, *now* I may be revenged. Orcs, orcs! Hold your lives cheap, for my time of repentance and scourging is over.'

'It is?' the Abbess said.

'I shall bring no sword but the Sword of Righteousness, and wear no armour but the Armour of Light!'

The Reverend Brandiman frowned. 'Pardon me, your Holiness, but I don't quite understand.'

'Ah. You are afraid, because you sense the Lady's power in me. Do not fear!' cried the elf. 'For I, whose name was once Amarynth, called Firehand; Sir Amarynth the Paladin-Mage and Commander of the Army of the Light, am myself again.'

280

He clasped his long fingers across the front of his ragged habit, already planning the new habits that he and his followers would wear: embroidered with a sword, and the silver crescent of the Lady, and perhaps made with integral hair shirts.

Amarynth continued, 'To descend to the Dark Lord's level must be a disgrace. But I hear the Lady of Light speaking through you, her humble mouthpieces. I clearly perceive that it is my *duty* to offer myself as this sacrifice, to save others from the terrible task – and to bring the sword of vengeance down upon those unclean orcs. It is my duty to stand for election. And, if elected, it is my terrible fate to serve as Ruler of the free World.'

He threw up his hand.

'The Crusade of Light is beginning!'

The Holy One's halfling priest and abbess looked at each other for a moment, mouths open, doubtless quite overcome with piety.

The road from Spine Gap travels south, branching once it reaches the north shores of the Inland Sea, but a part of it, at least, runs down the coast through the ochre-coloured farmlands and hunting preserves of the Southern Kingdoms until it becomes the main artery running into Graagryk.

The Duchess Magda Brandiman descended her coach's steps, extended her parasol and opened it. Its lace shaded her from the hammering midday sun; mage-spells woven into the fabric cooled her immediately. Two of her bodyguards checked under the coach. Two more melted into the background around the high brick factory walls.

Seeing Cornelius Scroop with the picket line, Magda signalled to him. 'Chancellor!'

The mage-wards on the industrial district momentarily lifted. Magda walked forward under a lowering sky of chimneys and black smoke. A stench of oil and coal assailed her flaring nostrils. But all the normal sounds – hammering, beating, shrieking iron, saws, earsplitting whistles – were silent.

Her fat Chancellor-Mage padded forward on large hirsute feet. 'Your Grace, the picket line refuses to let me through!'

His face above his wilting lace collar glowed purple. Magda waved him to silence, stepped past the halfling's rotund bulk, and beckoned to one of the workers on the picket line.

The halfling worker took off his flat brown velvet cap and held it in both hands as he approached her. Sweat soaked the underarms of his collarless shirt, even with his sleeves rolled up; and he wore no stockings under his knee-length velveteen breeches.

'Bring me your shop steward,' Magda directed.

'Yes'm.' The halfling nervously ducked his head. 'Bert! 'Ere, Bert! She wants *you*, Bert.'

Another halfling emerged from the fifty or so who stood clustered round the factory gates, placards drooping in the heat. The curly hair on his feet was grey, and there were lines in his round face.

'Bert van der Klump, your Grace,' he introduced himself. 'Official shop steward of the Graagryk chapel of the Associated Socialist Halfling Workers Unions. Look 'ere, your Grace. It says 'ere in the ASHWU minutes under section forty-three, sub-section thirty-seven, paragraph twelve, items seven, eight, ten, thirteen, fifteen and twenty, that—'

The halfling stopped, rubbing his fist across his forehead.

'What *does* it say?' Magda inquired interestedly.

'I forgets,' Bert van de Klump confessed. He looked from the Duchess to the Chancellor, back at his Duchess, and responded to the crinkling laugh-lines around the female halfling's eyes. 'Honest an' truthful, ma'am, I fink it says *refer to section nine, subsection four, paragraph twelve, point fourteen, above,* but I can't remember exactly. 'Owever, ma'am, the gist of it is as follows. We 'ere—'

He waved his hands at the halflings around the factory gate. They raised their placards and waved them, chanting enthusiastically. Magda read *Halflings Unite! You have nothing to lose but your chains!* and *Ducal Rule – What Is To Be Done?*

'We 'ere,' Bert repeated, 'are striking, your Grace, for a bigger slice of the cake.'

'*Outrageous!*' Chancellor Scroop, at Magda's side, wiped his forehead with a soaking handkerchief, his magery gone with his concentration. 'The city's budget is stretched to the utmost! We don't have gold to pay grasping, traitorous, blackmailing, malingering—'

'Oh, do be quiet,' Magda Brandiman said. 'Meister van der Klump, how would it be if I met your demands?'

She busied herself straightening her lace-work elbow gloves, and fluffing her silk gown's petticoats. The halfling in cap and knee breeches snapped his fingers, and he and a dozen of his co-workers went into a huddle. They emerged, sweating.

Van der Klump demanded, 'An' what h'exactly would be the terms of this 'ere settlement, yer Grace?'

'The ducal treasury will grant you all a further two tea breaks, every hour, with bakery goods fresh from the city's finest bakeries,' Magda said. She paused. Albert van der Klump's boot-button eyes fixed firmly on her face. She added, 'And *four* square meals a day at weekends in the workplace instead of the current three. What do you say, Meister?'

282

'Bert Klump, you ain't sellin' us out to the ducal-orcish consortium,' a worker yelled. 'We got our principles! No dealin' with the class enemy – *urk*.'

A placard dropped on to the worker's head from the picket line behind her and she sat down dazedly on the cobbles. The halfling with bulging muscles who carried the placard remarked gravely, 'Oops.'

Albert van der Klump hurriedly wiped his hand on the seat of his velveteen breeches and held it out to the halfling Duchess. 'It's a deal, ma'am!'

'Congratulations on your shrewd negotiations.' Magda jerked a ducal thumb at the vast brick armaments factories. 'Now get back to work.'

Albert van der Klump replaced his flat velvet cap on his greying curls. 'Workers of Graagryk! Three cheers for the Duchess Magdalene! Hip, hip—'

'HOORAY!'

Magda Brandiman turned on her heel and strode from the factory gates towards her closed coach, acknowledging applause with a wave of her lace-gloved hand.

Cornelius Scroop stumbled behind her. 'Your Grace, are you *mad*? That scum know we need the arms factories working night and day! They're a menace. They're undermining the fabric of halfling society! They'll just make further demands until they've bled the ducal treasury dry. And,' he added, 'the city can't afford *bakery goods*. Not for grubby little jumped-up peasants.'

'Aw, c'mon,' the Duchess protested. 'Let them eat cake.'

Cornelius Scroop sniffed with hayfever even mage-spells couldn't cure.

'Chancellor, I'll leave you here to sort out the practical details.'

Two well-built halflings in baggy breeches, and silk doublets that did not disguise the bulge of automatic pistol holsters, flanked the Duchess to her black-painted coach. She nodded to the one who held the door open and accompanied her inside.

Professor Julia Orrin looked up from where she lay across the seat, chewing her thumbnail, and throwing dice left hand against right. The female Man sat up, cracking her head against the roof as the coach set off. She tugged the lace froth back from her wrists and fanned her face vainly against Graagryk's heat, cheeks as scarlet as her frock coat.

'Damme if it isn't hot as the Abyss! Not like this in Fourgate.' She peered down at Magda, pushing powdered grey hair back from her wet forehead. 'Your Grace, are you *quite* sure you don't have relatives there? There was a halfling in the Abbey Park, looked just like you, couldn't *be* you, of course, she's a madam, but I used to frequent the bath-houses—'

'I briefly ran the *Gibbet & Spigot* tavern and bath-house in the Abbey Park last year, but had to give it up to resume my duties as Duchess.'

Julia Orrin's powdered brows lifted. *'Really?'*

'The barracks, Fyodor,' Magda ordered, removing her dark glasses. 'But go by way of the coaching inn. Professor Orrin will wish to return to the north today.'

'I will?' Julia Orrin narrowed her eyes. 'Then, madam, I warn you. We at the Visible College are examining very closely our commercial links with Graagryk. Very closely indeed. We may find it uneconomic to continue trading with you.'

'Uneconomic, or merely embarrassing?'

Midday sun pooled the black coach's shadow on the street. A form of minor magery polarized the windows against the southern sun, and another mage-spell chilled the air inside. The wheels rattled. Magda gazed out through the darkened window at one halfling outrider, spear at attention, riding his lizard-beast through Graagryk's deserted streets.

'It isn't a contract with Graagryk, ma'am. It's a contract with orcs. Questions are being asked. The College's board of governors don't like greenies.'

'That is not a term I care to have used in my presence.' Magda icily regarded the large, magic-scarred hands resting in the Man's lap. One finger sported a silver and lapis lazuli ring. 'I remember you from the *Gibbet & Spigot*. Rattan canes and mustard, wasn't it, Professor Orrin?'

At the female Man's expression, Magda smiled.

'Fortunately my professional discretion still applies. Now. The Visible College sells its nullity talismans to the orc marines, and you must be aware that the immunity to magical attack conferred on marines and their weapons is what makes them unbeatable. Like it or not, what you're doing is selling armaments to *greenies*.'

The female Man said stiffly, 'My colleagues and I prefer to regard ourselves as being in a defence industry.'

'Where does Graagryk's money go?'

Julia Orrin frowned at the change of direction. 'Don't see what concern it is of your Grace, but it goes into funding research. I specialize in pure research, myself. I'm proud to say that I doubt if I have ever created a spell that had any practical use whatsoever. Don't care to visit manufactories. We're not *interested* in commerce.'

'As long as you have enough money to purchase the expensive range of magical ingredients necessary for your research programmes.' Magda Brandiman removed a long ivory holder from her purse and inserted a slendor roll of pipe-weed. Her attendant bodyguard clinked steel and flint until a spark flared. Magda inhaled deeply, and blew out a plume of smoke.

'I used to wonder why you didn't just create the gold you need,' the Duchess said thoughtfully. 'Since it's well known that there are more alchemists in the Visible College than there are whores in the Abbey Park. Except, I suppose, that such an influx of gold would devalue the currency, destabilize the entire economy, and bring every mage and king of the South down on your back if you tried it. Even magic is subservient to economics and the Gross National Product . . .'

'We're northerners,' Julia Orrin said resentfully. 'The north is poor. Fourgate Council keeps us on a tight budget. Always has. No way we could manage without outside funding of some kind.'

Magda Brandiman drew deeply on her pipe-weed-holder. 'You have a permanent and almost inexhaustible source of revenue in the orc marines. As long as you continue to exclusively sell us magic-null talismans, the orcs will continue to buy. It's a growing business, armaments.'

The Professor-Mage dug in the capacious pockets of her frock coat, extracted a silver box, opened it, and sniffed a pinch of some substance up her right and left nostrils. 'That's – asschuuu! – essentially correct, your Grace. It would cost us too much time to sell the talismans to individual customers. And in any case, they're highly experimental technology. Probably unsafe. Civilians wouldn't use them without *far* more extensive testing. Assh*huu!*'

Julian Orrin wiped her streaming eyes and continued. 'Which are all good reasons why this commerce is becoming too risky for the Visible College to continue it. If we're found to be involved with gr— with orcs, then our reputations . . .'

Magda removed her pipe-weed stub, dropped it on the floor of the coach, and crushed it under one tiny heel.

'Let me introduce you to some of the facts of life, Madam Orrin. As far as the general public are concerned, dog-tag talismans are standard *protective* devices. It is not known that they *nullify* magic. If that were known a scandal would ensue, and enquiries would be made about the talismans' origin.'

'Madam,' Julia Orrin protested.

Magda continued relentlessly. 'The Southern Kingdoms can't damage the Visible College. They would be stupid to try. But in the face of public scandal – for example, proof of your selling proscribed magic to orcs – I think they might decline to sell you any magical ingredients you need for your research programmes. I really think they may do that.'

Professor-Mage Julia Orrin sat sweating and completely silent.

'And if your sources of supply dry up . . . well, as you say, you're a pure research institute. You don't produce a product. Nothing to prevent your bankruptcy, anyway. Madam Professor, the Visible College was lost from the first day, when you took my sons' money for nullity talismans – and didn't enquire too carefully to whom they would be sold.'

The Duchess Magdelene Amaryllis Judith Brechie van Nassau leaned forward and put her small hand on the Man's knee.

'Don't cancel a deal that's advantageous to both of our peoples. Don't worry about selling experimental magic to orcs. Your job is to worry about research. I suggest,' Magda said, 'that you return to the city of Fourgate and continue it. I'll handle the business end in Graagryk. I'm sure we'll continue to deal usefully together for many years to come.'

Magda sat back in her seat and smiled at the back of the frock-coated Man, descending to the steps of the coaching inn.

She remained gazing at the summer sky for some moments.

'Why', she murmured, 'couldn't *I* get the easy job, gallivanting around the Kingdoms running elections? *Orcs!*'

Beyond Graagryk the roads run south away from the Inland Sea, into the heart of the great and ancient Southern Kingdoms.

Ashnak chewed on the butt of an unlit cigar, his head lifting momentarily as he watched a wind-clipper sail over the roofs of the Serpent Temple in Shazmanar. In the great cities and civilizations of the south there are no ox-carts plodding dusty roads. The mage-powered ship's wooden keel brushed the tops of palms growing on the temple's roof-garden. The clipper spread more sail to catch the sun. Hull-down, it drove west.

'Very pretty,' the chief Serpent-Priest remarked.

General Ashnak, in full dress uniform of brown tunic, trousers and flat peaked cap, reassured him, 'Orcs don't mind beauty. We're broadminded. It doesn't offend us. Much.'

The orc gazed across the square at the Serpent Temple's candystick pillars, wide atrium, and snake-pattern mosaics.

'I'm officially requisitioning that building.' Ashnak belched. 'In the name of Ferenzia. Lieutenant Chahkamnit, make a note of the marine temporary campaign headquarters. Priest, let the towns-people know that voting will take place this afternoon, after speeches by Her Dark Magnificence, the Lord of the Empire of Evil.'

'Yessss . . .' The priest, naked but for chainmail groin-covering, hissed agreement and glided off towards the ochre-and-crimson-painted temple. His skin was curiously sheened for one of the Man-race.

The black orc lieutenant at Ashnak's elbow beamed. 'First-class accommodation, sir, what? Nothing's too good for Herself. Shall I see about mobilizing the orcs, sir?'

Ashnak growled, 'Get this set up at the double, L.t!'

'Absolutely, sir.' Lieutenant Chahkamnit saluted. 'Only too pleased to be of assistance. Over here, if you please, Corporal Hikz!'

Around midday, the General of the Orc Marines stood squat-legged on the roof garden of the Serpent Temple, surveying what could be seen of Shazmanar. The Shazmanarians thronged the main square, staring, with eyes that did not blink in the scalding southern light, at the five parked Bedford trucks and two M113 APCs under a palm tree. The Temple beneath echoed to the tramp of combat boots and the bellows of orc NCOs.

'General, sir . . .' a voice creaked.

Ashnak turned his heavy-jawed head. The midday sun shone on a skeletal orc lieutenant whose rotting black uniform and flesh were rapidly mummifying in the southern heat. One hand, on whose fingers no flesh remained, saluted. Pinpricks of red light burned in rotting eyes and sockets.

'Sir, beg pardon, sir.' Lugashaldim came to attention. 'The lieutenant wishes to have the general's permission to form the Undead marines into a new unit.'

Ashnak pulled a frond from the nearest palm tree, chewed on it experimentally, and spat it out. His dress-uniform jacket pulled tight across his bulging shoulders.

'And why's that, Lieutenant?'

'Sir, problems of being Undead, sir. We're magical. Can't wear nullity talismans.' The orc lieutenant made the kind of motion that in a living orc would indicate taking a deep breath. 'Can't use talisman-protected weaponry either, sir. Have to use it without the nullity talismans. That means the Special Undead Services have had to become very good at covert actions. Sir, I want permission for the Undead to form a unit that can act covertly in military *and* civil situations.'

Ashnak's beetling brows raised. 'Explain, Lieutenant.'

'Covert Intelligence Actions, sir, that's what I thought we could call ourselves. We've been working on new technology for our CIA élite force, too.' The orc lieutenant, enthusiastic, swung his backpack from his rotting shoulders and began to rummage through it. 'Here, sir.'

A skeletal hand proffered a miniature crossbow, almost lost in Ashnak's hand when the big orc took it. The Undead lieutenant held up a crossbow bolt, and a set of headphones.

'Put the headphones on, sir. That's it. Now if I take this crossbow bolt with me, over to the far side of the roof . . . that's it . . . you couldn't hear me now, sir, normally, sir, could you?'

Ashnak peered through palm tree fronds. The sun beat down on the roof garden. Only a faint smell of carrion gave away the presence of the orc lieutenant. 'Very clever, Lugashaldim.'

Lugashaldim thrashed back through the plants to emerge beside the orc general. 'It's a microphone, sir, fitted in the bolt of the crossbow. We can fire this from long-distance into a wall or a room, and overhear *anything* that takes place there!'

Ashnak leaned his elbows on the parapet of the roof garden. He pointed at a slit-windowed building on the far side of Shazmanar's main square. 'Target that second window on the left, Lieutenant. Let's see if this mother works.'

The Undead orc took the crossbow, swiftly fitted the bolt, raised it and sighted through one milk-blue dead eyeball, and fired. The bolt impacted.

'*Holy shit!*' Ashnak snatched the headset from his hairless, pointed ears. 'Next time you do that without a warning, marine, your balls are going to be on my breakfast table!'

'Sorry, sir. Didn't think, sir. Try it now, sir!'

Ashnak tentatively replaced the headphones and twiddled the volume control. His leathery forehead ridged as he frowned. Seeing that, the Undead orc frantically fiddled with the RT in his back-pack.

'Dead air,' Ashnak said. 'Not even an open channel.'

'No, sir,' Lugashaldim admitted.

The two orcs looked down from the roof garden at the distant window. The speck of the crossbow bolt was plainly embedded in the frame.

Ashnak inquired, '*Delicate* mechanism, is it, this microphone of yours?'

Lugashaldim looked at the crossbow in his skeletal orcish hand. 'Ah. Erm. Well . . .'

'Go away,' Ashnak said very softly, 'and don't bother me, marine. I have an election to win.'

A greater crowd had gathered down in the main square, many of them staring up, listening to the distant *whup-whup-whup!* of an

Apache helicopter gunship. Ashnak swung round, only to walk into the shining bones of his lieutenant.

'Sir!' Lugashaldim held out a black box. 'There's this, sir. In case of sabotage attempts by the opposite side.'

The orc general made a fist. His Undead lieutenant gabbled:

'It's a remote control device, General. Imagine the scene – one morning you leave your temporary campaign HQ, your driver starts the ignition of your APC, and *boom!*, there's an explosive device under it. I don't trust the Light not to use that dwarven rock-blasting powder of theirs. The CIA will *specialize* in anti-terrorist security, General.'

Ashnak unclenched his ham-sized fist and took the black box. 'This does what, exactly, Lieutenant?'

'It's a remote, sir. The other sensor is attached to the vehicle. It can remote-detonate any device that may have been placed under your vehicle, from a distance of up to one kilometre away. *Boom!* We lose an APC – but you're safe, General.'

Ashnak's large hairy nostrils flared. 'Hmmm . . .'

'I fixed up a test device under the last van, sir. If the general would like to activate the remote—'

BOOOOMM!

A pillar of black smoke and orange flame rolled up from the main square. Glass shattered in all the surrounding windows. Over the noise of screams, shrieks and running feet, Ashnak commented, 'Hardly what I'd call *covert*, Lieutenant.'

'But effective, sir. If that had been a terrorist device, we orcs would have taken no casualties from it whatsoever.'

Down in Shazmanar's square, healer-mages rushed in from the rest of the city, and bodies too fragmented for magery had cloaks and robes thrown over them.

'Yes,' the orc general remarked. 'You're right – no orc casualties at all. I *like* that. Very well, Lieutenant Lugashaldim. Form your Covert Intelligence Actions élite force, and keep me posted as to their progress.'

'Yessir, General, sir!' The Undead lieutenant departed, jaws gleaming. A squad passed him, doubling up on to the clear area of the roof; and the honour guard, led by a lean green orc, Corporal Hikz, formed up as the Dark Lord's helicopter touched down.

Darkness clung to the hot metal of the Apache helicopter gunship, muddying the bright southern sun. A slender form first emerged, cowled in glove-soft leather, a wine bottle tucked under one arm.

The orc saw, under the hood, green eyes glaring from a Man's face blotched with grey and black. The slobbering lips pulled back, and saliva ran freely down and dripped from the nameless necromancer's lumpy chin. The front of his robe was damp with spit and wine.

'Assshhnak . . . Behold our Mashter.'

The Darkness coalesced and oozed from the AH 64 Apache helicopter cabin, and hung, staining the tiles, behind him.

'This way, your Sable Eminence.' Ashnak addressed the Darkness, touching his talons to the gold braid on the peak of his cap. His medalled tunic clinked. 'Everything's set up.'

'*I will speak now. Summon the people of Shazmanar.*'

Ashnak descended through the labyrinthine passages of the Serpent Temple. The nameless followed, hood cowling his misshapen head. Darkness dogged their heels, impenetrable even to orcish vision.

'Thish better go right,' the voice of the nameless necromancer slurred.

'Herself in a bad mood? Damn whistlestop tours.' Ashnak kicked and booted the orc marine election HQ staff into rapid movement, medals and ribbons bouncing on his uniformed barrel-chest. 'Corporal, herd that crowd into the square and shut 'em up! Sergeant, I want that PA activated, and I want it *now*. Get your asses in gear, you orcs. Go, *go*, GO!'

A very few minutes later the crowd of serpent-eyed male and female Men of Shazmanar faced wooden posts erected in front of their Serpent Temple. Black hangings hung festooned from the structure, with occasional purple trimmings. Two squads of orcs in heavy boots and a great deal of metalware stood in stiff poses on the Temple steps. A banner strung from the wooden posts read 'VOTE FOR THE DARK LORD – YOU *KNOW* IT MAKES SENSE'.

A very large orc in a constricting brown uniform mounted the marble steps and cleared his throat. Black boxes at the corners of the square echoed his noise, so that all heard him clearly when he spoke.

'People of Shazmanar! Please give a great big enthusiastic welcome for your Powers of Darkness candidate in the coming election . . . *the Dark Lord!*'

The orc walked down the steps. A chill touched the gathered population of Shazmanar. There was a black-cloaked figure in front of the Temple now, and none of them had seen it come.

The figure raised pale hands and put the cowl back from its head. The material chimed, as if it might be metal.

Possession was having its effect on the body of The Named. Her rich yellow hair now caught the sun as a bleached white. Sepia-blue shadows haunted the fine-featured face. The rangy Man's body began to seem swamped in the folds of the black metalmesh robes.

Her eyes opened, lids rising to expose an orange glow.

'Hear Me, people of Shazmanar,' She said, 'for I have come to solicit your vote . . .'

Having heard the speech a dozen times before, Ashnak of the orc marines settled himself behind the Bedford trucks and lit up a pipe-weed cigar, cap pulled down over his eyes. The PA system brought him snatches of the speech:

'. . . and My aim will be to provide a number of healer-mages in every town who will perform their services freely, because they will be paid by My central government. My government will also be paying a wage to the crime-enforcement wizards, thus cutting down on bribery and corruption . . .'

The Shazmanarians muttered. Ashnak caught one hiss of 'Lunacsssy . . . !'

'I don't think She's quite got the gift of public speaking, sir.' Lieutenant Chahkamnit peered at the standing crowd. 'More used to giving orders, I suppose. At least they're not walking out on Her, sir.'

'They won't be doing that, Lieutenant. I have Kestrel and Vulture squads deployed at the exits of the square.'

The PA crackled. '. . . and free housing; together with weekly sums of money paid to those who have reached the end of their working lives. To enable My Dark government to keep these election promises, I shall, if I have your votes, institute a system of voluntary contributions of tiny amounts of money from each of you, which shall be called "taxes".'

A Shazmanarian called, 'Evil and corruptsssion!'

Ashnak yawned widely, exposing yellowing fangs and brass-capped tusks to the sun, and belched. A lizard scuttled past. The orc trapped its tail under his combat boot, popped the lizard in his mouth, and chewed contentedly.

'. . . and under My government, as I am committed to the principle of a multi-ethnic society, I shall ensure that all of us – serpent-people, orcs, liches, witches and enchanters – live together in unity and prosperity . . .'

Someone at the back booed.

'Watch the crowd. Single out the obvious troublemakers, Chahkamnit,' Ashnak directed. 'You'll be bringing them to me for interrogation.'

'. . . and in conclusion, may I add this. We face the greatest peril of this world's age. We all face an enemy whom even Darkness may, without prejudice, admit to fear. But, who is better able to deal with vileness than the Evil Empire? I say again: if elected, I will pursue with all speed the eradication of this dreadful force from the earth . . .'

Ashnak ground out his cigar. 'Stand by to see Herself back to the Apache, Lieutenant. I'll handle the rest of this.'

He prostrated himself in front of the Dark Lord as She passed, shrouded again in impenetrable Darkness and bad temper. A bell-like voice addressed him from the murk.

'Tell Me, My orc, is this something I cannot do? When I harangued the Horde in days gone by, they cheered Me loyally to the echo. Where is My error?'

Ashnak refrained from pointing out the Horde of Darkness's susceptibility to Dark magic (at least at the humble foot soldier's level) and the general inadvisability of appearing unenthusiastic whilst in the Dark Lord's Blasted Redoubt of the East.

'It's only because they're not used to You, Dread Lord,' the orc general said. 'They're overawed.'

'Ah. Yes. That must be it.'

The nameless necromancer cradled his baby-orc-skull wine cup, trailing in the Darkness's wake. From the dark of his hood, his voice slurred, 'Perchance it'sh your orcsh, Dread Lord. They do have a negative public image.'

'Yes,' the voice of the Dark Lord mused. 'I am disappointed in you, orc. I should not have made you My Field Marshal. You may consider yourself returned to the rank of General.'

'Ma'am.' Ashnak and the nameless glared at each other.

'Come!'

The Dark Lord departed. Allowing some minutes for the usual turmoil to subside, Ashnak shambled back up on to the Temple steps.

'Awriiight! Now listen up, people of Shazmanar. You all know how this here "election" works. Yesterday you saw the Light. Now you've seen the Dark. Now you're gonna *vote*. And you're gonna do it right. Ain'tcha? OK, Lieutenant, get 'em into lines.'

The afternoon sun beat down on Shazmanar's candy-twist architecture and flowing palm trees. The serpent-people in their mail groin-coverings hissed as orc marines, assault rifles slung over their brawny shoulders, herded them into long columns that wavered across the square. A squad of grunts scurried about with cardboard boxes full of mimeographed sheets, handing them out by the fistful.

'This', Ashnak waved a specimen sheet of paper above his head, 'is called a *ballot form*. It has "Light" and "Dark" written on it. You make your mark beside whichever one you want to vote for. If you cannot read, my orcs will assist you. Then you put the paper through the slots in these sealed boxes here. Then we count 'em up. Everybody got that?'

Ashnak strode down the steps into the square, elbowing his way to the marines guarding the ballot boxes. Lieutenant Chahkamnit sat with a carton of ballot forms beside him, marking the 'Dark Lord' box on each, and stuffing them into the sealed boxes.

'Well done,' the orc general remarked. He shot out a muscular arm, stopping a serpent-man from approaching the sealed box, and plucked the ballot paper out of the startled Shazmanarian's hand.

'Isss meant to be a ssssecret ballot!' the serpent-Man protested.

Ashnak unfolded the paper, furrowing his brow as he read it. '"The candidate I wish to elect is the Light candidate" . . .'

The orc shot out a hand, caught the serpent-Man around the throat, lifted him bodily, and threw him over the heads of the crowd. There was a trailing sibilant scream, and a thud.

'Wrong!' Ashnak reproved the Shazmanarian as the serpent-Man clawed his way upright. 'Now try again, you sorry mother, and this time get it *right.*'

The crowd hissed and muttered. From somewhere there came the *snk!* of a bolt-action rifle. As one, the Shazmanarians shuffled forward to the ballot boxes.

Under the gleaming eye of Ashnak, General Officer Commanding the orc marines, the city of Shazmanar proceeded to record their votes for the Grand Election to the Throne of the World.

6

THE FURTHER SOUTH-EAST from the
Kingdoms, the more the roads thin out and eventually vanish
altogether. Until, half a continent away from the Inland Sea, the
elven rainforests of Thyrion swelter under an equatorial sun.

In the back of the speeding river assault craft, marine Elendylis
Goldenfire abandoned the stately plucking of her harp and gave out
with three wailing chord progressions. Marine Illurian Swiftbow cut
in with a backbeat, and added a hard-driving guitar riff. The elven
music began to motor as the assault craft rocked crazily from side to
side on the foaming brown water.

'Move your ass, L.t!' Gunnery Sergeant Dakashnit bawled over the
noise. 'Gear up! What's the matter with you elves? Do you wanna
live *for ever?*'

'Funny you should say that,' Lieutenant Gilmuriel Hunt-Lord
remarked.

Starlight Squad, last of Gilmuriel's platoon to hit a dropzone, and
the command group he had chosen to go in with, sprawled among
heaps of equipment in the body of the assault craft and exchanged
laconic backchat as they geared up. Beads and bangles ornamented
the elf marines' combat fatigues, dulled with hard wear, muddy and
worn. Marines Dyraddin Treewaker and Belluriel Starharp wore
ragged silk scarves as headbands, and marines Goldenfire and
Swiftbow had adopted round wire-rimmed smoked glasses. A curious
sigil – a circle with a stylized three-toed bird's claw imprinted on it –

had been stencilled on their helmet covers. Corporal Silthanis Blackrose smoked a roll of Dakashnit's pipe-weed.

'You've certainly made these elves into marines, Sergeant.' Gilmuriel sighed in very reluctant admiration. He tipped his helmet back and scratched his pointed ears. 'Now – HQ says no chance of reinforcements for at least five days.'

'We ain't gonna get no help till the election's over.' Dakashnit straightened up and shook foam from her straight razor, having shaved her crest down to a regulation marine crew-cut. She emptied the soapy water from her helmet into the river. The orc then relieved herself into the helmet, tipped it over the side of the boat again, and emptied her pack of combat rations into it. Chewing, she added, 'L.t., we're always getting fucked by the politicians.'

The hulking orc grunt piloting the speeding boat muttered, 'Squeakies! Ain't no fucking use as marines! It's us orcs has to do the job.'

With heavy sarcasm, Gilmuriel fluted, 'I suppose a few hundred orcs are enough to hold back the Bugs' advance.'

The grunt said proudly, 'We're cadre troops. The marines' finest. OK, so we ain't here in force – just call us the thin green line.'

Dakashnit leaned over. 'Marines, these may be squeakies – but they're *my* squeakies. Let's hear some *respect*.'

'Uh, yessir, Sergeant, ma'am!' The orc steered the powerful boat in towards the bank. 'Here's your drop point.'

Engines throbbed overhead: helicopter support. The nose of the boat beached. The eight-elf squad pitched over the side into leech-ridden mud and squelched ashore. Gilmuriel didn't pause to watch the rest of the Forest King's expeditionary force hitting the waterline. The elf, fine-fingered hand grasping his automatic pistol, pounded across the open space and hit jungle cover.

Squatting in the shade of a fronded tree, the other elves clustered around her, Aradmel Brightblade murmured, 'We don't even know what this "enemy" is, Sergeant.'

'Isn't *what* they are that's important,' Dakashnit drawled. The dappled sun and shadow hid her even when Gilmuriel knew where he was looking for the orc. 'These Bugs butchered Moondream's squad, so we know they're hostile. All we need to know is – where they are . . .'

Two youngsters – Dyraddin Treewaker and Belluriel Starharp, neither more than three centuries old, to Gilmuriel's certain knowledge – abandoned interest in the mission and began discussing elven genealogies and the Lost Lands of the Oversea. Gilmuriel cuffed them.

'There is a term in the marines for this formation,' he snapped. '*Clusterfuck*. If you cluster up like that – we're fucked! The enemy will waste all of us with one burst. Now let us get sorted out for line of march.'

The jungle fronds of Thyrion dripped a humid damp. Gilmuriel took a deep breath, smelling the decay of leaves, the spoor of beasts, and the age of the great spiring trees. His elven instincts shrieked at him of a wrongness in the rainforest. A scent of evil beast, apart from orc; and metal, over and above the weapons of the elf marines.

The last sun to sift through the canopy illuminated Gilmuriel's blond hair and woodland cammo bandana. Weighed down under kit, he crouched with the black-haired radio elf beside him.

'Now listen up, you elves! This is our first real combat mission. We are to be in position on Hill 300 before dawn, dug in, with the rest of the company. Daylight will be the signal for the assault on the enemy. We're going to hold back the Bug advance from the City of the Trees.'

The damp vapours of Thyrion Forest wreathed. The slide and lock of M16 bolts sounded muffled under the heat haze and the omnipresent buzzing of insects.

'You may think the Forest King has sent us out to hold where no force could hold, to give up our lives in the hope it will buy time for the rest of the free peoples. If so, well and good. The long lives of the elven kind are not lightly given up, except in the cause of a great sacrifice.'

Dakashnit gave a baritone chuckle. She sprawled back in a bush, massive bow-legs spread, scratching at her crotch through ragged combat trousers. Thyrion's insect population swarmed over her black hide; the few that managed to bite through it falling off, poisoned.

'Last stand be buggered!' Camouflage paint irregularly striped the sergeant's craggy, grinning features. 'L.t., if it gets too hot, we're outta here. We're professional soldiers – we get *paid* for running away.'

Dakashnit slid silently to her feet, weighed down with ammunition belts, grenades and with a belt-fed General Purpose Machine Gun resting idly across one broad shoulder.

'Recap. Basic marine technique for reporting the sighting of hostiles. If you see *one* enemy . . .' Dakashnit raised a sharp-taloned finger. 'You hold up *one* finger. This is *two* enemy sighted. This is *three*.'

The orc held up four taloned fingers.

'This is *many*.'

Silthanis Blackrose solemnly nodded. Sergeant Dakashnit looked at him. 'Corporal, how many enemy is *this?*'

The tall, pudgy elf regarded the whole orc-hand held up.

'Don't know, Sarge,' he admitted.

'That', Dakashnit said, 'is *too many*. Now. Them Bugs is steaming west, towards the centres of highest population density. So let's go give 'em a hard time!'

Festooned with packs, water bottles, spare magazines, entrenching tools, and everything else they assumed useful, the eight tall and delicate-boned elves grinned back at their sergeant. '*Yo!*'

'Now you listen up,' Dakashnit repeated, in a tone that for an orc was gentle. 'Out here we're gonna be depending on each other. You screw up, you gonna get somebody else killed. Do you hear me? You watch your buddy's back. Your buddy watches yours. If anyone goes down, you tell me or the L.t. about it, and you don't *wait*. Now I don't wanna hear any more talk about nobly laying down our lives. We're marines! What are we gonna do?'

'Kick ass, Sergeant!' the tiny radio operator, Byrna Silkentress, squeaked.

Dakashnit beamed. 'That's what I like to hear. Keep your heads down and your eyes open. And just remember – a sucking chest wound is Nature's way of telling you to stay out of a firefight . . .'

Several hours of tactical night movement through another part of the Forest of Thyrion, which resembled exactly every other part of the Forest of Thyrion, brought them to within striking distance of their start-line objective. Gilmuriel paused on the edge of a clearing, letting his elvish vision read the map by starlight.

Aradmel Brightblade began a hymn of praise to the stars, and abruptly clapped her hand over her mouth.

The gunnery sergeant, night vision equally good, peered over Gilmuriel's shoulder. 'I don't reckon we're headed right, L.t.'

'We need no maps!' Gilmuriel folded his and returned it to his map-case. 'We are elves in the ancient forest of our forefathers. *This* way.'

After an hour and a half of increasingly slow movement, Gilmuriel was about to consult the map again and damn elvish instincts when starlight skylined a distinctive ridge, and vast goldentrees.

'Well, whaddya know?' Sergeant Dakashnit breathed. 'OK, you elves, let's see you dug-in quietly.'

'We are elves,' Gilmuriel objected. 'We shall take to the trees.'

'Man, I don't care if you take to drink!' the squat orc hissed. 'But we is part of a company attack, which is part of a brigade attack, which means we do *what* we're told, *when* we're told, and we was told to dig-in, not roost up in the trees like the fucking birds!'

Lieutenant Gilmuriel's eyes glowed golden in the forest dark. 'I didn't ask for an argument, Sergeant. *I gave you an order!'*

Dawn brought first the screeching and warbling of ten thousand birds, before light showed in the sky. Night had chilled the earth below the ridge: now it began to smell again of rot and decaying meat. Thyrion's trees are strong and wide. The eight elves, in buddy-buddy pairs among the branches, ate their waybread, a certain professionalism apparent. Four ate, four others attended to radio, weapons check and sentry duty.

A talon tapped a weapon. Gilmuriel automatically glanced towards the sound.

Sergeant Dakashnit sprawled on an outer branch, belly down, peering through the thinning leaves on the tree's east side. She tapped her shoulder and then her head. Gilmuriel moved lightly out to crouch beside her.

Dawn shone into the valley below the ridge.

'I smell something I don't like, L.t.'

Gilmuriel's gaze swept the ridge on the far side of the valley, seeking smoke, or any sign that the enemy were encamped where orcish Military Intelligence had reported.

The rising morning vapours drifted unchecked.

The sun growing warm on his face, Gilmuriel spat. 'That hill is as bare as a dwarf's bottom. There aren't any Bugs there.'

Dakashnit wordlessly pointed downwards.

The expected smoke plumes of the Elf Expeditionary Force lined the ridge they currently occupied. Gilmuriel smelled cooking fires, roasting meat. His keen sight distinguished dug-outs, trenches, camouflage netting—

'Mother of Forests . . .' the elf lieutenant breathed. *'Shit!'*

Morning sun glinted on the shining, sticky, dripping black carapaces of Bugs.

In every dug-out, every position . . .

'There's Bugs encamped all right,' Sergeant Dakashnit whispered. 'On *this* hill! We got a whole company round us, 'cept it isn't ours. L.t., that's the last time I trust elf instincts over a map.'

'That's the last time *I* trust Military Intelligence!'

Gilmuriel, heart pounding, watched the scorpion-tailed insectoids moving in dug-outs not twenty feet from the bole of the goldentree. The fronds of the forest plants shrank back from touching the blue-black carapaces, and shrivelled when a Bug brushed through them.

'I want fire support!' Lieutenant Gilmuriel whispered. 'I want tanks, mortars, artillery and fighter-ground attack!'

'It's all miles behind us, L.t., at the original map reference. Leastways, I *hope*. Shit, lookit that!'

A particularly large specimen of Bug, some eight feet tall, stood just below the tree the squad occupied. Morning sun striped its dripping jaws, powerful exoskeleton, and faceted eyes. At this close a range Gilmuriel could make out the straps of its body harness, and the pouches and packs hanging off it.

'HHHRRRASSHHHHH!'

Twenty Bugs poured from the nearest dug-out. Gilmuriel witnessed claws adjusting peculiar long-barrelled weapons, fixing straps and clips, and grabbing for equipment. The seven-feet-tall insectoids shambled into the open space under the tree and formed a straggling line, facing the large Bug.

'HRASSSH-*SKKKRRRAGHH!*'

The line instantly straightened. Bugs shuffled on their clawed hind feet. Gilmuriel surveyed the row of carapaced heads below him. Each quartet of eyes faced forward. Each pair of dangling skeletal arms hung down by the slumping thorax.

The large insectoid hissed, slime dripping from its jaws. Each Bug froze into immobility. It paced up and down the line, snarling sibilently. It stopped at one Bug to straighten a strap, at another to jingle a loose neck-harness, and at a third – its hiss rising to a furious pitch – to wave skeletal arms and spit slime.

The Bug dug its claws into its soft underbelly. They emerged holding a weapon. It slammed its exoskeletal heels together, scorpion tail jutting over its head at a strained angle.

'SKAHHHH – SRISSH-*KAAAH!*'

The line of Bugs faced east smartly, and jogged off into the insectoid encampment. Gilmuriel and the orc gunnery sergeant gazed down from the fifty-feet drop either side of the branch they stood on.

'Y'know, L.t.' Dakashnit scratched her head. 'That looks *familiar*, somehow . . .'

Gilmuriel shook himself and moved back to the main trunk of the goldentree, beckoning Starlight squad to join him.

Aradmel Brightblade chuckled under her breath. 'Hey, sir – tell the orc to go and crap in the Bugs' dug-outs, sir – it's called "area denial"!'

Dakashnit uncharacteristically ignored her. 'L.t., they got the ground sewn up down there. We ain't going anywhere.'

'Move with the shadowed silence of our ancient race,' Lieutenant Gilmuriel directed. He gestured at the surrounding goldentrees, and their broad branches that stretched away like paths above the forest floor. 'We don't need the earth. We're elves, Sergeant, and we're out of here!'

A long hour later, the elf marines descended from the trees.

'You're on point, Sergeant,' Gilmuriel said.

There was nothing from the orc but a soft 'Yo!', and when Gilmuriel looked, she vanished, blending with the rainforest's shadows. He led the marine recruits off down a faint track, ears pricked, elf-instincts at full stretch.

DAKKA-DAKKA-DAKKA-*FOOM!*

Bushes rustled. Gilmuriel heard a succession of thuds. He looked back from where he stood alone on the track. All twelve elf marines had dived into the bushes, only the shaking leaves marking their passage.

Gilmuriel abruptly ducked his head and slid into cover beside Corporal Silthanis. 'Get your elves up, marine! This is the real thing! Our first firefight!'

'I know that, sir.' The elf looked up at his lieutenant from under a too-large GI helmet with BORN TO SING stencilled on the cover. 'Lord Gilmuriel, let's go back. Call in the helicopter and let's go home!'

The bush under which Silthanis Blackrose cowered shook itself and became the orc sergeant Dakashnit, camouflage fatigues stuck at every point with tree-fronds and rushes. Her pig-like eyes gleamed under the rim of her kevlar helmet.

'I'll take a recon team down there, Lieutenant,' Dakashnit volunteered enthusiastically. 'Yo!'

The sound of real gunfire made Gilmuriel's stomach flip over.

'No, orc. We return to the main company, or better still, the City of the Trees. Byrna Silkentress, call the helicopter.'

With no rustle of leaves, the orc's GPMG swung up to cover Gilmuriel. 'Get down there and fire on the hostiles, L.t. The enemy might miss you. I certainly won't.'

Gilmuriel glared with the arrogance of fifty generations of High Elven ancestors. The orc, head sunk down almost between her shoulders, showed a yellow fang.

'There's elf recruits down there, L.t. I just saw. *Marines* don't leave their own. Even if they are a useless mob of squeakies. What are your guys down there gonna do to the Bugs, Lieutenant – *sing* at them?'

An unexpected smile broke on the elf's fine, aquiline features. He put one finger up, still with harp-string callouses on the pad, and pushed the machine-gun barrel to one side. Dakashnit noted that it now pointed directly at Byrna Silkentress. Assuming this to be an accident, she elevated her weapon's muzzle skyward.

TAKA-TAKA-*BOOM!*

'If there are other forest elves down in that mess, we must come to

300

their aid, of course. Very well. Gunnery Sergeant, line the recruits up for order of march.'

'Awrriiiight! Marines Illurian Swiftbow and Aradmel Brightblade, take the back door. If anything comes up behind us, I wanna know about it. Marines Dyraddin Treewaker and Elendylis Goldenfire, you're on point. The rest of you, five-metre spacing, don't close up, watch your buddies, watch for silent signals, and keep your fucking golden eyes open for the enemy!'

Gilmuriel took his place towards the centre of the line of march. A very un-elven sweat trickled down between his angular shoulder-blades, soaking the coarse cloth of his combat fatigues.

The orc sergeant reappeared by becoming a bush he had not noticed. 'L.t., take 'em up to the top of that ridge and we can make a killing zone of this valley.'

TAKKA-TAKKA-*FOOM!*

Shredded leaves spattered Gilmuriel's camouflage-painted features. A chunk of raw wood dripping sap caught him in the stomach and he sat down heavily. Rounds whipped over his head. Rolling and crawling, he made cover behind a moss-shrouded rock.

FOOM!

'Number and distance!' Dakashnit bawled, from behind another rock. 'Come on, you fuckwitted shit-for-brains marines! Didn't I teach you anything? Anyone see where that came from?'

'Over there,' a shrill elvish voice quavered. Belluriel Starharp.

'Over where?'

'Over *there!*'

'Over *where?* —oh fuck it,' the orc sergeant swore. 'This is what your training is devised to avoid, grunts. Give me a fucking *clock direction* on axis of march!'

Belluriel Starharp, sounding very bemused, asked, 'What is Time to one of the elven-kind?'

Gilmuriel called, 'Four o'clock, Sergeant.'

Back pressed flat to a rock outcrop, shivering, he found himself facing the rest of his squad. The elves lay facedown in a cluster in the leafmould of the forest floor, fingernails digging into the dirt. Only Corporal Silthanis had taken any reasonable cover: the tall, dark-skinned elf was scrunched down behind a fallen tree.

'First time under fire,' the orc sergeant sighed. 'Damn *squeakies.*'

BOOM! DUKKA-DUKKA-FOOM!

The orc broke cover, sprinting across the ground in a low crouch, seizing two elves by their sweat-soaked combat jacket collars and dragging them towards the rocks. *'Move your asses or you're dead meat!'*

Dakashnit threw Byrna Silkentress and the ex-healer-mage Ravenharp the White into the cover of the granite outcrops. She ducked her head, and shambled back across the open ground towards the recruits. Gilmuriel saw her jerk, miss a step, then run on at a crouch.

TAKKA-TAKKA-TAKKA-TAKKA!

Adrenalin fired him. He drew his pistol, winced at the feel of cold iron and replaced it in the holster; sprinted across the open ground of the killing zone – muzzle flashes to the right of the line of march: thirty metres – and dragged Aradmel Brightblade to her feet.

'Move your buddy into the rocks!'

The elf stared at him with glazed eyes. Gilmuriel backhanded her across the jaw, then sucked the skinned knuckles of hands not used to violence. Marine Aradmel ran for the rocks, on her own. The lieutenant got both hands under marine Illurian's armpits and dragged her, combat-booted heels jouncing, back into the granite outcrop.

DAKKA-FOOOMM!

'Fuck, man!' The orc sergeant hit the rock beside him, crouching down, her brawny shoulder pushed into the moss-covered granite. Her helmet was missing – out in open ground, Gilmuriel saw, with a smear of silver metal across it – and sweat shone in her cropped, bleached crest. 'You did *good*, L.t.'

The elf blushed a delicate rose at her praise.

Busily retying the red sweatband around her blood-stained brows, Dakashnit said quietly, 'Gonna have to assault through the enemy position. *Now*, L.t. Call us in some indirect fire support for when we've fought through.'

'Byrna Silkentress!' Gilmuriel signalled to his radio operator, crouched behind a rock five yards away. The tiny black-haired elf shivered and wept, a dark stain spreading at the crotch of her combat trousers. '*Marine* Byrna! Raise the artillery camp and call in fire support on this position – five minutes, on my mark – *now*.'

Trembling so that her fingers could hardly work the radiocom, the elf marine obeyed. Lieutenant Gilmuriel leaned back, tensed his thighs, and lifted himself to peer over the top of the granite outcrop. Only his blond hair, his eyes, and the tops of his pointed ears showed. 'Prepare to advance—'

KER-*FOOM!*

'—*what the fuck was that!*'

'Mortar, sounds like. I reckon we'll re-supply at Firebase Charlie,' Dakashnit speculated. 'Remind me to stock you guys up on mortars. Hey, squeakies! *Bug-bait!* Wake up. That's the fucking enemy over there. Start firing back!'

TAKKA-TAKKA-DUKKA-DUKKA-FOOM!

'Yo, man! *I see you, you son of a bitch!*'

The orc reared up, General Purpose Machine Gun grasped in her taloned paws, firing from the hip. The noise wrenched all breath from Gilmuriel's lungs. He refilled them to yell, 'Give that orc supporting fire, you miserable pointy-eared bastards, or I'll shoot you myself!'

'Way to go, L.t!' Sergeant Dakashnit fell back into cover beside Gilmuriel. 'Listen up, you elves – those are the Bugs that chewed up Baradaka's squad! Fireteam one, give 'em hell; fireteam two, advance under covering fire. *Go!*'

Gilmuriel, under cover of a ragged barrage from Silthanis and half the squad, loped at a crouch up to another granite outcrop. One glance over his shoulder showed him a hostile, running left to right, hitting cover—

The glimpse of black chitinous shell dripping with bodily secretions, the half-humanoid form with its scorpion tail raised high, shining blue-black and silver in the dapple leaf-light; the noise of the firefight; all this conspired to make Gilmuriel's stomach churn. The elf bent forward and vomited. 'We're fucking dead!'

'Fight through!' Dakashnit bawled, 'or we'll have our own fucking mortars landing on our heads – what the fuck is *that?*'

'*Magery!* No,' Gilmuriel corrected himself, elvish instincts screaming. 'No, it isn't . . .'

Across the leaf-strewn expanse of the Bugs' killing ground, the sun and shadow-dappled air twisted and somehow *opened*. A dark silhouette became visible within it. Too stocky for an elf, too tall for an orc. The shape of a Man, outlined in black fire.

The elf whispered, 'It has no smell of Good or Evil about it!'

Dakashnit hastily changed belts. 'Look at the Bugs, L.t. It's stopped 'em cold. They ain't got no fucking idea what it is either!'

The air folded, taking into itself green shadows and sunlight, becoming a whirling vortex of golden light. The Man-silhouette suddenly snapped into movement.

'Mother of Forests protect us!' Gilmuriel gaped, his jaw dropping. The three-dimensional figure of a Man appeared out of the vortex, facing the elf lieutenant, seeming to step backwards from something that was not the Forest of Thyrion.

'Holy shit!' Dakashnit half-straightened from her crouch.

The sounds of gunfire fell silent on both sides.

The orc's eyes gleamed, and all her tusks showed in a grin. 'Do you know what that is?'

The Man stood quite still, his polished brown combat boots crushing the leaves under his feet with undeniable solidity. He was

303

almost as tall as an elf, but broad across the shoulders and massively muscled. Gilmuriel let his gaze travel up the Man's body – brown-and-ochre camouflage fatigues; web-belt, pouches and pistol; commando knife; rubber-edged dogtag shining on a silver chain – until he reached the face. Sunlight dappled regular, square features, a strong jawline, and crew-cut hair glinting blond. The Man's piercing blue eyes met his.

'What is that?' the elf mumbled.

'That's a *real* marine!' Gunnery Sergeant Dakashnit brandished her GPMG. 'Just feel the aura on that! I ain't felt nothing like it since I was up in old Dagurashibanipal's caverns – I don't know where he's from, or how the fuck he got here, but that is one *genuine* marine. The finest killing machine ever devised by Man. The élite. The best.'

The orc straightened, as much as orcs are able, gripping stock and barrel of the machine-gun. She threw the GPMG bodily towards the Man. Smoothly and as if by long training, the Man raised his hands and the GPMG slapped into his grip.

Dakashnit called, 'Yo, m'man! Hostiles thirty metres to your rear! Chaarge!'

The smartly uniformed Man turned his head slowly. No hurry. No hesitation.

Ninety feet away, their chitinous heads weaving as if bemused by the vortex's visitation, the Bugs emerged slowly out of light cover. Thyrion's green fronds caressed sticky black carapaces, horns and clawed forelimbs. The slender scorpion tails curved up. Shadow slid across the belts and packs slung across their articulated thoraxes, glinting from the black metal of their weapons. One opened its vast jaws in a sticky, slime-dripping yawn. Gilmuriel shuddered.

'Hostile targets!' the orc called to the newly appeared Man. 'Take 'em out, marine!'

The Man's hands opened.

The machine-gun thudded to the jungle floor, ignored.

The uniformed Man opened his mouth.

'*Aaaaaaaaaaaaaaaaaaaarggggghhhh!*'

One large combat boot caught Gilmuriel and bowled the elf over as the Man barrelled past him. The Man sprinted at top speed, bawling, eyes glazed and wide with shock, mouth a square of fear.

'Wha'—?' Dakashnit mouthed. '*What?*'

'Fuck it!' Gilmuriel fluted, scrambling back on to his feet and signalling to his squad, ignoring the flabbergasted orc sergeant. He pointed after the running Man. 'You elves – don't ask questions – follow that marine!'

*   *   *

304

There are no roads to the east.

The Blasted Redoubt kills the land about its bastions. The dead shadows of those grim towers, those windowless high walls and courtyards where sun never shines, devastate the crop-yield for leagues around. The Redoubt itself is vast enough to create its own rain-shadow, so that one approaches from the West through a landscape of cracked earth, shrivelled moss, and cold desolation; and approaches from the east – but who knows what mud and storms lurk to the east of the Blasted Redoubt? Only the slaves of the Dark Lord ever travel there, and they are, for the most part, singularly reticent.

'All *I* can say', Ned Brandiman remarked grumpily, 'is that it's frightening the manticore.'

The wagon's draught-beast fluffed up its lion pelt, docked scorpion tail twitching, its Man's features showing distress. Ned threw it a tidbit of fried toad.

'Have no fear!' Amarynth Firehand called, striding beside the wagon, his ragged white habit tangling in briars. Thorns lacerated the elf's dark skin. His eyes glowing, the Holy One exclaimed, 'This is the ideal place to begin the Light's Crusade!'

Ned muttered, 'Ideal, my hairy left foot!'

'Mother Edwina!' Will Brandiman reproved. 'The Holy One is guided by the Lady of Light. If he says that we begin the Light's election campaign in the middle of desolation, in the Dark Lord's own fortress Redoubt; we, a company of barely two dozen, on a perilous journey from the rich, comfortable South and its plentiful supplies of *food,* for example – then that's exactly what we do.'

'Amen!' the good Abbess Edwina snarled.

The Holy Paladin Amarynth strode unmoved through the black land, his shaggy mass of dark hair flowing back from his pointed ears, in his hand a staff that glowed as white as his ragged monks' robes. The elf turned to look back at the wagons of the Mission of Light, his slender form silhouetted against the bastions, flying buttresses, walls, balconies, spires, towers, pinnacles and sheer masonry bulk of the Blasted Redoubt.

'On!' the elf cried. 'Onward!'

Tiny figures began to scurry along the Redoubt's parapets and into the shadow of the great West Gate. Ned's long sight detected orcs, their smaller cousins the kobolds, the giant wolf-steeds orcs use in battle, and the leathery fanged steeds-of-the-air unnamed in the West.

'Wonderful!' Ned looked back over his shoulder.

Behind the Mission of Light's wagon a dozen of the Holy Order of Flagellant Knights plodded along the desolate track. Each raised a metal-thonged whip and cracked it down on the back of the male or female elf in front. Periodically the leaders of the columns would swap with the back markers. The Mission wagon had been dogged for forty miles by vultures following the scent of the blood.

'Know what I think?' Ned observed, scratching under the hem of his nun's habit at his hairy bare feet. '*I* think we should've gone back and burned the Inn of the Sixteen Varied Delights, *and* that laundry, and *then* we should have left Graagryk for good.'

His brother whipped out an ebony comb, slicking his spell-dyed hair back from his brows.

'You can always burn down taverns that have thrown us out. How often does a halfling get a chance to enter the Blasted Redoubt?'

It crossed Ned's mind to ask, 'How often does a halfling *want* a chance to enter the Blasted Redoubt?', but the thought of ebony carvings, jet stones, sable furs and black diamonds – doubtless with no special guard on them, other than being in the orc-haunted, evil magic-spelled, heart-of-desolation fortress of the Dark Lord – made his eyes gleam in his chubby face.

'Take the reins,' Ned directed, handing the manticore's tack to his brother, and proceeded to freshen up his lip- and eye-paint. By the time the Mission wagon rolled into one of the Redoubt's outer court-yards he had repaired the worst ravages of travel, and brushed mud from his red habit.

Kobolds shambled from the shadows in increasing numbers, their eyes catching the light redly. The larger orcs herded them back with pole-axes and jagged black swords. Ned snapped his fingers at a wolf that stood several handspans higher at the shoulder than any halfling.

'Good doggie!'

'HRRRAAAGGGH . . .'

'Edwina, stop teasing that poor animal.' His brother, teeth gleaming whitely in the courtyard's gloom, stepped past Ned to address a hulking orc in a studded leather jerkin and black steel helmet: obviously one of the fighting Agaku. 'Good afternoon, sir. Allow me to introduce myself: I am the campaign manager for the Holy Paladin-Mage Amarynth, your Light candidate in the forth-coming election to the Throne of the World.'

The black-clad orc shuffled from foot to taloned foot, and scratched at his pointed, hairless ears with the spike of his pole-axe. 'Um . . . we've been supporters of the Dark here for generations. Don't want to be rude, but, well, isn't much point you coming here, is there?'

Ned raised his chin. Familiar with Man architecture as well as the townships of halflings, he was not unused to walls that towered up like cliffs, but the soaring masonry of the Redoubt courtyard lost itself in mist far too far above his head. It dripped with moisture; and the stench of excrement and the shrieks of the incarcerated echoed down from barred slit windows.

'My son.' Ned unclipped the whip from his spiked belt and cracked it. The noise echoed across the gathered heads of the Dark masses. Orcs twitched by reflex. He beamed at the Agaku. 'I know you won't disappoint a poor old woman – a poor old woman trained in the mage-craft of the Little Sisters of Mortification – and not hear our candidate. Will you?'

The orc shambled around, clawed feet kicking bones across the black cobbles. 'Silence! If anyone so much as breathes, I'll send his miserable carcass to the Pit! Dire wolves, you have free rein to harry any who speaks but the elf, be it bat, kobold, goblin or orc!'

Edwina smiled sweetly. 'Thank you.'

'Well done, our good and faithful servants!' the Holy One exclaimed, resting long-fingered hands on the heads of his halfling priest and abbess. In the abrupt silence, the Holy One paced across the courtyard and took his place on the cyclopean steps of the nearest tower entrance, looking out across the beady eyes, red pupils, snouts and twitching claws of his audience.

'Scum of the Blasted Redoubt!' the elf sang melodiously. 'Do you wonder why we have no fear, standing before you as we do in the heart of Dark's citadel? That is because you do not yet know who we are. We are Amarynth, who was a mortal elven paladin, but who you may now know as the Holy One, the Most Holy. We are the Son of the Lady herself!'

Ned abandoned the Mission wagon – there being no interrupting Amarynth once he had begun using *we* – and rejoined his brother on the other side of a locked postern door, inside the Blasted Redoubt. Black torches burned in wall cressets, nitre spidered the masonry, and the bronchial coughing of an orc guard echoed down from the upper reaches.

'Cellars, is my guess,' Ned said.

His brother nodded. 'If it was Men, I'd say tops of the towers. But orcs and Dark Lords, they think subterranean. Got your stuff?'

Ned guffawed. The nun's robe made packing throwing daggers, poisoned needles, fine mail gauntlets (for trying traps) and lockpicks easier than doublet and hose. Slits cut in the cloth under the arms aided easy access to them.

'Let's hit the shadows,' Ned said.

A sudden clatter of feet interrupted. Bare, hard feet. Torchlight glimmered first from the passage at their left, then from the passage

307

on their right. Six or seven orcs piled into the tower entrance's narrow antechamber.

'Ah,' Ned exclaimed. 'Good brother priest William, here are more souls who have yet to hear the word of our Mission.'

The orc in the lead growled, 'Oh, we've heard him. Promising the great last crusade against the Forces of Evil, your elf is. Says he'll field another Army of Light against the Horde of Darkness.'

Ned saw his brother momentarily squeeze his eyes shut, then open them, smiling a wide smile.

'Perhaps I can interest you gentlemen', Will Brandiman said, 'in contributing to the Holy Prayer Wheel Fund of the Mission of Light? Now, you're fighting orcs, I can see that, and the object of the Prayer Wheel is to heal all wounds caused in battle – no matter upon which side the fighter fought.'

''S not right,' the leading orc protested.

The Reverend Brandiman and the good Abbess Edwina exchanged glances. Neither benefited.

'Of course, if you don't *wish* to make a contribution to the Holy One's prayer-wheel,' Will oozed. 'Should you be *so* poor that you cannot afford a copper piece, a button, a shred, a bone . . . why then, you may take these . . . ah . . . *these* prayer-beads, for free. But search your heart, brother orc, and see if *you* can afford to deprive the world (for it will be you doing the depriving) of the benefits of the Son of Light's Holy Prayer Wheel.'

The orc's heavy brows lowered. He looked to have Agaku stock in him, Ned considered: a magnificent specimen of orc-hood some six feet high, with hulkingly muscled shoulders, and wearing nothing over his leathery green skin but a loincloth.

'He's war-mongering,' the orc accused. 'Your Holy One is. Promoting a war which only serves the interests of the Dark and Light Commands, and not the orc in the pit.'

Ned gaped up at the orc. The group of five or six other orcs crowded round, some brown-and-grey skinned, all wearing the odd scrap of mail or plate or nail-studded padded jerkins. Prick-ears flattened, and tusks and talons glinted.

'I'm sure you gentlemen have your point of view,' Ned said, a little breathlessly.

The leader orc loomed over Will Brandiman, reached down, and prodded him between two doublet buttons.

'I'm an official representative, me. I represent the Orc Pacifist Movement.' The orc waved a taloned hand. 'Us here, we're a OPM protest. We're protesting against your Paladin coming in here and telling us to fight. *He* don't go out with the foot soldiers, do he?'

308

The other orcs shook their heads in unison. Their leader continued:

'*He* don't have to trail a pole-axe over hill and dale, out of this lovely mucky land, and go down south where it's *green*. *He* don't get his balls shot off by some trigger-happy crossbow-elf. Not your Paladin! *He* don't end up hacking some poor Light sod to shreds just because he was in the wrong place at the wrong time, and it's him or you.'

Behind the large orc, his fellows began a guttural chant of 'Dark, no! We won't go! We won't fight—'

'GRAZHDNAG!' an orcish yell interrupted from outside the tower. 'Get your filthy, worm-eating scum down here or I'll flay you alive!'

The leading orc, Grazhdnag, cowered. His followers whimpered. They slunk past the halflings (ignoring Will Brandiman's outstretched hand, which still contained a string of Mission beads) and shambled out into the courtyard, from whence the sound of bone-cracking blows echoed.

'I'll teach you, you lazy scum—!'

Ned and Will listened briefly to the Agaku's voice, grinned, and split up, the better to cover more of the Blasted Redoubt's cellars in the available time.

On his fifth trip back – choosy now, the wagon's false bottom almost full – Ned Brandiman found himself climbing a narrow winding stone stair. He climbed until his calf muscles ached. At last he heard, through as-yet invisible windows, the voice of Amarynth rising to a peroration in one of the outer courtyards that, by experience, Ned had found to be merely a tiny satellite of the vast atriums, pits, coliseums, and air-shafts that pierced the mass of the Blasted Redoubt.

He reached the top of the steps and started down a corridor. Here there were torches, meaning concealing shadows, and he stayed in them by instinct.

An interior portcullis slammed down behind him. Ned leaped forward, grazing the back of his bare heel. He froze, listening; checked the trap-mechanism and discovered it to be ancient but well-oiled; decided that it had only cut him off from cellars already looted; and continued on.

Loud footsteps echoed down the corridor ahead.

An approaching shadow danced on the walls, distorted by the light from the black cressets; growing larger, taller, *much* taller than a halfling—

'Good lord,' Ned Brandiman observed, 'the press really do get everywhere.'

A female elf walking in the shadows of the Blasted Redoubt's black masonry halted, staring.

When Ned had last seen the elf she had been wearing the same leather bodice and thonged leather trousers, high boots and cloak; her dark braids tied around the brow with a strip of red cloth. A badge pinned on her vest over the upper slope of one breast now read *Warrior of Fortune*.

Perdita del Verro regarded Ned Brandiman with suspicion. 'Don't I know you, mistress?'

Ned himself had been stark naked at the time of their last meeting, and not known to be the owner of a Little Sisters of Mortification red habit. He removed his fingers from where they rested, through slit cloth, on a throwing dagger, and pitched his voice melodiously higher. 'I doubt we've met, my child, but we are all Sisters in the Light.'

'I must have seen you with the Holy One.' The elf narrowed her eyes. Her flyaway brows dipped, the frown accentuating the old scar on her left cheek. 'I'd like an interview – get to see him close up. Seems to me the Light candidate needs all the good press he can get in this election.'

Ned led her down from the tower and out into the courtyard. He kicked the back of the Mission wagon with his hirsute foot. 'Your Holiness, an elf of the press is here to interview you. Is it convenient?'

Amarynth, bent over and clutching the wagon's wooden frame with both hands, looked up irritatedly and gestured the attendant knight-priest to cease scourging the Holy back.

'Oh . . . very well.' Pulling up his monk's habit and slipping his arms into the sleeves, the Holy One looked at the female elf.

'Lord *Amarynth?* Paladin, it *is* you, isn't it! *By the Light!*' The elf blinked. 'Your campaign speech— I was too far away to tell—'

Regally, the dark elf stated, 'We were Amarynth, called Firehand, and are now the Son of the Lady on earth.'

'Amarynth the Paladin-Mage! You commanded the forces of the Light at Nin-Edin!'

Ned Brandiman ducked his head. The expected explosion failed to materialize. Ned, who never let a previously friendly meeting dictate the likelihood of a permanent alliance, congratulated himself on his caution when Perdita del Verro scowled and continued:

'Holy One, I'm extremely glad we've met. I was badly taken-in by those scum of Nin-Edin and their criminal allies. When I found out what they'd done in the mountains after the siege—'

'"After"?' Amarynth sounded surprised.

The elf lifted a brow, distorting the brawler's scar that crossed her cheek. Her voice echoed clearly across the courtyard of the Blasted Redoubt. 'You don't know, sir knight? Mother of Trees! While there's yet time before the election, then— I know something about the orcs of Nin-Edin that *you* ought to know.'

7

THE SEVENTH DAY before the final Election to the Throne of the World dawned bright and clear.

Early summer light chased down the masts of ships moored at Port Mirandus. Long shadows spidered from the beasts, Men and monstrosities loading craft to catch the morning tide. Shouts and the creaking of ropes echoed back from the warehouse frontages on the quayside, and leather-winged vampire gulls shrieked, soaring down the estuary of the River Faex that here flows into the Western Ocean. Haze, presaging warmth, drifted across the harbour's lapping, odorous waves.

'The Lord of Darknesh's orders are perfectly clear,' the nameless necromancer lisped primly, from under the concealment of his cowl. 'Send no relieving forces to Thyrion or anywhere else.'

'Damn it, Man, my marines are getting chewed up out there!'

Ashnak, General Officer Commanding the orc marines, spat over the side of his barge. An unlucky harbour fish rose to the surface, belly-up. 'We could send in support troops any time She lets us!'

A gloved hand went up to the hood, came down glistening with saliva. 'What an intereshting coincidence – since it takshes time to do the logistical planning for moving an army. Ready to move, are you, orc? I wonder what you were planning before She returned?'

Ashnak avoided that issue. 'All I know is, there's a damn good fight going on out there, and She won't let me – my orcs, I mean – join in!'

'Of coursh not. While the Bugs are advancing on the borders of the Southern Kingdoms, they're pressure to vote for Her Dark Magnificence . . . Orc, you will do no fighting until the elecshion's won, and your foot-soldiers must become used to dying while they wait.' The nameless necromancer whuffled a laugh. 'It'sh like old times – orcses to waste.'

The nameless limped off towards the silk canopies at the rear of the barge.

'And fuck *you*, asshole,' Ashnak grated.

Air flattened the water over the great fleet of up-river barges. The *whuck-whuck-whuck!* of an approaching Apache helicopter gunship aroused no curiosity. The dockhands of Port Mirandus are used to miracles.

'*Steady!*' Ashnak bawled into his headset microphone.

'*Oh, I say, sir, do give a chap some credit. I am doing my . . . best. There! There you are, sir.*'

Lieutenant Chahkamnit's voice fell silent over the radio link as the steel crate the orc pilot was lowering touched the deck of the rivership. The Apache hovered while two deckhands unhooked the load, then rose again, cable winching, nose down, rotors beating the water into circumferences of foam.

'*Park that damn thing on one of the air-support barges,*' Ashnak ordered, '*and get your ass back here, Chahkamnit! This travelling election circus should have cast off four hours ago!*'

'*Absolutely, sir. Just as you say.*'

Ashnak thumbed his headset off. Marine Commissar Razitshakra stood beside him on the rivership's deck, olive greatcoat hanging open in the southern heat, her peaked cap pulled down to her wire-spectacled nose.

'Prepare to interrograte the prisoner!' Ashnak barked, pointing.

'Sir, yes, sir!' Commissar Razitshakra enthusiastically snapped the steel crate's holding pins bare-handed. The front of the crate fell open. 'It's been too long since we've had some honest prisoner-torturing just for the fun of it, sir.'

A large body huddled in the close confines of the crate. It wore excrement-stained desert camouflage fatigues. Ashnak chewed more ferociously on his cigar and peered down at the broad-shouldered, big and solidly built Man; dirty with days of confinement, the stubble on his chin growing out the same blond as his crew-cut.

'On your *feet*, marine!' Ashnak snarled.

It rubbed at its streaming eyes. 'My name, rank, and number are Sergeant John H. Stryker – *sweet Jesus it's still fuckin' real!*'

'He speaks marine,' Commissar Razitshakra observed.

The Man stared out of the steel crate. 'This can*not* be real, man. I promise I won't ever do that shit again! I've got a wife and kids at home.'

'He checks out. Same aura as Dagurashibanipal's hoard, General.'

Stryker forced his big body to rise, straightening for the first time after six days' confinement in a metre-square steel crate. Staggering, filthy, on his feet; he felt the warm, stinking breeze of a harbour blow across his face. The skin around his eyes twitched, and his eyelids opened again.

A humanoid *thing* stood in front of him. Eight feet tall, muscled like a mountain; predator's fangs, leather-skinned, cat-quick, and with the frightening gleam of high intelligence in its piggy eyes. Even with its shoulders humped and long arms dangling, it stared Stryker levelly in the eye.

And there was a cigar jutting from its tusked nightmare of face.

It wore . . .

Stryker chuckled deeply. In his Stateside Germanic accent, he said, 'You guys can't fool me! Either this is the best shit I ever cut, or you guys are making a summer season movie. But I'm warning you – you shouldn't have messed with the Corps.'

Ashnak drew deeply, then blew the odd-smelling smoke from his cigar into Stryker's face. 'We *are* the Corps. What are *you?*'

'*Please!*' Stryker's stubbled chin began to twitch. His face crumpling, his eyes began to leak water. He sat down on the deck as if his hamstrings had been severed. 'Don't hurt me!'

'Show some guts, Man!' Razitshakra growled. 'You're a marine! Don't disgrace your uniform!'

'What's the matter with you, son?' Ashnak inquired, nudging the now sobbing Stryker with the toe of a combat boot. 'Anyone would think you'd never seen an orc before.'

The Man raised his stained face. 'A *what?*'

Razitshakra's whip ripped a channel across the back of his ribs, tearing his combat jacket and his flesh. He screamed, a full-blooded Man's scream, hand going up, and a metal-thonged whip coiled around his wrist, bloodying his knuckles. He grabbed the thong.

'*For fuck's sake, you can't do that!*'

Razitshakra tugged speculatively on the whip's butt, with no effort pulling him clear across deck.

'The traditional methods are the best,' she said thoughtfully. 'That's the Way of the Orc. To torture prisoners. I'll strip the hide from him and then, when's he's flayed, he'll talk.'

'I'll talk, I'll talk *now!*' Stryker scrambled across the barge deck. 'Hey, you just ask me – I'll tell you whatever you want to know! This

314

is too fuckin' crazy for me. I've never been in combat, never mind under heavy interrogation.'

'Never been in combat?' Ashnak's ridged brows lifted in astonishment. 'But you're a marine! Ah. I know how it must have been – you're a newly trained élite soldier, and you accidentally discovered a way through from your world to here, and your superior officers sent you to recce. Happens all the time. Right?'

'Hell, no!' Sergeant John H. Stryker wiped the sweat pouring down his strong, regular features, sprawled on his backside on the deck. 'I haven't had my hands on a gun in twenty years, and that was in basic training. I'm a *clerk*. I shift army gear and personnel. This gang of asshole kids jumped me. They totalled my jeep and they were gonna total me. I was gonna get the hell out, and then something *happened*—'

'You ran away from a brawl?' The orc commissar shuddered.

'Shit, there were dozens of the little bastards! For all I know they were carrying knives, of *course* I'm outta there! Look,' the Man's tenor voice protested plaintively, 'so far I've been kidnapped and dumped in the fucking *jungle*, for God's sake; seeing things I never thought to see outside of a trip. If I don't get back to Base I'm AWOL and they're gonna have my *ass*. And there's a load of Tornado spares that I *got* to get shipped through.'

'Support services,' Razitshakra remarked. 'Rear echelon.'

Ashnak snarled. 'We have the first real proof that there's a world where Dagurashibanipal's marines exist! Where you can get the weapons systems we only dream about. A heroes' world! And what do we get? We get *this*.'

Leather-winged birds gibbered and yawped over the estuary. Razitshakra unholstered a Desert Eagle automatic pistol, thumbed back the hammer, and placed the cold muzzle in Stryker's ear. 'I say we waste him, General, right now. He's useless.'

'Aw, why not . . . *fuck*.'

A cloaked figure with bodyguards paced up the gangplank.

Ashnak came smartly to attention and performed a parade-perfect salute. The Man chewed his large-knuckled fist, smothering a high-pitched giggle.

Razitshakra kept the muzzle of the Desert Eagle automatic pistol pointed at his head. The Man flinched each time the circle of darkness lined up on him.

'Yes, indeed,' Ashnak rumbled, 'I'm attempting to ascertain that very thing myself, your Dark Magnificence, how perspicacious of you to mention it. I believe this to be a marine from Dagurashibanipal's collection. One of my NCOs in Thyrion found it. Said it cracked up at the first sight of the enemy.'

315

Razitshakra muttered, '*Definitely* ideologically unsound!'

The hooded figure lifted pale hands and put the cowl back from its face. At this point Sergeant John H. Stryker of the US Marine Corps understood that he really should have read the four dollar ninety-five fantasy hack-and-slay paperbacks that turned up in the mess. Or at least watched more of the videos. *Thriller, Beaver* and *Private Eye* don't teach you rules for survival where orcs carry M16s. Or where women have glowing neon-orange eyes.

The air dirtied as if a cloud had passed across the dawn. Only She shone. Her gaunt face had shadows of the palest blue lining hollow cheeks and eye-sockets. A great starburst of white-blond hair cascaded back from Her smooth forehead. Smothered in heavy black robes, fragile, She gazed down at Stryker where he sprawled on the barge's deck.

Her voice like bells said, 'Curious and interesting.'

'Yes, Dread Lord.' Ashnak pointed at the barge fleet, the grunts crewing it, and the confusion apparent on most of the vessels. 'It appears to be a logistics expert, Ma'am. I thought we might see what it can do. Or we could try eating it.'

'No!' Sergeant Stryker added, as a confused afterthought: 'Sir!'

The Dark Lord said, 'You may accompany Me below, My Ashnak. Bring that with you.'

Ashnak saluted, gestured to the commissar, and set off down into the bowels of the Faex River barge. Under the prow cables hummed, strung up through beams and hooks to a portable generator. An acrid smell hung in the air. Ashnak moved forward to the laboratory benches.

'What have you got here, technician?'

Behind Ashnak, the Man whimpered. He shot a glare at Razitshakra, who put her taloned hand firmly over the Man's mouth. Blue eyes bugged, staring – so far as Ashnak could make out – at Tech-Captain Ugarit.

'Sir, General Ashnak, sir! Look at these babies!' Green spittle trailed down Ugarit's chin. The skinny orc's white laboratory coat pockets clinked with scalpels as he danced in place, head bobbing between Ashnak and the silent figure of the Dark Lord.

Ashnak supposed that, if you weren't used to it, Ugarit's habit of piercing his pointed ears with feathers and studs might be a little startling. The tall skinny orc wiped his hands down his blood-stained coat, eyes and fangs glinting in the light of naked bulbs; giggling and saluting. As he moved aside, Ashnak saw the dissected carapace of a Bug resting on the makeshift laboratory table. Sticky fluids flowed down on to the deck.

The Man whimpered, even through Razitshakra's muffling hand.

'Acid blood!' Ugarit enthused. 'Regeneration of parts! *Tiny* brains! They're perfect killing machines, your Dark Magnificence, perfect. Oh I do *envy* them so . . .'

The skinny orc dribbled again. Ashnak momentarily debated the wisdom of having moved Captain Ugarit from technical development to biological research.

'This,' the Dark Lord pointed, 'this is not flesh . . .'

Ugarit reached a heavily gloved hand into the mess on the bench, and extracted what looked to Ashnak like a steel mechanism.

'They *secrete* me-muhh-uhn-uhn-uhn—!'

Ashnak stepped forward and punched Ugarit firmly in the face. The orc's head bounced off one of the barge's beams. A daffy grin spread itself across his thin green features.

'They secrete *metal*,' he repeated, slightly more in control. 'They replace parts of their bodies with it. O Great Mistress, I think they can grow their own weapons. I think they can grow *our* weapons, now they've captured some to copy. Mistress, imagine if I could harness their growth mechanism, we could *grow our own armaments!*'

Ugarit reached back and rested fond gloved claws on the Bug's sticky shell.

'I always *wanted* to do cybernetic research,' the skinny orc murmured dreamily. 'Grafting parts. Inserting bits. This organic mechanism is so much simpler. Cyber-mech. That's it. Cyber-mech weapons systems . . .'

Ashnak looked at the Dark Lord. The Dark Lord's cowl turned in the general direction of Ashnak. She rested Her hand on Ugarit's bowed head. The sound of Her soft voice brought small rodents scurrying from the hold, spiders crawling from the beams, and Darkness to scurry about the orcs' feet:

'He is most ingenious, My Ugarit, is he not? Perhaps We should let him dismantle your captive marine. We might learn much from that.'

Ashnak ignored the snivelling from the Man behind him.

'Good idea, Dread Lord,' he said brightly. 'Thing's a disgrace to the marines anyway.'

'Look,' Sergeant John H. Stryker protested, 'I've seen a few videos, I remember how this is supposed to work! I come here, you train me, you make me into a warrior, I beat the shit out of your enemies; all that crap. Sir, I've *seen* those things fight. Never happen, sir.'

'Damn right,' Ashnak sniffed. 'Fancy you with a garlic sauce, myself. Very tasty, Man and garlic. Dread Lord, it's a pure waste of good meat to let the captain here have him.' He brightened. 'Unless we could have what's left over afterwards?'

Darkness hung and dripped from the underside of the barge deck, the electric bulbs spawned sepia and blue shadows, and a constant rustling of invisible homage sounded around the Dark Lord's bare robed feet.

Stryker gabbled, 'You're the ranking officer here, right, ma'am?'

Her narrow lips twitched up at the corners.

The Man stumbled on. 'And you've got a conflict situation here? And a presidential election? That takes planning. I can plan! I'm shit hot, ma'am. What I can do is make sure you and every other unit gets where they're meant to be, when they're meant to be there. *Really,* ma'am.'

'It is intelligent enough to eavesdrop. Well.' The Lord of Darkness wrapped Her thick black robes closer about Her body. The hold's smell of spices was overlain with a thicker scent. 'One *might* delay dissection, I suppose . . .'

'Yes, Dread Lord.' Ashnak resentfully ignored his rumbling gut.

The Heart of Evil shook back the pale hair from Her face, that seemed child-like amongst the heavy robes; and She smiled, holding out one of Her long-boned hands in front of Her, and turning it from side to side in examination.

'It is strange,' She said, 'to inhabit a female body, after so many aeons.'

The arcing electric bulbs in the hold illuminated Her gull-wing brows, delicate tiny ears and shapely mouth.

'There must be many things One can do with a female body,' the Dark Lord said. Her speculative gaze lingered on General Ashnak, who came to attention and a terrified eyes-front; then passed to Biotech-Captain Ugarit, who giggled; Razitshakra (obliviously reciting cantos from the Way of the Orc to herself), and finally fixed on John H. Stryker. She smiled.

'Have that boy washed,' She ordered, 'and sent to My cabin.'

'Yes, Dread Lord!' Ashnak remained with his head bowed until She had departed for Her quarters. 'Commissar Razitshakra, you heard the Dark Lord. While you're doing that, interrogate the Man carefully. You may cause it pain, but don't damage it. Dismiss!'

Biotech-Captain Ugarit followed Ashnak back up on to the deck. Ashnak's despairing gaze travelled across the orc marine barge fleet, still not ready to cast off and direct their prows up the River Faex. Up the river, through all the townships and cities and the capitals of the Southern Kingdoms, on the last and heaviest stages of the Dark Lord's election campaign. And only seven more days . . .

'Sir,' Ugarit pleaded, 'may I have him, sir? Just a tiny bit, sir?'

'Well, I suppose She wouldn't miss a toe or a finger, or one of the smaller organs,' Ashnak mused. 'On the other hand, we—'

'General, what's that?' Ugarit, his dirty white laboratory coat flapping around his ankles in the river breeze, suddenly snickered, whinnied, and pointed.

'Don't interrupt *me*, you puking excuse for an orc ma—' Ashnak stopped, speechless. 'Pits!'

A cloud of dust rose up over the bank of the River Faex. Delta mud, dry as a bone in this summer season, kicked up sky-high. Following the plume down to its base led Ashnak's eyes to a black blob, travelling at high speed towards the moored barge-fleet.

'That's an armoured vehicle.' Ashnak's nostrils flared, failing to catch the scent of any magic. 'That's one of *our* armoured vehicles.'

Ugarit removed from his lab-coat pocket a miniaturized radicom, held it to his skinny ear, and shook it. 'Sir, they can't get it to identify, General, sir!'

Ashnak vaulted the poop deck rail, landing heavily and squarely on the lower deck. He strode to the barge rail nearest to the quay. 'Perimeter guards!'

A rachetting roar shook the earth and sky. The plume of dust switched direction, turning towards the river, trailing clouds of black exhaust. Juddering at its top speed of 30 mph, swaying, gun dipping and rising in a vain attempt to compensate for the terrain, a T54 Main Battle Tank swung down on to the quayside.

Before Ashnak could bellow a warning over the comlink, and with orc marines leaping into the water out of its way, the speeding tank rocketed down the bank, on to the wooden jetty in front of the barge, ground up a spray of timbers in its treads, and shuddered to a halt, its metal casing three feet from Ashnak standing at the barge rail.

The wooden piles of the quay groaned, cracked, and sank two yards with a sudden jolt.

Ashnak surveyed the banks of the River Faex. Dockworkers fled the wooden quay as the whole length of it swayed. Orc marines who had plummeted off the side swam, in full kit, back towards their own barges. Anxious signals jammed the radio frequencies, coming from further down the fleet.

'Get me artillery support!'

'Yessir!' Ugarit squeaked.

Ashnak leaned his horn-skinned elbow on the rail of the barge, and rested his massive-jawed chin on his hand. The steel hatch of the T54 flipped open. Ashnak raised his free hand, holding his .44 magnum officer's pistol.

A small figure stood up in the hull hatch of the T54 Main Battle Tank. The wooden beams and pilings of the quay creaked, snapped, and sank another foot, tilting the tank's nose towards the swirling black waters of the Faex. The figure ignored this. It saluted snappily, and gave a joyous cry.

'Sir, General Ashnak, sir!'

Ashnak suspiciously narrowed his deep-tilted eyes.

The helmeted figure, visible from the waist up, saluted again, and cried shrilly over the noise of the river birds, 'Sir, General Ashnak, *sir*. Major Barashkukor reporting back for duty, sir!'

Ashnak's you-can't-fool-me-dickhead-I'm-a-marine expression vanished. *'What?!'*

'Sir, it is me, sir, honest sir!'

The orc standing in the T54's hatch pulled off its helmet. Long hairless ears sprang momentarily upright, then drooped in the heat. A broad grin spread itself over only-too-familiar features.

Ashnak stared.

The small orc wore the remnants of a desert camouflage jacket, and one glove only. His other hand and arm seemed covered in shiny silver – no, were *made* of silver metal. And his eye . . .

The small orc's right eye had been replaced by a metal socket and zoom-lens, which whirred as he focused in on his general, and flashed in the dawn sun of Port Mirandus.

Ashnak thumbed back the hammer of the pistol he held. 'You sure as hell don't look like any kind of orc to me, boy.'

The small orc cyborg's face brightened. Both his ears perked up. 'Sir, the major can explain that to the general, sir!'

'You'd damn well better be able to!'

As Ashnak drew a bead on the figure in the tank, the dock timbers groaned and gave further way. The rear of the tank dropped a yard. The upper casing of the Main Battle Tank was now below Ashnak, the gun swivelling to aim straight between the large orc's eyes.

'And don't point that thing at me, you dumb-ass excuse for a marine!'

'Sir, yes, sir!' Barashkukor exclaimed happily. He hitched himself further up out of the T54's hatch, by the mounted machine-gun. 'Sir, it was a terrible experience, sir.' The small orc watched Ashnak out of the corner of his one eye. 'Worth a medal, sir, do you think?'

'Get on with it!'

'Yessir! Well, it was like this, sir. In attempting to immolate myself and the hostile Bug, I omitted to remember that petrol evaporates.' The small orc, unmistakably Barashkukor despite alterations, sighed

320

wistfully. 'There was a flash-burn, not much else. So I expected them to tear me to pieces, sir, same as they did my corporal, but I guess it was having the corporal to practise with gave them ideas, sir, and they more or less put me back together. Not altogether correctly, I have to say, but I think I was an experiment—'

The T54 dropped bodily by six feet. The black waters of the Faex washed around its treads, suspended on the last few pilings of the collapsing dock.

'Well, sir,' the orc continued obliviously, looking up at Ashnak, 'after that it was my duty as a marine to escape, so I let them prod me about a bit, and then when they lost interest – well, I think it was more like, put me on one side for lunch – I cammo'd myself up and hid in the desert. Tell you the truth, sir, I don't think they can smell very well, and they don't have magic, so they didn't find me. I made my way back to Gyzrathrani. Couldn't get through on the comlink, and the Gyzrathrani weren't being very cooperative, so I told them their OT64 needed a test-drive . . .'

Ashnak leaned over the barge rail, looking down.

'*That* is not an OT64 armoured personnel carrier.'

'No, sir. Beg to report, the OT64 broke down seventy miles north of Gyzrathrani. I commandeered another vehicle.' The small orc major coloured. 'A camel, sir, I believe they call it. Nasty spitting creature. That got me as far as the edge of the Endless Desert. Damn things don't taste like much either, sir. Then I ran into a contingent of Gargoyle Marines and got their airborne tactical wing to bring me as far north as Aztechia. Couldn't reach you on the com, sir, the radio operators didn't seem to believe who I was. So I borrowed a despatch rider's motorcycle.'

Barashkukor felt in the ragged combat jacket's pockets.

'Think I've still got his despatches on me somewhere, sir. That broke down two hundred miles back, near the High Ranges. Well, sir, the garrison there still wouldn't put me through to you – said I had to be an imposter, or some sort of *monster*.'

The small orc looked hurt.

'Not my fault if the Bugs put me back together with metal. It *works*, sir. Well. Most of the time.'

A fresh wind swept across the estuary of the Faex River, bringing the homely scent of vampire-bird dung, ogre cooking-fires, and sweating orcs. Ashnak raised one beetling eyebrow.

'I'm a reasonable orc, Barashkukor. I just know there's a good reason why you turn up here in one of my tanks and trash it beyond repair. I just know it. So tell your old general – you "borrowed" the tank from the High Ranges?'

321

Barashkukor saluted again, catching his ear with the steel fingers of his right hand, and wincing at the pain.

'Not exactly, sir. I borrowed a Cobra helicopter gunship from the High Ranges. But you know how I am about flying, General. It sort of . . . it . . . it developed a severely reduced flight potential.'

'It crashed.' Ashnak covered his eyes with his free hand. He thoughtfully weighed the pistol he still held. 'And then you took a tank.'

'Nossir.' Barashkukor swallowed audibly. 'Then I commandeered a military hovercraft, sir, to come up the coast of the Western Ocean to Port Mirandus. It, er, sank, sir. I didn't do anything to it, sir, honest! I think those machines have a design fault.'

'How far did you get, marine?'

'Lalgrenda, sir.'

'*Then* the tank?'

'Nossir. Another APC from Lalgrenda to Kaanistad. The engine burned out on that one. Then I borrowed a staff car. That was fine.' Barashkukor's eye gleamed, and his socketed lens whirred. 'Rolls-Royce Silver Shadow with armoured chassis, sir. Sweet as a nut. Drove like a dream.'

'That', Ashnak pointed at the T54 Main Battle Tank, the water now lapping halfway up its filth-crusted sides, 'is not a staff car.'

Barashkukor rested one gloved and one steel hand down on the rim of the hatch. He regarded the tank thoughtfully.

'Not a staff car, sir, no, sir. The Fourteenth Armoured Troll Division at Vendivil wouldn't believe my identity either, sir, so they shelled the staff car. I got out all right, though. *That* was when I decided I needed armoured capability to get to you, General Ashnak, sir, so that's when I commandeered this tank from their motor pool. Unofficially. I did leave a chitty.'

The small orc took a deep breath, and immediately coughed, regretting it. The River Faex, as the hot sun warmed it, began to hum.

'Lots of essential information for you, sir, about the Bugs, sir! That's why I had to get back to you, General.' Barashkukor drew himself up, standing waist-deep in the hull hatch of the sinking T54, his single eye fixed on Ashnak and glowing with hero-worship. 'Sir, did I show enough initiative, sir?'

The T54 Main Battle Tank lurched and settled deeper into the greasy water.

'I did my *best*, sir,' the orc major protested.

Ashnak carefully thumbed down the hammer and replaced his pistol in his belt holster. He braced both hands on the rail of the barge and leaned over.

'Abandon armoured submersible!'

'Sir, yes, *sir!*' The small orc clambered up out of the hatch.

Ragged brown desert-camouflaged combat trousers clung to his skinny leg, rolled up at one ankle. He wore only one combat boot. His other leg, from thigh to foot, shone brightly in the sun. Ashnak stared at the steel bones, tendons, pulleys and plates.

'I'll be right—' *whirrr-clk!* '—right with you, General Ashnak, sir!'

The small orc hitched himself out of the hatch, skinny buttocks pointing at the sky, then straightened up, picked up his helmet and crammed it down over his long ears, walked across the casing of the T54 as the tank shuddered, juddered, and – among the scream of splintering timber – sank beneath the surface of the river. Barashkukor flexed his small legs and sprang.

His normal orc-leg pushed feebly. Barashkukor's cyborg-leg, Ashnak noted with some interest, flexed and sprang with vicious speed.

The small orc shot up and sideways.

'HEEAAARGGGH!'

Barashkukor smacked into the side of the barge two feet below Ashnak. The large orc reached down, seized the small orc marine officer by the seat of his combat trousers, and dragged Barashkukor up and over the rail. He dropped Barashkukor on the deck.

'Salute when you see an officer!' Ashnak roared.

Barashkukor's helmet rolled in small circles on the deck of the barge. The small orc's ears flattened in the blast. Hurriedly, whirring and clicking the while, Barashkukor got to his feet, made a vain attempt to smarten his uniform and combat boot, and directed a salute in the general direction of Ashnak. 'Sir!'

The cyborg-orc wavered dizzily as he stood upright.

Bio-technician Ugarit wiped his hands down his white lab coat and edged closer, eyes gleaming as he studied the metal leg, hand and eye of the orc officer. 'May I, General? May I have him? *Please* may I?'

'Sir!' Barashkukor's right eye whirred, focusing. He edged away from the skinny orc technician.

'Well, well, well . . .' Ashnak reached down, purring.

The large orc hooked a talon in the back of Barashkukor's collar, hoisting him three feet into the air. He dangled the small orc in the hot southern air, turned him from side to side, inspected him above and below, held him out at arm's length, and dropped him back on the deck.

Unable to prevent himself, Ashnak showed all his fangs and brass-capped tusks in a beam.

323

'Welcome aboard, Barashkukor! Welcome back! Between the Dark Lord and the Bugs – you got here just in time for the fun.'

North-east of Port Mirandus, far up the River Faex, the great Royal Hall of Ferenzia was packed, mostly with Men, which meant every elbow was at face-height, and Will Brandiman twice nearly lost an eye to an unguarded rapier-hilt. He shouldered his way through mail-clad hips, tassels, the tops of high boots, and the horned helmets of a party of dwarves.

In front of him, an elf smoothed down the lapels of her military-cut civilian tunic, touched her brown hair to make sure her glossy braids flowed back behind her pointed ears, and turned to a contraption on a tripod.

'This is Perdita del Verro, your *WFTV News* reporter at Ferenzia, capital of the South, covering the arrival of the Light candidate in the forthcoming election, the Holy Paladin Amarynth Goddess-Son. With the election only six days away, and the promised scandalous revelations about to be disclosed, tension here is steadily mounting—'

Will Brandiman slicked back his glossy black curls, from which the grey had again been removed with dye-spells; arranged his plain white collar and tightly buttoned doublet, and smiled directly over her shoulder at the camera lens as he passed. Like all *WoF*'s recording equipment it had *Made in Graagryk* stamped on it.

'"Kinematographic theatres",' he murmured. '"To bring images of the news to one and all, across the Southern Kingdoms." I wonder if I could interest Mother in carrying broadcasts from the Good Abbess Edwina and the Reverend William, appealing for the Holy Prayer-Wheel Fund . . .'

He arrived at his vantage-point on the steps of the first gallery.

'I don't know about you,' a gruff contralto said in his ear, 'but I feel like a young halfling let loose in a chocolate factory!'

Ned Brandiman's red habit bulged more than Will remembered it to, especially around the waistline. He had the suspicion that if he picked his brother up and shook him, the wimpled halfling would clink.

'I've told you before about purses,' Will reprimanded. 'We're here for much bigger game.'

Ned's powdered and painted face creased with laughter-lines. A brown curl escaped from under the edge of his wimple and he tucked it back. 'Brother, be sensible. *We've robbed the Blasted Redoubt.* There aren't any challenges left! Even taking Magorian's Regalia would be taking sweetbreads from elflings.'

'What I really like about this', Will observed, obliviously, 'is that the only thing that orc bastard thinks he has to worry about is the Dark Lord's election chances. And the Bugs.' He rubbed small calloused hands together. 'Little does he know!'

A shrill blasting of silver trumpets shook the chamber. Dirt sifted down from the gothic vaultings. The Royal Hall was only brought out and dusted for occasions of extreme ceremony, Will remembered (from the coronation of High King Magorian, which had also been profitable for purses), and now sweltered behind pointed ogee windows which did not open, and behind vast oaken doors which were currently shut.

'Hail Amarynth! Hand of Fire, Goddess-Son!'

The great double doors banged open to another screech of brass. Will, from the first gallery rail, watched the Ferenzi nobles – vastly uncomfortable in the ancient but traditional formal wear of doublet and skin-tight hose, fur robes, tippets and liripipe hats; *none* of which seemed overly suited to midsummer in the south – turn their noble heads first for the breath of cool air that enterd down the central aisle, and then for sight of Amarynth Firehand.

'As you know, I'm not talking about worldly profit, Mother Edwina,' Will observed quietly. 'There is a more satisfying spiritual spoil to be had.'

Ned's plucked eyebrows raised. 'Is *that* what you call it?'

'Trust me,' Will said smugly. 'And keep on your furry little toes, brother.'

Dust motes filled the regulation sunbeams that spotlit the throne at the far end of the Hall, under the rose-window; flashing back from King Magorian's golden armour (which, close-up, Ned Brandiman had established to be only gilt) and from the white flowing locks of the High Wizard Oderic.

A rhythmic tread shook the granite floor of the Royal Hall.

Twelve Flagellant Knights in full plate harness clashed through the double doors and down towards the throne. Somewhere in the centre of their banners and ostrich plumes Will detected the dark-skinned Holy elf paladin. He bowed as deeply as the rest of the assembled nobles, in case Amarynth should have his eye on his priest and abbess, and with his head down muttered to Ned, 'Is it there?'

'Under one of the knight's cloaks. Never one to miss a dramatic moment, our Holy One.'

'O great Nobles of Ferenzia!' the elf cried, his high voice quietening the Royal Hall completely. 'High King of the South, Magorian of glorious fame!'

'Mpph, what?' The High King sat up, scratching at his balding scalp.

The High Wizard Oderic patted him comfortingly on the arm, and stepped forward on to the marble floor before the throne. 'Great Amarynth, your return to the councils of the wise is most welcome.'

'But I bring fell news,' Amarynth replied as if rehearsed. Will Brandiman, who had spent much of the past three days rehearsing him, found his lips moving in the shape of the next words: *a foul crime has been committed—*

'A foul, murderous, impious and vicious crime has been committed!' Amarynth exclaimed.

'Everybody's an improviser,' Will grumbled.

He noted the hot and thirsty assembly, who had assumed themselves there merely for a formal welcoming of the Light candidate to the great and honourable city of Ferenzia, jewel of the south, et cetera and et cetera, straighten up and begin to take notice.

The elf bowed deeply to the throne, moving to where another sunbeam illuminated the much-worn granite flooring. The light shone from his brown pointed ears, his glossy black starburst-hair now fastened back with a silver fillet, his plain white habit (made from Archipelago silk), and his ivory staff.

'Listen to a humble pilgrim!' Amarynth beseeched.

Will Brandiman caught the Holy One's eye, and nodded reassurance.

'Without more ado,' the ex-Paladin cried, 'High King Magorian, must I bring to your attention a most foul and despicable crime! My Lords, the other candidate in this heretical election—'

Amarynth's brown nostrils flared. His high cheekbones coloured bronze, and he began to pant.

'That blasphemy! That *He*, the epitome of Evil, dare appear in a female form to mock my mother Goddess, the Lady of Light! Blasphemous mockery!'

Will Brandiman filled his chest and sang out resonantly, '*Amen!*' Several others of the assembled Knights Flagellant, and a number of the Ferenzi nobles, echoed him. And, as Will had calculated, the sound of a familiar voice recalled Amarynth to his script.

'My Lord High King, I bring to your knowledge a crime against peace and humanity, for which the perpetrator must be arrested and tried.'

The elf swept back his ragged flowing hair, his eyes blazing.

'When I was an elf of war, I laid siege to a wilderness fortress, Nin-Edin of the North. The story of that is familiar to all. The orcish filth of that fortress held out, by some devilry, until I and my army were recalled.'

One or two of the younger, more fashionably dressed Men smiled. The beefy, gorget-wearing old campaigners watched impassively.

326

'We marched', Amarynth continued, 'instantly to the relief of Sarderis. Infantry and cavalry, we fell upon the remnants of the Evil Horde, and freed the city. In doing so we had undertaken a forced march, and come from Nin-Edin to Sarderis in a time never beaten. And – our baggage train followed. Followed us far more slowly, and with but one junior mage, because as you know, the baggage train is sacred under the rules of war.'

The Royal Hall came alive and electric with attention. Will caught Ned's eye, and the Good Abbess grinned. The two halflings at the gallery rail then composed their faces to righteous indignation.

Amarynth Firehand dropped smartly to one knee. He had not yet, Will assumed, become accustomed to not wearing armour. Will saw the dark elf wince.

'Great King,' Amarynth fluted, 'it is known far and wide that the baggage train of the Army of Light perished that day, butchered in the Red Gullies. It is known, and yet none know how. Was it deserters from the Horde, stray beasts and monsters, or even reinforcements for the orc-filth? Because all perished – and none of them, my lords, was above the age of fifteen – because all these *children* perished, there was no way to know.'

Amarynth paused.

'But now there is!'

Almost without moving his lips, Ned Brandiman murmured, 'Every old theatrical trick, eh, Will?'

'If it works, don't knock it.'

Amarynth filled his lungs and shrilled melodiously, 'The atrocity was committed by the orcish filth of Nin-Edin themselves!'

The Royal Hall buzzed with voices, one or two raised in shouts, demanding answers, justice and revenge in about equal measures. The High King Magorian's head rolled to one side and he began to snore quietly.

Oderic stepped forward, sweeping his formal grey robes about himself. 'But this is a most serious accusation, Lord Amarynth. What proof have you that this is true?'

'You ask *us* for proof?' The elf's face contorted. 'We, who are the Son of the Lady on earth?'

'I knew he'd go haywire somewhere . . .' Will Brandiman rubbed his knuckles across his eyes. He sighed. About to slip out of the gallery and go down to Amarynth, he stopped as one of the Knights Flagellant moved forward, uncovering what had been concealed by his silken cloak.

In a subdued voice nonetheless audible in that silence, the Knight said, 'High Wizard Oderic, here is your proof.'

The wizard moved forward, leaning on his staff. Will heard a most satisfactory gasp from the assembled nobility of Ferenzia.

The Knight Flagellant had left off his steel arm-defences so that the body he cradled should suffer less pain. What he carried in his arms was a Man-child no more than nine or ten years of age. Her skull seemed swollen and her eyes huge, and her upper arms, under her shift, could have been encircled by finger and thumb. She leaned her head listlessly against his breastplate.

A scar crossed her face, shattering one eye socket. It wept yellow fluid. At some point her hair had been red, but it had been shaved back so that the continuation of the scar across her skull could be stitched, and now grew out in patches.

All her bones stood out sharp as a bird's breastbone.

'Look!' Amarynth Firehand seized the Man-child, grotesquely, by one leg. He raised the thin limb. An angry red-and-black scar across the back of her knee showed where her hamstrings had been cut.

'They took her maidenhood.' The elf lifted the child's chin. 'Kyrial, speak. Tell what you have told to me.'

The child's face screwed up. Water rolled out of her eye.

'The orcs lay with her,' Amarynth said, into the appalled silence, 'as they lay with all: prisoners, and those whom they had killed in their first attack. Kyrial, elf-friend, speak. Say how you escaped them.'

The Man-child began visibly to shake. She wore a grey shift, under which her body was bones rolling in a thin covering of skin. Her hands and feet appeared uncommonly large. She mewed.

'Say,' Amarynth persisted.

'. . . hid . . .'

The child's voice was ugly, dissonant. The white-haired wizard approached, his face kindly.

'Speak, my dear. Where did you hide?' Oderic frowned. 'You must tell us, you know.'

The child huddled against the metal breastplate of the Knight.

'Where?' Oderic queried.

The Knight Flagellant tucked Kyrial's head against his shoulder, where his cloak cushioned his armour. Soothing, he whispered something to her, then raised his head. 'Sirs, she hid herself in a pile of butchered bodies, most of them companions she had grown up with, and passed as a corpse. There was no one to rescue her. She lay three nights that way.'

Amarynth said, 'One hundred and fifty youngsters rode in charge of my baggage train. All were butchered. Raped, then murdered. We had thought there were no survivors. But here is Kyrial to swear, on her oath, who is responsible for the atrocity of Red Gullies. And who it is should answer for this crime against the rules of warfare.'

Will savoured the silence in the Royal Hall of Ferenzia, appreciating vicariously the *frisson* of horror.

Oderic, a tear rolling down his lined face, lay his hand on the Manchild's head for a brief moment. Will caught a movement out of the corner of his eye: Perdita del Verro circling down from the far gallery for an additional close-up with a hand-held newsreel camera.

Oderic spoke up. 'Poor innocent! Lord Amarynth, how came she to you now?'

The Holy One turned to his Knight Flagellant.

Prompted, the elven knight said, 'She was found wandering, many months ago, my lords, by a family of dwarves. They tended to her in the mountains. She had no speech. Not until I came across her by chance did she speak and say *Red Gullies*. But since then, she has refused to eat, and starves herself to death.'

At the mention of the Red Gullies the child began to cry.

'She shall be made a Ward of Ferenzia,' the High Wizard Oderic proclaimed, 'we shall care for the poor child. But, my Lord Amarynth, I think you have the right of it. The best care will be to bring to justice the evil filth that did this act!'

Will whispered, 'Awriiight!'

'But you have not heard all,' the Holy One, Amarynth, said. 'Beloved child, speak what else remains.'

The scarred child's head rolled back loosely.

'The name,' Amarynth prompted. 'You heard the orcs call a name, elf-friend. Speak it now. You heard them shout their leader's name. Speak it to us now. *Speak.*'

'"*Ashnak*".' An ugly, weak, but unmistakable noise. '"Ashnak".'

With grim satisfaction, Amarynth held the High Wizard's shocked gaze. He said triumphantly, 'Ashnak. The orc "General". The same filth Ashnak who is henchman to the Dark Lord – and who now acts as His campaign manager in the election to the Throne of the World.'

Riot. Every Man in the gallery turning on his neighbour and yelling, every Man in the main body of the Royal Hall clamouring for instant justice, instant vengeance.

'Get out of *that*,' Will Brandiman exulted. 'He may be our stepfather. But I haven't forgotten the dungeons of Nin-Edin.'

'No,' Ned Brandiman agreed. 'No, Will. Nor have I. Brother, he should have realized. We make bad enemies.'

The stewards and officers tried in vain to restore order to the Royal Hall of Ferenzia. The High King Magorian sat up and blinked at the court. Oderic, High Wizard, rapped his mage's staff on the granite floor.

'My lords and kings of the South! Be not hasty!'

The wizard's white hair gleamed in a shaft of sun, slanting down from the hall's gothic heights. He placed one arm carefully on the shoulder of the scarred child, weeping in the Knight's arms. 'My lords, it is hard, in the face of this, but we must beware of haste. We must beware of folly – of condemnation without proof.'

Oderic shook his head wisely.

'And so I will say this to you. We may rightly now demand of Evil that there is held, immediately – *before* the election – a tribunal. A fair and just tribunal to find out the truth of the Red Gullies atrocity, and to bring the true culprit to justice. We demand the immediate arrest of the orc General Ashnak for a war crimes trial!'

8

T HE EVENING SUN slanted level and
gold across the outlying halfling suburb of Ferenzia. A large orc in
urban combats, forage cap jammed between his pointed ears,
regarded the round brightly painted doorholes, the thronging hairy-
footed population, and the fly-posters stuck up on all the vast oak
tree boles that dotted the market square, with sour distaste. The
posters all, without exception, read *Vote for the Light!*

'Only four days to the election, sir,' Barashkukor reminded his
commanding orc. 'Surely She'll let us fight the Bugs after that, sir?'

The general of the orc marines glanced down at him. Barashkukor's
chest swelled with pride in his smartly pressed green DPM combats.
His polished cyborg hand and leg gleamed. His cyborg eye whirred.

'It still isn't the true Way of the Orc! All this voting and peaceful
campaigning. It just isn't *orcish*. We should be out fighting Bugs!'
Marine Commissar Razitshakra took off her steel-rimmed spectacles,
polished them, and put them back on her snout.

The three orcs in green DPM camouflage combats stood in the
main street of the halfling district, pistols firmly holstered, assault
rifles slung over hulking shoulders. The street was jammed with
wagons and pony-and-traps piled high with halfling refugees from the
Bug advances into the Eastern Kingdoms.

'Begging the general's pardon.' Barashkukor stood even more
smartly to attention. 'The commissar's right, sir. Don't know when
my marines last had a real mission, sir.'

331

Ashnak's bass baritone voice grated, 'Are you questioning my judgement, Lieutenant?'

The small orc paled several shades. 'Sir, no sir! Wouldn't dream of it. Just wish you'd send us out on combat missions. Those orcs out fighting in Thyrion and Gyzrathrani and Shazmanar, they can't hold the Bugs back for ever. They need us, sir!'

'What we're going to do', the large orc general growled, 'is win this election as fast as possible.'

'How can we do that, sir?'

Ashnak's eyes glinted. 'I may just have a dangerous mission for you *personally*, Major. Volunteers only. I *can* trust you to volunteer?'

'Erm . . .' Barashkukor swallowed audibly. 'Yessir! You can rely on me. Erm. How dangerous *exactly*, sir?'

Razitshakra nodded her head judiciously. 'Ah, the true orcish spirit. I only wish I could join you, Major Barashkukor, but my political duties keep me from the battle.'

Barashkukor looked up at his general. The large orc's craggy face creased into an evil grin. Barashkukor snickered.

'Alternatively,' Ashnak said, laying an extremely heavy hand on Commissar Razitshakra's shoulder, 'I may just have a mission for *you*. Barashkukor, where's that halfling?'

'Over here, sir.' The small orc walked back to the APC parked between a covered wagon and a halfling delivery cart. Ragged halflings whose belongings were scattered, abandoned, on every road from the east and south of Ferenzia, moved aside to avoid him. Tiny spurts of steam hissed from the knee-joint of his artificial leg, and a *whirr-click!* sound followed him across the road.

He heard Ashnak, behind him, remarking, 'I think you'll find that this mission accords with your political duties, Commissar. Since it's a matter of ideology.'

'I'm your orc, sir!' Razitshakra snapped to attention, eyes gleaming behind her spectacles. 'Trust me, sir, I have a firm grasp of orcish ideology. If that's what this mission requires, I can do it! I can promote the Way of the Orc—'

'You certainly can,' Ashnak sighed.

Barashkukor clicked his way back across the dusty road, his steel hand clamped firmly on the shoulder of a fat, hairy-footed halfling. The halfling wiped sweat-plastered curls from his wet forehead.

'Just remember,' Major Barashkukor jerked his free orc-thumb back at the APC, 'that the rest of your spawn, er, family, stays in there until your return. Their health is dependent on your good conduct.'

'Don't 'urt me, sir,' the halfling pleaded. His brown eyes sought the orc general's forbidding face. 'I's always been a secret supporter of the Dark, honest, governor.'

'I'm sorry to hear that.' The big orc frowned. 'You may not be useful to us after all. Major Barashkukor, warn the cook to prepare a garlic and herb sauce tonight, for basted halfling.'

'I means, I *pretended* to be for the Dark,' the halfling gasped. 'Really I'm a solid Light voter. No one stauncher.'

'Then now's your chance to prove it.' General Ashnak nodded at the town hall, some blocks down the street. Most of the thronging halfling population, swelled by the influx of refugees, had vanished inside. A straggling line of shaggy ponies and ricketty carts parked outside gave the clue that a town meeting was in progress. 'The major has told you the message you have to deliver?'

'Oh, yes, governor.' The halfling puffed out his chest, pulling his food-stained jerkin awry. 'You can rely on Alfred Meadowsweet. I goes in to the town meeting, and I tells them "This here's from the Halfling Popular Front". Then I shouts "Long Live Amarynth Firehand!" and I leaves. Must say I think it's good of you to deliver packages for the Light, what with your being on the other side and all, sir.'

'Think nothing of it. We may be sworn to Evil,' the orc general said righteously, 'but that doesn't mean we're not honourable. In our own way. Commissar Razitshakra, you will act as escort for Master Meadowsweet to the town hall. I think what he has to deliver is a little heavy for a halfling.'

Razitshakra's heels clicked together. She scowled at the general of the orc marines. 'Yessir! Of course, sir. Sir, what are we doing helping the Light's election campaign?'

The large orc tightened his talons on the commissar's shoulder.

'Isn't there something in the Way of the Orc about questioning the decisions of one's general?' he purred. 'Because if there isn't, marine, I suggest you write it in. *Now!*'

Razitshakra's pointed ears flattened back against her skull. She straightened her peaked cap. 'Sir, yes, sir!'

Barashkukor whirred and clicked his way to the APC, pausing only to hit his steel knee with a hammer that he extracted for the purpose from a pouch on his web-belt. He staggered back again, skinny legs bowing under the weight of an ammunition box. He set it down heavily, raised his head, and looked for his general.

From the far side of the street, Ashnak called, 'You may remove the package now, Major. Commissar Razitshakra, carry it for Master Meadowsweet.'

333

Razitshakra's 'Yessir!' echoed across the street as Barashkukor joined Ashnak.

The large and the small orc marched smartly towards their APC. Barashkukor's cyborg eye whirred, extended itself on a jointed steel arm, and gave him a view back down the street. Halfling officials at the town hall door were talking to the orc marine commissar and Alfred Meadowsweet. Barashkukor retracted his eye, quickened his pace, and scrambled adeptly up and into the APC after Ashnak. He showed his fangs at the female halfling and four brats cowering in one corner.

'Shall I order that herb and garlic sauce anyway, sir?'

The large orc looked shocked. 'Of course not. What are you thinking of, Major?'

'Sorry, sir.' Barashkukor's shoulders slumped. He raised a contrite face to his general. 'I should have remembered – for young halfling meat, it's chili pepper and rock salt.'

Ashnak's snarl widened into a pleased smile. Barashkukor extended his cyborg eye up through the APC's hatch.

'Mission entering the town hall now, sir.'

'. . . fifty-eight, fifty-nine, sixty.' Ashnak pushed a button on a device hanging from his webbing.

KER-FOOOMM!!!

The halfling mother and her children screamed. Debris rattled down against the outside of the APC for some moments.

'Anti-personnel charge,' Ashnak explained.

Barashkukor, having retracted his eye just in time, crammed his GI pot down over his long ears and stuck his head outside. The long, muscular arm of his general pushed him up and out into the evening sunlight.

Smoke drifted across the street. Halflings and the odd dwarf ran in panic. Bricks, wood and broken glass covered the cobbles; and had embedded themselves in the round, painted halfling-hole doors. Healer-mages flapped and bustled around the smoking heap of bricks and mortar that was all that remained of the town hall building, their white robes splashed and dripping with red.

'Now if *that* doesn't convince them to vote for Herself,' the orc general Ashnak remarked, 'then I'm a half-elf.'

Barashkukor picked himself up and dusted his combats down. He nodded smartly. 'Very clever, sir. If they blame Amarynth and the Light, they'll vote for us. And if they think it was done by the Dark, they'll vote for us to stop it happening again. Sir, well done, sir!'

'And another advantage . . .' The large orc's voice trailed off.

A singed and blackened figure shambled up the road towards the

334

APC, green hide smoking, long olive-drab greatcoat hanging in smouldering rags, and wire-rimmed spectacles dangling smashed from one pointed ear.

Orc Political Commissar Razitshakra, swaying on her bandy legs, saluted up at Ashnak filling the hatch of the APC.

'Truly orcish, sir!' she enthused. 'That's what I *call* politically correct! Can I do the next mission too, sir?'

'How fortuitoush,' a voice remarked.

Barashkukor, turning, was startled to see a figure cowled in a patchwork leather robe. A dozen Ferenzi troopers in striped hose, carrying halberds, accompanied the figure. It slowly reached up and put the hood back from its head.

Level sunlight through the explosion's dust shone on grey, black and fish-belly white skin. Ragged black hair surrounded a face now almost pleasant, by orc-standards. Barashkukor had some difficulty in recognizing the nameless necromancer.

'Sir,' the small orc acknowledged, startled, but nevertheless according him the respect of a soldier for an ex-employer.

'General Ashnak!' the nameless necromancer cried, slobbering round the tusks that twisted his mouth awry. 'You stand accused of crimesh against peasch and humanity!'

The great orc frowned. 'Accused of what?'

'"Crimes against peace and humanity",' Major Barashkukor deciphered helpfully. He watched his commanding officer blush the colour of basalt.

'Thank you,' Ashnak said gruffly.

'It'sh a charge, not a commendation!' the nameless necromancer spluttered. 'You're under arresht!'

Barashkukor fingered his pistol in its belt holster and looked enquiringly at Razitshakra, who swayed, singed and cross-eyed; and then at Ashnak. The big orc rested his hand on the machine-gun mounted by the APC's hatch.

'Can't say I'm impressed by magical firepower these days,' the orc general drawled. 'Not even the nameless necromancer's.'

The disfigured face twisted. It was several seconds before Barashkukor worked out that this orcishly handsome member of the Man race was smiling.

'But it ish not I who arresht you,' he said. 'I hold the authority of another.'

'The Light?' Ashnak's upper lip lifted over his fangs as he snarled at the Ferenzi guards.

Barashkukor pulled his cap straight between his drooping ears. His steel leg clicked and emitted a jet of steam as he stepped forward, positioning himself between the APC and the nameless necroman-cer's escort of Ferenzi troopers.

'The Lords of Light have no military jurisdiction over the orc marines,' Barashkukor proclaimed primly, unfastening his pistol holster.

'But I do not shpeak for the Light,' the Man slurred.

Behind Barashkukor, Ashnak gave a guttural cough. 'So who *is* trying to arrest me, if not the Light?'

The nameless necromancer drew his skin robe about his hunch-shouldered body, snuffling a little with triumph.

'Why,' he said, 'General Ashnak, you are placshed under arrest now by the authority of the Dark Lord Hershelf.'

The silence of evacuated territory pervaded the root tunnels below the City of the Trees. Lieutenant Gilmuriel Hunt-Lord signalled fireteam one of Starlight squad to halt.

'Fourteen!' he called, voice squeaking with exhaustion.

'Nine!'

The challenge being a number over ten, and the correct response a number under it, the blond elf sighed in relief and advanced down the corridor.

Carved out of the thick roots of aeons-old trees, the polished tunnel walls gleamed gold in the near-darkness. Wood-grain swirled, looped and waved. Faint light came up from under the circular tunnel floor, across which thinner roots had been trained and grown into walkway gratings. Gilmuriel's boots fell on pierced wood so ancient it rang hard as metal.

'Yo, L.t!' A lean, green-skinned orc with corporal's chevrons on his sleeve advanced to meet Gilmuriel. Several orc marines in mechanic's overalls followed him.

'Corporal Hikz, your patrol's overdue.'

'Sorry, sir.' The lean orc corporal saluted. 'Sir, nothing much to report. The sq— the inhabitants have all cleared out of the city. The place is practically deserted.'

'Practically?'

'We discovered a small Man-child last night, sir.' Orc Corporal Hikz gestured at the corridor's walkway root flooring. 'Under those gratings. Plucky little yellow-haired thing she was, sir. Obviously in hiding from the Bugs.'

Gilmuriel looked at the five or six orcs behind Hikz. 'And what have you and your orcs done with the Man-child, Corporal?'

'We ate her, sir.'

'What!'

'And very tasty she was too, thank you, sir.'

'Well done, that orc!' Sergeant Dakashnit appeared silently in their midst from a side corridor, showing all her tusks in a grin. As Gilmuriel belatedly turned to give the challenge, fireteam two of Starlight squad limped into view.

'Tried taking the radio up to tree-top level,' Dakashnit jerked a gnarled thumb at marine radio operator Silkentress. 'Can't raise the rest of the platoon, or the company. All the firebases east of the river have been overrun. Saw Bugs in at least battalion strength – they're across the city perimeter and headed this way *fast*.' The female orc removed her steel helmet and wiped her shaven head. 'This is what we in the marines call a target-rich environment.'

Gilmuriel frowned. '"Target-rich environment", Sergeant?'

Corporal Hikz said, '"Overwhelming enemy forces", sir!'

sssssssssssssssssszakkk!

Gilmuriel's pointed ears pricked at the sound of firing. He looked swiftly from side to side.

'That lateral corridor leads to the supply rooms,' he said crisply. 'Down this way is the Plant Room. I'm assuming that will be one of their objectives. Corporal Hikz, I think it's time for you to deploy your experimental weaponry here. The rest of the squad will set up an ambush from the supply rooms.'

With every impression of being amazed by his decisiveness, Gunnery Sergeant Dakashnit saluted. 'Corporal Blackrose, recce the supply rooms and access tunnels.' She paused. 'Corporal Hikz – that wouldn't by any chance be Tech-Captain *Ugarit's* experimental weaponry, would it?'

'Yur,' Hikz said laconically.

'Oh, *shite* . . .'

HHHHSSSSSSS-*ZK*-FOOM!

Over the bustle of the squad reconnoitring the nearby tunnels, and Hikz' mechanic orcs cracking open the crates they carried and rapidly assembling machinery, Lieutenant Gilmuriel Hunt-Lord heard the sound of the Bugs' incomprehensible weapons firing.

'Move it!' he fluted. 'Hikz, what *is* this new weapon?'

The lean corporal emerged from under a stout steel tripod, brandishing a spanner. 'Tech-Captain Ugarit calls it a *smart-weapons system*. Basically a heavy machine-gun, sir. Marine Karakingat!'

Hikz scrambled up on to his feet, kicking the large mechanic orcs out of his way. A rather smaller orc in a desert camo forage cap staggered down the tunnel from the direction of the Plant Room, draped in heavy belts of ammunition which he slung around his thin

337

neck, over his arms, elbows, and around his waist, and still managed to trail them on the ground.

'Sir, smart ammo, sir!' Karakingat saluted, dropping the belts on the wooden grating at Gilmuriel's feet.

Gilmuriel squatted down. The belts of ammunition gleamed gold, catching the tiny amount of light elf eyes need for vision.

'The gun,' Hikz slapped the heavy machine-gun on its tripod. It reeked of oil. 'Got *laser sensors*, sir, that's what the Tech-Captain calls 'em. It'll lock on to anything that comes within its range, acquire a target, and blow the fuck out of it. On its own – no operator. Called a *smart gun*, sir. This is the ammo for it. That can track a target *after* it's been fired, sir. Karakingat, start bringing up the rest of it!'

The ammunition appeared bulkier than Gilmuriel was used to. A small panel set into the side of each round glowed with a liquid crystal display of targeting calculations.

The LCD blinked, shifting from numerals to letters.

. . . 46-453-56 . . . SIR. SHOOT ME AT THE BASTARDS *NOW*, SIR . . . 647-3 . . .

'Smart ammo,' the elf lieutenant commented.

He glanced up the corridor. From somewhere far above, in the outbuildings that clung to trunks two hundred feet above the forest floor, the sound of firing echoed. The Bugs would be entering the vast goldentree trunks whose chambers and grottoes had been a city since the Sea's withdrawal, unaccounted ages past.

'Load it up!' he ordered.

'Yessir!' The orc corporal fed one belt into the heavy machine-gun and hooked up the next belt for automatic reload. 'Marine Karakingat, prepare for weapons-test!'

'Sir, yes, sir!' The small orc perked up his ears, rolled up the sleeves of his combat jacket, and began to flick triggers, bolts, and carriers back and forth.

'Checklist correct, sir!' Marine Karakingat peered down the cluster-barrels of the weapon. 'Ready to go—'

DAKKA-DAKKA-DAKKA-*FOOM!*

'Arrrgh!' Karakingat vanished. Green spatters splashed the far end of the root corridor.

'He's been fired,' one of the large mechanic orcs remarked.

'Ah . . .' Corporal Hikz sighed. 'We'll never find another orc of his calibre.'

Hikz' ridged brows furrowed as he looked down at the second ammunition belt in his hands. 'Sir . . .'

Gilmuriel looked over the orc's uniformed shoulder. The LCD display on the next rounds ticked past:

338

'Even smarter ammunition,' the elf lord commented. 'Do what you can, Corporal. Sergeant! Do we have a KZ set up?'

'We can make this corridor a killing zone, L.t., and fall back through the supply rooms to the water-pumps.'

'Then let's roll!'

HHHHSSSSSSSH-*ZK*-FOOM!

'*Contact!*'

Chunks of wood ricocheted. A line of brilliance opened, as if the world had cracked apart to show the sun. Blue-white, it seared down the corridor and impacted.

FOOM!

'Targets twelve o'clock, fifty metres low, down corridor!'

'Seen!'

'Seen!'

'Seen!'

'How many?'

'Thirty-plus!'

'Fall back by fire and movement!'

'*Grenade!*'

FOOM!

'Contact *six* o'clock! Thirty metres. *They're behind us!*'

'ERV! Go, go, go!'

'One elf down!'

'Mother of Forests, *carry* him! Move out! Go, go, *go!*'

BOOM-BOOM-BOOM-BOOM-BOOM!

'Hostiles fifty-plus!'

'Team two pull back!'

'*Arrrgghhhh!*'

'Go, go, GO!'

Lieutenant Gilmuriel pounded across a lateral corridor, the back-flashes of weapons lighting the gnarled walls and the pierced gratings. The deep roar of the smart-gun hammered at his ears. Elves ran past and fell into the shelter of side-turnings, waited until the next team ran past, and gave covering fire.

Gilmuriel slammed into the cover of the Plant Room doors. Elven combat boots thudded past him. The crouching elf, sweat-stained woodland camo bandanna tied behind his pointed ears, cradled his automatic pistol and stared back up the smoke-filled corridor. His elf marine squad hugged the scant cover of wall niches. Orcs in overalls and BDUs shambled back out of the haze.

The hefty bulk of orc sergeant Dakashnit slammed in beside

Gilmuriel, her M16 stinking of hot metal. Ejected ammunition cases rattled across the gratings. She looked up and down the corridor, and then at the wooden-gated Plant Room beside her.

'If we close these doors, L.t., will they hold?'

'Not against those weapons. What *are* they?'

'Fuck knows, L.t.!'

BOOM-BOOM-BOOM-BOOM—

The hammering fire of the smart-gun abruptly cut off. Gilmuriel peered through the haze. Torch-beams cut the smoke, dazzling him until his elvish sight adjusted.

The beams dipped, crossed, jabbed towards the Plant Room. Sharp hisses of command echoed down the corridor. The first glint of a blue-black carapace brought Gilmuriel's pistol up. Dakashnit closed her large taloned hand on his arm.

'L.t.' The orc had a strange expression. 'Look at that. It's a textbook advance . . .'

Gilmuriel looked down the wood-walled corridor at the twelve or fifteen insectoids tactically advancing, bulge-barrelled weapons held at the ready, hugging their hard exoskeletons into every piece of cover. Rapid commands passed between them. They advanced down the hundred metres of exposed corridor with frightening speed.

The elf lieutenant shook the orc's hand off. 'Sergeant, pull yourself together! Those Bugs are history!'

Dakashnit protested, 'But look, L.t., they ain't no different from *us*. They're soldiers.'

Gilmuriel bared his teeth in a maniacal grin, sighting his pistol. 'OK, so they're *military* history!'

FOOM!

Narrow beams spattered across the hardwood ceiling and seared down into the walkways underfoot, hissing and sparking electric-blue down their lengths. A dozen more hostiles appeared through the smoke from slowly smouldering goldentree roots.

'Pull out!' Gilmuriel bawled. *'GO!'*

BOOM! BOOM!

Grenades covered their escape. At the next RV point, Gilmuriel sank panting against the wall of a six-corridor intersection. Marines Aradmel Brightblade and Ravenharp the White sprinted into the open space, the twisting, screaming body of an elf carried between them, and laid her down. The lieutenant stepped over debris to stare at Byrna Silkentress. A beam of spitting light had caught her directly across one cheek, bubbling her dark skin. Another shot had glanced across her belly, not deep enough to sever her body in two, but deep enough to split the peritoneum wall beyond repair.

The wounded elf writhed, bulges of flesh pressing out between her slick fingers as she tried to hold her intestines inside her body-cavity. Blood soaked her combats sopping-wet.

'Shit!' Aradmel Brightblade moaned. 'Oh, shit, man. I *told* her to run through.'

'Brightblade!' Gilmuriel snapped. 'On guard, that corridor, now!'

Marine Ravenharp the White knelt down by Byrna's side, his hand going to touch the dog-tags fused into the flesh of her neck by the blast. 'I used to be a healer-mage . . .'

'Magery won't work for marines.' Gilmuriel dragged another word from his increasing marine vocabulary, appealing back over his shoulder to Dakashnit. *'Medic!'*

The orc sergeant looked at him blankly. 'What's a "medic"?'

'Please!' Byrna Silkentress screamed. *'Please!'*

Gilmuriel's hand slipped, wet with the ropes of her spilling intestines. He wiped his fingers on his combat trousers and drew his automatic pistol. With one hand he turned her head away. He placed the muzzle of his automatic pistol on her skull at the base of her neck and squeezed the trigger. A slew of blood and bone punched out her skull from eyes to crown, splattering the corridor wall with red tissue. Byrna's body relaxed.

'Marine Starharp.' Gilmuriel swallowed bile. 'Take over radio duties.'

'Yes, sir.' Removing the rig from Byrna's body, Bellurial's long-fingered musician's hands shook.

'Enemy seen?' Dakashnit questioned the squad harshly. 'Come on, assholes! I'm gonna get the rest of you out of here alive if it kills me. Enemy seen?'

'Not seen.'

'Not seen.'

'Not seen!'

Eighteen hours later, Lieutenant Gilmuriel and the elf marine squad patrolled from the lower to the upper levels of the root tunnels. Nerves stretched, ears pricked; hands slick on rifles.

'If it were an ambush we'd have hit the kay-zee by now,' Dakashnit advised. 'L.t., I think the Bugs did a sweep through the area and that was *it*. They haven't occupied the city at all. They're gone.'

'Leaving hostile forces behind them?'

'Uh-huh.' The orc looked thoughtfully at marine Starharp. 'See if you can raise HQ now, L.t. Send a despatch.'

'Saying what?' Gilmuriel Hunt-Lord stood aching, weary, and filthy in the city of the Elven Lords. Above him vast ancient canopies reached for the sun; capillary action drank up moisture from the

341

roots; but the whorled chambers and high platforms of the City of the Trees lay deserted, blood-spattered, home only to bodies and the circling carrion eagles. A persistent smell of burning stung his eyes: the slow fires that, once begun, would smoulder for decades before finally burning the City to the ground.

'They're not holding territory,' Dakashnit said.

'They're not holding *this* territory, Gunnery Sergeant . . .' Without turning, Gilmuriel spoke to Bellurial Starharp. 'Raise HQ, marine. Advise them to plot the Bugs' advance – use satellite observation to find out exactly where they are. Inform them there's a possibility the Bugs may have a specific objective to which they are advancing.'

9

'CERTAIN IRREGULARITIES HAVE
come to light', the Dark Lord stated, 'about your conduct in the late
war. *And* your administration of My election campaign.'

'Must be some mistake, Ma'am.' Ashnak shifted his massive
weight from foot to foot, now bare of combat boots. The chains
fettered to his wrists and ankles clinked.

The black canvas walls of the Dark Lord's Dark Pavilion flapped in
the night wind. Silver embroidered sigils of Evil glinted in the electric
light. The outside generator hummed.

'And I am under no illusion', the Lord of Nightmare added, 'as to
the strength of those chains.'

Ashnak was wearing the fetters more from a sense of appropriate-
ness than from coercion. His hand-to-hand fight with the Ferenzi
guards had also been in a spirit of play, resulting in no more than
their minor maiming.

'Yessir, Ma'am!' He brought his bare heels down on the pelts and
carpets that covered the earth six-deep in the Dark Pavilion. His
combat trousers slid an inch or so lower about his hips, his belt and
webbing having being confiscated. The electric light gleamed on his
bald head. 'Not planning to escape, Dread Lord. Nothing to be afraid
of. I'm innocent.'

The Dark Lord laughed; a soft sound that killed the night insects
buzzing around the lamps. She sat enthroned in a chair of basalt
subtly carved with all the creatures that slide, or creep, or sting.

Masses of paperwork covered her stone desk. Her face showed violet-shadowed, beautiful, and dire.

'There remain only two days before the final accounting of votes . . .' She said. 'Ah. Brother.'

The tent flap was pulled up by one of the guards outside – not an orc marine, Ashnak noted – and the cowled figure of the nameless necromancer strode in. Oderic, High Wizard of Ferenzia, followed him, trailing a cloud of blue pipe-weed smoke, and leaning on his staff.

The wind blew chill across the encampment of Evil that lay outside Ferenzia's Royal Quarter.

'Orcs!' The High Wizard Oderic stared at Ashnak, knocking his pipe out on the edge of the Dark Lord's table. Without waiting for permission he eased himself down into one of the plush chairs. 'Only goes to prove what I've always said about them, m'dear. Orcs are all well and good, I dare say, in their own lands to the east, but would you want your daughter to marry one?'

There was an eye-contact between the nameless necromancer and the Dark Lord of which the white mage seemed utterly unaware.

Ashnak drew himself up as erect as is consistent with the sloping posture of an orc and bellowed resonantly, 'I demand a trial to clear my good name!'

The white-haired wizard guffawed.

'But you see,' the Lord of Darkness said, 'orc Ashnak, it is not a matter of *your* good name, it is a matter of Mine. You were one of My Horde Commanders. I cannot have My reputation soiled by atrocities you may have committed without My orders.'

There was no direct response to make to that which would not result in his head being on a pike before dawn. Ashnak settled for falling to his knees in a multiple rattle of chains. The impact of his weight shook the ink-stand on the stone table. He held up his fettered hands in a suitable attitude of appeal.

'Rather than bring disgrace upon my Mistress I will fall upon my own sword! But,' Ashnak added hastily, catching the gleam in the necromancer's eye, 'that would not clear You, Dread Lord, of the accusations of electoral corruption. That can only be done by bringing me to trial and proving me innocent as soon as possible – Ma'am, you're going to need the orc marines very shortly, since the last situation report on the Bugs gave their position as being just south of the Faex River.'

'We need not worry about that,' the Lord of Darkness said. 'My brother the nameless, you have had some experience with these orc soldiers. I hereby appoint you the authority of My name. Take over command as their general.'

Ashnak came up on to his taloned feet with all the speed and strength of a great orc, rock-sized fists clenched, chain taut between them. His voice hit tenor in outrage. *'No!'*

'Orc Ashnak, you will not defy Me!'

Ashnak's breathing slowed. His granite-coloured hide rippled, blood-gorged muscles relaxing. He dropped his taloned fists back in front of him. 'Ma'am – I'm thinking of my orcs. The nameless necromancer has no experience of marine combat! He'll get my boys killed.'

The nameless necromancer sprayed spittle across the Dark Pavilion. 'What are orcsh *for?* Battle-fodder! You have been acting above your station for too long now!'

The Dark Lord said, 'Mage Oderic of Ferenzia, you see that I am willing to commit My servant Ashnak here to the Light's trial.'

The wizard looked up from searching through the pockets of his tweed robe for pipe-weed. 'High King Magorian has decided to appoint my humble self as the judge. I have the trial scheduled for the fifth day after New Moon. That's ten days from now.'

The nameless necromancer spoke from the darkness of his cowl. 'That is not accsheptable, mage of the Light. The trial must take plasch now, *before* the electshion to the Throne of the World. My Mishtressh the Dark Lord demandsh it – as your War Leader.'

Just so there should be no mistaking the intention, the nameless necromancer paused for an obligatory two heartbeats before adding, 'The marinesh are not yet fully mobilished. It would be unfortunate if they were not available to use againsht the invaders.'

Ashnak caught the featureless orange eye of the Dark Lord with a look that spoke volumes, mostly about the nameless necromancer's failing acquaintance with subtlety.

'Hold the trial tomorrow,' the Dark Lord suggested.

'Ah, very well. If you insist.' The wizard conjured up, with a flick of yellow-stained fingers, pipe-weed and a burning match. He lit his pipe. 'Shall we say th— *hkkk! hkkk-hkkkk! kah!* —the Hall of Justice, at ten?'

Ashnak, who had no doubts whatsoever about the Light's verdict, rehearsed a number of possibilities and reluctantly dismissed physical mayhem. He allowed his massive shoulders to slump. 'Am I to be held in military custody, then, Ma'am?'

'And have the marines report your unfortunate escape? I think not—' The Lord of Night and Silence halted, Her delicate head tilted to one side as if listening. 'Let them enter.'

The flap of the Night Pavilion was drawn back again by braided silver cords. The wind brought Ashnak the scent of troll-flesh and metal from the door guards, overlain by a pervasive corruption, and a very familiar smell of halfling.

Magda Brandiman marched across the fur pelts and lifted an armful of broadsheets up on to the stone table. 'Latest election edition of *Warrior of Fortune*, Dark Lady. Hot off the presses. I also have some information too recent to have made the news.'

For some reason that Ashnak could not fathom the Dark Lord and the female halfling glared at each other for a moment in silence. Magda's fur-short hair slicked up like a cat's under the electricity. The Dark Lord leaned back, pale hair and shadowed face framed by her black robes.

'We were not aware of your interest in broadsheets.'

'Graagryk had need of a newsheet with inter-Kingdom circulation,' the Duchess said, 'so I made it my business to acquire one. It is a recent purchase.'

The halfling had the appearance of having come from a social function to the press room, before coming to the Dark Pavilion. Her arms were ink-smudged below the sleeves of her black gown, and her diamond tiara had been shoved back to make room for a green eyeshade.

'And this is one of my sources in the military,' Magda said crisply. 'Lieutenant Lugashaldim of Covert Intelligence Actions.'

The Undead orc wore dark glasses, a black beret on one side of his flesh-stripped skull, and a sleeveless black vest apparently made up entirely of pouches and pockets. 'Dark Lord, Ma'am! General Ashnak, sir!'

'I won't intrude on your private conversations.' The white wizard Oderic eased himself up out of his seat with palpable reluctance.

The Dark Lord said, 'We have nothing to hide in this matter. Duchess of Graagryk, you may speak.'

'Lugashaldim,' the halfling prompted. Magda stood on one leg, momentarily leaning her hand against Ashnak's hip for balance, and scratched the sole of her hairy foot. Her other hand, resting against his skin, made the finger-speech movements for:

—Watch. Wait.

'Lieutenant Lugashaldim, you may regard this as a debrief,' Ashnak said.

'Very well, sir.' The Special Undead Services orc put the heels of his rotting boots together. 'It recently came to the attention of the CIA that a smear campaign was being conducted against the general during the present election. We have thoroughly investigated this, and I can now announce that there is no foundation in it whatsoever.'

High Wizard Oderic grunted sarcastically. 'And the evidence, foul Undead creature, what of that?'

Lugashaldim's gaze remained firmly fixed on the Dark Lord. 'Ma'am, the Light candidate Amarynth has *no* substantial evidence against General Ashnak – the supposed written confession of the witness Kyrial cannot be found. The Man-child herself has vanished. As for the halfling Meadowsweet and his family, they or their inheritors can't be traced either. Lord Amarynth has no one willing to come forward and testify, Ma'am.'

Ashnak, having a reasonable idea as to why no written evidence could be found, and where the witnesses might have gone, smirked.

'But there is the noble elf, Perdita del Verro,' Oderic protested.

'Regrettably,' Magda Brandiman said, 'as I discovered, upon Graagryk's purchase of *Warrior of Fortune*, the previous owners seem to have sent Mistress del Verro to cover the bush wars in the Drowned Lands, five thousand miles to the West. Even more regrettably, we can't contact her while she's on board ship for the two-year voyage. She could be anywhere on the Western Ocean. I fear she will not be able to return in time for the trial.'

'How regrettable,' the Dark Lord remarked drily.

Ashnak picked his nose to cover a broad grin.

'But,' the Dark Lord added, 'I'm afraid I cannot expect the Light to take our word for lack of evidence.'

Magda's hand slid into Ashnak's, gripping his gnarled fingers. He looked down at the top of her head and pulled her close for a moment. Between their bodies her fingers moved again:

—Don't give up hope!

'You still agree to a trial, then?' Oderic sounded surprised.

The Lord of Dead Aeons closed Her long lashes over Her glowing eyes, sitting as still as any effigy in the Halls of Those Who Sleep.

The nameless necromancer's hood turned towards Oderic. 'What She has said, sho let it be!'

'Well, well. Goodness me.' Oderic, still standing, blew a succession of smoke-rings, each a further degree of colour up the spectrum than the last. 'I'll inform the jury of the new time for the trial. No, no, don't bother to see me out. I know my own way.'

After the guttural challenge of the troll guard ceased, the nameless necromancer spoke again; hobbling away from the stone table. 'Lich orc, you are now under *my* command. You will come with me and tell me all you know. Your Grace of Graagryk, goodnight.'

The necromancer held up the tent flap pointedly. Magda dropped a very formal curtsy to the Dark Lord and walked out without a backward look. Lugashaldim, after glancing at Ashnak for guidance, followed her.

'And take off that shilly talishman!' The nameless pointed at the marine-issue dog-tag slung around Ashnak's bull-neck. 'Dark Lord, I shall return for the orc prishoner in just one moment.'

Ashnak thoughtfully tested the chains between his wrist fetters. The metal groaned. Troll Irregulars are stronger than common orcs, though not stronger than great orcs. The Royal Quarter of Ferenzia is not that far from the military encampment of the orc marines.

'I would find you,' a voice whispered, dry as the husks of dead bees. Lashes lifted and the Dark Lord once again watched from Her great basalt throne.

Nor is it far from the Dark Pavilion to the orc marine camp where the retributive powers of the Lord of Night and Silence are concerned.

'Since I have consented to play this game, I will not lose it now. If it is My pleasure that you be sacrificed to make My name good in the eyes of fools, then so be it. You are Mine, little orc.'

The black robes rustled like leaves, and a pale hand upon which the sword callouses were long healed reached out.

Ashnak by tensing his muscles snapped the fetters around his wrists. He reached up and broke the chain of the marine-issue dog-tag, and dropped the nullity talisman on to the stone table before Her implacable gaze.

The same night wind that tugged the guy ropes of the Dark Pavilion whistled through Ferenzia Station.

The Reverend Will Brandiman tucked his marine-surplus radio rig back inside his doublet, and leaned out of the steam train's window. 'There they are, Ned – right on time.'

His brother stuck a wimpled head out of the window as the train hissed, chugged, and screeched to a halt on the southern-incoming platform. The air under the high panelled glass station roof smelled of steam, grit and food-stalls. A crowd of brightly dressed halflings, elves, dwarves and Men thronged the platform, all illuminated by the spitting naphtha flares. Their waving banners read VOTE LIGHT, VOTE AMARYNTH! and AMARYNTH FOR THE THRONE OF THE WORLD!

'There's upwards of five hundred', Ned marvelled, 'on the platform alone. Are all of them Mother's rent-a-mob?'

Will tapped the radio rig. 'That's what she says. An audience for us.'

The two halflings looked at each other as doors banged open down the length of the election express special, echoing in the vast interior space.

Ned grinned. 'Let's do it!'

Will slicked back his dyed black hair, still leaning from the train window. He touched the transmit button on the radio. 'Hairfoot to Grace, we're coming in, do you copy?'

'Grace to Hairfoot, copy loud and clear. Take it away, boys.'

Cheers echoed. Four fat dwarves unrolled a red velvet carpet towards the Holy One's carriage. Will ducked back into the train and made his way forward, Ned at his heels.

'Your Holy Paladinship.' Will bowed. 'Your people wish to greet you.'

'And so they *shall* greet us.' The dark elf Amarynth, Holy Son of the Lady, stood accoutred in a white robe sewn with pearls. Diamonds fastened back his shaggy mane of black hair above his pointed ears. 'Come, let us descend.'

A flurry of Flagellant Knights descended first, clearing the crowds back. Will assumed a pious expression and clasped his hands before his breast, treading in a stately manner down the small flight of moveable steps to the platform. A muttered curse at his back informed him that Ned had trod on his habit's hem again.

Questions came rapid-fire from the crowd:

'Your Reverendship, will you say a few words for the press?'

'This way, Reverend – smile for the camera!'

'How's the campaign going?'

'Mother Edwina, will you say something for the women of Ferenzia?'

Will held up his hands soberly. The thronging crowd of halfling ballad-singers, Human gossips, dwarf rumour-mongers, and an elven broadsheet camera-crew formed a half-circle around the train steps. 'Gentlemen! Ladies! One at a time, please!'

Mother Edwina picked up his skirts and walked to join his brother, whip and handcuffs jangling on his chain belt. 'Good people of Ferenzia! It is not *we* who should speak to you. Behold – the Lady's Son himself, your Light candidate. *Amarynth!*'

Flashbulbs popped and the general decibel-level of questions rose to screaming pitch. The crowd behind the press waved their banners, chanting '*AM-A-RYNTH! AM-A-RYNTH!*' The Holy One appeared in the train door, paused for a moment, then swept down the steps and on to the red carpet.

'We stand before you filled with Light and hope!' The elf spread his arms. The sleeves of his white robe flashed back the naphtha lamps' illumination. 'In two days the final accounting is due – our victory, that will wipe the treacherous forces of Darkness from the face of the earth!'

349

Reverend William Brandiman and Mother Edwina proceeded to orchestrate the taking of questions, Will with half an eye on the guardsmen shepherding Ferenzia's enthusiastic general public. The gate from the platform into the main body of the station was hopelessly blocked. Will searched the broadsheet gossip-mongers for any familiar face.

In the second rank of the crowd, effectively concealed by Men's legs and the skirts of their doublets, Magda Brandiman stood with notebook and quill in hand, a slouch hat pulled down over her eyes.

'There.' Will nudged Mother Edwina. The wimpled halfling followed his gaze.

'I see, brother. Mother Edwina will call on her for a question after the dwarf has finished.'

Will took a deep breath to steady himself. The Holy One's answer to the dwarf interviewer's question seemed unusually extensive. He glanced up at Amarynth.

'. . . And furthermore,' Amarynth said, 'in the certain knowledge of our victory, we have an announcement to make. A most important announcement! It should perhaps wait – but we are so anxious that we cannot.'

Amarynth Firehand beamed, first at the crowd of journalists and then directly at Will and Ned. The Holy One stepped forward in the expectant silence.

He sank gracefully to one knee in front of Ned Brandiman.

'Mother Edwina!' Amarynth Firehand began. 'We know that your Order, the Little Sisters of Mortification, is not an Order that forbids congress with members of the opposite sex. Indeed, many of the Little Sisters even marry. Oh, Edwina, marry *me!*'

A fury of flashbulbs burst, tripod-cameras catching the expression of stunned amazement on the halfling features of Mother Edwina. Someone behind Will said, 'Aw, that's so sweet!'

'You must know how we feel!' Amarynth exclaimed. 'Edwina, our feelings cannot come as a surprise to you.'

Ned Brandiman regarded Amarynth for a confused moment. 'You're an elf. I'm a halfling. It would never work.'

'But it will!' the Holy One protested, holding out a beseeching hand. 'Edwina, make us the happiest of elves! Say yes!'

The crowd of elves, dwarves and Men around Will scribbled furiously, glancing from the Light's candidate to the halfling in her red nun's habit. Will belatedly shut his open mouth. A Man muttered excitedly, 'Headline: LIGHT CANDIDATE PROPOSES TO GOOD ABBESS, WEDDING OF THE YEAR, question mark!'

The Good Abbess Edwina stood on the station platform, her

350

motherly wrinkled face catching the naphtha lights. The night wind blew around the skirts of her red robe. The silver tip of her whip gleamed. For a long moment she stood perfectly still, gazing into the eyes of the kneeling elf, which were just on her level.

She reached up slowly and pulled off her wimple, disclosing tight brown curls and a fair amount of chin-stubble.

'I'm a *male* halfling,' Ned Brandiman pointed out gruffly.

'No one of us is perfect,' Amarynth shrugged.

The elf's response was drowned in the flash of bulbs and the screech of questions, and a baying howl from the crowds at the platform gate. They broke the guards' cordon and flooded in. The Knights Flagellant moved forward and scuffles broke out. Will Brandiman stepped back in among the journalists, effectively concealing himself, and stripped off his tight black doublet. He reversed it to show the scarlet lining, and struggled to get his arms back into the sleeves.

'Amazing,' a familiar voice commented. Magda Brandiman removed her slouch hat and passed it to her son, standing revealed in an evening dress and fur stole; the picture of a socialite halfling. '*Much* more effective than planting a question about the Reverend's financial irregularities. Amarynth might have wriggled out of that. This is his political death.'

'Mother, it was nothing to do with us!' Will tugged the hat down over his eyes and pointed to where the dark elf and the defrocked Abbess were being pushed and shoved. Ugly noises sounded from the crowd. 'Let's get Ned out before real trouble starts.'

The halfling smiled, tiny crow's-feet wrinkling in the corners of her dark eyes. 'There's always an old favourite,' she murmured, moving to the opposite platform's edge, striking a sulphur-match, and dropping it into the litter between the rails.

Will filled his lungs and bellowed. 'FIRE!'

The stench of burning rags filled the air and the crowd panicked. Will elbowed his way between the dwarf correspondent and the elf camera crew, caught Ned's arm, pulled; and the two halflings rolled and dived and dropped down between the edge of the platform and Amarynth's election special express. Ned tore his habit to tunic-length and wiped off his face-paint. Heads ducked down, they loped along under the train and exited on the far side, merging with the crowd disembarking from a northerly stopping train, and slipping out on to the far platform.

The Duchess of Graagryk's coach departed from the outside of Ferenzia's main station, her Grace naturally enough not wishing to be involved in the riot that, beginning on platform seven, spread out

351

from there and before the night's end had barricades up in fifty streets of the poorer quarter. The Duchess's coach, as well as its driver and complement of halfling bodyguards, acquired two new coachmen, who rode in the chilling air without complaint as the coach jolted over the cobbles towards the Royal Quarter.

'I don't know, Will.' Ned Brandiman shook his head. 'I'm not saying I won't accept him. It was just so sudden. A girl likes to have time to make up her mind.'

Will Brandiman perched beside Ned on the tiger's seat at the back of the coach, watching the dark streets of Ferenzia jolt by. He put his head in his hands. His voice came muffled to Ned. 'What I say is, never marry an elf who refers to himself in the plural, that's what I say.'

'Well . . .' Reluctantly, Ned conceded. 'There may be something in that.'

The ducal coach left the cobbled streets of the Royal Quarter, the horses' hoofs muffled on the turf of the Royal Park where the forces of Darkness were encamped. The Duchess Magdelene Amaryllis Judith Brechie van Nassau leaned from the window and spoke briefly to the kobold and dire-wolf guards.

She alighted in front of the Dark Pavilion, and entered.

By the time she reappeared Will had engaged in dice-throwing with the kobold guard, and was the proud possessor of two saw-tooth daggers (with spikes on pommels), a wyvern-skin ration bag (with split seam), and four copper coins of indeterminate value. The red eyes of the kobolds glowed at this total pillage of their wealth. Will tactfully palmed his other set of loaded dice and lost a double-or-nothing last throw. He joined Ned and his mother in the coach.

'Well?'

'I could have had a *beautiful* bride's gown,' Ned mourned. 'With ribbons.'

'Brother, be quiet!' Will scratched at his itchy hair, determined to remove the dye-spell as soon as possible. 'So, Mother, what's happening?'

Ned added, '*And* those little flounce-things, with lace . . .'

Magda Brandiman struck flint to steel, the light blossoming in the dark body of the coach. As the vehicle clopped away she lit a thin black roll of pipe-weed, placed it in her pipe-weed holder, and inhaled deeply.

'We've done you a considerable favour,' Will pointed out. 'That routine with the prayer-wheel was good for months yet. Ned and I could have been rich. Richer. Comfortably off, even.'

'And afforded a wedding gown with a train,' Ned Brandiman put in. 'Twenty yards of the best Archipelago silk.'

Will elbowed his brother halfling firmly in the ribs. 'As a favour to our mother, we sink the Light's election candidate – yes, I know it wasn't us, precisely, but we were going to. I'd prepared a marvellously touching speech where I broke down and confessed to Amarynth's forcing me to extort money from the pilgrims.'

Slightly miffed, he added, 'It was really good, for a rush job. Shame. However, the chances of Amarynth Firehand winning the election to the Throne of the World are slender now, to say the least, and we want to know, Mother – what did the Dark Lord offer you as a reward? And how much is our share of it?'

Chiaroscuro shadows chased across Magda Brandiman's lined, sallow face, and the swell of her small breasts under her evening gown. She frowned, exhaling pipe-weed smoke. 'That Bitch! I know exactly what She's after, She doesn't fool me for one minute. Which is more than I can say for a certain starry-eyed orc . . .'

Will frowned. 'Mother, I think you'd better tell us about this. What have orcs got to do with it?'

Magda Brandiman turned her head, her delicate profile appearing against the window as the grey of false dawn streaked the sky over Ferenzia.

'I may have misled you, son,' she confessed. 'Removing Amarynth wasn't the Dark Lord's idea. It was mine. It occurred to me, you see, that with no rival in the election, and Her victory therefore certain, it wouldn't be necessary for my Ashnak's trial to go ahead.'

'Oh, no,' Will Brandiman groaned. 'Ashnak!'

'The evidence against your stepfather has been, shall we say, mislaid. And She doesn't need a propaganda victory with Amarynth Firehand disgraced. *But*,' Magda snarled, 'will She cancel his trial? She will not! Ten o'clock this morning, it goes ahead.'

'You mean *we've* just attempted to help that – *orc* – out of trouble?' Will Brandiman demanded. He glared at Ned for help, but the brown-haired halfling leaned back in the jolting coach seat and hummed a wedding march. 'Mother! How could you?'

'I couldn't count on your voluntary assistance.' Magda Brandiman stubbed out the pipe-weed on the gilt frame of the coach window, scowling. 'I begin to see it now. I'm a fool. There's no way She'll stop the trial or settle for any verdict less than *guilty*. With my Ashnak out of the way She controls the marines. And they're the only thing now that stands between us and the Bugs.'

The condemned orc ate a hearty breakfast.

Morning sun shone down from the grille into the tiny cell the Order of White Mages allot their prisoners. Ashnak blinked as the sun moved across his eyes. Fathoms of spellcast chain rattled as he rolled off the plank bunk and on to his bare feet.

'*Urrp!*' He scratched his crotch through his ragged combat trousers, chains rattling again, and relieved himself against the cell wall. The sun's heat raised a malodorous warmth. The orc beamed and belched again.

'General Ashnak!' A thunderous banging sounded on the door, to be succeeded by the rattle of keys, and the heavy oaken door swinging open.

A small orc in smart brown uniform tunic and breeches backed through the doorway, holding a silver breakfast salver in one steel- and one orc-hand. A clean white towel hung over his arm, and he jauntily wore a tall white cook's hat.

'Good morning, General, sir!' Major Barashkukor said. 'How would you like your witness?'

Ashnak chuckled. 'Well done!'

The small orc whipped off the domed cover of the salver to disclose sizzling haunch of halfling, crisped to a dark brown. Ashnak seized and sank his teeth in it, saying through a full mouth, 'That'll do nicely . . .'

'Last of the young Meadowsweet spawn, sir.' Barashkukor assumed an expression of modesty. 'Cooked it myself. Glad you like it, sir. I told the Order of White Mages it was deer-haunch, sir, and they let me through. After they'd insisted on tasting it first.'

Ashnak stripped the succulent meat to the bone, broke the bone and sucked the marrow, the chains on his wrists hardly hampering him at all.

'What about my other order?' he rumbled.

'Yessir!' The small major unbuttoned his uniform jacket and removed a spare set of dog-tags. He held the nullity talismans in his hand for a bewildered moment, then scrambled up on to the bunk and passed the chains over Ashnak's heavy head, dropping the tags down under the fettered orc's ragged marine sweatshirt. 'There you are, sir.'

Staves clashed down the passage and a dozen of the white-surcoated Ferenzi Order of Mages appeared. The female Man who was their leader scowled at Ashnak, who wiped the last halfling-grease from his chin and drew himself up to his full stature.

'You!' she said harshly. 'To court, now, and no tricks. My mages will burn you where you stand if you try anything. I would welcome the chance to wipe you from the face of the earth.'

Ashnak regarded their tall ironwood mage-staffs and bared brass-capped fangs in a smile. 'Kiss my ass!'

'Excuse me, madam.' Barashkukor belatedly climbed down from the plank-bed, removing and folding his towel and chef's hat. Under the chef's hat he wore a flat peaked cap with major's insignia. 'I am Major Barashkukor of Five Company. According to marine regulations, appointed the Prisoner's Friend.' He beamed at Ashnak. 'I am even now preparing your defence, sir.'

The white mage looked down at the orc, her serenely beautiful features wrinkling in disgust. With no more words the mages fell in around Ashnak as he left the cell, Barashkukor at his heels, and strode down the echoing tunnels of the prison.

A covered bridge took them from the prison to the court. The noise of a crowd could be heard through the bridge's ventilation slits. Ashnak's deep eyes glinted in the gloom. He quickened his step, forcing the mages to run to keep up. His chains dragged three or four yards behind him, sweeping away the dust of ages.

'Here . . .' Panting, the head of the Mage escort handed Ashnak over to the court ushers at the entrance to the courtroom. Most of the ushers were halflings. The two who approached Ashnak were orcs with DEPUTY USHER stencilled across their fatigues.

'As you suggested, sir, I mentioned to the lads that they might like to come along.' Barashkukor beamed up at the gallery on the left of the door, his cyborg eye whirring. Upwards of two hundred orcs packed the tiered seats, their elbows, shoulders and knees crushing the dwarves, elves, halflings and Men sitting in with them. The orc marines threw nuts and offal and chorused barrack-room songs. Their whistles and orc-calls echoed through the court's high vault. The grunts chanted, *'Ash-nak! Ash-nak!'*

'How very touching.' Ashnak let his eyes sweep the courtroom – the witness-stand in front of the judge's bench, the desks for prosecuting and defence counsels, and the twelve good Ferenzi and true sitting in the jury box. Members of Ferenzia's general public filed in towards the last gallery seats.

'Oh, it's such a shame . . .' A female dwarf wept copiously as two orc grunts helped her towards a seat. 'He didn't do it, he's a *nice* boy . . . He's my only support in my old age!'

'Your *support?*' one hulking, granite-skinned orc queried.

'Aw, she wants Court Four,' the other grunt said, his ugly features clearing. 'Thoin Bardsbane, the dwarf axe murderer.'

'My little boy!' the old dwarf female wept, tears trickling into her beard. 'He didn't do it!'

'Haven't they hanged Thoin Bardsbane already?' the first grunt remarked.

'Naw.' The second orc paused. 'Hung, drawn, *and* quartered.'

The female dwarf broke into a howl and buried her sobbing face in a kerchief. The two orcs in green fatigues escorted her back out of the courtroom. Their voices came faintly to Ashnak:

'When did that happen, then? I never seen a quartered dwarf.'

'You missed it. Sunrise, that was. Pretty good, too . . .'

A staff tapped on the tiles behind Ashnak and he turned to see a grizzled orc sergeant-major intercept a white-haired old Man in grey robes. ''Ere, you! No weapons in the Hall of Justice!'

The old Man seemed to become even more hunched and bent. Leaning on the gnarled oak, he quavered, 'Would you deny a feeble old man his staff?'

The orc sergeant-major guffawed.

'No you don't, granddad, I've been had like that before!' The orc plucked the staff away, snapped it over his knee, and tossed the pieces back out of the door.

'But, but—'

'If you can't walk, crawl!'

Ashnak watched the old Man crawl on all fours up the gallery steps. Then he turned his head and nodded. The orc ushers slammed the outer doors of the courtroom on the White Mages and shoved bars into place.

Ashnak twisted his hands in the spellcast chains, pulled, and snapped the steel links. He stripped the fetters away, muscles bulging, and took a pistol from Barashkukor which he shoved under the waistband of his combat trousers.

'You!' Ashnak strode forward, pointing at a halfling usher. 'Call this court to order. I will not suffer this unruly behaviour.'

'But— But— But—'

'That's *contempt*.'

FOOM!

'I will not stand for contempt in this courtroom!'

To orcish yowls of applause, Ashnak blew smoke from the Colt .45's muzzle. He loped up on to the judge's bench and seated himself in the carved, high-backed chair. Ashnak donned a pair of half-spectacles abandoned on the bench and gazed righteously down into the court, bald head and peaked ears gleaming.

'Clear up that mess!' At the snap of his fingers, six more halflings rushed forward with buckets. Ashnak turned his heavy-jawed head towards prosecuting counsel's desk.

'You! Counsel for the Prosecution.' Ashnak's bushy brows

lowered. His deep-set eyes gleamed over the half-spectacles. 'Why have you not yet made your speech?'

A small curly footed halfling in brown breeches, the only being as yet sitting by the prosecution's desk, first looked over his shoulder, then all around, and then back at Ashnak. *'Me?'*

'State your case!' Ashnak roared.

'But—' The halfling stood, nervously smoothing down his waistcoat. 'But, your Honour, I'm a *witness*, not the counsel for the prosecution.'

'*That's* contempt!'

FOOOOMM!

Ashnak looked over his half-spectacles at marine major Barashkukor, standing smartly to attention behind the defence's table. 'Let that witness take the oath.'

Barashkukor poked around on the floor and finally held up the halfling's severed hand.

'Does he swear to tell the truth, the whole truth, and nothing like the truth?'

Barashkukor looked enquiringly down at the mess. 'He does, sir.'

'Good. And what does he have to say?'

The cyborg orc rapped out: 'The general didn't do it, your Honour!'

'Is that right?' Ashnak asked the witness.

Barashkukor picked up the severed head and nodded it vigorously. 'That's right!'

Ashnak seized up the heavy gavel that lay on the bench and bashed it down. 'Not guilty – case dismissed!'

Deep-throated orcish cheers rang out, and the orc marines threw their forage caps and steel helmets up into the air, sometimes even catching them again. The Ferenzi who sat in the gallery huddled down into their seats in blank-eyed bewilderment and terror.

'You can't do this!' an outraged juror protested from the jury box. The Man's plum-coloured doublet matched his complexion. 'Shedding blood in the house of justice – it's intolerable!'

His neighbour juror, a blue-eyed elf, pulled the Man's sleeve. 'Sit down! Mother of Trees, it was only a pair of halflings!'

'*Cease!*'

Simultaneously with the mage-enhanced voice that rang out in the courtroom, the barred doors burst inwards. Orcs tumbled backwards. The *slam!* of the doors produced instant silence.

'This circus is ended,' the same voice said bitterly.

Oderic, High Wizard of Ferenzia, paced into the courtroom, leaning on his mage-staff. Twenty of the wizards of the Order of the

White Mage followed at his heels. The gimlet-eyed old man glared at the rising tiers of seats. The twenty mages in white surcoats faced the rows of hunched orcs festooned with bandoliers, saw-toothed daggers, stick grenades, magazine pouches, pistols, M16s, Kalashnikov rifles and at least one General Purpose Machine-Gun. The orc marines stamped, catcalled, whistled and yowled.

'There *will* be a trial,' Oderic insisted. His fingers flashed with mage-fire. 'Orc, step down from the bench. It shall not be forgotten that you are intimidating the Light's witness.'

Ashnak bared odorous fangs at the wizard. 'There isn't enough of him left to intimidate!'

He moved the Colt .45 automatic pistol to the small of his back and shuffled down from the judge's bench, making certain at all times that he faced Oderic, and joined Barashkukor at the defence's desk.

'Didn't think we'd get away with that one, Major.'

'Worth a try, sir.' Barashkukor's long ears straightened. 'Don't want it to come to outright war if we can help it, sir, we're going to need these lads in the near future.'

Ashnak nodded thoughtfully. He bellowed up at the stands, 'Ten*HUT!*' and then, when the two hundred orcs snapped to attention in disciplined silence, added, 'At ease! Stand easy!'

'The prisoner will refrain from giving orders!' Oderic snapped as he mounted the judge's bench. He looked down at the carved seat and wiped it with his robe before he sat. The white wizard glanced at the halfling detail mopping up the floor and sighed. 'That violence was ill done, orc. Especially since I am to be your judge. I do not approve of the waste of good halflings. Clerk of the court! Swear the jury in.'

A middle-aged Man began to move along the line of jurors with one of the Sacred Tomes. Ashnak turned in his chair and glared up at the orcs behind him. He coughed.

A scuffle among the armed orc marines disclosed a somewhat cramped Duchess of Graagryk. The dark-haired female halfling stood up in the middle of a row of orcs in green DPM, her black leather gown and diamond-ornamented plume holder catching the sun pouring in through the court's great windows.

'I appeal!' she called.

Oderic said testily, 'It is customary, madam, to leave the appeal until *after* the sentence.'

Uncrushed by his sarcasm, Magdelene Amaryllis Judith Brechie van Nassau of Graagryk spoke with a penetrating clarity.

'I appeal to the highest justice of Ferenzia on behalf of my husband.'

'You have it.'

'No,' she corrected. 'We do not. High Wizard, on capital matters Ferenzia has an ancient and honourable tradition. The defendant may apply for, and be granted, the right to be tried by the highest justice in the land. We demand to be tried by the *Royal* justice. Mage, I demand as judge for my husband – the High King, Magorian himself!'

The High Wizard's eyes bulged. 'But he's—'

'Yes?' the halfling Duchess said sweetly. She fluttered her eyelashes. 'You were about to say, he is the High King, and therefore well-known to be a great and *wise* judge?'

'Er . . .'

'Of course you were. I really don't need to remind you that this is within our legal rights, do I, your mageship?'

The Duchess of Graagryk seated herself again, her dignity somewhat spoiled by six hulking orc marines leaning across to slap her on the back and growl 'Yo!'

Oderic scowled, got to his feet, held a muttered conversation with the captain of the Order of White Mages, and then stomped from the court, his staff crashing down on the tiles and dying into the distance. Ashnak leaned back in his chair and put his hands behind his head, and his bare feet on the table.

'It'll work, sir, won't it?' Barashkukor said stoutly.

Ashnak bit off a toe-claw and flicked it. It spanged off the bald head of a middle-aged dwarf, who winced and clapped a handkerchief to the bleeding wound.

'Steady on, sir. That's counsel for the prosecution.'

'The hell you say.' Contented, Ashnak slid back in his chair and closed his eyes, listening to the orcs in the courtroom chanting 'Yo the marines!' The halfling ushers attempted verbally to restrain them from the floor of the court, unwilling to venture up the steps. The mages of the White Order watched with a dispassionate contempt.

A faint knocking sound impinged on Ashnak's consciousness. He opened his eyes, turning his head to look out of the courtroom's open window.

A stark frame of wood rose towards the morning sky.

A gallows.

The gibbet was already complete, and the hammering came from an elderly Man fitting the trapdoor below the noose. Ashnak noted a number of orc marines in off-duty fatigues lounging around the gallows.

'Are you sure you're getting a long enough drop?' a squat orc marine lieutenant asked, her voice coming up thinly to Ashnak from the square below.

'Tear 'is 'ead off if it's wrong,' an orc grunt added. 'Won't it, ma'am?'

The elderly Man spat out another nail and hammered it in. 'I'm sure you're right, mum. Don't 'ee worry none! Begging yur pardon, I'll have 'un set up a treat by the time the orc hanging's due. He's a big 'un, so I'll be sure and drop a few sandbags through first and check, mum, now's you've been so kind as to mention it.'

A fanfare of trumpets drowned out the noise of hammering. Ashnak lumbered to his feet as the High King Kelyos Magorian entered, holding the arm of a squire, and was escorted by his helmeted and mailed guards to the judge's bench. Ashnak saluted. Barashkukor threw out his chest and sprang to attention, the steel fingers of his right hand touching the peak of his flat cap.

'TenHUT!' the small orc bawled. The orc marines in the court joined the standing citizens of Ferenzia in what Magda Brandiman had demanded as a politic show of respect.

There was, Ashnak noted, no sign of Oderic.

'. . . mmm, and I hadn't finished breakfast *either*,' Magorian grumbled. He irritatedly swatted at his elf squire, who continued to button him into a long black judge's gown. 'Damme, what am I here for, Kalmyrinth?'

The elf straightened the long curled horsehair wig on his sovereign's head and stepped down from the bench. 'You are presiding over the trial of orc General Ashnak for war crimes, sire.'

'Oh, *good!*' Magorian brightened. 'If he's sent down, then all of those damned greenies will leave. That means property prices in the Royal Quarter will stop falling. Guilty!'

The bald dwarf prosecutor stood up at his desk. 'No, sire, we have to hold the trial first. *Then* we can hang him.'

The High King subsided into his robes, blue-veined hands shaking, and gestured at no one in particular. 'Let the case begin!'

'Your justicular Majesty,' the dwarf began, walking out on to the floor of the courtroom. He turned to the jury box. 'Distinguished citizens of Ferenzia.' He turned towards the gallery seats. 'Lovers of justice. I am Zhazba-darabat of the Deep Mountain, and I appear for the prosecution. Today you will hear the details of a most heinous crime. The orc before you—'

Zhazba-darabat's gnarled finger stabbed up at Ashnak, lounging in his chair at the defence's desk.

'—this orc, most trusted general of Her Dark Majesty, an orc long experienced in the hardships of war, stands accused of the greatest offence a soldier can commit. Citizens, this orc has committed a massacre of helpless civilian baggage-handlers, against all the

360

civilized rules of warfare. He has butchered witnesses to his crime. And he has interfered with the running of the great Election to the Throne of the World, to wit, by causing explosive atrocities among the voting population.'

'Objection!' Barashkukor bounded to his feet.

Magorian looked down at the small orc. 'Ah. Um. On what grounds does the counsel for the defence object?'

Major Barashkukor frowned. 'He shouldn't say that sort of thing about my general!'

Magorian's sandy eyebrows raised. 'Well, I admit, it does seem a little harsh . . . What?' The High King held a hand cupped to his ear as the Man clerk of the court whispered. 'Ah. It appears that counsel for the prosecution is *obliged* to do this. Well, well.' He beamed encouragingly. 'I shall make sure you have your turn later on, Major, have no fear of that.'

The dwarf prosecutor sighed and wiped his face with a large handkerchief. Ashnak gave him a wide unnerving grin. At his imperceptible hand-signal the orc marines in the gallery began to crash the butts of their rifles against the floor.

'WE WANT ASHNAK! LET THE GENERAL SPEAK!'

The Order of White Mages moved across the floor of the courtroom in a businesslike manner, and the High King Magorian picked up his judge's gavel and banged it down with a fine disregard for aim. 'Order! *Order!*'

'Mine's a pint!' a very small orc grunt in the front row yelped.

'Oh, good grief.' An enormous orc sergeant leaned down from behind, and brought his fist down smartly on the grunt's skull. The grunt's long ears jolted bolt upright, then wavered and crossed as the small orc subsided to the floor.

Marine Commissar Razitshakra, who had been sitting next to the grunt, looked at the bench beside her. 'This seat needs cleaning – pass me a halfling.'

After a small scuffle one of the halfling ushers was seized and passed hand-to-hand, protesting, over the orc marines' heads, down to Razitshakra. She wiped the leather cushion first with its curly hair, and then with its hairy feet. 'Anyone want this seat?'

Lieutenant Chahkamnit looked down from three rows above. 'Er. No. Not right now.'

The marine commissar scowled. 'Anyone want this halfling, then?'

'Nah,' a corporal said. 'It's been used.'

'I've got a bap,' a hopeful voice remarked from the back row.

'*Silence!*' The captain of the White Mages let go a bolt of fire that singed the ceiling and had the Ferenzi citizens cowering in their seats.

The unimpressed orc marines looked at Ashnak and, at his signal, subsided.

'Your majestic Honour,' the White Mage protested, her blond hair swinging as she spun to face the bench, 'you simply cannot allow that rabble to behave like this!'

'Mmph?' The High King looked up from doodling with a griffin's-feather pen on his notepad. 'Is that all the case for the prosecution?'

Prosecuting counsel Zhazba-darabat marched across the court-room floor to the bench, stepping over a number of cables marked OFFICIAL DO NOT REMOVE. The dwarf stared up at the edge of the bench, with no line of sight to the judge. 'Your honour—'

'What?' Magorian blinked rheumy eyes, gazing around. 'Has the little fella finished? You, orc, whatever your name is. Do your bit.'

Barashkukor bounded to his feet again. 'Objection!'

'What is it *this* time?'

'I'm not ready yet.'

Magorian glowered. 'State your case, greenie. And make it quick. I want my dinner.'

Ashnak shifted in his chair, the metal bulk of the Colt .45 pressing against his spine. Through slitted eyes he watched the mages of the Light.

'M'lud.' Barashkukor straightened up from behind the defence's desk. He exchanged his peaked cap for a horsehair wig whose long side-flaps dangled down to his web belt. 'M'lud, the defence's case is as follows. General Ashnak didn't do it, it wasn't him, and besides he was somewhere else at the time! I would now like to call a character witness.'

Magorian's sandy eyebrows raised. 'Oh . . . very well.'

Barashkukor marched out into the floor of the court. 'Call Lugbash!'

A halfling usher opened the doors and bawled down the corridor. *'Call Lugbash!'*

A distant voice echoed: 'CALL LUGBASH . . .'

Ashnak leaned one muscular arm over the back of his chair and spoke to marine commissar Razitshakra in the gallery's front row. 'Who the fuck is Lugbash?'

Before the commissar could answer, a hunched orc in a ragged dress and shawl hobbled into the court. Barashkukor gallantly offered her his steel arm as she climbed up into the witness stand.

'I remember Ashnak,' she crooned, without provocation. ''E were a lovely little orc, 'e were. I was his nanny, you know, the dear sweet thing.'

Barashkukor clasped his hands behind his back. 'And in your

opinion, Nanny Lugbash, is your charge capable of committing the acts of which he is accused?'

'What, my dear little Nakkie?' The orc's shawl slipped and she grabbed at it, but not before Ashnak had caught sight of a lantern jaw and corporal's chevrons. 'Of course 'e couldn't, dearie. Never did anyone any harm, and *such* a good little orc. Always ate his meals. Ate the plate, come to that. And the dog . . .'

'No further questions,' Barashkukor said hastily. 'I would now like to call as a further character witness Bio-tech Captain Ugarit—'

'No, you wouldn't,' Ashnak growled.

'— no I wouldn't. Erm.' The orc major turned on his heel. The ends of his wig flew out, swatting a halfling usher. He strode back to the desk. 'I will now claim precedent!'

'"Nakkie", indeed!' Ashnak rested his hand across his eyes as Barashkukor busied himself digging out a heap of tomes. The faint knocking of the gallows-maker's hammer became more pronounced.

'Don't think it'll work,' a dubious orc voice remarked in the square outside. 'That crosspiece is far too high. And look at that strut. Shoddy workmanship, I calls it.'

'Rubbish!' another orc proclaimed. 'Superb piece of execution engineering.'

'Sez 'oo?'

Ashnak glanced out of the window as the work-Man stood to one side, avoiding the orcs swinging punches at each other.

'Kind of you to say so, gentlesirs. *Most* kind,' the Man said, tucking another hammer away on a loop on his carpenter's apron. Ashnak heard the Man add under his breath, 'When it comes to gallows, *everyone's* a h'expert . . .'

Ashnak turned back to the courtroom as Zhazba-darabat drew his long velvet robes about him and began unearthing books from the prosecution desk. In a voice too low for the judge to catch, the dwarf growled, 'I have witnessed centuries of precedent, orc. How skilled in law are you?'

'Erm . . .' Barashkukor shot a haunted look at Ashnak, swallowed, and hauled a book out from the bottom of his pile. 'I cite the unanswerable case of *Hashbanipal Shadowtree vs. The Blue Elves.*'

The dwarf slammed a heavier tome down. 'I contradict you with *Meliadis the Savage vs. Brukgug Halforc.*'

'But I quote *Bishop Filgrindibad vs. The Secret Masters of the Halls!*'

'And I return: *Mistress Shulikan vs. Dolf, Dexis and Durundibar!*'

Barashkukor flicked back the ends of his wig, stunning another halfling, and appealed to the jury. 'I therefore cite the unanswerable precedent of *Berendis vs. All the Elves of Thyrion!*'

Several of the jurors applauded. Those who had been glancing from Barashkukor to Zhazba-darabat rubbed their necks.

'*Alaric Bonegrinder vs. The Red Paladin Hugon!*' Zhazba-darabat cried triumphantly. 'And what do you say to *that*?'

The small orc scrambled up on to the pile of books already cited, steel leg glinting, and thumbed another tome, rocking precariously. 'I will answer that with – erm – with . . .'

'*Order!*' Magorian's gavel crashed down. The orc sergeant in the third row glowered at the front-row grunt. Only a pair of orc ears remained visible, and they did not so much as twitch.

There was silence, apart from the growing noise of the brawl outside in the square, which seemed to have attracted a number of non-orc combatants.

'I rule those precedents out of court,' Magorian quavered. 'If you think I'm going to sit here and listen to all that rubbish, you're much mistaken. Counsel for the defence, do you have anything else to say?'

'I can't wait,' Ashnak rumbled under his breath, his bloodshot gaze fixed on the small orc major. Behind him, Razitshakra chuckled. Ashnak looked over his muscular shoulder.

The orc marine commissar rested her elbows on the front row of the gallery. 'Don't worry, sir,' she murmured. 'I've rigged the jury.'

Ashnak glared red-eyed at the jury box. Seven well-fed Men, an elf, two halflings, a dwarf and a half-elf. 'Those aren't our people.'

'No, no, sir; I've *rigged* the jury.' Concealing her movements from the White Mages, Razitshakra briefly drew open her greatcoat. Ashnak saw the commissar's free hand held an M57 firing device.

'Claymore mines under the chairs, sir.'

One of the floor-cables ran across from the gallery to the jury box. Studying them, Ashnak noted beads of sweat on the foreheads of the Man and halfling jurors. Even the elf looked a little uncomfortable.

'Nice work, Commissar,' he approved.

Several shots sounded from the square, over the noise of brawling. The White Mage captain scowled and ordered half her force outside. She fixed Ashnak with a challenging glare. Ashnak flicked an imaginary piece of lint from his ripped combat trousers.

'My client', Barashkukor proclaimed shrilly, 'was somewhere else entirely at the time when the said atrocities were committed. M'lud, I am my own witness here – at the time in question, the general was observing my handling of a T54 Main Battle Tank in the Faex River.'

Magorian looked doubtful. 'I don't think you *can* be your own witness, counsel.'

'Oh.' The small orc's face fell. Then he brightened. 'Very well. I never did trust paperwork. I'm an orc of action, I am. Call the T54 Main Battle Tank!'

The same halfling usher flung open the door to the corridor. *'Call the T54 Main Battle Tank!'*

'CALL THE T54 MAIN BATTLE . . . *WHAT?'*

'I don't think you can do that.' Magorian looked from the clerk of the court to the Captain of the White Mages. 'Can he do that?'

Whatever answer he received was drowned out by the grinding roar of a main battle tank. The orc marines in the gallery cheered, banging their weapons on the floor. A grunt carrying a red flag on a stick walked in through the courtroom door.

Ashnak stood as first the gun-barrel, then the tracks, and finally the chassis of a T54 tank ground into the courtroom. Since it was not more than a few inches wider than the door, it did no more than knock large chunks out of the doorframe. The tracks ripped the tiled flooring to shreds.

The T54's motor chugged, coughed and idled. A broad-shouldered orc grunt in a steel helmet flipped open the lid and leaned his elbows on the hatch, one arm close to the mounted machine-gun.

'Officer on deck!' Razitshakra bawled from the gallery. The orc caught sight of Ashnak and saluted rigidly. Ashnak returned the salute.

'I demand you rule this tank out of court!' Zhazba-darabat screamed.

The High King Magorian regarded the battered doorway. *'You* rule it out of court!'

The dwarf prosecutor threw all his papers up into the air in disgust. 'Your Honour, I object!'

'Why?' Barashkukor asked smugly. Zhazba-darabat marched up to the small orc and glared at him, nose-to-nose.

'Because it isn't even the same tank, that's why! *Your* T54 Main Battle Tank is at the bottom of the Faex River, isn't that right, Major?'

Flustered, the orc major muttered, 'It's a *representative* T54 Main Battle Tank.'

'No such thing!' The dwarf waved his arms, appealing to the bench. 'It couldn't testify, even if it *could* testify!'

Magorian scrubbed shaking fingers through his thinning hair. 'What was that again?'

'I said—'

Uproar broke out, each citizen of Ferenzia trying to out-shout the orc marine sitting nearest them on the merits of a tank's testimony. In vain the Order of White Mages used enhance spells to bolster their calls for silence.

'Silence in court!' the High King Magorian's voice cracked. *'Silence in court!'*

Ashnak raised his head. 'I think I can help you there.'

He snapped his fingers.

FOOOOOOOOOMMMM!

The T54's 100mm cannon fired. The window glass imploded. A substantial section of the vaulted ceiling fell in, scattering the gallery and the floor of the court with wreckage. For a moment there was silence broken only by the moans of Men, elves, dwarves and halflings bleeding from the ears.

Ashnak reached up and pulled a large chunk of cotton wadding from his right ear, and another one from his left ear. *'That* brought the house down.'

The smoke cleared to show High King Magorian waving his gavel in a dazed manner as he sank out of sight. '*I said silence in court, dammit . . .*'

Barashkukor pulled several yards of cotton wadding from his ears. The other orc marines followed suit. Barashkukor brushed debris from his horsehair wig. 'M'lud, I rest my case.'

A small voice quavered from under the judge's bench. 'The jury may retire . . .'

Seven Men, two halflings, a dwarf, an elf and a half-elf left their seats at a run and pelted out of the court, knocking aside the stunned mages. The Captain of the Order of White Mages signalled her Men to sit down on the jurors' vacated chairs, and tend to their wounded.

DAKKA-DAKKA-DAKKA!

'Arrrgh!' The body of a brawling Ferenzi Man hit the floor, blown *in* through the windows from the fight in the square.

'On second thoughts . . .' The High King Magorian scrambled into view behind the judge's bench. 'General Ashnak, I hereby pronounce you as thoroughly innocent as it's possible to be, and completely exonerated of every accusation ever brought against you. Now, or in the future. Will that do?' the old Man added, stumbling down from the bench on the arm of his elvish squire.

'That', Ashnak said over the cheers, yowls, and automatic rifle fire of the orc marines, 'will do just fine, your Honour.'

In the square outside, over the noise of brawling, Ashnak clearly heard the gallows-builder's yell. 'What's that you say, gentlesirs? A verdict of "innocent"?'

There was a pause.

'Oh, *fuck!*'

'ASH-NAK! ASH-NAK! *ASH-NAK!*'

'We did it!' Magda exclaimed, hurtling down from the gallery and into Ashnak's embrace. He kissed the female halfling with enthusiasm.

'We did, sir, didn't we?' Barashkukor, dazed and starry-eyed, beamed at his general. 'I told you you could rely on me, sir!'

The Ferenzi citizens bolted for the exit, and the Order of White Mages did not even look up from their commandeered jury seats. A crowd of cheering orc marines lifted Ashnak and bore their commander on their shoulders out of the courtroom.

'Congratulations, sir!' Marine Commissar Razitshakra shook Barashkukor firmly by the hand. The small orc's wig fell off. 'Politically correct in every respect.'

Barashkukor weaved out of the courtroom between Razitshakra and Lieutenant Chahkamnit.

The small orc grunt in the gallery front row blinked his way back to consciousness. Staggering to his feet, he made for the door in the wake of the cheering marines. A metallic object caught his foot.

The orc bent down, picked it up, and looked at it thoughtfully. The cable trailed behind him as he stepped into the corridor, closing the doors behind him, and squeezed the device's handle twice.

BOOOOOMMM!

'*Arrrrrgghhhhh!*'

Ashnak glanced back down the corridor at the brick dust drifting out of the courtroom. He raised his jutting eyebrows, then shook his head.

'*Yo!*' The hefty orc grunts carried Ashnak shoulder-high out into the square, where the midday sun shone on Ferenzi citizens still busy brawling. Off-duty orc marines stood and watched as if they couldn't think what all the fuss might be about.

'*Hold!*'

Ashnak looked over the head of the crowd towards the voice. He slapped the shoulders of the marines carrying him and slid down to the cobbles, taking the clean urban combat jacket Barashkukor was holding out and putting it on.

'Honour guard, tenHUT!' he rasped. The orc grunts around Ashnak, Magda and Barashkukor trained their M16s on the crowd, and on the High Wizard Oderic who forced his way through at the head of a column of mages and fighters.

'Reconvene the court,' Oderic shouted to Magorian.

The High King blinked at the sunlight, squinting in the direction of his High Wizard. 'You've got to be joking!'

'*I have a new witness.*'

Ashnak looked at Magda, who shrugged, and at Barashkukor, who paled. The White Mages behind Oderic parted their ranks.

A shambling, hunched figure in patchwork leather robes limped forward. The temperature in the sunlit square dropped twenty degrees. The sweet scent of decay made Ashnak's nostrils twitch.

The nameless necromancer put his hood back from his deformed face.

'I am hish witnesssh! I can vouch for your criminal actions at the halfling bombing, "General" Ashnak.' The nameless smiled, yellowing tusks drawing his mouth out of shape, and wiped away a string of drool. 'You and your accomplices. I have sheen it all. I wasss there!'

Ashnak put his rock-sized fists on his hips and glared under lowered brows at the nameless. One hand inched towards the gun in the back of his belt. '*That's* contempt . . .'

'Sir! I say, sir!' The lanky Lieutenant Chahkamnit interrupted, marine radio in hand. 'I rather think you ought to hear this, don't you know?'

Ashnak listened.

He held the radio out so that Magorian, Oderic and the nameless necromancer could hear the frantic broadcast:

'*—Bugs are past the south-eastern suburbs of the city! Repeat, our security is compromised, we have hostiles in Ferenzia itself; the Bugs are past the south-eastern suburbs of the city! All units alert!*'

'Lady of Light!' Oderic suddenly leaned on his staff, his face seeming that of a Man decades older than his one hundred and twenty years. 'How could they come on us so unprepared?'

The nameless necromancer rounded on Lieutenant Chahkamnit. 'Mobilize the marines!' he ordered.

The black orc scratched uncomfortably at one peaked ear. 'Awfully sorry, sir. I really don't think I can do that.'

'*What?*'

The nameless necromancer elbowed past the stunned High Wizard Oderic. Ice formed on the cobbles of the sunlit square. The brawling ceased in mid-blow. The nameless ignored Chahkamnit and loomed over Barashkukor, yellow bile dripping from his fangs.

'Major, *you* will mobilizzze the orcses!'

The orc's cyborg eye glowed ruby. 'With respect – I don't take my orders from a civilian.'

The edges of the sky above Ferenzia's rooftops darkened. The midday sun blurred. The head of the nameless necromancer swivelled, as he glared round at the mob of three hundred orc officers, sergeants and grunts.

'Is thissh a time to mutiny, with the fate of the world at stake?'

Ashnak finished buttoning his urban combat jacket and tucked it into his trousers. Orc batmen fitted him with combat boots, webbing, and pistol holster while he stood bow-legged in the square outside Ferenzia's Hall of Justice. His hairy nostrils widened, sensing the acrid stink of inhuman invaders.

''Snot *our* city,' an orc grunt remarked.

An orc captain in the crowd's front rank, General Purpose Machine-Gun resting over her shoulder, shouted, 'This isn't a mutiny! We're awaiting orders from our commander.'

The High Wizard Oderic of Ferenzia stared at Ashnak. The white mage swore. He threw his staff down on the sorcerously iced cobbles. The white oak, made brittle, snapped into four pieces.

'That's politically correct,' Commissar Razitshakra confirmed. 'We're waiting for orders from Joint Chief of Staff Ashnak. Or we marines don't do anything – except pull out of Ferenzia.'

10

A GREAT STRETCH of land lies between Ferenzia and the north-eastern hills. The colour of the plain changes as if a great shadow is passing across the sun.

The sun shines unhindered.

The blackness on the face of the earth crawled, crept, advancing forward with slow irresistibility: exoskeletoned Bugs marching in their hundreds and their thousands. The crackle of living-metal weaponry hissed through the air.

Unbroken, the lines of Bug soldiers pressed on towards the high ground. Orc vehicles and marines were visible in clumps, clusters and retreating bands. Mortar fire covered their retreat. A line of helicopter gunships strafed the Bugs and wheeled away, firepower lost in the morass of chitinous bodies.

Unit by unit, company by company, horde by horde, the approaching thousands of Bugs flowed towards the orc marine battalion in the hills. Weapons splashed fire against the granite ridges. Smoke rose up against the sun.

'Sir, look at the *range* on those things!' Major Barashkukor gaped at the figures the head-up display on his cyborg eye gave him. 'We don't have the firepower to deal with that!'

'There's a battalion of us, and fifteen thousand of them. Where's the problem?'

Ashnak drew on his cigar and exhaled a plume of foul-smelling smoke in the direction of the Lord of Night and Silence.

'Thinking of going into battle, Dread Lord?'

Rank upon rank of great orcs, common orcs, wolf-riders, kobolds, hobgoblins, dark elves and lich riders lined the ridge, their ragged banners darkening the sky. Before the Horde of Darkness, a great palanquin of bone – the yellowed rib-cage of some Dragon of the elder world – was supported on the shoulders of six Gnarly Trolls. Black pennants and horse skulls dangled from its corner posts.

The Dark Lord sat on Her throne in the palanquin. Her ash blonde hair shadowed copper and cyan in the sunlight. She wore a black armour, polished as ebony, fluted and pierced and decorated.

'They do not announce the formal election to the Throne of the World until tomorrow.' She leaned Her chin upon Her hand, Her armoured elbow denting the skull of one of the troll palanquin-bearers. 'Having played the game thus far, I do not wish to lose it.'

Ashnak shoved his steel helmet up from his brows. 'Now that's what I want to talk to you about, Ma'am.'

A detachment of elf hussars rode up, sabres jingling, and broke formation to disclose High King Magorian, Oderic and the White Mages. A band of Knights Flagellant rode up in their wake, but without Amarynth Firehand.

'Just taking up a stronger position.' Oderic puffed on his pipe, and with the stem indicated the pass through the north-eastern hills to the country beyond. 'Going that way . . .'

The Dark Lord abruptly signalled to Her trolls. They set the bone palanquin down. She leaped lithely to Her feet with the clatter of full plate harness. Her black steel-gauntleted hand fell on Ashnak's shoulder. He bit back a groan, legs bowing even more than is natural.

'Let Us talk,' the Dark Lord said, and Her spell of inaudibility flickered around them, stinging Ashnak's dog-tag into searing pain. 'You have a request, little orc, do you not? Amuse Me by telling Me what it is.'

'Quite simple, Ma'am.' Ashnak assumed a bluff, military manner. 'Don't want other units getting in the way of my marines. Bugs will make cat's meat of us if that happens. You'd better put me in charge of the lot – before I have to pull my forces out. Give me the rank of Supreme Commander, Ma'am.'

'Supreme Commander of the Horde,' She mused. 'I have not appointed one of those in aeons.'

Ashnak coughed. 'Not exactly, Ma'am. I mean Supreme Commander of the Dark *and* Light forces.'

The Dark Lord laughed, a sound like subterranean bells. The nullity talisman around Ashnak's neck broke into powder under the weight of the one magic of the Lord of Darkness.

'There are at least five other major spearheads of Bug attack, Ma'am, other than this one on Ferenzia. You need the orc marines. Unless you're planning to just wipe out all the Bugs like *that*.' Ashnak snapped his talons.

'The magic of obliteration is not a subtle magic. Yes, little orc, I could. But if I wipe these Bugs from the face of the earth, I shall in turn destroy the city they are in, and the land upon which they walk, so great is my power. No, my Ashnak. You shall have to face them in battle.'

She broke the spell of inaudibility and turned back to Her palanquin.

'White Mage!' She cried. 'I and My Horde shall accompany you back into the hills. My orc, in whom I am well pleased, is appointed over you all, to the command of this battle. Your people shall obey him as they would Me, or else suffer the same penalties.'

'But, but,' Oderic stuttered. 'But—'

The vanguard of the Evil Horde began to march on into the hills, drums thumping and horns blaring, with the Lord of Dead Aeons in the bone palanquin.

'She didn't like that, Supreme Commander,' Barashkukor said.

'*I* did.' Ashnak shifted his cigar to the other side of his mouth. He grinned. 'Awriiiiight! Let's get this show on the road – officer meeting, my tent, *now!*'

Dust rose up from the plain north of Ferenzia. Weapons and carapaces glinted through the murk. Dust rose up from the low ridges, canyons, gullies and cliffs of the hills. Below every ridge, concealed in every hollow, orcs and other marines in combat drab crouched with their weapons. Infantry battalions, field artillery groups, land-mine companies; signals, engineers, anti-aircraft, anti-tank and missile batteries; and behind them the auxiliary services, motor transport, fuel supply, repair workshops, bakery and butchery . . .

Cobra gunships and Hueys criss-crossed the midday skies above Ferenzia, flying nose-down over peaked roofs and spires. Radio traffic filled the air. Surface-to-air missiles roared into the sky.

'We have a go situation!' Sergeant John H. Stryker of the US Marine Corps put the jeep into a skidding handbrake turn and brought it around in front of Ashnak's field command tent, five miles to the north of the city. 'Sir, everyone and everything is where it ought to be, sir – on time, sir!'

'Fuck me,' Ashnak said as he leaped down from the vehicle. 'Well done, Sergeant. Maybe you Otherworld marines do have your uses.'

372

Followed by Barashkukor, the great orc strode into the command tent.

'I want recce reports on the Bugs' firepower and tactics. Then I want a confirmation of the assault plan; and rehearsals, if performed. Then I'll give orders. Any questions?'

Lieutenant Chahkamnit, Commissar Razitshakra, Biotech-Captain Ugarit, Sergeant Dakashnit, Lieutenant Lugashaldim and the higher-ranking general staff, seated on rickety chairs around comlinks and map tables, shook their tusked heads. The canvas-filtered sunlight gleamed on one marine, not an orc, tall and skinny, in a uniform decorated with beads, scarves and silver trinkets.

'I've got that report on what it is we're facing here, sir.' The hard-eyed elf Lieutenant Gilmuriel lounged to his feet. He snapped slender fingers. Ugarit cranked the handle on a kinematographic machine. A jerky moving image flashed on the pull-down screen.

'I don't know what the Bugs call 'em,' Gilmuriel drawled, 'sir. We call this one a "blaster".'

A bolt of charged particles seethes through the air of Thyrion, exploding at the point of impact; taking out three elf marines. Another elf seems caught in a beam of wavering air. Her body explodes in a rain of blood.

'That's a "disruptor",' Gilmuriel continued. 'They use that one a lot. That thing there—'

A black cylinder of metal hovers in the air, above the ruins of the City of the Trees.

'—we call that a "hunter" missile. It has the instincts of an elf, to track and follow its quarry. Explosion has a two-hundred-metre radius. Couldn't get footage of the "homing" grenades they use, sir. This . . .'

The elf glared at Ugarit. The skinny orc clicked the kinematographic machine rapidly, removed a slide, and replaced it the other way up.

A wavering bolt of energy tracks across an open jungle clearing, impacts on an armoured vehicle, explodes, and knocks the APC forty feet into the air.

'"Plasma gun".' The elf leaned one foot up on a chair, resting his elbow on his knee and his chin in his hand. He wore a brightly patterned scarf as a headband, and his pointed ears were pierced with silver studs. 'If they can see us, man, they can hit us! There are heavy weapons versions of that. And a contra-gravity harness, sir, I'm certain.'

Ashnak scowled. 'What's their armoured capability? What about airpower?'

The hefty black orc sergeant beside Gilmuriel stirred.

'Ain't seen nothing else but infantry, sir,' Dakashnit said. 'Their flight capability is jump-packs. No troop transporters. No ground vehicles, less'n they got some of ours. Hell, Commander, they don't *need* 'em.'

'Well, we've had about all the time for rehearsals we're going to get—' Ashnak swung round.

Dust-covered and sweating, the nameless necromancer stumbled into the tent and shambled into the circle of orcs. '*Talking?* You orcs should be out there fighting! You shall pay for thish disobediensche.'

Ashnak took two swift paces forward and loomed over the necromancer. '*Sit. Down.*'

The nameless found himself sitting in one of the folding chairs.

'About bleeding time, too,' Ashnak growled. 'My troops have moved out of the assembly areas to the forming-up points and start line. You, Lord Necromancer, can get the Light's troops off their asses! I'm committing the Light to the attack in Ferenzia itself. Hold 'em as long as you can, then pull back.'

The necromancer glared. 'That is a task for marines!'

'I've got more than enough problems,' the big combat-clad orc snarled, 'without fighting through built-up areas. Get those lily-livered sons of bitches down there! Those Bugs are throwing fuck knows what against us! You're gonna hold 'em up enough so's we can take 'em on their way north out of the city, here on this line of hills. Any questions?'

There was silence in the command tent. The nameless necromancer slobbered and hissed, standing and drawing himself up to his full height.

'Sir?'

A hand went up at the back.

'Sergeant Stryker?' Ashnak said.

The blond Man sood. New combats and weaponry made him the very image of a marine. His muscular frame bulked as large as any there, except the largest orcs. The nameless necromancer sniffed suspiciously. That would be the Otherworld marine's aura, Ashnak guessed. He gestured for the Man to continue.

'Well, it's just this, sir.' John H. Stryker shifted his feet uncomfortably. His blue eyes met Ashnak's.

'I know the Bugs are supposed to be these homicidal, mindless, alien psychopaths and killing-machines,' John H. Stryker said, 'but has anyone ever tried just *talking* to them?'

Some thirty minutes later, at a forward gun position on the edge of the line of hills, the small orc major said, 'It *might* work, sir.'

Ashnak ducked down behind the sandbag walls. 'Are you out of your mind, Major?'

'Nossir!' Barashkukor protested. His cyborg eye whirred, left its socket, and extended on a jointed steel rod. With some care the small orc extended it over the sandbags of the hillside gun emplacement.

Having chewed up the Light's armoured infanty in the streets of Ferenzia, and mangled the crack elf cavalry on the plain beyond, the Bug soldiers were just becoming visible through the haze. Walking towards them, carrying a white flag on a pole, Sergeant John H. Stryker of the US Marine Corps strode down the track from the hills.

'A brave Man!' Barashkukor enthused. 'A true marine! Don't you think so, Supreme Commander?'

'I think the Dragon's Curse has a lot to answer for.' Supreme Commander Ashnak lowered his binoculars and grunted, crouching over the orc marine with an RT backpack, phoneset in his other taloned hand. 'At odds of fifteen to one against us, I'll try anything. Let's hope the Visible College's translation talismans work, soldier.'

The distant figure of John H. Stryker reached his goal.

Barashkukor focused his extended eye.

'I see him, Supreme Commander! He's . . . he's talking to them!'

Heat haze jumbled the air. As if through running water, Major Barashkukor watched the blond crew-cut Man sergeant.

The Man stood before a semi-circle of Bugs gathering around him. They towered over his six-feet height by eighteen inches or more. The sun gleamed blue from their black carapaces and dripping jaws. Dust stained their hard exoskeletons, and their black living-metal weapons were dull shapes of menace.

Stryker drove the pole of the truce flag into the dirt.

Barashkukor watched the Man wave his arms. Through the heat haze, it was visible how his lips moved. The great carapaced heads of the Bugs dipped and swayed. One extruded foot-long inner jaws and salivated.

The saliva burned holes in the earth.

'They're not attacking him, sir! They're listening to him!'

Barashkukor's cyborg eye tracked left and right. Through the dust, the light kept flashing back from harness, weapons and chitin shells. The advance line of Bugs wavered, slowed . . .

'It's working!' Barashkukor jumped up and down on the spot. His eye-stilt jerked to and fro.

The Supreme Commander (Dark and Light Forces) lifted his head from the radio set. 'Mission successful, Major?'

In the sharply focused view of Barashkukor's metal eye, the Bugs around Sergeant John H. Stryker stepped towards the Man on their skeletal hind legs. Their shining heads rose up, and they raised their clawed forefeet patiently. Stryker turned. Even over the long distance Barashkukor could see the broad smile on the Man's face.

The orc's long ears perked up and his small tusks gleamed. *'Supreme Commander, sir, mission successful! —oh.'*

Stryker's head exploded in a rain of meat.

The Bug who had impaled him on an extensible rigid tongue let the body drop. The other Bugs moved in, jaws dripping, feeding quickly and messily.

'Oh, well.' The small orc sighed. His eye whirred, sank down, and clicked home into its socket. 'Not entirely successful, sir. They ate him. *Incoming!'*

CRAAAACK!

A wavering bolt of blue fire impacted with the hillside forty yards away. The explosion threw up dirt and bedrock. Two or three pieces of debris bounced off Barashkukor's helmet where the small orc crouched in the corner of the emplacement.

'Time we got *serious* about this,' Supreme Commander Ashnak announced. 'Command group moving back. Go, go, *go!'*

'I'll drive, sir!' Barashkukor leaped lop-sidedly into the jeep after the rest of the grunts and pushed his cyborg foot down on the accelerator. The vehicle jolted down the far side of the hill, spraying showers of dirt and grit. Barashkukor whooped, one steel and one orc-hand wrestling with the wheel. Ashnak tightened the strap on his helmet.

'Forward unit engaged!' the orc marine radio operator yelped. She listened to the headset and added, 'Captain Hashnabul reports a problem, Supreme Commander – the grunts keep stopping to invent suitable tortures for Bug prisoners.'

Ashnak's helmet cracked against the rollbar 'Dammit, tell them they're not supposed to be taking prisoners anyway!'

'Oh, they don't have any prisoners yet, sir. They're just inventing the tortures . . .'

Barashkukor spun the wheel and ran the jeep up an impossible slope. The vehicle's wheels spun. The small orc reached out and seized a juniper stump with his cyborg arm and pulled, and the jeep pivoted and came down on a path made by the tracks of tanks. One of the orc marine runners left the vehicle on the bounce, and Major Barashkukor somewhat reluctantly stopped to let her climb back on board before he gunned the engine and shot off again.

'Isn't this thrilling, sir?'

'Thrilling,' Ashnak growled, recovering his cigar from the body of the jolting vehicle. He jammed it in the side of his mouth. 'Dammit, Major, can't you get any *speed* out of this thing?'

CRAAAAAAAAAAAAAACKK!

White plasma-fire split the dust and exploded against the cliff in front. One-handed, Major Barashkukor spun the wheel. The jeep swerved violently, successfully avoided the landslip, and jolted on towards the rear of the orc marine company.

'For you, Commander.' The RT orc passed the handset over to Ashnak.

'Lieutenant Chahkamnit here, sir. I say, what an absolutely cracking good show this is, sir!'

Ashnak chewed his cigar. 'What's your position, Lieutenant?'

'Directly over yours, sir.'

The big orc caught hold of a strut and leaned out of the jeep, gazing up at a blue afternoon sky that appeared completely empty. 'Can't see you, Chahkamnit.'

'No, sir, of course you can't. I'm piloting the stealth dragon, sir.'

Barashkukor's cyborg eye whirred into the infra-red. While his orc eye watched the road, his lens swivelled to study the heat-outlined shape of a dragon large enough to cover Ferenzia itself.

'Painted it with blue radar-reflective paint,' the Major approved. 'Smart idea, sir.'

Ashnak spat out the remnants of his chewed cigar. 'Take her down, Lieutenant Chahkamnit. Start giving me some fighter ground-attack!'

Another voice spluttered from the RT handset:

'Hai-yah, yo! Comin' in NOW!'

The jeep swerved wildly as both Ashnak and Barashkukor attempted simultaneously to watch the sky and the road. The small orc pointed with his orc-hand, steering with the metal one.

'There, sir!'

A squadron of winged white horses wheeled over the hills in perfect formation. Stark against the blue sky were the Hellfire missiles under each wing. Their riders, mail byrnies flashing in the sun, the wind whipping the fur of their leggings and their long yellow braids, dug their heels into the flanks of the pegasi, urging them on with shrieks and cries.

'Going in!'

The Valkyrie marines peeled off and pitched down towards the plain. A laser-guided missile fired and left a searing trail across the sky. A bolt of blue light leaped up from the plain's dust. The Valkyrie marines folded their wings as one, dived for speed, and came in low and hard over the target area. A female voice crackled over the RT:

'Dah dah-dah DAH dah, Dah dah-dah DAH dah . . .'

Barashkukor dragged the jeep's wheel round and steered behind a granite ridge, jouncing out into sunlight at the end of it. His commanding officer's hand smacked him smartly across the back of the head. His helmet rang.

'—and *stop* when I tell you!' The great orc leapt from the slowing jeep and loped across to a squad of grunts at the end of the ridge. Sun glinted through the ribs of the Special Undead Services.

'Give me a sit-rep,' Supreme Commander Ashnak demanded.

Lieutenant Lugashaldim saluted, skeletal fingers touching his rotting beret. The lenses of his sunglasses reflected unearthly shapes in their curve.

'Setting up a crack sniper squad here, sir.' The lich orc marine indicated the rest of the Undead grunts nestling into hollows in the rock, overlooking the plain below. 'See, sir, the main difference between an orc who'll make a good sniper and an orc who won't is heartbeat. Shakes the sights, sir. Well, naturally enough, Undead orcs make the best sniper-teams.'

Ashnak nodded his tusked head. 'What results are you getting?'

'Following the standard procedure, sir. Shooting to maim, not kill, so that the enemy will have to risk fire to rescue the injured soldier, with subsequent effect on their moral.' The Undead orc removed his sunglasses. Pinpricks of red shone in his mummified eye sockets. 'All very well, sir, but these Bugs don't seem at all bothered by their mates being wounded. They just leave them writhing, sir.'

'Keep shooting to maim, in any case,' Ashnak ordered. 'It'll have a good effect on *our* lads' morale.'

'Sir, yes, sir!' Lugashaldim sighed. 'Only wish I had more of the SUS on hand here. As it is, sir, we're only a skeleton staff.'

'How many of you are there?'

'Just the nine, sir.'

The *crack!* and *whumph!* of mortar and artillery fire shook the hills. Puffs of dirt shot up on the plain below. Major Barashkukor gunned the jeep's motor as soon as his commanding officer vaulted back into the front seat, and sped off, overtaking a column of T54s deploying to the front.

Hooves thundered behind Barashkukor. The small orc jerked his attention back to the road. A troop of black horses split to gallop past the jeep, hoofs cutting the earth. The riders, black cloaks swirling to disclose shining spiked black armour, spurred their thundering steeds. Barashkukor coaxed a tad more out of the engine, keeping level.

'Where the fuck do you think *you're* going?' Ashnak bawled, deep orc-voice rising above hoofbeats and whining gears.

The hood of the last rider slid down. It disclosed rat's-tail black hair, and a piebald grey-and-black face snarling in a rictus of fear.

The nameless necromancer freed one patchwork-gloved hand from the reins to point wildly down at Ferenzia and the plain.

'We've been overrun! We're all going to die!'

Ashnak's upper lip pulled back from his tusks in a snarl. 'You're a *necromancer*, dammit. It isn't death – it's a learning experience!'

The troop of black riders kept pace with the jeep, hoofs kicking up the heavy golden dust. Barashkukor glanced sideways. His commanding orc, squat in urban camouflage battledress, held the front bar of the jeep with one hand, and with the other unbuckled the flap of his pistol holster.

'I've got a forty-five calibre Colt automatic here that says you're going back to the front line!'

The black riders wheeled and plunged away down a trail that led back into the hills, where anyone might conceal themselves and hide from catastrophic defeat. The nameless necromancer, his silver-threaded leather robe flying, snarled an obscenity at Ashnak.

'Fly, fool of an orc! Or stay here and die!'

FOOM!

'Good *shot,* sir!'

Barashkukor's metal eye extended above his helmet and stared back down the road. A riderless horse fell back, reins trailing. A dark figure slumped on the dirt track in a splash of intestines.

'He'll be back,' Ashnak said. 'Yo! Here, Major. I said *here*. I *said—*'

An orc fist impacted on the side of Barashkukor's helmet.

'—STOP!'

Airbursts and groundbursts shook the world as Barashkukor slewed the jeep to a halt in an artillery emplacement. Camouflage netting blocked the sky, filling in the gulley. The battery of guns faced the plain below. The small orc slipped the jeep's ignition keys into his pocket and followed his commanding orc over to the forward observation post.

'Estimate—' *whirr-clk!* '—upwards of sixteen thousand hostiles, Supreme Commander.'

The radio orc and the runners clustered around Ashnak as the great orc surveyed the plain below through field glasses. Writhing lines of marines and Bugs became visible through the dust, then vanished again. Monitoring headquarter's radio traffic brought a constant stream of situation reports. Barashkukor picked out an elvish voice among the radio traffic.

'*I don't care if it is orders, Sergeant! Marines never retreat!*'

'*No, L.t.,*' Dakashnit's laconic voice answered Lieutenant Gilmuriel. '*'Course not. Think of it as "advancing to the rear".*'

379

Without looking, Supreme Commander Ashnak snapped his talons for the handset. 'Ashnak to command post, Ashnak to command post. Commissar Razitshakra – keep pulling 'em back. Get 'em *out* of there. Over.'

'I copy, Commander.' Razitshakra's voice crackled. *'Command post to all units, repeat, command post to all units. Fall back. Repeat, fall back now!'*

Orc gun crews pounded past Barashkukor to their stations but did not fire. Bio-tech Captain Ugarit emerged from the back of one of several Bedford trucks parked under the camouflage netting. The skinny orc spotted Barashkukor, stared fixedly at the major's metal arm and leg, and began to drool.

'Tech-Captain!'

Bio-tech Captain Ugarit sidled past Barashkukor and approached Ashnak. Dust, oil and less recognizable stains covered his long white coat and the uniform beneath. A succession of studs, chains and feathers dangled from his pierced, pointed ears.

'Sir!' The skinny orc tugged at Ashnak's sleeve. The Supreme Commander lowered his field glasses. Ugarit gabbled, 'May I try it, sir, please may I; never get another chance like this, sir, *please*?'

'Wait.' Ashnak lifted his field glasses again, studying the plain.

The roiling dust began to clear now, a light breeze blowing from the east. Thin lines of light seared criss-cross. The woodpecker-rattle of automatic fire sounded incessantly. Cordite stung. The heavy cough of artillery rang out further down the line of hills.

Sixteen thousand Bugs advanced towards the orc marine defensive positions.

Supreme Commander Ashnak regarded the battle.

'Captain Ugarit, are we loaded up?'

The skinny orc saluted with the wrong hand. 'Yes, Lord General!'

Ashnak lifted the radio orc's handset to his tusked mouth. 'Artillery crew, on my mark – *fire!*'

A thunderous barrage broke out over Barashkukor's head. The small orc rapidly retrieved the chunks of cotton wool from his uniform jacket and stuffed them into his ears. The gun muzzles recoiled, carriages jolting; and the suck and concussion of the air beat at him, the noise resounding in his torso and testicles.

WHOMMMMPH!

The bright afternoon shook. Barashkukor staggered to the forward observation post and peered through the gaps between the sandbags.

At first the battlefield appeared no different. Then, from the craters of the artillery strikes, Barashkukor noticed a yellow mist drifting across the plain.

Helicopter gunships whipped overhead, rocket motors spurting from the missiles they fired. Barashkukor followed their tracks to the earth below. More sluggish and low-lying yellow fog caught the breeze and drifted away from the missile strike areas.

'*Ranging shots are good.*' Supreme Commander Ashnak's voice approved. '*Bio-tech Captain Ugarit, continue to target according to previous strikes.*'

'You got it, Commander!'

Barashkukor stared at Ashnak. The big orc leaned his elbows on the sandbags and turned his glasses on the uneven ground between Ferenzia and the hills. The sun, hardly an hour past noon, filtered in beams through the slowly drifting mists.

The small orc thumbed his helmet radio. '*Sir, what is that, sir?*'

'*That, Major,*' Ashnak's voice crackled over the radio, in Barashkukor's cotton-blocked ear, '*is chemical warfare. Mustard and nerve gas. That over there is sarin and tabun, mostly, with some lewisite, and a little anthrax for entertainment value.*'

WHOMPH! *FOOM!* WHOMMPH!

'*Oh, yes! Oh, yes! Took it from Dagurashibanipal's hoard, I did. Adapted it! Lots of lovely dead Bugs to play with. I've genetically tailored it for them and not us, we're safe, but they're not!*'

Filled with irresistible emotion, Major Barashkukor seized the gibbering Ugarit's hand and shook it firmly. 'Oh, well done!'

'Thank you . . .' Ugarit retained a vice-like grip on Barashkukor's metal hand, whipped out a magnifying glass, and began to subject it to close scrutiny. Barashkukor wrenched it away.

'*Commander Ashnak to command post – give me the field units' situation reports.*'

Commissar Razitshakra's deep orcish tones over the open channel broke with emotion. '*Commander, the Bugs are dropping right, left and centre!*'

The small orc major leaped for the sandbagged wall, his cyborg leg propelling him smartly upwards. Clinging to the top of the emplacement, Barashkukor focused his long-distance sight on the battlefield.

'It's true, sir! It's true! They're going down! We've done it!'

The great orc said grimly, 'Now let's put the real barrage down. Captain Ugarit!'

Barashkukor, amazed, stood up and pushed his helmet back on his head. His long ears sprang upright. 'No, sir, *wait.*'

The small orc scrabbled down, lost his grip, and fell heavily on his commanding officer's boots. He got to his feet, pointing excitedly towards the plain. 'Sir, what's that?'

Far out on the plain, visible to technology-assisted eyes, a unit of

381

thirty or forty Bugs clustered on high ground. Burning trees and buildings marked the hill as one of the outlying hamlets on the road from Ferenzia to the north. The yellow fog swirled about the foot of the rise, clinging to the low-lying earth below the one or two hovels left standing.

None of the Bugs were firing their weapons.

One Bug, taller than the rest, its exoskeleton a gleaming ebony, held something in its front claws. As Supreme Commander Ashnak stared through his field glasses, he recognized John H. Stryker's pole and white pennant.

The Bug raised its arms and frantically waved the white flag.

'Cheeky *bugger!*' the orc major yelped. 'Land the next barrage smack on that position, sir. Of all the nerve – offering to surrender to *orcs.*'

Bio-tech Captain Ugarit yelled, 'Artillery group, depress elevation—'

· Ashnak brought his fist down on the top of Ugarit's head. The skinny orc folded like a dropped brick. Ashnak rumbled, 'All artillery units on stand-by. Repeat, on stand-by. *No one* fires without my order.'

'But *sir!*' Barashkukor protested.

Supreme Commander Ashnak surveyed the battlefield outside Ferenzia, the white flag, and the clouds of nerve gas even now dissolving on the slight easterly breeze.

He picked up the radio handset.

'All units – cease fire! Say again: *cease fire.* Commissar Razitshakra, I'm taking a unit out to grid reference oh-seven-three nine-eight-zero. I'm going to accept the enemy's surrender.'

11

THE YELLOW-WHITE Class G star seared down through the smoke of burning trees and native buildings. Two rotor-driven flying machines rested on the scorched fields. A cordon of indigenous life forms surrounded the blitzed village on the hill, their curiously separable weapons pointed at the Jassik soldiers. Hive Commander Kah-Sissh regarded the hot, smelly, fleshly body of the nearest indigenous life form – so suitable for incubating eggs – and clicked his mandibles in regret. His salivating hiss sounded above the susurration of the wounded, and the rotors of the natives' flying machines:

'I am Hive Commander Kah-Sissh.'

'Supreme Commander Ashnak,' the life form growled. 'Pleased to make your acquaintance.'

Fifty metres away a Jassik soldier rolled, black carapace shredding in the clinging yellow gas. Exoskeletal limbs sprouted, malformed; desperately attempted to re-grow. She finally dissolved into a metallic black sludge, self-repair mechanisms run wild.

Hive Commander Kah-Sissh spat, 'It is our dishonour to surrender ourselves to you, indigenous life-form!'

The native scratched with taloned manipulators at the division of its bifurcated trunk.

'That's "orc" to you.' Its tusked head lifted, staring up at the Jassik Hive Commander, and it jerked one of its opposable thumbs at the only native hovel left standing in the area. 'Inside!'

383

The translation device that the other native had carried burned against Kah-Sissh's thorax. He understood. The novelty of studying these creatures other than to kill them momentarily took his interest.

Hive Commander Kah-Sissh looked up at the three-storey building, set like an island here where two major roads crossed: north-south and east-west. A creaking wooden panel suspended on the frontage bore a two-dimensional image – one of the native beasts of burden, portrayed as rearing in an anatomically unlikely manner.

'I consent.' Hive Commander Kah-Sissh hissed an order. Thirty exoskeletal Jassik heels clicked down on to the dirt. The command escort's lines straightened up smartly, their carapaced heads jutting forward in a uniform position, odorous slime dripping down and eating into the soil at their feet. Kah-Sissh's thorax expanded with a desperate pride.

'Battlemaster! Flightmaster! To me!'

Two of the largest Jassik stepped out, black metal harnesses glittering on their articulated thoraxes, disruptor and blaster power cables growing from their backs. The raised marks grown into the chitin of their shoulders marked them as high-ranking officers, suitable to accompany Kah-Sissh into disgrace.

'Awright, awright!' The native life-form did something to its dead-metal weapon that made it click. 'I'm not running a goddamn party here. Get your Bug asses inside there, sharp!'

The Battlemaster and Flightmaster followed Kah-Sissh into the low-beamed structure. The Jassik Hive Commander picked his way distastefully through the overturned chairs, tables, and broken glass of what was obviously a shell-battered civilian hostelry.

'This will suffice for the Immolation of Disgrace,' Kah-Sissh announced, seating himself in the middle of the floor and gazing down at the fleshy bipeds.

'Not in this here inn, you don't!' a portly native of the Man variety announced, bustling out from behind the long bench that stretched the length of the room. ''Scuse me, master orc, but are these . . . "visitors" with you?'

Kah-Sissh watched Supreme Commander Ashnak draw himself up to his full height and glare round the interior of the inn. 'This is where I'm holding our top secret, highly confidential peace negotiations. Any objections?'

There was a clink of glasses from seats in a niche by the chimney that Kah-Sissh took to be the local heating-source. Several much smaller natives, the curly hair on their pedal extremities grizzled and grey, raised button-black eyes to the orc.

'Holding peace negotiations, is it?' one remarked.

''Oo's stopping you, boy?' another commented. 'So long as us halflings gets a quiet drink, we doesn't care. Does we, Walter?'

'That us don't, Matthew. That us don't. Got better things to do than listen to orcs.' The more elderly of the halflings grumbled, sinking its mouth into a tankard. 'By the Light! But it's getting hard to find a good pint, what with the war an' all. I recall as how you used to get a good pint at The Dog and Leggit—'

Hive Commander Kah-Sissh tapped the translation device hanging from his thorax, and despite himself queried: '"The Dog and Leggit"?'

'Ar,' the elderly halfling, Walter, replied. 'Inn over at Bremetys, that were. Called that on account of you threw up over the dog, and then you legged it.'

Kah-Sissh eventually decoded the small natives' hissing expirations as amusement.

'Cider was better in The Dragon's Nest,' the third halfling drinker remarked, from a seat at the back of the snug. 'Whatever 'appened to The Dragon's Nest?'

''Undred and fifty five millimetre, six rounds of,' Walter remarked dolefully. 'Drink ain't never been the same since this 'ere danged *fighting.*'

The portly Man bustled across the inn floor and bowed to the orc commander, his gaze sliding sideways to Kah-Sissh. 'If you gentlesirs will wait just one moment, I'll set you up a table. Dick! Tom! Drat it, where have those lads gone?'

Kah-Sissh watched as the portly innkeeper stomped into the back of the building. His keen hearing caught the Man's muttering:

'. . . don't know what it's all coming to; all we had to contend with in the old days was cloaked strangers in hoods, and sometimes a disappearing halfling or two; the odd black rider; t'isn't like we had all these new-fangled *Bugs* to put up with . . .'

The outer door banged. A smaller uniformed orc entered and marched up to its commander. 'Supreme Commander Ashnak, sir, you *can't* agree to let these things surrender! We can wipe them out to a Bug, sir. Strategically it's the only thing to do.'

The small biped lowered its voice, its eyes on Kah-Sissh. The Hive Commander noted how its spindly ears drooped, under the rim of its dead-metal helmet.

'We're orcs, sir,' it whispered. 'We can't go around sparing enemies. The grunts will never stand for it. We'll never live it down!'

Another of the orc-bipeds strode in, completely ignoring Kah-Sissh and the other Jassik. This one wore a long, olive-drab garment over battle-stained fatigues; and peaked headgear.

'Barashkukor's right, sir. It isn't the Way of the Orc, sparing enemies. Why have you stopped the battle? We ought to massacre—'

The large orc commander pointed his dead-metal weapon at the ceiling and pulled the trigger.

FOOM!

A proportion of the ceiling vaporized. Chunks of plaster drifted down, whitening the Hive Commander's battle-scarred carapace. Kah-Sissh brushed himself clean. The halfling drinkers in the hearth-snug glanced up momentarily, then returned to a game they were playing with black-and-white spotted counters.

'I protest!' Kah-Sissh hissed. 'The dignity of these proceedings is severely impaired, Supreme Commander Ashnak, by your continued failure to observe the correct ceremonies.'

The large orc ignored Kah-Sissh, rounding on his underlings. 'If I say these are peace negotiations, these are *peace* negotiations. Are you receiving me, marines?'

'*Sir, yes, sir!*'

'Good . . .' The orc bared his teeth as more be-weaponed orcs entered the inn, taking up covering positions at the hostelry's windows. They had an encouragingly exoskeletal appearance – but it was not, the Jassik Hive Commander noted with regret, natural to the species.

'We have not surrendered to an honourable enemy,' Kah-Sissh announced to the Battlemaster and Flightmaster.

'No, Hive Commander.' The Flightmaster extended her jaws, acid saliva etching the hostelry's wooden floor. 'Are they are of sufficient honour even to witness the Immolation of Disgrace?'

Before Hive Commander Kah-Sissh could express his opinion, the large orc stomped across the floor towards the Jassik. He pulled out a chair from the table a young Man had just set upright and covered with a white cloth, and seated himself; throwing one booted hind limb over the chair's arm, his battle-stained peaked cap shading his deep-set eyes.

'Welcome to the peace talks,' he announced jovially.

'My Swarm Commander is damaged,' Kah-Sissh mourned. 'Regretfully, therefore, we cannot treat with you, orc commander.'

'No kidding?' The Supreme Commander grinned, a not-particularly reassuring sight. 'I've got an orc here who's just aching to try out our full range of biological and chemical warfare devices on your other Bug divisions. Isn't that right, Bio-tech Captain Ugarit?'

A muffled 'Yessir!' came through the glass faceplate of a breathing mask worn by a skinny green biped.

The Supreme Commander frowned. 'Ugarit, you're certain that nerve gas out there is harmless to orcs?'

'Oh, yes, Supreme Commander! Completely and utterly sure, Supreme Commander! Absolutely and totally – *awk!*'

The big orc regarded the breathing mask that he now held in his large paw, sniffed at it, and slung it over his shoulder. It bounced off a sleeping quadruped in the corner, which fled, yelping. The skinny green orc clasped its fingers over its mouth, enormous eyes staring at Kah-Sissh.

'I'm sure you'll see your way clear to negotiating,' Supreme Commander Ashnak surmised.

'Excuse me, gentlesirs.' The portly Man innkeeper looked out from a door behind the bar. 'Times is hard, master orc. All we has of the menu is pony stew, and none too fresh, either.'

'Pony stew? My favourite. Serve up, innkeeper!'

The Battlemaster looked across at Kah-Sissh from where she sat with one exoskeletal arm about the shoulders of the Flightmaster.

'You want *my* opinion,' she said crisply, 'the Immolation of Disgrace is out. Waste of time with these "orcs", Hive Commander. Wouldn't make any impression on them at all.'

Kah-Sissh rattled his jaws in a sigh. 'I refuse to accept that, Battlemaster, until it is proven beyond all doubt.'

The orc commander took a container from the approaching young Man servant and drained it, slopping half the contents down his splotch-patterned battle gear. To Kah-Sissh's complete confusion the orc then took out a roll of dried vegetable matter, set fire to one end of the cylinder, put it between his jaws, and inhaled the smoke. The Hive Commander's metal-enhanced jaws sensed alcohol and toxins; a possibly flammable mixture.

'It's like this.' The orc exhaled a plume of smoke. 'You guys can quit fighting now and we can come to an agreement. A mutually beneficial agreement. Or else my grunts abandon the truce, carry on fighting, and you're fucked. Do I make myself plain? —*URP!'*

The weight of the translation device on Kah-Sissh's thorax was negligible now. The language of the orc came to him almost naturally. With a sigh, bowing to the inevitable, the Hive Commander expanded all the plates of his thorax, drawing in the oxy-nitrogen atmosphere, and copied the orc's ceremonial eructation:

'URRRRP!'

The orc commander picked himself up off the floorboards, and set his chair upright again. The smaller orc rushed up with a brush and whisked it down his commander's battledress, recovered the peaked cap, and handed it to the big orc.

'*OK* . . .' the orc supreme commander beamed. 'You're getting the hang of this. Let's talk.'

Kah-Sissh inclined his carapaced head. 'I do not understand, commander. You have sent a hive-sibling of yours out to me, to teach me your manner of surrender. You have killed my hive-kin. What else is there to discuss except our extermination at your hands?'

The Flightmaster added, 'The Jassik are never defeated!'

'You see, sir?' The small orc, Major Barashkukor, appeared again at the table. A white cloth was draped over his arm, and he pushed a wheeled trolley on which sat porcelain bowls and a container of steaming liquid. 'Marines are marines, sir, even if they are Bugs. One lump or two?'

Kah-Sissh watched the orc pour yellow liquid from the container into the bowls, add a white liquid (that the Hive Commander's sensors informed him was mammal-derived) and two small crystalline lumps. The orc major placed the bowl on to a second, much shallower bowl, and extended it towards Kah-Sissh.

'Allow me, Hive Commander.' The Battlemaster took the two bowls in her front claws, picked up one, her smallest claw jutting out, and sipped. Lights flickered across her living-metal battle harness. 'Non-toxic. Mmm . . .'

The orc Supreme Commander reached across to a glass container on the trolley. 'I'll have something stronger.'

Supreme Commander Ashnak knocked the top of the container off in a shower of shards, and tipped a darker brown liquid down his throat. Hive Commander Kah-Sissh watched the orc for a moment to see if another ceremonial eructation was required. It apparently was not.

Kah-Sissh took his own set of bowls from Major Barashkukor, and sipped delicately. 'There is nothing to discuss except the manner of the Jassik's extermination.'

'Now that's where you're wrong, son.'

Kah-Sissh hesitated. His metal-assisted mandibles twitched on the air. Lights flickered on his body harness and he touched the devices with the tip of one claw. He lowered his shining black head until his faceted eyes were on a level with Supreme Commander Ashnak's face. '*Wonderful* beverage . . . what isssh it that you call it?'

The orc stared at Kah-Sissh, who beamed back at him. The small orc major interrupted the silence.

'Tea, Hive Commander, sir. It's called "tea".'

'Marvellous.' Kah-Sissh extended his dripping jaws in pleasure. His faceted eyes glimmered. 'Where was I? Oh, yes. Our honour requires us to perish, now, at our own hands. Each and every one of us. *Qweep!*'

The big orc scratched at his bald head and peaked ears, and drew on the smoking vegetable-matter again.

'I've been watching you boys,' Ashnak said affably, 'on satellite. You're not from around these parts, are you, son? I co-ordinated reports from my combat units, and plotted the directions you guys have been coming in from. Well, some of you came out of Thyrion, and some of you from Gyzrathrani, and some from the Antarctic Icelands. But that's not the interesting part.'

Hive Commander Kah-Sissh extruded his dripping jaws slightly, then retracted them. 'I will sssay nothing more than is required by the honour of war. *Qweep!*'

'That's our commander!' The Battlemaster waved her own tea-dish in an extravagent claw. 'Perish at the height of military glory! No prisoners! *Qweeeep!*'

'Riiight . . .' The orc commander looked somewhat askance at Kah-Sissh, picked up the tea-bowl, and sniffed at it. The small orc major and the skinny orc technician looked at each other, looked at the bowls, shrugged, and shook their heads.

Kah-Sissh beamed at the Battlemaster, and the empty space beside her. Momentarily sobered, he looked for the Flightmaster.

A female orc voice explained, 'That's called *double top . . .*'

The Jassik Flightmaster, her carapaced head bent so as to avoid the plastered ceiling, stood beside the squat orc in the long coat and spectacles. Both faced the wall of the inn, where a small concentric-ringed target hung. The orc pointed, lifted another tiny fletched arrow, and hurled it at the target.

'*Qweep!* I see, I see!' the Flightmaster exclaimed excitedly. She extruded from her chitinous underparts a large black living-metal weapon, hefted it up on to her shoulder, aimed, and pulled its trigger.

HHZAAAKKKK!

The hanging target vanished, as did a sizeable chunk of the wall.

'Game!' the Flightmaster exclaimed sibilantly.

Kah-Sissh noted the orc commander glance over his shoulder, catch the eye of the female orc, and murmur 'Let the Jassik win,' before turning back to the conference table.

'As I was saying.' Ashnak's voice rumbled deep enough to vibrate through Kah-Sissh's thorax. His dark eyes gleamed. 'You Bugs are coming in from the four corners of the earth. I want the answer to one question. My orcs have plotted you and those six other Bug divisions on the map table, extending your lines of advance to see where they intersect, and what your objective is. Now answer me one thing, Hive

Commander – why is it that all your forces, without exception, are headed straight for the middle of the Inland Sea?'

'Ah, the Sssssea . . .' Hive Commander Kah-Sissh sighed. He was peripherally aware of the small orc major refilling his tea-bowl. He lowered his mandibles and drank, finally lifting his shining head to survey the orc supreme commander.

'Your ssseas are too deep,' Kah-Sissh explained, careful with a speech that seemed to contain entirely too many sibilants. 'And your lakess are too cold. We need a ssufficiently ssshallow, warm and large body of water.'

All the orcs gathered behind their commander, the squat female peering through her wire-rimmed lenses; the skinny technician and the small major gazing wide-eyed at the Jassik.

'What in the name of the Dark do you need a *sea* for?' the orc commander demanded.

Expansive in the admiration of his new friends, Kah-Sissh waved a claw and elaborated.

'This is a cold world, Commander, and I find it ssuch a trial to be continually breathing oxygen! Had our starship not broken up in your star's gravitational field, we should not have sss-set claw upon your pathetic little world. But we fell in our escape pods as our great ship broke up and burned . . .'

The skinny orc leaped from foot to foot, and bent to whisper something in Supreme Commander Ashnak's pointed ear. Kah-Sissh hummed pleasurably to himself. The Battlemaster slumped against his chitinous shoulder, half-full tea bowl slopping from her claw as she buzzed in deep slumber.

'So why,' the orc persisted, 'head for the Inland Sea?'

Kah-Sissh shrugged. 'It is most suitable for incubating a ship-egg.'

'A *ship* egg?' the orc said. 'A ship-*egg?*'

'A starship-egg.'

'Yo!' The skinny orc technician slavered in an almost-civilized fashion. 'They can grow weapons! They can grow star-travelling ships! Wonderful!'

'There is the difficult matter of finding a beast large enough to serve as host.' Kah-Sissh inhaled again the warm, pungent smell of the orc bipeds. 'Then it is merely a matter of subduing this paltry planet while we wait for the ship to grow, then off again to the stars, and further worlds to conquer for the Hive!'

A low buzzing sounded from the other side of the inn room. Kah-Sissh looked across the expanse of overturned chairs and broken window glass. The Flightmaster, audibly asleep, had curled up under a table with the four-footed furry quadruped sleeping on her thorax.

390

Hive Commander Kah-Sissh took a coldly oxygen-scented breath, compressed his thorax-plates, and began to wail a Jassik drinking medley.

'Hive Commander – I say, *Hive Commander!*' The big orc stood, glaring up into Kah-Sissh's mandibles as the Jassik beat time with one waving claw. 'Now don't you fade out on me, boy!'

A dose of cold air shocked Kah-Sissh back into coordination. He rattled his mandibles sulkily at orc Major Barashkukor, who had opened a window.

'We ssshall not perform the Immolation of Disgrace,' Kah-Sissh remarked, his tone petulant. 'It would be wasted on such savages. We are the Jassik, proud and noble warriors!'

The orc major and technician simultaneously muttered something that sounded to Kah-Sissh very like, 'Psychopathic mindless alien killing-machines!'

'So tell me,' the orc commander demanded, 'if all you needed to do was get from your crash-sites to the Inland Sea, why butcher your way through from there to here?'

Hive Commander Kah-Sissh, hurt, protested, 'We *like* killing things.'

Supreme Commander Ashnak and Major Barashkukor exchanged glances.

'I can identify with that, sir,' the small orc remarked.

The big orc sat down at the table and put his head in his hands, only sitting up when the Man landlord emerged from the kitchens with a bowl of burned muscle-tissue, steaming odorously.

'Pony stew?' Supreme Commander Ashnak offered.

Kah-Sissh hissed a nauseous moan. In order to bring dignity to the proceedings the Jassik Hive Commander rose on to his hind limbs, clicked his claws, and began the delicate movements of the Dance of Lesser Victory Concealed In Overwhelming Defeat. The Battlemaster fell over, snoring. Kah-Sissh caught his foot in one of the drinkers at the bar (halfling and tray going flying) and sat down in a clatter of living-metal weaponry. He raised his great head to find himself surrounded and covered by the dead-metal implements of the orc marine guard.

'About our deal,' the seated orc commander, Ashnak, said through a mouthful of dead, cooked flesh.

Hive Commander Kah-Sissh's faceted eyes glimmered. 'Our Swarm Master perished, but there are other Hive Commanders such as myself, and they, be assured, will dance the Immolation of Disgrace, and burn your paltry continent down to the bedrock!'

'Nerve gas,' the orc reminded him. 'We can dust off every one of your divisions, son.'

391

Kah-Sissh froze.

The orc smiled. 'I like a Bug that's susceptible to rational argument.'

'Peasants – *qweep!*' Hive Commander Kah-Sissh gathered the remnants of his dignity and rose from the floor, folding his exoskeletal limbs so that he seated himself again before the negotiating table. 'Rest assured, we ssshall not live to be your ssslaves.'

'Now who said anything about slavery?' The orc's beetling brows raised affably. He leaned both elbows on the table and smiled toothily up at the Jassik warrior. 'Access to the Inland Sea could be one of the terms of your surrender. If you want to grow your "ship-egg" and get your Bug asses off my world, then I sure as hell won't object.'

'In return,' Kah-Sissh said sharply, 'for what?'

'Ah. Yes. Believe it or not,' the big orc purred, 'there *is* somehing that you Bugs can do for me and the lads . . .'

The G-type star declined as the planet turned. Shadows lengthened.

Outside, Jassik warriors waiting at attention accepted with comradely gratitude the beverages offered by the local military life forms.

Before long, Jassik warrior songs hissed up to the stars.

Under them sounded the deep rumble of armoured divisions pulling back, of infantry regrouping, of air support patrolling the neutral ground between the two waiting armies, and of the occasional interchange of friendly fire.

12

'H ARD A-STARBOARD!' SUPREME
Commander Ashnak bellowed. 'Hard a-port! Lower the jib! Man the
tops'l! Pull, ye lubbers, *pull!*'

The quinquereme *SS Gibbet and Spigot* out of Graagryk heeled
into the wind. Massed ranks of orc rowers in DPM battledress and
steel helmets heaved on the oars, sweating under the cloudless,
windless blue sky.

Ashnak paced up and down the central walkway of the ship,
cracking his oiled leather whip. 'You're meant to be *marines*, aren't
you? Pull!'

He strode aft, past the glistening muscled backs of orcs stripped
down to combat trousers and boots. The galley's drummer kept a
rhythmic oar-stroke, to which Ashnak had been attempting to encourage the marines to sing sea-shanties. As a result, the port-side grunts
were giving a spirited rendition of 'How Much is that Shoggoth in the
Window?', loudly challenged by the starboard-side rowers chorusing
'Daddy Wouldn't Buy Me a Balrog'. The quinquereme wavered on a
somewhat indirect course across the limpid waters of the Inland Sea.

The waves glowed pearl-blue under a blazing sky. Ashnak lifted his
binoculars, spotting the wheeling pegasi of the Valkyrie marines
some klicks to the north, and the vast shadow of the stealth dragon on
the waves to the east. Twelve more galleys and sixteen sailing ships
kept a parallel course to the *SS Gibbet and Spigot*. There was no sign
of land.

Ashnak loped up on to the poop deck. 'Steady as she goes, pilot!'

Lieutenant-Colonel Dakashnit (a battlefield promotion) leaned on the vast spoked wheel, swinging it with one muscular black arm. She grinned and touched her GI pot. 'You got it, m'man!'

Major-General Barashkukor also saluted his commanding orc. 'Sir, flagship of the Graagryk Navy proceeding as you ordered, sir. We are entering deep waters now, sir . . .'

The small orc's features paled. He fixed Ashnak with bulging eyes, abruptly about-faced, and leaned over the back of the poop deck. Ashnak regarded his heaving shoulders. Ignoring the retching sounds, he slapped Barashkukor on the back. 'Well done, son!'

The patter of small but heavy feet warned him. Ashnak turned in time to catch a half-orc halfling as it hurled itself at his leg. He scooped the child up, threw it up into the air, and (after a split second's hesitation) caught it again. With its tiny taloned hand in his, Supreme Commander Ashnak crossed the poop deck.

'Pepin, sweetheart, don't annoy your father while he's working.' Honorary Colonel-in-Chief Magdelene of Graagryk absently patted the curly footed tot's head, avoiding its milk-fangs with practised ease. 'Go and play with your brothers and sisters.'

Magda Brandiman reclined at her ease in a long, cushion-padded chair resting on the deck. An orc stood behind her with a parasol, shading the Honorary Colonel from the sun; and Magda leaned back, the wind whipping her hair, and sipped from a tall glass full of alochol and fruit. Her infants sat at her feet, playing 'Hang-orc'. Her mirrored Raybans reflected Ashnak as she turned her head.

Ashnak gallantly kissed her free hand. 'We've been at sea for five hours, my love . . .'

'Trust me.' Magda hitched down her mirrorshades and gazed at her orc over the rims. 'Would I lie to you? Just keep on this course.'

The quinquereme wheeled again. Dozens of orc marines swarmed up the rigging, letting out the meagre sails to assist the rowers. Ashnak watched them swinging one-handed from ropes, rifles still slung across their backs. It became apparent that the port-side orc sailors were setting up an assault course through the lines and sheets.

'Splice the mainbrace!' Ashnak bellowed happily. 'Ship ahoy! Yo, ho, ho!'

The spate of orders had little or no effect on the ship's crew. The colour of the water under the *SS Gibbet and Spigot* changed to royal blue, and white foam flecked the waves. A line of orc marine rowers, their oars abandoned, leaned over the ship's side, vomiting. Ashnak noted those who threw up over the windward side for possible demotion.

394

'Sssupreme Commander . . .'

Ashnak turned at the hissed sibilants. The midday sun gleamed from the blue-black carapace and black metal harness of the Jassik Hive Commander. The Bug had wedged its long body and exo-skeletal hind legs into the corner of the poop deck, claw-hands gripping the rails.

'When . . .' Kah-Sissh lowered his shining head. 'When will this ssstorm abate, Commander?'

'That's "Admiral of the Fleet" to you, Kah-Sissh,' Ashnak said, cheerfully slapping the Bug on the back. He winced and blew on his palm. 'Storm? What storm? This is good sailing weather, this is!'

The Bug's faceted eyes dulled. Kah-Sissh's head slumped on to the rail, dribbling a thin trail of slime from extensible jaws.

'Our guest isn't well,' the big orc observed. 'Probably time for another meal. Barashkukor! Send down to the cook for some fat pork and poached eggs – and the remains of the jellyfish, if there's any left.'

'You're a cruel orc, my love,' Magda Brandiman observed.

'Nothing of the sort.' Ashnak held Major-General Barashkukor over the side by one leg to avoid the vomiting orc spraying him, and grinned toothily. 'Can I help it if I'm a good sailor? I'm a marine!'

Ashnak dropped Barashkukor back on the deck and drew a deep, satisfying breath. Under the smell of orc sweat and vomit, his hairy nostrils caught the scent of sun-hot wood and rope, of spices from the *SS Gibbet and Spigot*'s last commercial voyage, and the alien tang of the Jassik's bodily fluids. A whiff of pipe-weed made him look round.

'Man, you better come up with something soon, sir.' Pilot Dakashnit, now smoking a cigar, lazily spun the wheel. 'Them Bugs don't do at *all* well on water, but we still got six divisions of them sitting out there in the neutral zone, and patience is something they ain't got, sir.'

Ashnak donned his cocked hat, planted his bowed legs widely apart, and put his hands behind his back, gazing forrard. 'Trust me, soldier, I'm an orc.'

'*Stealth dragon to flagship, stealth dragon to flagship, over.*'

Admiral Ashnak stuck one hand into his naval topcoat. He removed it, holding a radio handset. 'Flagship receiving.'

'*I say, sir, wonderful view of you from up here! Life on the ocean wave, eh, what?*'

Ashnak stared up at the empty sky. 'Are you sure you're happy in your work, marine?'

'*Oh, yes, sir. Tophole! Well, you know what they say, sir. Life's a bitch, and then you fly . . .*'

Ashnak growled.

'*We may have just what you need*,' Wing Commander Chahkamnit's voice crackled hurriedly. '*Bearing zero nine three relative, sir. Distance five miles.*'

'Course change to zero nine three degrees!' Ashnak whooped.

The three grunts manning the tiller put their heads together, muttering. The largest counted on his fingers, pointed decisively, and declared, 'That way!'

The quinquereme wallowed, orc marines scurrying, no more than half a dozen falling overboard. The galley's bow bit deep into the waves. The oars rose and dipped furiously. A marine with flags semaphored wildly to the rest of the fleet, and the other ships began to wheel about and follow the SS *Gibbet and Spigot*'s wake.

'Man the guns!' Ashnak bellowed. Crews scurried towards the galley's ballistas, rail-mounted crossbows and six-inch naval artillery.

Magda Brandiman put down her empty glass. The halfling rose from her chair, smoothing down her white sun-dress, and walked elegantly across the deck to stand beside Ashnak, her head level with his belt-buckle. She put one hand to her sun-hat in the stiff breeze.

'I'm going forward,' she announced.

Ashnak strode down the central walkway behind the female halfling. A number of the orc marine rowers whistled and cheered, which the Colonel-Duchess of Graagryk acknowledged with a wave, never missing her footing. Ashnak loped up behind her into the bow.

'*THAR SHE BLOWS!*'

Ashnak fingered his ringing ear. He then wiped his talon down his naval jacket and glared at Tech-Colonel Ugarit. The skinny green orc hung over the rail, bow-wave intermittently soaking his white lab coat, pointing and yelling.

'*Thar she*—'

Ashnak seized one of the skinny orc's legs, and lifted. Ugarit vanished over the ship's side.

'—*heeaaarggh!*'

'I heard you the first time,' Ashnak growled.

The big orc leaned on the rail. Some yards below, Tech-Colonel Ugarit (having landed on the upper tier of oars) was clambering back up towards the ship's side. Ahead, there was nothing but the open sea. White waves flecked the deeps.

'Not seen, sir!' the elven lieutenant Gilmuriel reported to Ashnak. His golden eyes appeared slightly crossed. Ashnak looked at the elf marines, their dog-tags removed, who clustered round the enormous retro-fitted harpoon launcher that occupied all of the galley's bow-space. Most of the elf marines were leaning over the side of the ship.

'Sorry, sir,' Gilmuriel added, wiping at a stain on his woodland camouflage. 'You really need the Sea Elves for this, sir— *blehh!*'

Ashnak sidestepped smartly.

'Do I have to do *everything* myself?' The great orc leaned precariously over the rail, staring ahead through rubber-armoured binoculars. A sibilant hiss and Magda Brandiman's gracious greeting told him they had been joined by Hive Commander Kah-Sissh.

'There, sir.' Major-General Barashkukor tugged his commanding orc's sleeve. 'Sir, there, sir!'

'Where?'

'There!'

'I said – oh, fuck it!' Ashnak picked the orc major-general up by the back of his collar. 'Point, dammit!'

Ashnak followed the direction of the small orc's quivering finger. He narrowed his beetle-browed eyes.

At first the orc saw nothing. The Graagryk Navy appeared to be passing through a shallower part of the Inland Sea, brownish weed floating some distance under the surface. Ashnak slitted his eyes against the sun flashing off the waves. Salt crusted his nostrils as they flared to scent the air.

'Nothing!' he swore. 'Magda, woman, you told me the Kraken had been sighted here in the Inland Sea – well, where *is* it?'

Major-General Barashkukor continued to point, his skinny fingers shaking. The small orc made a mewling sound, dangling from Ashnak's fist, and a thin trickle of liquid spattered down on to the deck. Ashnak dropped him and leaped up to stand on the *SS Gibbet and Spigot*'s prow.

'*There*,' Magda Brandiman said.

From high on the prow, Ashnak looked across the waves to the fleet's smaller galleys and sailing ships. A pearl mist dulled the sun. The mass of shallow-water weed stretched out around the fleet to the horizon.

The brown weed's tendrils waved, thick as redwood trunks.

The brown weed opened one lazy golden eye and stared up at Ashnak.

Ashnak stared down at the vast, sea-encompassing coils of the Great Kraken.

'*Yo!*' The orc beamed and sprang down on to the deck. Ashnak strode to where, towering over the diminutive female halfling, Hive Commander Kah-Sissh stood on the quinquereme's deck. He grinned up at the exoskeletal Bug.

'Your egg needs its host living.' Ashnak jerked his thumb over his shoulder. 'New marine-issue harpoon system. Visible College magic, sleep-inducing weapons, guaranteed to put out *anything*.'

Tech-Colonel Ugarit, having regained the deck, dripped and muttered something about *field-tests* and *prototype models*.

Ashnak slapped Lieutenant Gilmuriel on the back, seized the elf marine's collar to prevent him ricocheting overboard, and bellowed, 'Load up and fire! Barashkukor! Signal all ships to fire at will! Go, go, go!'

Two hundred orc rowers dug their heels into the boards, backing oars. Rashes of signal flags broke out on the lines. The orc marine crew of the *SS Gibbet and Spigot* hurtled to their stations, unearthing from the cargo hold league upon league of fine, magic-woven netting.

Ashnak, holding his cocked hat on with one taloned hand, sauntered back across the deck to stand with Magda Brandiman. Nets whisked into the air, opening and falling; a rain of harpoons darted out from every ship of the Graagryk fleet. Ashnak craned his squat neck to look up at the Bug.

'Son, if you got any complaints, now's the time to tell me. Once we've caught it, we sure as hell ain't going to throw it back.'

Hive Commander Kah-Sissh hissed with pleasure, dripping acid slime on the quinquereme's deck. 'It will suffice.'

Magda Brandiman leaned on the rail and watched a vast golden eye close. 'I think we can probably consider the peace treaty ratified now, Hive Commander. Don't you?'

Orc marines cheered. Water flashed, dropping in diamonds from the raised oars of the quinquereme. Vast scaly tentacles broke above the waves, and subsided. The less speedy ships of the Graagryk Navy closed in, adding their own magic-assisted stun harpoons to the mêlée.

Major-General Barashkukor looked thoughtfully up at his supreme commander.

'Sir, what do you think, sir? Could we have a campaign medal struck for the Great Kraken Hunt, sir? Could we, sir? Please, sir? —*OW!*'

Half an hour later, Admiral of the Fleet Ashnak, upon returning to his cabin, found the door ajar. Desert Eagle pistol in hand, he kicked the cabin door open.

A male halfling, black hair showing a plentiful crop of grey, sat cross-legged on the admiral's chair behind the desk. His black doublet and breeches and yellow ruff showed some travel stains. A rapier and dagger were visible at his waist, and there was an additional bulge under one armpit.

'Stepfather,' Will Brandiman greeted Ashnak.

The big orc slammed the cabin door shut. With a nasty gleam in his eye, he advanced on the halfling.

'Ned knows I'm here,' Will said. 'I don't know where Ned is, exactly. Something to do with Archipelago silk, I believe. Anyway, he'll be only too pleased to tell Mother that I didn't accidentally fall off a galley, if I don't show up after today.'

Ashnak crossed the cabin in a stride, opened the drinks cabinet, and downed half a bottle of Spice Isles brandy without blenching. He wiped his mouth on the gold-embroidered sleeve of his naval jacket. 'Whaddya want?'

'Is that any way to speak to your stepson?' Will Brandiman enquired. 'You should be pleased that I'm taking an interest in your work, Father.'

'Don't', Ashnak said, 'push your luck.'

Will Brandiman smiled a slick smile and slipped down from the chair. He rested his shoulder against the edge of the admiral's desk.

'Nice set-up for taking the Kraken,' Will approved. 'Got the whole Visible College running round supplying you, I see. Funny how anxious they are now to work for the Great Peacemaker Ashnak, isn't it? Be a shame if any evidence came to light that would start the Red Gullies war crime scandal up again, what with the Dark Lord's coronation as Ruler of the World coming up and all.'

The orc shoved his Desert Eagle automatic pistol back in its holster. 'You're bluffing.'

'Probably,' Will Brandiman agreed. 'But I'm a generous halfling. I'm not asking for favours. Not really.'

'*Well?*'

'Funnily enough, stepfather,' the stowaway halfling said, 'there *is* something you can do for me . . .'

Ashnak stripped off his jacket, kicked off his seaboots, and thudded down into the admiral's carved chair. His bright eyes fixed on the halfling with unwavering bale.

'What is it this time? Grand larceny? You're stealing Ferenzia because it's not nailed down? Well, I got news for you, boy. This time the answer's "no!"' The Great Peacemaker Ashnak showed his tusks in satisfaction. 'Frankly, son, I wouldn't piss on you if your hair was on fire. Now, *out!*'

Overhead fire had stripped the glass from the paned roof of the great Assembly Hall of Ferenzia. Warm air and the smell of morning drifted in. Repair-magics slowly knitted silicon together. Orc marines with buckets and mops, under the direction of a sergeant-major, cleared the rubbish away, whitewashed the more immovable heaps of masonry, and set out official lettered marine signs reading KEEP OFF OF THE RUBBLE.

'He's through here, sir.' Major-General Barashkukor pointed.

Orc marines in ceremonial studded-leather armour stood around the Assembly Hall's panelled walls. They sloped arms with pole-axes as Supreme Commander Ashnak entered.

'Nice touch,' Ashnak approved.

'Thank you, sir!' Barashkukor saluted. 'Traditional ceremonial weapon of the orc, the pole-axe. The M203 grenade-launcher attachments were my idea too, sir.'

Ashnak strode across the Hall to where the High King Kelyos Magorian slumped in a carved chair at a table.

'You're about to miss the first convocation of the World Parliament, your Majesty,' Ashnak rumbled.

Kelyos Magorian raised his balding head. He screwed a monocle into his eye, staring up at the two orcs; the smaller one in a tailored and be-medalled brown tunic, with more gold braid on his peaked cap than it could fairly carry; and the large orc in urbans, web-belt sagging under the weight of pistols, grenades, spare magazines, and formal hand-axe.

'Go away,' the High King said. 'Damned greenies! Spoil the game. Two sugars!'

His halfling servant filled a steaming porcelain bowl from a silver trolley beside the oak table, placing it by Magorian on the green cloth covering. The elderly Man muttered, moving the bowl away from copses of dyed-green lichen and contour-carved miniature hills.

'Ha!' Magorian spilled dice from his blue-veined fist and peered at them through his monocle. 'The Horde routs! The Light wins, dammit.'

Ashnak reached across to the halfling servant's trolley and grabbed a fistful of biscuits. Chewing, he lowered his tusked head and studied the table. The myriad model warriors were set out in much the same array as the previous Hallows Eve's Last Battle.

'*Parliament*,' he reminded Magorian.

'Think I'm going to watch that damned female now She's been crowned Ruler of the World? Damned right I'm not. They don't need me now. Going to retire and do what *I* enjoy. Fight these battles the way they *should* have gone.' The High King Magorian blinked fiercely at the orc. 'The Light wins. *Always*. I've proved it!'

Ashnak snapped his fingers. A very large orc corporal trotted up, a voluminous blue velvet and ermine robe clutched in her arms. Her squad's combat boots pounded the parquet floor as they approached at the double.

'By the numbers,' Ashnak ordered, 'High King Magorian, for the parliamentary sessions: *dress*. Regal crown of Ferenzia: *on*. Squaaad . . . wait for it, wait for it . . . to the Opticon, High King Magorian, marine escort: *march!*'

Ashnak and Barashkukor strolled out of the Assembly Hall in the wake of the grunts and a protesting High King.

'That the last one, Major-General?'

'Sir, yes, sir! We've rounded them all up. We have the full legal complement for the new World Parliament, sir.'

Bells battered the bright summer air, ringing out from the only cathedral left standing in Ferenzia after the Bug invasion. Walls demolished, suburbs flattened, the Lake Fleet burned at the quayside; Ferenzia was just recovered enough to welcome in delegates from all corners of the civilized land.

Ashnak loped to his jeep, Barashkukor at his heels, and hauled himself into the vehicle. He demanded, 'Where's Magda?'

The skeletal orc driver in the black beret and assault vest surveyed Ashnak through dark glasses. 'The Colonel-Duchess said something about the press, sir, and getting the WFTV cameras into the Opticon.'

CIA Chief Lugashaldim slammed the vehicle into gear and they roared off through the Ferenzi streets, engine noise racketing between the high buildings, crowds hurling themselves out of the jeep's path.

'I understand Magda Brandiman Enterprises (Graagryk) Limited has the monopoly on parliamentary broadcast pictures, sir. Three silver shillings colour, two copper groats black-and-white.'

Ashnak rested his chin on his fist. 'That's my Magda . . .'

The jeep hurtled through war-torn Ferenzia, held up in places by the various on-going victory parades – the Sixth Elf Hussars, the Dwarf Sappers and Miners Brigade, the Eagles (Ferenzia Eyrie, 1st Tactical Wing) – until at last it pulled up outside a domed masonry building with two wings.

'Opticon surrounded by honour guard, as you ordered, sir.' Major-General Barashkukor bustled Magorian towards the arched entrance. Ashnak strolled after, taking the salute from the cordon of heavily armed and flak-jacketed orc marines.

The shelling and street-fighting had by some fluke passed the interior of the Opticon by, doing no more than knock a level of dust from its endless shelves of books. Above the books, on the unshelved wall-space, great fresco maps gleamed intact, picturing in blue and gold and ochre paint the kingdoms of the South and North, and the Wild Lands to the east, and the Land Beyond the Western Oceans.

Sunlight filtered down through the circular window in the top of the central dome.

One beam of light illuminated the Throne of the World.

Plush benches had been set up in the gallery space. Ashnak pointed at the front row of benches to the right of the Throne, under the star-painted ceiling of the West Wing.

'That'll do for His Lordship.'

Barashkukor hustled the elderly hero forward.

A library-hush muted the noise of the Light delegates – Men, dwarves, elves and halflings – shuffling on to their benches. Ashnak caught the eye of one elf, the marks of age shocking on his face, seated between the Mayor of Sarderis and a Snake Priest of Shazmanar. 'Inquisitor Elinturanbar.'

'You do not belong on this side!' the long-dying elf hissed. 'Come not near! We shall bring justice down on you one day soon.'

The races of Darkness – trolls, witches, necromancers, Undead, kobolds and the rest – scrambled for places on the benches on the left-hand side. Ashnak's hairy nostrils flared. At the centre of the front bench a figure slouched, its leather robe a patchwork of hands and limbs, eyes and lips, all tanned and sewn together with silver wire.

'Lord Necromancer,' Ashnak acknowledged, out of sheer habit.

Dirt and dried blood stiffened the nameless necromancer's skin robe. What could be seen of his tusked face under the cowl had a greenish, decaying cast. He creaked.

'Ssscum!' the nameless hissed. 'Traitor to thish side of the House. Do you think you can betray the Dark by letting the Bug-filth live, and not yourshelf live to bitterly regret your *mercy?*'

'*Ain't* you pissed off,' Ashnak grinned. 'Nothing to do with missing the victory celebrations due to being dead, of course.'

'*Bah!*'

Light gleamed down from the Opticon's dome on to the first World Parliament. The Dark delegates crowded each other unmercifully; whistling, throwing dung, and hauling the books down from the shelves at the back of them, and reading the more dubious passages aloud.

'Call them to order!' Oderic, High Wizard of Ferenzia, demanded as Ashnak approached him.

Ashnak surveyed his grunts, who were mostly leaning up against the panelled seats and bumming pipe-weed from the delegates; and the Order of White Mages, who strode about in their Sun-ornamented surcoats attempting to reduce the chaos.

'No point,' Ashnak rumbled. 'They'll quieten down soon enough when – yo! There!'

Outside, a sparkling blue sky shone over the Dread Lord of Dead Aeons as She descended from Her bone palanquin, surrounded by cheering Ferenzi and the Horde of Darkness.

The Dark Lord entered the vast, book-dusty hall of the Opticon. Black dire-wolf furs swathed Her head to foot. Under the cloak a tight-fitting black silk robe rippled, slashed to the thigh, and belted with a jewelled waistband. Intricate steel-and-silver jewellery clasped Her arms and Her ankles. Her ash-blond hair gleamed, Her head uncovered and unadorned.

Cheering crowds pressed in close behind Major-General Barash-kukor's cordon of orc marine guards at the double doors, waving flags, and chanting:

'DARK LORD! DARK LORD! DARK LORD!'

Ashnak hitched up his web-belt and combat trousers, and ambled across the floor of the Opticon to the Dark Lord. 'Your Parliament assembled, Ma'am, for the first free, frank, and democratic exchange of views between Your loyal government and Your loyal opposition. As soon as they can make their minds up which is which.'

The Dark Lord surveyed the benches to left and right of the Throne, Her delicate profile turned to Ashnak. 'Shall I preside well, do you think, little orc? This power has been so long in the achieving, I think I have forgotten what it was I would do with it.'

'Buck up, Ma'am!' Ashnak removed his forage cap, coming solidly to attention. 'You just do what every other Ruler of the World's done and You'll be all right – reward a few, hang a few, and tax everything that moves.'

She laughed, a sound of ancient amusement. 'You advise Me well, orc. Perhaps I shall make you My chancellor.'

Ashnak grunted non-committally.

'Or perhaps I shall *not* . . . There is something I wish to have done, after this. It is a proud and lonely thing to be Ruler of the World. Therefore I shall not sit upon My throne alone. I shall take a companion, a consort. Mine will be thought a strange choice, but I have seen, and in seeing desired, and desiring, must have. Shall it be thought strange to raise a commoner, and one not of My own race? Then so be it. And, orc Ashnak – you know the one.'

'Erm.' Ashnak sweated in the sunlight filtering down from the Opticon's central dome. 'Really, Ma'am?'

The Dark Lord frowned. 'Don't be coy.'

'I suppose,' Ashnak grated, salt sweat trickling into his eyes, 'I could hazard a guess, and while I'm sensible of the honour, Dread Lord, I really don't think I—'

The Dark Lord spoke over his mumbling.

'We have met few enough times, of course, but often enough to spark My desire. And she is not, after all, a complete commoner.'

'I— *she?*' Ashnak barked.

The Dark Lord turned Her ancient, humanly beautiful face towards the orc as She paced towards the Throne. 'Why yes. Ever since the night she came to My tent, I have known that I must have Magdelene, Duchess of Graagryk. My beautiful Magda! Be so good as to inform her that we will wed, after I have settled affairs in Ferenzia and quietened the south. You, Ashnak, may be best orc and give away the bride.'

Ashnak growled, 'She's married.'

'She's divorced. I have said so: so let it be. We shall', the Dark Lord added, 'have to think of a suitable role for you, also, in this new world, little orc. Some backwater province that needs a junior governor. Of course, the orc marines will be disbanded . . .'

'Ma'am!' Ashnak saluted, his gaze sliding across the seats and registering, in the upper gallery, the Duchess of Graagryk's cameras.

To the ringing of the White Mages' silver trumpets, and the fluttering wings of a thousand released black doves, the Lord of Darkness advanced up the hall of the Opticon and stood before the Throne of the World.

The marble floor tiles ceased under the central dome. Four Men of the Order of White Mages knelt there, where, surrounded by its marble dais, a fang of ancient continental bedrock jutted up. Living rock: around which first the Opticon and later Ferenzia itself had been built. The black stone breathed antiquity.

Hands older than the city of Ferenzia had carved this basalt outcrop into a throne. Ancient winged and scaled beasts ornamented each of its corner as supporters. The seat shone with intricately chiselled flowers, fruits, vines and corn-ears. The massive back of the throne rose up to a point, every inch carved with wings, eyes, globes and solar discs.

The Dark Lord lifted Her arms, letting Her wolf-fur cloak fall. She stood, slender and tall, in Her clinging robe of ebony silk, Her jewelled belt flashing in the sunlit, dusty air. As She seated Herself, lounging back on the piled velvet cushions, Ashnak picked up Her robe and took his station to the left of the Throne of the World. High Wizard Oderic reluctantly stood to Her right, in his arms an onyx-and-diamond crown.

'Behold,' Oderic of Ferenzia cried, 'the first democratic parliament of the Ruler of the World.'

'No, sssister!' a voice lisped from the front row of the Dark delegates.

The nameless necromancer hunched and slumped his way to his feet, and on to the floor before the Throne. Ashnak rubbed his mouth, tasting the sudden metallic flavour of wizardry.

'We have both of ush been betrayed, sister! Now – *avenge* us!'

Orc marine squad leaders watched Ashnak for orders. He held up a restraining hand, his eyes on the Throne.

The Dark Lord lounged against one of the Throne's carved arms, Her black robe falling back from her calf, knee and thigh. Her skin glowed sepia-pale in the dusty light. Her orange eyes flared.

'What, little Man? Do you challenge Me?'

'*Sssister* mine!' the nameless necromancer appealed. 'I know your schpirit, your ssoul, still lives within that body. Wake, wake, and take your body back!'

The Dark Lord's chin dipped towards Her silk-clad breast. She looked up from under Her brows at the suddenly silenced parliament.

She spoke.

'You who were My greatest enemy, you who were called The Named – look now and see what I have made of you. I have kept your spirit alive within Me until now, so that you may see Evil ruling from the Throne of the World.'

'Madam President!' A black-bearded dwarf raised his hand from the Light's back benches. Ashnak recognized Prosecuting Counsel Zhazba-darabat. 'You mean, "Evil presiding over this democratically elected assembly".'

'Of course,' the Dark Lord purred. 'Now. You who were called The Named, behold your shame, and your brother's extinction for daring to challenge Me!'

The Dark Lord's featureless orange eyes dimmed. Her cyan- and sepia-shadowed face contorted. Ashnak, meeting Her gaze, saw green Man-eyes suddenly stare out wildly at the crowd.

The orc drew his pistol, assuming a combat stance, but did not fire.

The rangy female Man slid her hands down a body clothed in silk. She sprang to her feet, bare feet stumbling as if she had anticipated the restrictions of armour. An expression of horror, revulsion, and triumph appeared on the face of The Named as she saw her brother, yet unharmed.

The Dark Lord blinked, and, without giving The Named time for any last words or actions whatsoever, snuffed her soul out like cracking a flea.

She opened Her eyes again, that glowed like the fires of sunset, and smiled down at the nameless necromancer. 'Was I to gloat, and in so doing give her time to repossess Me? Was that your plan? I know what commonly becomes of Evil at the end of tales – but I am not so stupid.'

A fork of black lightning stabbed down from the Opticon's dome.

Ashnak blinked away the after-images, holstered his pistol, strolled across the black and white tiles, and studied the smoking heap of bones that was all that remained of the orcs' ancient master. As he watched, the bones disintegrated into dust.

'Corporal Hikz, give those tiles a going-over.' He faced about as the grunt scrubbed at the stone. 'Well done, Ma'am. Speaking as head of the security presence here, I admire good, quick work.'

The Dark and Light parliamentary delegates settled back into their seats under the great gold-and-blue wall maps, glaring at each other across the chamber.

The Ruler of the World spoke.

'Is that *all?*' She said.

The Dark Ruler lay back between the wing-carved arms of the Throne of the World. Its feather- and eye-decorated stone back rose high above Her: Her ash-pale hair, and Her child-delicate face, and bare shoulders.

'Is that all . . . ?'

The Ruler of the World pointed, with one sepia-shadowed hand, at the gallery of the Opticon and the walls above it.

'You do not know how petty all this seems to Me. What is pictured there?'

Her hand indicated the great blue-and-gold wall maps, with the green hills and farmlands of Ferenzia, Gyzrathrani, Fourgate, Graagryk, Sarderis and the rest painted in intricate detail.

'Half a hundred petty kingdoms, a few stretches of wild lands, some uninhabitable territories at the poles, and a flooded continent to the west. Number it, it is easily numbered. What is it all to me, who with the mere thinking could turn it all to molten rock . . .'

Her bell voice chimed in the Opticon's dome. The substance of the air shivered, as if all the Powers – Earth, Water, Air, Fire and Void – were brought unwilling into that chamber.

'And you . . .'

The gaze of the Dark Ruler swept across the tiered seats. Specks of sunfire gleamed in Her pupil-less orange eyes. Bereft of speech and movement, the races of the earth stared back at Her like animals caught in torchlight.

'No,' She said. 'It is not worthy of Me to commit genocide against such inconsequential beings.'

A tension left the air, the Powers fading.

'Always I have fought for the mastery of this Land. Again and again I have thrown My forces of Darkness against the Light. Finally, I am victorious! But when I have the victory, what have I won? The lordship over furrow-grubbers, axe-swingers, and beast-handlers. Farmland, wilderness, and not a city worthy of the name!'

The Mayor of Sarderis made as if to speak, caught Her gaze, and was silent.

The Dark Ruler of the World smiled.

'There are none left, are there, to challenge Me?'

A red-eyed kobold in a mailshirt spoke up from the tiers of Dark delegates. 'Ma'am, we appreciate that as Dark Lord and World Ruler You expect regular challenges to Your power – but this House requests that we deal first with the budget for Lower Shalmanazar, and the submitted paper on Waterworks and Canals, *and* the Evil Races (Suffrage) Bill.'

The Dark Lord rested Her elbow on the arm of the Throne, and Her chin in Her hand. From the pinnacle of the world She gazed down.

'Already,' She said, 'already I am bored. You do not have the greatness of soul to know *how* tedious I find this muddy world of which I am Ruler.'

Ashnak chewed his cigar, checked the position of his marines, and moved forward. 'Got a priority matter for you to deal with, Ma'am. Before these Bills and suchlike. If I may . . .'

'Do what you will, My orc!'

Ashnak jerked his thumb over his shoulder. 'You've met Hive Commander Kah-Sissh.'

Delegates leaned forward on their benches as the double doors of the Opticon were flung open.

A squad of twelve Bug insectoids approached across the floor of the Opticon, bearing on their chitinous shoulders the body of a Jassik warrior twice their size. Upright, the exoskeletal body would have touched the domed ceiling. Now the black chitin was matt and dull, the faceted eyes dim, the great claws motionless. A vast array of black living-metal clustered on the dead Jassik's body, no lights flickering on it, all dead and still.

Hive Commander Kah-Sissh trod delicately across the floor before the Throne, and folded his legs into an obeisance. 'Great One, Ruler of this world.'

The Dark Lord glanced down at the Bug, and then at Supreme Commander Ashnak. 'What is this?'

'It's a dead Bug, Ma'am.'

'I can see that!'

'A mostly dead Bug,' Ashnak corrected himself. 'Isn't that right, Kah-Sissh?'

The Hive Commander unfolded, in response to a nudge from the orc's combat boot, and said hastily, 'All but dead, Great One. This is our Swarm Master, who was damaged as we came to this world. You would call him our Emperor. His mind is damaged, dead, and cannot be healed. His body yet has a kind of life in it, but it is fading fast.'

The Ruler of the World rose from Her throne, pacing down to the floor of the Opticon. Her orange eyes glowed. The great body of the Bug towered over Her. She surveyed its chitinous carapace.

'Ashnak, be so good as to tell Me why you are bringing dead Bugs into My court?'

The dwarf Zhazba-darabat coughed. '"Parliament".'

Orange eyes turned to the Light benches. 'What?'

'"Parliament", World Ruler, Ma'am. Not "court".'

The Dark and Light delegates looked at each other, nodding their heads in complete agreement.

'Into My *parliament*,' the Dark Lord hissed, Her fists clenching at Her sides. Her silk robe slid across Her long legs as She paced the length of the dead Jassik, and then back to the Throne's dais. She turned Her head, gazing at Her supreme commander.

'*Well?*'

Hive Commander Kah-Sissh, nudged again by Ashnak's boot, spoke. 'This is the Emperor of all Jassik. Emperor of those who are here, and of those who rule, in his name, the myriad worlds of the stars. He leads us from world to world, plundering and pillaging, subjecting all to Jassik control. He leads the holy war, across stars uncounted, forging an empire of worlds too many to be numbered!'

'Wait!' The Dark Lord stared at Kah-Sissh's back and the Jassik's multi-barrelled disruptor. 'What discourtesy is this, orc Ashnak? I was under the impression our foes had agreed to throw down their arms.'

Ashnak shrugged. 'Bit difficult with cyber-grown weaponry, Ma'am. We're doing the best we can.'

Hive Commander Kah-Sissh drew himself up, towering over the assembly. 'I am bound by a warrior's honour to keep the terms agreed at the peace negotiations.'

The Jassik rubbed his claw across his chitinous skull between his faceted eyes, as if he found the Opticon's light uncomfortable.

'For some reason, I do not entirely *remember* all the conditions,' he added, 'but nonetheless, I hold to them!'

The Dark Lord seated Herself again on the Throne of the World. She shot a sharp glance at Ashnak. 'I ask again: why have you brought this body here? I am not in the healing vein today.'

'Our ship-egg is on the point of hatching.' The alien hive commander stood on his exoskeletal hind limbs. Sun gleamed on his articulated thorax, domed head and acid-dripping jaws. His faceted eyes held a thousand reflections of the Lord of Darkness. 'Within hours we must leave this petty world. The Jassik Empire must continue on its conquering way.'

'"Petty" world?' the Dark Lord mused. 'That is not something it is tactful to say to Me.'

'No, Ma'am.' Ashnak glared at the hive commander. 'What Kah-Sissh *means* to say, Ma'am, is that the Jassik need a Swarm Master to lead them. This one is destroyed in mind, but only damaged in body. Dread Lord, the Jassik offer You the body of the Swarm Master to possess – if You will become their Emperor and lead them from world to world, conquering as You go.'

A silence fell on the parliament. Ashnak's gaze swept Oderic's scowling features, Magorian and the White Mages; the Ferenzi nobles and people; the creatures of the Horde . . .

The Ruler of the World's gaze returned from the same survey.

'What do I rule, here?' She asked. 'Some half a million creatures. Yes, little Kah-Sissh, I have been speaking with your Jassik companions of the worlds that lie beyond the stars. The many, *many* worlds.'

An orcish voice spoke up from the rear of the Opticon.

'It's quite all right if you refuse, Ma'am,' Major-General Barash-kukor called, almost on cue. 'They've said that if you don't want the post, they'll offer it to someone else.'

'*Will* they, now . . .'

The Dark Ruler of the World stood, jewelled belt blazing in the Opticon's sunlight. She turned Her gaze upon the tiers of seats.

'And who would accept this offer? You, Magorian? To be a hero again in a body not betrayed by age? Or you, Oderic who thinks he is a wizard, to gain the knowledge of the stars?'

Her gaze swept on.

'My br— My necromancer would have taken this chance, out of courage or desperation. What of you, nobles of Ferenzi? Dwarves, will you study the engineering of the stars? Halflings, will you carry your thievery to other worlds? Elves, will you visit those stars of which you sing? Ah, you see that I see into you all. There is not one of you who can answer Me.'

The Dark Lord's gaze lowered to the marble dais at the foot of the Throne.

'Not even *you*, little orc. Come, confess it before your fellow warriors and be shamed. You will not take the offer of a Jassik Emperor's body. Your bowels loose at the very thought.'

The orc Supreme Commander shrugged, shifted uncomfortably from combat boot to combat boot, and avoided his grunts' eyes. 'Ah. Well. That is . . .'

The Dark Lord's voice seared. 'Shall I *make* you take the offer? It is in My power so to do.'

Rapidly concealed anxiety showed in the orc's porcine eyes. With a more genuine discomfort he said, 'No, Ma'am!'

The Dark Lord laughed.

'It would be a fitting reward, to dispossess you of your orcish warriors. But that I can in any case do. Let Me think . . . Yes. Curiously enough, little orc, there *is* something you can do for Me.'

A Darkness began to fill the Opticon.

Out of it, Her voice said, 'I here proclaim Ashnak of the Agaku to be My regent, to rule this petty world in My absence!'

Ashnak's tusked jaw sagged.

Her voice laughed.

Darkness swirled, stinking of rot and bone, smelling of spices and cherries and the east wind. The unseen dome of the Opticon creaked. The shrieks and cries of the delegates fell, muted, as if into infinite void.

Abruptly, Darkness vanished.

Ashnak swiped at his eyes that streamed in the sudden sunlight. All the elves, Men, kobolds, witches, dwarves and other delegates in the chamber rose to their feet, shouting; and then suddenly fell silent.

Lights ran across the black metal body of the Swarm Master.

Hive Commander Kah-Sissh and his Jassik escort folded and fell, making obeisance on the tiles.

The Swarm Master rose.

His articulated armoured body hung suspended between chitin-metal limbs, weapon-muzzles gleaming. His faceted eyes glimmered with an ancient amusement.

He spoke, His voice ancient and familiar:

'None of you are worthy of Me . . . You and this world are too poor in scope for My ambition. What, is there no more world left for Me to conquer? Are there no worthy enemies? I go now to rule an Evil Empire beyond your comprehension! Little beings, amuse yourselves in this dungheap that is also Mine, for I shall not return to it, beg Me though you may.'

The Emperor of the Jassik moved on metal-chitin limbs. He lowered his acid-dripping jaws towards the discarded body of the female Man that lay between His feet.

410

'I have a *universe* to conquer!' He hissed.

The Jassik's Swarm Master picked up The Named's limp body in one foreclaw, bit her head off, and, escorted by Jassik warriors, paced regally out of the Opticon, chewing.

Will Brandiman glanced up at the sign over the door – *Wrestling Emporium*, and in smaller letters A DIVISION OF MAGDA BRANDIMAN ENTERPRISES – and trotted past the bouncers into the club. A welcome fug of pipe-weed smoke and small beer hit his nostrils. He paused for a moment, eyes becoming accustomed to the dim light. There were no uncurtained windows to let the morning in.

'Ned?'

'Over here, Will.'

Halfling-sized and Man-sized tables filled most of the floor. The club's arc-lights shone on the roped arena, on a dais, in which two mud-spattered dwarves wrestled in three inches of black slime.

'Foul!' Ned Brandiman bawled, thumping his fist on the table. His red wimple was pushed back, showing his curly brown hair and his stubbled cheeks. He grinned up at Will.

'Good, isn't it?' he said happily.

The ex-Son of the Lady, Amarynth Firehand, also looked up from where he sat, his arm around Ned Brandiman's red-habited shoulders. 'Ah. Brother-in-law William. Do you approve?'

With a roar, the smaller of the wrestling dwarves flipped the other over, kneeling on her shoulders and rubbing the black mud into her beard. Will waited until the ringing cheers had died down before he said, 'Dwarf mud-wrestling, Holy One?'

'No, no. I am no longer Holy.' The elf lowered his eyes. 'The Lady of Light has told me how unfit I am. Now I must wallow in sin and depravity, tasting every vice, until my knowledge of evil is perfect. Only then dare I call myself Most Holy again.'

Will reached over and poured another measure of arrack into the elf's cup. 'I feel it could take you some while, Ho— Lord Amarynth.'

'Nor am I to be called Lord, or Knight, or Paladin. I am simply Amarynth, owner of *The Azure Roc*. But,' Amarynth said, cheering up, 'at least I am able to share my new life of shame with someone for whom I care deeply.'

Ned Brandiman blushed.

'I'd like to borrow Ned for a while,' Will said, 'if I may.'

'Certainly.' Amarynth lifted his dark cheek for the brown-haired halfling's kiss, flicked through his programme, and turned back to the wrestling ring and the dwarves. He frowned. 'It says here, the next

411

act to audition involves "water sports". I still don't see how they're
going to get a shower into the ring . . .'

Ashnak stood for a moment grinning an inane, stunned grin.

'Aw*riiight!*' he roared, over the tumult of the Light and Dark
delegates. 'You heard the Lady – from now on, I'm the boss here!'

An orcish voice shouted above the confusion, 'Hail, Regent
Ashnak!'

'*Never!*' Oderic, High Wizard of Ferenzia, stomped forward from
beside the Throne of the World. 'The Light cannot accept this! We –
we will crown Magorian King again!'

Sunlight blazed down into the Opticon, glaring back from the wall
maps, the bookshelves and the rich robes of the halflings, Men, elves
and dwarves who stood up and shouted from the Light benches:

'No orcs! No orcs!'

The armed orc marines lining the walls grinned, readying their
weapons.

'NO ORCS!' The same sun gleamed from the black mail, dagger-
hilts, sallet helms, and dark velvet gowns of the Dark delegates:
kobolds, witches and Undead all scrambling to their feet.

Ashnak raised his beetling brows. 'Whaddya *mean*, "no orcs"?'

The red-eyed kobold waved her dagger. 'Orcs are just big and
nasty. What sort of treatment will you give the rest of the Horde?
You'll just enslave us!'

'Oh, ho!' the High Wizard Oderic bellowed in triumph. 'Even
your own Evil side won't accept you, *orc!*'

A gang of Trolls on the back benches began to chant, 'Orcs out!' A
somewhat desperate elven chorus on the opposition benches sang in
counterpoint, 'Bring back the Dark Lord!'

A knife shattered against the Throne of the World, beside Oderic's
hand, drawing blood and severing a tendon. Ten, twenty, fifty
metallic hisses: swords drawn from their sheaths. Men in mailshirts
under their velvet robes leaped up, overturning chairs. Dark dwarf
delegates upturned benches with a crash. An elvish blade flashed: a
minotaur screamed: a White Mage bellowed a word of Power. An
ebony spatter of blood fell on the tiles.

DAKKA-DAKKA-DAKKA! *FOOM!*

Chaos froze. Halflings shaking their fists, dwarves standing on
benches and shouting, Men using their superior lung-power to be
heard: all froze into silence. The assembled Light and Dark delegates
sank back into their seats, or stood among the wreckage, all eyes
turned to the Throne of the World, and the great orc now sitting on
it.

412

'Thank you, Lieutenant-Colonel.' Ashnak nodded to Dakashnit. The black orc grinned and lowered her AK47. A fine layer of plaster sifted down on to the Opticon's library shelves. The map of Lesser Gyzrathrani now had a line of dinner-plate-sized holes just above the Endless Desert.

Ashnak sat back, rumpled camouflage uniform stretching to contain his large body. He pushed his forage cap back on his head, and scratched his crotch. The smell of sweating orc drifted across the Opticon. Sitting with both arms resting across his camouflage-trousered thighs, combat boots square on the Throne steps, and pistol in hand, Ashnak's eyes swivelled down to survey the World Parliament.

'*I'm* in charge here,' he stated flatly.

Oderic spun on his heel, white hair flying, pointing to the orc marines at the door and around the walls. 'We will never submit to your military dictatorship!'

The Dark kobold gibbered. 'Tyrant! Dictator!'

Ashnak's powerful head swivelled, taking in the recalcitrant kobolds of the Blasted Redoubt and the stubborn trolls of the Horde, the mutineering witches of the wastelands, and the revolting wild orcs of the mountains.

'"Tyrant" . . .'

He let his gaze travel from the furious white wizard to the comotose ex-High King; from Shazmanar's Snake Priests to Gyzrathrani's wary warriors, from the elves of Thyrion to the halfling bankers of the Ferenzi suburbs, and the city stockbroker-dwarves.

'Yo! I *like* the sound of that.'

Orcish voices bawled 'Yo!' across the Opticon. Marines beat the butts of their rifles against the floor. Magorian woke up long enough to mutter, 'Damned greenies!'

'Let me tell all of you something about orcs.' Ashnak's smile was almost affectionate. 'If you're born an orc, every race's hand is against you. Every Dark Leader that happens along thinks, I need an army, what about a few thousand orcs? They're brutal, efficient, cheap, and there's always plenty more where they came from.'

Oderic sneered, 'Foolish creature, what else is there to do with you? You live in filth, you *are* filth.'

Major-General Barashkukor stepped forward, protesting. 'Anyone would think orcs lived in Pits by their own choice.'

'Dammit, we do!' Ashnak thumped his fist on the stone arm of the Throne. 'I'm proud to be an orc! I came out of the Pit the nastiest, toughest object you could ever wish to see – the necromancer's army made me a junior sergeant on the spot. I fought my way up to captain

413

in the Horde; I've held command of the marines; now I've got the Throne of the World, and I'm keeping it! You ain't got the orcs to kick around any more!'

Voices screamed in unison:

'*Orcs out! Orcs out! ORCS OUT!*"

Ashnak gazed down at five hundred rioting Dark and Light delegates with the identical desire for dead orc in their glowering eyes.

'I don't think it's a popular decision, sir,' Wing Commander Chahkamnit remarked.

'I'm not asking them to like me! Time for a couple of volleys into the crowd,' Ashnak purred. 'How convenient that we've got all the ranking delegates from the Northern and Southern Kingdoms in the same room—'

'FREEZE, MOTHERFUCKER!'

Ashnak saw first the glint of the Brandiman Enterprises camera in the gallery below the wall maps, and then the sunlight flashing from the muzzle of the sniper's rifle beside it, held by a halfling in the red habit and wimple of a Little Sister of Mortification.

Ned Brandiman kept his eye to the sights. 'Make a move, orc, and I'll blow your heart out.'

The orcs around the Throne shuffled back from Ashnak.

He glowered and opened his mouth to bellow.

Another voice called, 'Not so fast, orc!'

The Opticon fell silent. Ashnak gazed towards the open doors. A small, curly haired figure stood in the gap, the light of the sun behind him.

The figure moved forward, black silhouette becoming a halfling in the velvet doublet and gold fillet of a Graagryk prince. The sun shone down on his black curls, streaked with grey, and his hands that he held out empty before him.

'Gentlemen,' Will Brandiman said. 'Let's be sensible about this.'

The Prince of Graagryk walked with an easy swagger, thigh-length cloak swinging with the weight of coins sewn into its hem. He kept one hand on the swept hilt of his rapier as he marched down the aisle between the benches and halted before the orc supreme commander. He turned to face the delegates.

'Commander Ashnak would do a fine job as Regent.' Above protests, Will added, 'Even though I have experience of him as my stepfather, I still say that. But – if he took the job, he'd have to kill most of you to do it. Because none of you will be ruled by an *orc*. Right?'

Yowls of agreement echoed from the Opticon's dome. Ashnak

414

snarled, brass-capped tusks flashing. He stood up, great-shouldered and powerful; the sun gleaming from his insignia of rank. 'Asshole halflings!'

'I am,' Will Brandiman said, 'a reasonable halfling. So are we all – elves and Men, kobolds and Undead – so are we all, reasonable beings. Gentlemen, ladies, we're a *Parliament*. It's our job to debate, to discuss, to agree, to compromise. Am I right?'

Two or three voices dissented, the rest murmured agreement.

'We're civilized people,' Will continued, striding to stand on the edge of the marble dais, a move that still didn't put him on a level with Ashnak. The great orc glared and fingered his pistol.

'We're civilized people, and the days of warfare are over. Commerce needs to continue, trade needs to flourish, harvests need to be – er – harvested,' the Graagryk prince said. 'I suggest we delegate the post of Regent to a compromise candidate who shall be acceptable to us all.'

A much-battered dwarf elbowed his way out of a crowd of Undead. Zhazba-darabat drew himself up and with dignity remarked, 'President.'

'Pardon?' Will said.

'Not "Regent", sir. President.'

'A compromise *President*,' the halfling reiterated, 'who we can all find acceptable.'

'I'm going to make you eat your own testicles!' Ashnak snarled.

'I knew you'd come round to my way of thinking.' Will Brandiman's eyes flickered to the gallery.

Ashnak's command officers went into a huddle behind the Throne. The phrase 'not the Way of the Orc!' drifted out of the group. A fist went up, and came down on the commissar's head.

'Behold!' Will shouted.

Another figure appeared in the Opticon's doorway, silhouetted against the light.

Will bellowed, 'I suggest for Ruler – President – of the World, one whose allegiances are both to the Dark *and* the Light. People of the South and North, give your support to the one best able to preside over a World Parliament and a Federation of All Races.'

The figure became a short-haired halfling in a smart dove-coloured executive suit and gloves, high heels tapping as she walked down between the rows of benches.

Ned Brandiman cried from the gallery, 'Magdelene of Graagryk!'

Ashnak strode out to the centre of the floor, furiously chewing his cigar, and glaring down at Magda Brandiman.

'See!' the female halfling cried, before Ashnak could speak.

'Ashnak the Great Peacemaker concedes to the forces of democracy!'

There was a silence. The Dark delegates looked at each other, and then at the Light delegates. The Light delegates looked at High King Magorian, and then at each other. They all looked at Ashnak.

'*Long live President Magda!*' Albert van der Klump, shop steward, took off his top hat and unhooked his thumb from the armhole of his waistcoat, and waved his fat cigar enthusiastically. Cornelius Scroop, Chancellor-Mage of Graagryk, and militia Captain Simone Vanderghast pounded the backs of the seats in front, starting a roar of applause that spread rapidly across the Parliament.

Scanning the benches, Ashnak began to count the many, many faces who had at one time or another been customers of Magda Brandiman Enterprises Ltd.

'Well, my love.' The female halfling held up her pipe-weed holder for him to light her thin cigar. 'That was one of the longest twenty minutes of my life . . .'

His pointed ears ringing with the cheers reverberating through the Opticon, Ashnak stared through the many hats tossed into the air. The gallery was empty now.

'Just to get your attention, my love,' Magda apologized sadly. 'No one will ever accept the rule of an orc. You know that. Prejudice is stronger than guns.'

'But—!'

The great orc's shoulders fell very slightly.

He nodded to his edgy troops to stand down.

As delegates across the Opticon sat down, or recovered their chairs and benches and sat down, Magda Brandiman turned to the House.

'I don't look on this as a position of power,' she said, rich voice echoing. 'I'm thinking of it as a business opportunity. Factories, industrial bases – *all* the Kingdoms can be as rich as Graagryk! Everyone can share the economic boom!'

Magda drew on her pipe-weed and expelled a plume of smoke.

'And pleasure is my business, too. If we work at it, we can make this land the pleasure capital of the world! There are whole territories in the Black East and the Drowned Lands of the West to be opened up. We *can* build a city worthy of the name, and we can all share in its riches! And no more of this antiquated Dark and Light nonsense – it's bad for investment.'

'MAGDA! MAGDA! *We want Magda!* WE WANT MAGDA!'

Will swept the velvet cap from his greying curls, leading the cheers that rang out until they shook the dust from the Opticon's bookshelves. Magda went into the crowd, shaking hands and professionally smiling.

'Shee-it!' Ashnak reached up and wrenched his jacket collar open. Buttons spanged off and lost themselves on the marble tiles.

The High Wizard Oderic hitched up his long white robes and sat down on a corner of the dais beside Ashnak. Dispiritedly he conjured a pipe, pipe-weed and a match.

'That does it! I'm – *hkk! hakkk! hk!* – I'm retiring.' The High Wizard glared up at the orc. 'I've had enough. Going to write my book. Always said I would; now I will.'

Ashnak fingered one hairy nostril. 'What book's that, then?'

'The history of an Age,' Oderic said, puffing smoke rings that lurched, lop-sided, into the air. 'I'm going to tell the *real* story about halflings, orcs, the Dark Lord and the final victory. The halflings are going to be cheery and moral and know their place; the orcs will be cowardly, and they'll lose; there won't be *any* mention of arms-trading, and at the end of it the Dark Lord will be male, and very, very dead!'

The great orc snorted. 'Nahhh.'

The white wizard coughed, and finally smiled. 'But you see, master orc, Good *is* triumphant. In a somewhat unorthodox manner, I grant you, but none the less – Order is restored.'

'Bah! Ashnak stomped away across the Opticon.

'. . . But it's disgraceful,' Political Commissar Razitshakra protested, pointing at the orcs who, with assault rifles slung across their shoulders, were happily mingling with the parliamentary delegates. 'The grunts don't seem to mind peace at all!'

'Hey, m'man.' Lieutenant-Colonel Dakashnit's rich tones echoed under the domed roof. 'Soldiering's much more fun when no one's shooting at you.'

'Supreme Commander, sir!' Lugashaldim saluted skeletally. 'Sir, Madam President Magdelene has asked if myself and Commissar Razitshakra can be seconded to her, sir, on temporary duties. She wants us to head her secret police.'

'"Police"?' Ashnak exclaimed.

'Uniformed officers of visible integrity who keep the government in power,' Razitshakra explained. 'She's not having any of them, sir. Just secret police. That's the same as regular police, but without the uniforms and the integrity.'

The great orc sighed gloomily.

'Got some news, man.' Dakashnit saluted lazily. 'Seems as how not all of the Bugs have left with the starship. But no need to worry, S.C. It's Hive Commander Kah-Sissh and his squad who've stayed. They want training.'

'They want our training?' Ashnak asked.

'Yes, sir! Well— that, and the tea. Permission to turn 'em into Bug Marines, S.C.?'

Ashnak growled, 'Hell, why not? What does it matter now?'

He tugged at the crotch of his combats. Then he reached across, removed Major-General Barashkukor's braid-encrusted peaked cap, and tapped his cigar ashes into it.

'Didn't want to be World Ruler *any*way,' Ashnak grunted. 'It's a Staff job.'

'Ah. Stepfather . . .'

Will Brandiman, standing just out of the orc's reach, cricked his neck to look the great orc in the face.

'You little rat!' Ashnak hissed.

The halfling beamed up at the orc who towered over him. 'Think of this as being our revenge on you, Ned and I, for the dungeons of Nin-Edin.'

'Damn you!'

'Quite probably,' Will agreed. 'But the moral is – don't fuck us over. Ever. Halflings have long memories, master orc. But you'll have enough time to think about that. Since you're not going to be occupied with world government.'

The great orc stood under the circular hole in the Opticon's roof, bathed in sunlight. A slight odorous steam rose from him. He wiped his nose, and his eyes glinted as they fixed on the colonel-duchess.

'Hellfire! She didn't take much persuading to do this,' Ashnak said bitterly.

The halfling raised a small eyebrow. 'She didn't take much persuading to save your ass. She didn't take much persuading to do the only thing that would stop you being lynched. Oh, and you would have been lynched – Ned and I would have made sure of that. But . . .'

Will Brandiman waved his hand at the Opticon floor below the Throne of the World. Five hundred Dark and Light parliamentary delegates elbowed each other in the rush to speak to Magda.

Orcs in camouflage fatigues with assault rifles stood in clusters, at ease, drinking from their water bottles. Each grunt carried with ease the weight of weapons, spare magazines and grenades.

'If you're so pissed off,' Will said softly, 'waste her. You're armed. You could still stage a violent coup. But you'll have to take Mother out first. So go ahead – do it.'

The orc did not move.

'You're a marine.' Will's tongue flayed. 'That's what marines do, isn't it. Go ahead! *Take* power.'

The strings of the halfling's ruff already trailed loose. He scratched irritably at the embroidery-stiffened collar of his doublet. Will looked towards the Order of the White Mages' wizards shuffling about in the background, hastily repossessing the onyx-and-diamond crown. A priest of the Sun gabbled his way through the coronation oath.

'I can't.' Ashnak shoved his hand deep in his combat jacket pocket, brought out another cigar, and bit off the end. He spat on the Opticon's tiled floor. 'Damn it, halfling, *I can't.*'

'That's what I thought,' Will said smugly. 'Villains always fall short of the mark at the end.'

'Fuck off and *die.*'

Ashnak straightened his shoulders, chewed his unlit cigar, and watched as, to the cheers of both sides of the House, in the Opticon of Ferenzia, upon a Throne older than cities, Magdelene Amaryllis Judith Brechie van Nassau of Graagryk, Duchess and Colonel, took her place as President of the United Northern and Southern Kingdoms and effective ruler of the world.

13

T<small>HE AUTUMN SUN</small> burned the dew off the stone walls inside Ferenzia's colossal stadium, the largest in the Southern Kingdoms. The cheering grew louder as the *whup-whup-whup* of a Bell Iroquois HU-1 helicopter thrummed above the velvet-draped stone tiers. The roar of the marine march-past and All-Forces victory tournament echoed to the skies. A single-prop Ferenzi airship puttered in, wavering as the Huey passed it, sporting a contingent of elf musketeers.

'My hero!' a northern dwarf breathed, her hands clasped to the breast of her shining mailcoat, over her rippling beard.

Major-General Barashkukor, in formal black combats and stetson, strode forward from among a crowd of dwarf and halfling females, flowers in their beards and hair respectively. They scattered rose-petals over the small orc and blew kisses.

He waved the mob away as he approached Madam President Magdelene's box, and saluted his honorary colonel. 'Magnificent show, ma'am.'

The World President sat on the straight-backed chair overlooking the arena, her many advisers one row behind. The female halfling wore a peach-coloured executive suit and gloves, and a small hat with a spotted veil.

'Make the most of it, Major-General. It's probably the last one.' Magda Brandiman regarded the sunny ranks of citizens with a jaundiced eye. 'The House had the nerve to pass the Marine Reserve

420

Force (Disbandment) Bill today. Not a thing I could do. The defence budget is slashed by 50 per cent because the marines are "uneconomic" without a war.'

'We could always start one, ma'am,' Barashkukor suggested thoughtfully.

'With what?' She leaned her chin on her hand. 'You're running low on equipment from Dagurashibanipal's hoard, and arms factory production is being cancelled from the beginning of next month.'

'Oh.'

'My sons have left the city,' Magda sighed. 'Last heard remarking that they'd robbed the Blasted Redoubt, outwitted the Dark Lord, and out-thought the marines, so what is there left to do? There are no worthy adventures left for them.'

She cast a sardonic eye up at the orc.

'I know how they feel, Major-General. *I* miss adventuring. I haven't done anything seriously illegal for months. Only politics, and every politician is crooked, so that hardly counts. You see, it's become my business to support the status quo. More and more responsibility piled on . . . That means it's me who has to worry about whether Ashnak—'

She broke off in mid-sentence.

The small orc smoothed down the bare breast of his tunic.

'Would have liked a medal,' he said. 'Sure General Ashnak would have awarded me one, if circumstances hadn't intervened.'

His lower lip began to quiver.

Magda waved her advisers away and leaned forward. 'Tell Magda all about it?' she invited.

Barashkukor sniffed. 'I'm worried about my beloved general, ma'am! He's up north in the Nin-Edin fort, *brooding*, he won't give the marines orders, he just shuts himself up all the time, and now—'

'He's either going to retire gracefully, or he's going to wreak bloody revenge,' the World President said. 'I know which my money's on. It's me who has to worry about it. And . . . Barashkukor, I haven't seen or heard from Ashnak in a month.'

The small orc wiped his nose.

'You have now, ma'am. That's why I'm here. I've just had a message through from the north. It wasn't very clear, ma'am. The general is calling a meeting, wants you there too – he says he's going to make some kind of an announcement.'

Magda bit her lip.

'Call that Huey down,' the colonel-duchess ordered. 'Whatever it is, I wouldn't like us to get there too late.'

* * *

421

The Demonfest mountains rose higher to either side as Wing Commander Chahkamnit swung the Huey up from Sarderis and through the Nin-Edin pass. Fog clung to the peaks. Water spattered the viewscreen. Visibility decreased as they contour-flew the pass up to Nin-Edin. The wind blowing through the helicopter was icy.

'Splendidly bracing, ma'am, what?' Chahkamnit bellowed from under goggles and ear-flapped flying helmet.

'Cold enough to freeze a rock-troll's ass,' Magda snarled. 'Didn't Ashnak's message say *anything* else, Major-General?'

Barashkukor held on his stetson by main force. 'No, Colonel, ma'am. Only that he wants all of us here, right now.'

In the main body of the Huey, CIA Chief Lugashaldim, Master Sergeant Varimnak and Lieutenant-Colonel Dakashnit sat morosely jammed elbow to elbow. Commissar Razitshakra read a tattered paperback. It was not clear whether she had been summoned, or merely attached herself to keep an eye open for examples of unorcish behaviour.

CRUMP!

'Nice landing, Wing Commander.' Magda swung herself down from the Huey's cockpit. The machine stood, less than levelly, on the earth of Nin-Edin's outer bailey. A gothic mist swirled around the battlements, and poured down from the mountains, hiding the inner keep, and the outer gate.

'Brings back memories, ma'am,' Barashkukor said, disembarking with the other officers. His eyes shone. 'First time I ever handled a marine weapon, it was right here in this compound. Me and Marukka and Duranki and Azarluhi . . . All dead now, ma'am. Fallen on the field of battle.'

Barashkukor dusted his small snout violently on his sleeve. 'Wonder if it wouldn't have been better, ma'am, if the general could have found an honourable death in a firefight . . .'

Magda glared at the snivelling orc. 'No, it bloody well wouldn't!'

'Falling in battle is the Way of the Orc, ma'am,' Commissar Razitshakra observed, putting her paperback in her greatcoat pocket and wiping the fog from her dripping peaked ears and round spectacles. 'The Way of the Orc doesn't say anything about reserve lists, pensions, or retired marine officers. Or anything about sulking—'

'As far as I'm concerned, Commissar,' Dakashnit drawled, 'you can shove that up *your* ass and whistle Dixie!'

The halfling and the group of orcs tramped up the hill towards the inner walls, and the shattered gate that still stood unrepaired, although now a section of marines guarded it. Magda heard Master Sergeant Varimnak sigh.

'Remember the siege?' The Badgurlz marine elbowed Lugashaldim in his stripped ribs. 'Hell, man, that was good! That elf – she could swing a whip like she'd been *born* to it.'

The Undead orc took off his dark glasses, gazing up at the battle-stained keep now visible through the shifting fog. '*I* remember the Fourgate commando mission, and how brave General Ashnak was. He wouldn't hear any arguments – he insisted on returning to this besieged fort, no matter what the personal danger . . .'

Commissar Razitshakra made a note in her book, muttering something about not quite remembering it that way. Lugashaldim ignored her. He patted Magda's arm with a gloved skeletal hand.

'Ma'am, to think he should come to this. Skulking in a garrison in the middle of nowhere; drinking, I expect, and . . .'

At her other side, Chahkamnit stuffed his flying goggles in his bomber-jacket pocket and crouched down to put his arm around Magda's shoulders. 'I say, ma'am, I wouldn't give any of that a thought if it was me. The old general's ticketty-boo, take my word for it. He'd never do anything silly.'

Magda straight-armed the lanky black orc, who sat down hard on the earth.

'You're getting on my nerves!' she snarled. 'Damn it, whose husband is he? I know Ashnak better than any of you.'

A great orc stepped out from under the split masonry arch of the inner gate, into the swirling fog.

The general officer commanding the orc marines wore a ragged pair of combat trousers, and had obviously been wearing them for some time. His boots were scuffed, and his web-belt hung low, pulled down by the weight of his .44 Magnum. Fog pearled and shone on his bald head, peaked ears and deep brow ridges.

Barashkukor saluted energetically. 'Sir, you said you had an announcement to make, sir!'

'Did I?' An enigmatic expression crossed the orc's craggy features. He reached down a taloned finger and touched the shoulder of Magda's suit.

Lugashaldim, Varimnak, Dakashnit and Chahkamnit exchanged wary glances. Bewildered, they regarded their large, filthy commanding orc. Ashnak stepped out of the gateway, striding past them down the hill.

'Follow me,' he ordered.

The caverns under the mountain echoed to boots, and the hissing arc lights that orc marines had strung up on cables. Although chill, it was still warmer than the fog-shrouded mountainside above.

423

Colonel-Duchess Magda van Nassau quickened her pace, heels clicking, to keep up with her orc general. The other orc officers followed, muttering asides to each other as Ashnak led them deeper into the dragon's caves.

'Will spoke to me before he left Ferenzia.' Magda glanced up. 'He holds that the orc marines were bound to come to grief eventually in any case – *hubris*. And Good always winning in the end, as it does.'

Ashnak's eyes glinted. He chewed on his unlit cigar. 'It ain't like that.'

'Comparative Good,' Magda amended. 'I'm the first to admit, my love, that I'm Good compared only to, say, a seriously bored Dark Lord who might take up continental destruction for the fun of it.'

The corner of the orc's mouth twitched. 'True. But it *really* ain't like that.'

'What do you mean?'

'Let me show you.'

With Barashkukor at her heels, and the rest following, Magda entered the central cavern of Dagurashibanipal's caves. She stared up at the crystal stalactites that were all that remained of the dead dragon. Cables looped across the floor. More arc lights burned, warming the cavern's chill air.

Ransacked and bare, the halls of the dragon's hoard stretched out before her.

'I've found it, I've got it, I've—' The voice of Tech-Colonel Ugarit set off crystalline echoes. He hopped from one foot to the other, grinned a sickly grin at Ashnak, and backed away until his skinny frame was flattened against the cave wall.

'I'll *eat* you,' the great orc threatened.

'Not yet, my love,' Magda pleaded. 'You've found something here? What?'

Lieutenant-Colonel Dakashnit eyed the gibbering Ugarit sardonically. 'Probably some super-duper new weapons system, man. That right, General? You thinkin' of blowing the fuck out of people?'

Ashnak sighed. 'Don't encourage him. He's been wanting to take that *"nuclear"* stuff off the shelves for months and see what it does.'

'Found!' the skinny orc squeaked. His eyes crossed. He went into paroxysms of excited giggles. 'Found?!'

Ashnak stepped forward, removed the tech-colonel's helmet, and dropped his fist on the skinny orc's skull. Ugarit staggered back against the cave wall.

'It isn't a weapon that I've discovered. Not exactly . . .' Ashnak raised his head, momentarily distracted by the line of holes across the cavern roof.

'First time I ever fired an AK,' the great orc remarked in melancholy tones, pointing. 'Nearly did for Imhullu! Ah, you wouldn't remember him, Magda my love. A nest-brother of mine. Fell at Guthranc.'

Magda threw herself forward, embracing the orc's big muscular thigh. She fisted one hand and punched him on the painful pressure point of the inner leg. 'Don't you even *think* about doing anything stupid! I'll have your ass!'

Ashnak smoothed her chin with a horny finger.

'Is that what you thought?' He shook his head, gazing at the lugubrious faces of his officers. 'Don't be ridiculous! I'm an *orc!*'

Barashkukor gazed around the cavern.

'Does take you back, sir, doesn't it? Remember when I was a scrawny little grunt, sir, and you were training us? And then we marched off to war with Captain Shazgurim, and Captain Zarkingu's band? Those were the days! But I guess those days are gone, sir. I'm beginning to think we were better off in the bad old days in the necromancer's tower, with pole-axes. We weren't redundant then. I guess I miss the Dark Lord, sir. At least we had the Light to fight . . .'

Ashnak looked, not at Barashkukor, but at the diminutive halfling beside him.

She said, 'You've *got* something . . .'

'Fuckin' A!' Ashnak grinned.

The orc general turned on his heel and marched off, boots clattering noisily in the cavern. Magda trotted to keep up with him. Ugarit skipped in her wake, digging his fists into the pockets of his white coat. His pierced and studded ears jingled as he hopped from foot to foot, shrieking.

'Paradigm anomaly! It's so simple! Paradigm anomaly!'

In a daze, Magda stumbled after Supreme Commander Ashnak and his orc officers, living and Undead, further on into the cave system. She was aware at one point of Barashkukor taking her arm to help her down scree-slopes her heeled shoes could not cope with. She kicked off the shoes and walked bare and hairy-footed. At some point she discarded the veiled hat.

She passed through ancient and measureless caverns now stark with the raw light of electricity. She stumbled around pillars and down stairways of an underground city of some hapless race the dragon had exterminated. Grunts with AK47s and M16s stood guard at every corner, every corridor. Barashkukor, Lugashaldim, Varimnak and Dakashnit were too bemused to return their salutes, which Razitshakra made careful note of.

At last, so deep below ground that the knowledge of the

mountain's weight was an immense pressure, she walked through the newly opened entrance to a hall.

Large enough for six dragons, the roof soared vast and high above her head. She walked out into the expanse of cavern floor, tiny in the great space.

Carved masonry archways set into the walls led out of the cavern.

Winds blew out of the archways.

Magda's nostril's flared, catching a hundred mingled scents; all strange, all unknown. An orc behind her swore, breathlessly. Magda stared.

Each elaborately carved stone arch opened into a different place.

The light of strange suns striped the cave floor. Yellow, white, amber, cerise . . . A flood of sunlights: rich with the heat of summer, pale with the chill of winter; none of it the dank mist and fogs that hung in the Nin-Edin pass.

Magda walked forward until she stood on one threshold. The stone was cut in strange geometries. The aura of draconic mathematics breathed from the rock. A yard in front of her bare, hairy feet, the paving stones of some strange summer-hot city wept tar into the gutters.

She stared back over her shoulder.

Other thresholds opened into rich fields, forests, seas; and cities of every kind, from monumental white stone to vast glass-and-steel towers. She smelled the mingled scent of a hundred worlds. A hundred Otherworlds . . .

Ugarit shrieked, 'Dimensional portals! Wormholes in space! Parallel dimensions!'

'Is he all right, sir?' CIA Chief Lugashaldim swallowed. His bony jaw creaked. 'Am *I* all right, sir?'

Magda with difficulty turned her back on the magnificent threshold and walked to Ashnak. She reached up and took the orc's hand.

'You found this,' she growled.

Ashnak stood easy. 'I knew it had to be here somewhere.'

Magda shook her head. 'I know that Dagurashibanipal was a collector. Very powerful, even for a dragon. A collector of militaria. But what—'

Ugarit stopped hopping, dusty and brilliant-eyed and slavering. 'Antiquarian militaria!' he sneered. 'Very little truly modern stuff. You know how dragons are.'

The bewildered orc officers wandered through the Cavern of Portals, gaping. Varimnak was so far away as to be almost out of sight, and she had not exhausted the number of gateways yet.

Ashnak smiled, showing brass-capped tusks. 'I knew that the

426

dragon collected weapons of war from all the Otherworlds that necromancers and wizards see in their visions. She *went* there, or sent her golem, and she brought matériel back. And then she died, and cursed her hoard, and we've had the Dragon's Curse ever since.'

Major-General Barashkukor, shocked, cried, 'You haven't found a way to get rid of it, sir?'

'Good god, no!' Ashnak scratched deep in the cleft of his buttocks, and hitched up his combats again. 'Dagurashibanipal raided the Otherworlds, from these caverns under the Demonfest mountains. The gateways are *still here*. They had to be! How else could Sergeant Stryker have got here?'

Ashnak shrugged modestly.

'He arrived here at least a year after Dagurashibanipal was killed.'

Magda shook her head. 'And I thought you were skulking up here, planning some noble suicide . . .'

'I'm an orc, damn it!'

More amazed than seemed tactful, she said, 'Don't tell me you and the tech-colonel came up with this idea on your own?'

Ashnak said smugly, 'I'm not just some dumb grunt.'

'I've been observing Stryker's world – that one, over there. Colonel-Ma'am, the one you were looking at,' Tech-Colonel Ugarit dribbled. 'That's *really* weird. And there's more than one world. There are *hundreds!*'

Barashkukor clipped the tech-colonel's ear with his steel hand. Ugarit cackled. The Undead orc and the other officers began to drift back from the gateways, their expressions dazed.

'Slight exaggeration,' Ashnak demurred. 'There probably aren't more than fifty worlds that orcs could survive in. Some with a higher technology level than us, some lower.'

As if hypnotized, Magda padded barefoot back across the sun-warmed stone to the threshold of Stryker's world. She sniffed the strange air.

'Smells like the mechanized warfare division.' The halfling wrinkled her nose. Carefully, leaning forward, she moved her head across the threshold. There was a faint sensation of *give*, as if some transparent meniscus had been penetrated. Sound battered her ears. She stared at the vehicles thundering along the city's paved streets and across a teeming bridge towards her; at the high glass towers beyond, and the gothic clock tower of a building next to the sluggish brown river.

When she turned her head, the cavern behind her had become invisible. She drew back. Rock-chilled air engulfed her, cold after the sudden exhaust-laden summer.

'You know what this means . . .'

427

Major-General Barashkukor, cyborg eye whirring, stared gob-struck at the dirty blue sky, and the red vehicles crossing the iron river bridge. Commissar Razitshakra scribbled furiously; Sergeant Varimnak nudged Dakashnit in the ribs, and indicated with a nod of her heavy-jawed head where two young females of the Man species broke from the crowd to lean on the bridge rail, and winked. Wing Commander Chahkamnit gaped. Lugashaldim's red eyeless sockets glowed. Ugarit beamed.

Ashnak regarded Stryker's world. 'I don't believe we need worry about an occupation for orcs. Dagurashibanipal seems only to have been interested in worlds completely obsessed with war.'

'Good show, sir!' Wing Commander Chahkamnit shaded his eyes against the yellow sunlight and watched a flight of Tornadoes hurtle across the dirty sky.

'I say, sir, what about that!'

Magda took Ashnak's hand and gazed into that new world's rising sun.

'I do have an announcement to make.' The great orc looked at his fellow orc officers, and then down at Magda. 'There was something I once told you of, my love. When the Dark Lord touched my soul. Never let on to Her, of course, but it did show me what, as an orc, I really am.'

Major-General Barashkukor assumed a military erectness. 'Sir, a member of a proud and noble but misunderstood warrior race, sir?'

The great orc thought about it for a second.

'Not really,' Ashnak said. 'More like, a mean motherfucker who loves big guns. I *don't* want to be World Ruler. All I want is to go on doing what I enjoy. I intend to carry on being an orc marine. And I intend to take the marines on missions to as many of these worlds as I can.'

'Me too,' Magda said unexpectedly.

The black orc Dakashnit grinned, and muttered something under her breath about dumbfuck halflings

'Damn it, my Vice-President can take over here.' Magda gripped Ashnak's large hand and grinned. 'Hell, orc, I'm an officer in the marines too – this time I'm coming with you!'

'*Yo!*' Ashnak swung Magda Brandiman up into his arms, waltzed a few bow-legged steps on the cavern floor, kissed her and stepped back as she kicked him smartly.

'My love,' the big orc said gravely, 'I thought I would at least have to *ask*.'

Barashkukor seized Supreme Commander Ashnak by the taloned hand and shook it vigorously. 'Oh, *sir!*'

428

Magda tugged her tailored skirt straight.

'Of course . . .' Her eyes narrowed. 'If John Stryker accidentally came through to here – then others can do that too. Accidentally. Or deliberately.'

'They can't see us! Can they?' Tech-Colonel Ugarit suddenly whimpered and cowered, turning cross-eyed to survey the cave of dragon-sized arches. 'We may even now be under scrutiny for attack!'

Commissar Razitshakra snapped her notebook decisively shut. 'Then we'll have to get our retaliation in first! Supreme Commander, sir, I volunteer to accompany you!'

'I thought you might,' Ashnak remarked.

Magda speculated demurely. 'I'm sure the Otherworlds will see the point of trading with the Orc Marine Armaments and Leisure Services Company – once we've given a small-scale demonstration.'

'If they don't,' Barashkukor offered, 'we can always give a large-scale demonstration . . .'

'Congratulations!' Ashnak walloped Major-General Barashkukor's shoulder. 'You just volunteered for the first mission, too. And I *will* see there's a medal for you in this.'

'Oh, sir, *thank* you, sir!'

Wide-eyed, ears jutting bolt upright, Barashkukor surveyed the Cave of Portals, and the many worlds. 'I can see it now, sir. Missions! Campaigns! Wars! Crusades! Empires!'

CIA Chief Lugashaldim mused, 'Employers of mercenaries. Regimes to destabilize . . .'

'Worlds', Commissar Razitshakra said, 'to which we can take the Way of the Orc!'

'R & R,' Master Sergeant Varimnak muttered. Dakashnit bellowed laughter. She elbowed Wing Commander Chahkamnit. 'I love it, man! New worlds to conquer, and she's already thinking about her—'

'Oh, I say!' Chahkamnit blushed.

'I can see it too.' Ashnak grinned. 'Rape. Pillage. Massacre. Atrocity . . .'

Ashnak threw back his head, hairy nostrils flaring, scenting the winds from the arcade of worlds. The great orc in filthy camouflage battledress put his arms around Magda Brandiman as the Otherworld sunrise shone brightly into the eyes of the orc and the halfling, and the other officers.

'Yo!' Ashnak yelled. 'It's an orc's life in the marines!'